Fat Guys
Don't
Wear Stripes

Fat Guys Don't Wear Stripes

by
Dick Dunham

QUINLAN PRESS
Boston

Published by Quinlan Press
131 Beverly Street, Boston, MA 02114

Printed in the United States of America, 1988.

Library of Congress Cataloging-in-Publication Data

Dunham, Dick, 1942-
    Fat guys don't wear stripes.

    I. Title.
PS3554.U4667 F38   1988   813'.54   88-42933
ISBN 1-55770-100-8

For Linda, my wife.
For Kelly and Michael, my children.

ACKNOWLEDGEMENTS
I want to thank Ron Gollobin, who inspired me to write.
Chuck Kraemer, for helping me learn to write. Helen Desmond,
for her crime research. And my agent, Dennis Campbell, for his
unyielding and faithful belief in me.

Fat Guys
Don't
Wear Stripes

1

Ten more minutes to go.

Sonuvabitch! I'm not going to make it. Not tonight.

I pedalled faster. Sweat ran down my face onto the floor, soaking the carpet under the bike. Sitting back, I changed position on the seat. It didn't do any good, not when the seat was already halfway up my ass.

Who the hell designs these pieces of shit anyway?

The doctor told me, Joe, you want to live — exercise. You're not getting any younger. You're forty-four, overweight, and getting uglier by the day. Stop eating all that junk food, he told me.

I told him, I'm a cop for Chrissakes. I work nights. Where are you going to find a good meal at midnight? You don't have a lot of choices.

So bring a salad to work, he told me. I'm not a rabbit, I told him. I need substance. He said I had enough of that already.

I told him I didn't like the way he treated me — I was changing doctors. He said he didn't give a shit, and handed me a 1700 calorie-a-day diet.

Asshole.

I looked down at the timer attached to the handlebar. Seven minutes left. I took in several deep breaths to keep from passing out. My legs ached; my chest was on fire. I tried to concentrate on the music coming out of my headset. Luciano Pavarotti's aria from Puccini's *La Boheme,* "Che gelida manina", but all I could think about was this giant fat guy with a beard stuffing himself with lasagna and wine, wishing it was me.

Footsteps thundered down the basement stairs. My daughter, Jessica, stuck her head beneath the railing.

"Dad," she said, "There's a call for you. I think it's Lieutenant Bailey."

"What?"

"I stopped pedalling, took off the headphones, and tugged vainly at my teeshirt; it was clinging to the fat around my waist like wet toilet paper. Jessica repeated what she had said.

"What does he want?" I said. "Doesn't he know I'm on vacation?"

"Since when did that matter?" Jessica replied.

"You're starting to sound like your mother," I said, grabbing a towel, wiping my face. "Where is she by the way?"

"She took Jeffrey to karate." Jessica frowned. "You okay, Dad?"

"Yeah, why?"

"You look awful."

"So everyone keeps telling me."

"No. I mean it. Your face. It's bright red. You're not going to pass out or anything like that are you?"

"No, I am not going to pass out."

"You don't have to be so sarcastic about it. I was just asking."

"I'm sorry. You want to make your dear ole Dad a cup of coffee?"

"No. I'm busy." She went back upstairs.

So much for dear ole Dad.

I finished toweling off. When I thought I could breathe well enough, I went upstairs and picked up the phone.

"You forget I'm on vacation?" I said.

"Fuck your vacation," Lieutenant John Bailey said. "You know the last time I had a vacation?"

"No, and I don't give a shit either."

"Two years ago — took three lousy days. You've had a week."

"And I've got one more."

"Wrong."

I pushed what hair I had left away from my forehead and sat down at the kitchen table. I looked out the window; the rain was coming down heavy, washing away the grass seed I just planted around our new aboveground swimming pool. Sonuvabitch!

Lieutenant Bailey let go one of his hacking coughs. "Get over to Dorchester," he said. "Codman Square — in back of the Latin Academy. Your partner's holding the scene."

"What happened?"

"Some maniac put a bomb under a Channel Eight television news truck and blew it into next week. There's three people dead, maybe more. One of them was that reporter, Susan Howell."

It took me twenty minutes to get from Milton to Dorchester. The traffic at Pierce Square in Lower Mills was gridlocked; nothing moved on Dorchester Avenue. I had to make my way through back streets until I found Washington Street. When I finally got to Codman Squre, the traffic still wasn't moving. I flashed my lights and blew my horn at the black uniformed cop wearing an orange raincoat, refereeing traffic in the middle of the intersection. I rolled down my window and the sounds of the city rushed in. So did the acrid odor of smoke coming from behind the Boston Latin Academy a half-block away.

"Hey, Bro!" I yelled to the black cop, flashing my lights on and off.

The cop glared at me. He must have been new on the force. He didn't know who I was.

I took out my gold badge and waved it at him. "Detective Sergeant Knight," I said. "Homicide. Think you could move some of those cars so I can get through?"

The black cop came over to me, looked at my badge then at my corroded brown Plymouth. "You got a siren in this piece of shit, Sarge?" he said.

"No. But if you're nice to me, I'll let you peek under the hood and see my gorilla."

The cop looked at me. The rain and the traffic did nothing

for his humor. He muttered something obscene, then put his whistle between his lips, and walked away. A couple of minutes later there was a hole in the traffic big enough for me to crawl through.

In the parking lot behind the school, the crowd was everywhere — so was the press. They were like swarming flies. I couldn't remember when I'd seen so many cameras. The cops had most of them behind barricades, but I knew damn well that as soon as they saw me, all hell would break loose. And it did.

"Sergeant Knight! Sergeant Knight!" they called out as I stepped over the yellow tape with CRIME SCENE — KEEP OUT printed on it.

Reluctantly, I stopped and faced them. Before I could blink, a zillion microphones were in my face, and a zillion questions hurled at me from a zillion different reporters.

"Sergeant Knight. Can you tell us what happened?"

It was a standard stupid question.

"There was an explosion," I said.

"How many are dead?"

"I don't know. I just got here."

"Do you know what caused it?"

Another stupid question.

I held up my hands. "Look. Give me a break, alright? When I know something, I'll let you know something."

I walked away from them, ignoring their shouts.

What was left of reporter Susan Howell lay underneath a painter's drop cloth which the rain had pressed down into her bleeding eye sockets and gaping mouth. Shards of glass crunched under my shoes as I stepped around a side panel that said "NewsCenter 8" in large red letters.

"What the hell is this, Jake?" I said to one of my detectives wearing a tan raincoat, kneeling next to the corpse. "Couldn't you find anything else to cover the body with?"

Jake Callaghan stood up. Rain dripped from the visor of his Scally cap. "Hi, Joe," he said. "How was your vacation?"

"It sucked." I pulled the collar of my raincoat tight against my fleshy neck. "What happened?" I said, looking around.

"Looks like dynamite," said Jake. "And a lot of it."

"You touch anything?"

"No."

"Good. Let the bomb squad handle it. They know what to look for. How many are dead?"

"Three. Reporter Susan Howell, and two technicians." Jake took out a small note pad from inside his suit jacket. "Eddie Clark and Paul Collins. What's left of them is over there. Sorry about the drop cloths but it was the only thing we could find. Tommy grabbed them off a paint truck. He said the stiffs wouldn't mind."

"That figures."

"He's your partner."

"Don't remind me."

I looked down at Susan Howell. Blood seeped through the cloth and mingled with the colors of the paint. She worked nights. Came into our office now and then looking for scoops. A real looker. Good reporter. Too bad.

"Who identified them?" I said.

Jake nodded toward the coffee shop across the street. "Some photographer from Channel Eight. Tommy's talking to him now."

Crouching as low as my joints would allow, I leaned over Susan and peeled back the cloth. I swallowed hard. "Jeeszus H. Christ!"

I felt a dull ache deep in my belly. Her brilliant blonde hair didn't look blonde anymore. Her skin — where there was skin — was scorched. I replaced the cloth and stood up. "The M.E. been here yet?"

"Yeah," Jake said. "He's with Tommy in the coffee shop. Want me to send someone over?"

I shook my head. "No. What about Channel Eight? They been notified?"

"Yeah," Jake said. "Warren called them. Someone's supposed to be on the way over."

"Where's Warren now?"

"Checking out an old lady across the street who thought she saw someone running from the scene."

"What time is it now?"

"Three-fifteen."

"Pictures been taken?"

"Yeah."

"What about Joe Latina and his bomb squad?"

"On their way."

"Alright. Keep everybody back. I want everything left the way it fell."

Jake nodded. "What about the bodies, Joe? They've been here a long time? Want them bagged?"

"No," I said. "You want a coffee or doughnut?"

"No, thanks," Jake replied, patting his trim waist. "Trying to cut back."

"Fuck you," I said. I knew what he was thinking. Jake used to be fat like me until he started working out. Now he was worse than a reformed smoker.

Jake stared at my shirt under my jacket.

I looked down at myself. "What's the matter?" I asked.

Jake said. "Anyone ever tell you that fat guys are not supposed to wear stripes? Up and down stripes are okay, but not the ones that go around like that. Makes you look fatter than you already are."

"Who gives a rat's ass, Jake. I like striped shirts."

"We've noticed. You must have a lot of them — and such pretty colors."

"Kiss my ass." I started across the street.

"By the way," Jake said, "We got a good lead on that punk from the Dog Posse gang. The girl he shot talked to me and Warren last night. Gave us a good description."

"So pick him up," I said, stopping and looking back.

"You kidding me? We'll need an army to get him out of Roxbury. You know what those fuckin' Jamaican punks are like."

"They're kids, Jake. Kids."

"They've got guns, Joe. And lots of 'em."

"We'll talk about it later."

I could smell it as soon as I walked in the coffee shop — Tommy Sanders' miserable, rotten, cigar. Sonuvabitch! It was enough to make you puke.

I ordered coffee at the counter and gazed down at the giant sweet roll in the glass case. It was begging me to eat it, but I resisted. I went over to the table where Tommy was and sat down.

Tommy was happy to see me. "Joe, you're back. How was the vacation?"

"Lousy," I said. "Where's the medical examiner?"

"In the bathroom," Tommy said. "Aren't you glad to see me?"

"It's only been a week for Christ's sakes."

Tommy Sanders was forty-three, with mischievous hazel eyes, and a hairdo that reminded everyone of Friar Tuck; bald spot on top, long on the sides. He was six one, a couple of inches taller than me, but not quite as fat.

Tommy said, nodding to the man sitting next to him. "This is Stanley Jones from Channel Eight. He's the chief photographer. He said he got here right after it happened."

"Detective Sergeant Joe Knight," I said, shaking hands. "You know Bobby Dunn?"

"Jones stared at me blankly through his black-rimmed glasses. His skin was pale, his hair light red, graying on the sides. He nodded.

"Best cameraman in town," I said. "One of the few guys in your business I'd trust. What's he doing now? Haven't seen him on the streets lately."

"He's left news and gone over to production," Jones said. "Working on the nightly news magazine show."

"He still bitching?"

"Of course."

Smoke from Tommy's cigar came at me. I tried to wave it away as I watched the cigar dance between his lips. There was always something erotically sick the way it stuck out of his little round mouth, poking through his multicolored mustache and full beard.

"Will you put that rotten thing out," I said.

Tommy looked at me, disgusted. "You going to start nagging me again for Chrissakes?"

"I never stopped."

"No shit. Smokers got rights too you know?"

"You want to kill yourself, that's your business. But don't kill me. How many times do I have to tell you that?"

Tommy shook his head. Reluctantly, he put out the cigar. "Asshole," he muttered.

"Thank you," I said.

"Fuck you," Tommy said.

The waitress came over with coffee and filled our cups. After she left, I said to Jones. "How'd you hear about it? On the scanners?"

Jones nodded.

"Where were you when you heard it?"

"On Blue Hill Ave — near Franklin Park."

"How long did it take you to get here?"

Jones looked toward the street, his eyes glassy. "Five minutes. Perhaps six."

"What did you see?"

"Thick smoke. People screaming." He paused a moment to gather his thoughts. "And my colleagues . . . scattered over the parking lot."

"Anything else?"

He gave me that what-a-stupid-question look. "No," he answered.

Jones' words were clipped and precise; each carefully thought out. I think he was trying hard not to cry.

"We checked a dozen witnesses," Tommy broke in. "No one saw anything before the explosion. Warren is checking out some ole lady."

"Anyone checking on Warren?"

Tommy grinned. "I hope she's got a strong heart."

I drank some more coffee. "What were they doing?" I said to Jones. "Covering a story?"

Jones took a deep breath to gather himself. "I heard Susan say on the two-way that they were going to lunch. That was around one."

"I checked the Golden Crown down Talbot Ave.," Tommy said. "They ate lunch and left around two. The first call came in around two-fifteen."

Doctor Jacob Katzman came out of the bathroom. He was a German Jew, short and round with no hair — and one of the best pathologists in the business.

"Hi, Doc," Tommy said. "Your rhoids acting up again?"

The doctor shook his head in disgust. Like Otto Preminger, he spoke with a phony German accent. "Jokes," he said, pulling a chair beneath him, sitting down. "Always with the jokes, Tommy." He wiped the moisture from his wrinkled face with a handkerchief. "Sergeant Knight, I do not like it when bodies are left out in the rain. I do not understand why your people insist on keeping them at the scene."

I drank the last of my coffee. "The last time your morons bagged a body from my scene," I said, "they walked all over it. Picked things up — got their fingerprints over everything. We had a helluva time sorting out who was who. Nothing moves until I say so."

"And when will that be, Sir Joseph?" Doc asked.

I looked outside. "As soon as the bomb squad gets through," I said.

The doctor stood up. "I have better things to do with my time than to sit here and debate with you," he said. "My people will remain — release them when you can. You will have my results tonight."

The doctor went out into the rain.

"Sergeant," said Jones. "There are some very expensive items still intact on the ground out there. Can I take them before they get stolen?"

"Like what?" Tommy asked.

"The camera for one. It's an Ikegami 79D. It's worth about forty thousand dollars."

"Not now it isn't," Tommy said.

"There's also a microwave unit and two portable radios. There could be a few other things still salvageable."

"When the bomb squad is through checking everything, take it," I said. "But make sure we know what it is."

Jones got to his feet. "Is there anything else?" he asked.

"We'll be in touch," I said. "Who's coming from your station?"

"The news director, Bill Lombardi, and Jill Rodney, the assistant news director."

"Did you take any pictures of the scene?" Tommy said.

"Yes," Jones said.

"Can we get a copy of the tape?" I said.

"You'll have to ask the news director."

"I will."

Jones left.

I waved the waitress over again.

"What did you do on your vacation?" Tommy asked.

"Nothing much," I replied. "Did a little work around the house. Planted some grass around the pool. Drove a few nails — things like that. The kids drove me crazy — I forgot how much they argue and fight. How's everything with you?"

"Sue still thinks I'm the biggest asshole that ever lived."

"You are."

"Our kids are driving her insane. Other than that, everything's great."

"You do any work while I was gone?"

"Of course. You know that guy Lawrence Wagner from Toronto — the guy who had his prick bitten off? Well, he died last night. He woke up long enough to give me a partial description of the broad who did it. She's maybe in her late teens or early twenties with blonde hair. Wagner said she had a body that wouldn't quit and she talked real soft."

"She rob him?"

"He still had his wallet."

"She show up again?"

"If you mean has she bitten off any more cocks, no. At least none's been reported." Tommy chewed on the end of his cigar. "Maybe she found some food stamps."

"Anything's possible."

The coffee came. We drank.

Tommy said, "Can you imagine having your prick bit off right in the middle of the only head you've probably gotten in twenty years? Christ. They must be still scraping his eyeballs off the dash.''

I smiled. "You check out the bars in the Zone?''

"Yeah. We staked out a few of them a couple of nights but came up empty. It's a waiting game now — see if she bites again.''

I looked at the counter. I really wanted that sweet roll. My eyes fell on the destruction outside. "What do you make of the bombing?'' I said.

"It could be just some nut pissed off at the news media,'' Tommy said. "I can see how it could happen — you been watching the news lately?''

"I try not to.''

"There's too fucking many of them,'' Tommy said. "Christ. You see the way they stormed around Joe Kennedy the other night. The poor sonofabitch could barely breathe with all those microphones and cameras sticking in his face. Look what they did to you when you showed up. I saw you squirming. If you ask me, they all suck. I've never met a reporter I could trust.''

I nodded my agreement.

Outside, Jim Latina and his bomb squad finally arrived. I paid the waitress and followed Tommy across the street.

The rain had turned to mist, but it did nothing to cool the humid August air — it remained heavy and oppressive. I took off my jacket and watched Latina and his boys go over everything with expert fingers. Tommy went off to bullshit with a couple of cops, and I stayed close to Latina.

"Anything yet?'' I asked him.

Latina stopped what he was doing and looked at me as if I had two heads. "I just got here for Chrissakes, Joe. Give me a break, alright?''

"Okay, okay, you fucking prima donna. I was just asking.''

Latina shook his head and went back to work on his hands and knees, sifting his fingers through the rubble. Ten minutes later, he found what he was looking for.

"Just what I thought,'' Latina said smugly, showing me the charred remains of a miniature timing device. "A remote control unit. Effective range of two hundred and fifty yards, depending on line of sight. Cute — and cheap."

"Can you tell what explosive was used?"

This time, I had three heads. "Dynamite," Latina said. "Six or seven sticks. Effective. By the look of things, the dynamite was placed dead center under the truck. The poor bastards never knew what hit 'em."

I looked down at the timing device in his hand. "Where can you buy something like that?" I said.

"Any electronics store sells them for about twenty bucks," he said.

Latina handed me the remote control unit, and grinned. "Better get going, Sarge," he said. "There's about one thousand and twenty-three billion electronics stores in the Boston area. Have fun."

"Thanks," I said. Smart-ass sonofabitch. "What about the dynamite?"

"What about it? There's nearly two hundred kinds."

"What difference does it make what kind it is? Dynamite is dynamite. What I want to know is where did the guy get it."

Latina looked at me. "You just can't buy the shit over the fuckin' counter, Knight. Knowing the type could narrow it down a little. Save you a whole lot of running around."

"Gee, that's swell of you, Jim," I said. "Thanks for thinking of me." I knelt down and toyed with some debris. "How are you going to tell what kind it was in all this crap?"

"Simple. If you know what you're looking for — and we do."

I straightened. "Of course," I said. "How stupid of me."

Latina said. "My guys found nitro resin on the frame. They're running some tests on it right now. I'll know the type in about twenty minutes. That quick enough?"

I smiled and said, "Yeah." Then I asked, "What about the bodies? You through with them?"

"Yeah," Latina said. "Too bad about Susan Howell. Great lookin' broad. Ever talk to her?"

"A few times," I said. "She always got the story straight at least."

I looked to my right. Tommy was talking to a short, blonde women in a dark raincoat, and a gray-haired man with a mustache and a three-piece suit, who was standing under a black umbrella.

When I walked up to them, Tommy had on his sad-face look.

"This is Detective Sergeant Joe Knight," Tommy said to Jill Rodney and Bill Lombardi from Channel Eight. "He's in charge of the investigation."

We shook hands. "I'm sorry," I said.

Jill Rodney couldn't speak. Her blue eyes darted from me to the wreckage then back to me.

"Do you know what happened, Sergeant?" Bill Lombardi, the news director asked, his voice choked with emotion.

"It was dynamite," I said flatly. "We're ruling it a homicide."

"Was she married?" Tommy asked.

"Yes," the news director replied. "To Jack Adams."

"The sports guy from Channel Three?" Tommy said. "Yes."

"Has anyone contacted him?" I said.

Lombardi said, "I called Channel Three's news director. He said Jack was out of town on an assignment. He left an emergency message with the hotel where Jack is staying."

Jill Rodney ran her fingers back through her long hair that went down to her shoulders. Her eyes were filling up. "Why?" she said. "Why would anyone do such a thing? It's . . . insane."

The bodies were being stuffed in green rubber bags. Jill turned away and buried her face in her hands. I thought she was going to be sick.

The news director didn't look either. "Do you have any suspects?" he asked, taking in a couple of deep breaths.

"No," I said. "Not at this time."

"It had to be a maniac," Jill Rodney said, turning around to face me, anger now in her voice. "Who else would do such a thing?''

Tommy said to me as he walked away, "I'll call Channel Three and see if they made contact with Jack Adams yet.''

I nodded.

"Anyone call your station claiming responsibility?'' I said to the news director.

"No,'' Lombardi said.

"It's early,'' I said. "Give them time.''

I reached into my back pocket and pulled out my wallet. Taking out a card, I noticed the coffee stains on my new Jack Nicklaus Golden Bear striped golf shirt. Shit!

"Here's my number,'' I said, handing Lombardi the card. "I can be reached there anytime. You get any kind of crank calls, I want to know about it.''

Lombardi glanced at the card. "Of course, Sergeant,'' he said.

"By the way. Wasn't Susan Howell the one who broke the Chelsea police story?'' I said. "They caught them stealing from a food store or something?''

Jill Rodney wiped her eyes with a handkerchief. "Yes, she did. She nearly want to jail because of it — for protecting her source. But that was two years ago.''

"Was she working on anything like that now?''

"No, I don't believe so,'' Jill said.

"What about the two technicians? Clark and Collins?''

"I don't know anything about their personal lives, frankly,'' Jill said. "As far as work is concerned — they were dedicated workers who did their job well. They were very well liked by everyone.''

The bodies were loaded into the medical examiner's van. We watched the van drive off.

Jill Rodney held on as long as she could. Finally, she broke down and cried.

Bill Lombardi put his arm around her.

"Will that be all, Sergeant?'' he asked. "I think we should leave now.''

"I have some more questions,'' I said. "But they can wait. What about tomorrow? I can come out to the station.''

"Of couse, Sergeant," Lombardi said. "Jill and I will be in at nine. Earlier if you like?"

"No. Nine is okay."

I saw Latina walking toward me. I excused myself and met him halfway.

"It was blasting gelatin," Latina said, a cocky smile spread across his face. "It's a plastic, rubber-like explosive made by adding seven to ten percent of nitrocotton to nitroglycerin — some wood pulp and sodium nitrate."

"Speak English for Christ's sakes," I said.

"It's sold as straight gelatin — used for blasting under water," Latina said. "That tell you anything?"

"No," I said.

"Didn't think so," Latina said. "Try MacFarland Industries up in Lynn. They sell a lot of it."

I said. "Damn, you're good."

He said. "I know."

2

Tommy said he had a couple of things to check out and took off. I went back to the office to file the report on the bombing.

Lieutenant John Bailey pushed away some papers and stained coffee cups on my desk, sat down on the edge, picked up the black and white photos of the bombing and flipped through them.

"What a mess," he said, looking at the photo of one of the technicians. "Jesus Christ. It must have been a helluvan explosion. I mean — look at the size of this guy. To make a guy that big look like that...."

"John," I said. "Haven't you got anything else to do for Chrissakes?"

The chief of homicide put down the photos. "Sorry about your vacation, Joe," he said. "You want me to put someone else on this?"

I looked up at him. "You're the zoo keeper," I said.

"Tell me about it," the chief said. "Take a look at this." He handed me a report Tommy Sanders had filed two days ago on a black kid found hanging from a tree in Roxbury.

"It was a suicide," the chief continued. "Look how that moron partner of yours spelled suicide. S-e-w-e-r s-i-d-e. Can you believe that?"

I smiled. "Yes. I can."

"Oh, yeah," the lieutenant said. "While I'm thinking about it — clean off your desk tonight. The painters are coming in tomorrow."

"You're shitting me." I looked around the room. Too bad. I was going to miss the faded green walls and chipped dark green woodwork — especially the giant water stain in the flaky ceiling over my desk. "They going to do something about the floor?"

"You got something against warped floors?"

"I guess not. I kinda like the way they creak."

"Look at this place. It stinks. There's trash everywhere. The cockroaches live off you guys. Why don't — "

" — you be more like Jake Callaghan," I broke in, finishing off what we've all heard a zillion times before. "Jake's a kiss-ass-goodie-two-shoes."

"He's a good cop and you know it. He's always saying great things about you. Besides, he's the best rumor spreader I've ever had. You want the world to know — tell Jake."

"I don't trust anyone who's got a thirty-two inch waist."

"Mine's a thirty," the chief said. "What about me?"

"What about you?" I said. "You're wasting away for Chrissakes. You've got a drunk's red face from all that scotch you drink. You piss so much you had to move your desk next to the comode. You've hardly got any hair. Your teeth are yellow and crooked. You're forty-six, but you look sixty."

Lieutenant Bailey stood up. "Anything else, fatso?" he said, indignant.

"Yeah. See a doctor before its too late." I took a long look at him. "Because we love yah, and we don't want anything to happen to you."

"Too late, you sonuvabitch. He's already seen me."

"And?"

"The chief put his boney hands in his pockets. "I'm dying," he said matter-of-factly. "It's cancer."

"Don't kid me," I said, trying to conceal my shock.

"I don't kid. You know that. Not about this anyway."

Both of us fell silent.

"I've got six months," the chief said. "Maybe a year if I stop drinking."

I could barely talk. "Then stop drinking," I said.

"Bullshit. If I'm going out, it'll be with a smile on my face."

I tried to write something down in the report. I couldn't.
"I don't know what to say."

"Say you're sorry for making my life miserable all these
years — you and your asshole partner."

"Does Tommy know?"

"No one knows — not even Stella." John looked out the
window. "Despite what I say, I love this job. I want to go
out on my own, not kicked out like some useless piece of
shit. I'm not looking for sympathy. I just thought you ought
to know."

"I'm not sure I wanted to know."

"Don't go soft on me, Joe. Not now." John Bailey headed for the door. "See yah later," he said. "Make sure that
report is on my desk by morning." He stopped and looked
back. "I don't like the feeling I'm getting on this one.
Something's not right."

My eyes went out of focus, water came out of the corners and ran down my cheeks. I wiped them away quickly
with the back of my hand.

"I know," I said. "I feel the same way."

It was nearly five-thirty by the time I finished the report.
I had called MacFarland Industries but they were closed.
I made a call to Channel Eight and talked with a guy named
Sollintari who said he was the news assignment editor. I
asked him if anyone called to claim responsibility for the
bombing. He said no.

He asked me if he could send a crew over to do an interview. I said no. How about tomorrow, he said. No, I said.

I called Channel Three. The news director told me they
got in touch with Jack Adams. He was taking the first
available flight back from California.

The news director asked me if I'd agree to an interview.
I said, no.

Warren Dolan called me and said that the old lady he
checked out was full of shit. From where she sat in the window overlooking the parking lot, she couldn't possibly have
seen the explosion. The school building was in the way.

In fact, Warren said, the woman was half deaf — she probably didn't even hear the bang.

I told Warren what Latina said about the dynamite. I said we had a lot of checking out to do tomorrow, so don't plan anything.

Tommy called and said he was going for coffee and a sandwich. Did I want anything? I said I didn't feel like eating. He knew something had to be wrong with me and wondered what it was. I told him nothing was wrong. He didn't believe me.

Tommy also said if I wasn't doing anything later on, we could pick up the warrant for Julio Pasquez. He heard Pasquez's girlfriend was hiding him in her apartment on Center Street in Jamaica Plain.

Pasquez was a sleazy, drug-crazed Puerto Rican who killed two kids a month ago — cut them to pieces with a butcher knife. Tommy and I had been looking for the bastard ever since. We almost had him one night near the Forest Hills MBTA station, but the sonofabitch was fast as hell. No match for two fat guys. He made it on the train before we had a chance to blow his brains out.

I told Tommy I'd pick up the warrant at headquarters and meet him at the Dunkin Donuts on Center Street at nine. He said make it eleven-thirty. I asked him why so late and he said he had something to check out. When I asked him if he had something going on the side, he laughed. A fat shit like me, he said — no way. He wasn't convincing.

I called home. My son Jeffrey answered.

"Hi, Dad," he said sadly.

"What's the matter, Jeff?"

"Nothing," he said.

I said, "Something's the matter. What is it?"

After a brief silence, he said. "You were supposed to take me to the Red Sox game tonight, remember?"

I sat back in the chair and rolled my eyes. "Aww, Jeff," I said, feeling like an instant jerk. "I'm sorry. You're right."

Jeff cut me deeper. "They're playing the Yankees, Dad."

"I know, son. What can I say? I blew it."

Then a thought struck me.

"Why don't you call Uncle Paul and see what he's doing. I could swing by Fenway and drop the tickets off at the service gate. How's that sound?"

"I don't know, Dad. Seems like a lot of bother."

Typical.

"Then don't go, Jeff," I said, irritated. "Stay home."

"Yeah. I think I will. There's a movie I want to see on TV anyway. You want to talk to Mom?"

I let out a sigh. "Sure. See yah later, Jeff. I love you."

"I love you too, Dad. Here's Mom."

I waited a moment.

Victoria came on the line.

"Hi, Hon," she said. "Where are you?"

"At work."

"I thought you had another week of vacation?"

"So did I."

"What happened?"

"Do you really want to know?"

"No. Not really."

"Thought so. I'll be home late. Don't lock the door."

"Did you bring some veggies to munch on?"

"No," I said.

"Why not?"

"Because I hate them."

"They curb your appetite. And they're good for you."

"No, they're not."

"Alright. Forget I said anything."

"It's forgotten."

"You forgot about the baseball game I see?" Victoria said.

I knew that was coming. "I know. I said I was sorry. Something came up."

"Doesn't it always?"

"Let's not go into all of that again. It couldn't be helped. Why don't you turn on the news. You might see me."

"No, thank you. The news depresses me," she said. "Besides, you look so much fatter on television."

"Thanks."

"You're welcome. I've got dinner cooking. I've got to go. Take care of yourself, alright? I love you."

"I love you too. See yah later."

We hung up.

I went downstairs to the booking area. A bunch of cops were sitting around the TV waiting for the news to come on.

"Helluva scene out there, huh Sarge?" the desk officer said. "How many dead? Three?"

I sat down on the wooden bench. "Yeah — three," I said.

"I saw the news bulletin a while ago," another cop said. "They said it was Susan Howell. Great looking broad. Too bad."

"Served her right," Charlie Finlanson said from across the room. "She fucked some good cops in Revere a couple of years ago. Just to make herself look good. She was always stickin' her nose in places it didn't belong."

I glared at Charlie. He was the biggest loud-mouthed asshole on the force. He hated me as much as I hated him. I waited for him to say something more. He didn't.

The news came on.

". . . . topping our news tonight at six," news anchor Patricia Day began, her voice tight and full of grief. "Three people are dead in an apparent bombing in the Codman Square section of Dorchester. . . ."

Co-anchor Brett Jacobs broke in, also noticeably shaken. "Channel Eight reporter Susan Howell died instantly this afternoon in an apparent bomb explosion that tore through a Channel Eight television news van. Also dead are technicians Edward Clark and Paul Collins — all victims of a vicious and senseless attack. Thus far, no one has claimed responsibility for this heinous, cowardly act. . . ."

I watched the video tape taken at the scene. There I was. In front of a zillion microphones holding up my hands, looking stupid and fat.

"Hey, Knight," someone called out to me. "You losing weight? You look a lot slimmer on television."

Everyone laughed.

I ignored the remark.

"What's the scoop, Joe?" patrolman Larry MacDonald asked, a veteran bike officer and friend. "You got any idea who did it?"

I turned around. "No," I said.

Larry twisted his long mustache. "The commissioner call you yet?"

"Not yet."

"He will."

"I can't wait."

"I'll keep my eyes and ears open," Larry said. "Bike around the area and see what I can dig up for you."

"Thanks, Larry," I said. "I need all the help I can get."

The officer on the desk yelled across the room. "Hey, Joe. There's a phone call for you. It's the commissioner. You want me to switch it upstairs?"

I glanced at Larry. He smiled. "That didn't take long," he said.

I stood up. "Don't you miss homicide?" I asked.

"Nope."

I patted Larry's black leather jacket on the back, felt the bulletproof vest underneath. "Nice jacket," I said.

Larry smiled. "Keeps me alive."

Upstairs, I sat down at my desk and picked up the phone. "Sergeant Knight," I said.

"This is Commissioner Roberts," Frankie snapped. "What the hell is going on, Joe? Why wasn't I notified about the bombing?"

Frankie Roberts had been a street cop at one time, and not a very good one. His friend the mayor said Frankie was the best man for the job when he appointed him commissioner. Everyone thought because he came from the streets he would make a great commissioner. They were wrong.

"I'm sorry, Commissioner," I lied. "I was busy. Besides, I saw some of your people there. I thought they might have told you."

"They didn't. I was at a meeting at city hall all day with the mayor."

Stupid sonuvabitch. No wonder you weren't told.

"No one called the mayor either," Frankie said.

"Calling people is not my responsibility, Commissioner," I said. "Or have you forgotten procedures?"

"Don't get smart with me, Knight. Where's your report?"

"On Lieutenant Bailey's desk," I said.

"I want it."

"Right now?"

"Yes. Right now. I'll be waiting in my office."

I checked my watch. 6:20 pm. "I'll be there in ten minutes," I said reluctantly.

"Make it eight," Frankie said.

The crosstown traffic wasn't bad over the Broadway Bridge. I went up Herald Street, turned right onto Washington, left across Arlington to Berkeley. When I got to headquarters, a bunch of cruisers were parked in front of the building, so I backed up and double-parked a little way down from Columbus Ave.

I walked past a baby-faced police cadet at the front desk inside headquarters and took the elevator to the sixth floor. Lieutenant O'Keefe, the commissioner's I-know-everything-about-everything man was sitting at the desk guarding the commissioner's office.

"Hey, White Knight," O'Keefe said. "How's it going out there?"

Not too many people called me "White Knight" — mainly because I didn't like it. O'Keefe knew that, and that's why he said it — like he was jealous I had a nickname and he didn't. I could give him one if he wanted. Ass-kisser.

"People are still killing people," I said. "No one's going to lose their job."

He grinned and said, "You hope."

The commissioner's door opened and a young woman with auburn hair who I'd never seen before came out. She said her name was Nancy from public relations. I had a hard time looking at her face, which wasn't bad — her breasts were better. Huge and tight against the green dress she wore.

"Sergeant Knight," she said with a brilliant, white teeth smile. "You can go in now."

I glanced at her breasts one more time. Sonofabitch.

I went in and closed the door behind me.

Frankie Roberts was sitting behind his large oak desk in the corner of the thirty-foot square, dark paneled room. Flags of Massachusetts and the United States stood on posts behind him.

"Take a seat, Knight," Frankie said. "That the report?"

I dropped the yellow folder on his desk. "Not much in it," I said, sitting down in the brown leather seat in front of the desk.

Frankie Roberts had short gray hair and a gaunt face. His blue eyes were sunk in under a protruding forehead that seemed frozen in a constant frown. He had narrow fingers and a thin neck. His white shirt and red tie seemed several sizes too big around his throat.

"You're right," Frankie said, going over the report. "There's nothing here but a bunch of bullshit. This all you could come up with?"

"For now, yes," I said.

"The mayor's not happy. You know that don't you?"

"No, I didn't."

"The press were just in here, throwing questions at me like a bunch of panicked lunatics. They wanted me to go live on television, for Chrissakes. What the hell could I tell them? I didn't have any answers. You know, the press won't let this die easy. They're going to be all over us until we find out who did it. You'd do the same if it were cops that got killed."

I glanced at the painting of a sailing ship on the wall. "I suppose so," I said.

"You know damn well you would. The press are assholes enough without something like this panicking them. I want some answers, Knight. And I want them fast. Drop everything you're working on, or give them to someone else."

"I can't do that, Commissioner. I'm close to solving some cases that I've worked on for months. I can't let them cool down."

"I don't care. You do whatever you have to do, but find out who did this. Understand?"

"If you say so, Commissioner."

"I say so." Frankie looked down at the report. "That's all, Knight. Keep me informed."

On my way out, I stopped by records and picked up the warrant on Julio Pasquez. I said hello to a couple of cops I hadn't seen in a while and went to my car.

My stomach growled at me, begging me to shove something in it. It wanted a pepperoni pizza bad, it settled for a plain dry tunafish on whole wheat at Legal Seafood at the Park Plaza hotel.

I went back to the office and made a few more phone calls until it was time to meet Tommy. It was shortly after eleven by the time I reached the Dunkin' Donuts on Center Street in Jamaica Plain. I was coffee'd out so I waited in the car.

Twenty minutes later, Tommy showed.

"You got the warrant?" he said getting in.

"Yeah," I said. "How was she?"

Tommy grinned. "What are you talking about?"

I looked at his cigar. "What did I tell you about smoking that thing around me?"

Tommy rolled down his window and made an attempt to blow the smoke out. "Get off my ass, alright?" he said. "It helps me think. Kicks in all the brain cells."

"I thought when you farted it did that?"

Tommy gave me one of his looks. "It's eleven-thirty," he said. "The asshole should be there by now. Let's get rolling."

Tommy pulled out his .9mm Beretta, removed the clip, and took out the bullets.

"What are you doing?" I said.

"Changing rounds. These department issue bullets are fucking useless. Remember when that black guy in Hyde Park tried to run us over? I shot at the tires and the bullets bounced off. Fucking things things didn't have enough powder in them to cut through horseshit, let alone rubber.

So I bought my own bullets.''

Tommy loaded the clip with hollow-point supervells.

"Those will do it," I said, starting the car.

"I hope so," Tommy said as he inserted the clip.

It was still hot; the rains of the past few days did nothing to cool things down. By the time we got to Oakview Terrace, across from South Huntington Avenue, our shirts were soaked with sweat, and not just from the heat.

I shut off the headlights and rolled the Plymouth to a stop a block from Oakview Street.

"Where's the house?" I said.

"Three doors down on the right," Tommy said. "Yellow building. Top floor. Above the fish and chip shop."

"How do you know Pasquez is there?" I said.

"A little bird told me," Tommy said. "After I kicked the shit out of him."

"Nice touch."

"I thought so. You ready?"

I opened my door. "Let's do it. You go first."

"What else is new?"

We walked along the sidewalk in the yellow-orange spill of street lamps. When we got to the fish and chip shop, Tommy looked up. "The lights just went out," he said quietly. "They must have gone to bed."

A weathered old man with white hair and a dirty green shirt and blue jeans came out of the shop, closing and locking the door behind him.

"You're too late," the old man said to us.

"What do you mean?" I asked.

"I'm closing," he said. "You want food, you go down the street."

I breathed again.

"How many people live in the apartments upstairs?" Tommy asked the old man.

"Why? You planning to rob them?"

I showed the old man my gold badge. "No. Answer the question."

The old man squinted at my badge. "You're cops. That's great."

Where were you a coupla weeks ago? Bastards robbed my store. I nearly got killed for Chrissakes.''

"Just answer the question," I said.

The old man looked at us another second. Then he said, "There's a couple living on the second floor. I don't see them much.''

"What about the third floor?" Tommy asked.

"A young girl lives there. Mexican or Puerto Rican — same difference. I think she's a whore.''

"Why do you say that?" I said.

"I see men going up there all the time. I think they're doing drugs or something.''

Tommy took out a mug shot of Julio Pasquez and showed it to the old man. "Ever see this guy go up?" he said.

The old man took the photo and turned to the light spilling out from his store. He looked hard at it for a long time. "Yeah," he said finally. "I've seen him before. Seen him a lot in fact.''

"Is he up there now do you think?" I said.

"I don't know. He could be. What do you want him for?"

"Tell you what," I said. "Go to a phone and call this number. Tell whoever answers there's some officers in trouble at this address. You got it?"

"Yeah, I got it. But who's in trouble?"

Tommy pried open the door leading to the staircase. "We are," he said.

I followed Tommy up to the second floor landing. It was dark. The only source of light came up from a naked bulb in the ceiling downstairs. The place smelled worse than Tommy's cigars.

Tommy took out his Beretta. I took out my .38 Smith and Wesson.

Tommy spoke softly. "We get to the door — I yell police, then we break in the door."

"Okay," I whispered, "but don't hurt yourself. Remember the last time you tried it."

"Don't remind me."

We crept up the filthy stairs to the third floor. The

wooden steps creaked and groaned under our feet. We stopped. It was completely dark now. I put my hand on Tommy's back to be sure of where he was.

"You ready," Tommy whispered.

"I'm never ready," I whispered back.

Tommy rapped on the door. "Police!" he shouted loud enough for the whole world to hear. "Open up!"

Silence.

Then we heard muffled shouts and racing footsteps inside the apartment.

Tommy hit the door hard. The stairs were narrow. No room for two of us on the landing.

Tommy hit the door hard again. The door gave way, spinning on its hinges. We rushed in.

We saw Julio going out the window. He was naked except for the large automatic he carried. A thin, naked Spanish woman about eighteen years old started screaming at us from the bed. She was sweaty.

"Get out you fuckin' pigs!" she yelled at us. "What the fuck you do'n! You can't break in here like that!"

"Shut the fuck up!" Tommy said to her.

Julio's eyes were huge and panicked. He kept them on us while his ass slipped further out the window.

"Hold it right there, Julio!" I shouted, raising my snubnose, aiming it at his face. "Don't do it! Your mother will puke when she sees what's left of you!"

Julio didn't listen. He went out the window to the fire escape, but not before he shot three quick rounds at us.

One bullet hit the door frame next to me; wood fragments shot through the air. Another struck metal somewhere and ricocheted, smashing the glass of a photograph on the wall. We never saw the third — Tommy and I were both kissing the floor.

When we looked up, Julio was gone.

"Sonofabitch!" I shouted and got to my feet. "Go down the stairs, Tommy! I'll take the fire escape!"

I went out the window. I could see Julio ahead of me, almost at the bottom. I took the crooked metal steps two at a time, knowing any moment the stairs would give way and take me down with them.

I reached the bottom. There was a high wooden fence to my right. If Julio went over it, he was gone. End of chase. I took a chance and ran toward the street. There he was, his sweaty naked body glistening in the orange light.

Julio sprinted down the sidewalk. He still had the gun.

I ran after him.

I heard Tommy shout something at me from behind. Something like "Go get 'em tiger!" I couldn't tell — I was breathing too hard.

Julio took a look back at me as he crossed the street. It was a mistake. A car came down on him fast. Julio crashed into the fender, the impact hurling him back onto the curb.

I stopped running and collapsed against a lamp post. My chest and legs were in pain. My breath was so spent I thought I would puke; so I went limp and let air fill my lungs.

Julio was in obvious pain. When I got to him, he looked up at me and screamed. "You miserable fuckin' pig! Look what you did to me! My leg! It's broken!"

I reached down for Julio's gun laying next to him and picked it up. "Gee, that's tough shit, Julio," I said. "Better luck next time."

As I straightened up, I felt the worst pain I'd felt in years. I doubled over and crumbled to the pavement. Julio had kicked me in the nuts.

He took off running. I struggled to my knees.

I managed to raise my arms, pointed the barrel of my .38 at Julio's back. I had him in my sights.

I couldn't pull the trigger.

3

I got home around three and went straight to the bathroom, dropped my pants, and checked myself in the full-length mirror behind the door.

They were still there. Swollen and hurting like hell, but they were there.

I looked at the rest of me. I looked old. My ratty silver hair needed a wash. My eyes were tired, the hollows beneath dark and stretched — not enough sleep for too many reasons. I took off my shirt; not only did it have stains, the sleeve was torn.

I undressed, shut off the bathroom light, and slipped quietly into the bedroom.

Some light from the hall spilled in on Victoria. She was naked; one of her breasts had slipped from beneath the sheet. I looked at her for a moment. A little heavier than when I married her twenty-two years ago, Victoria was still lovely. Her blue eyes had remained bright and alert, her clear soft skin didn't have a wrinkle, and her light brown hair showed only a trace of gray.

I opened the hamper and threw in my dirty clothes.

"You're late," Victoria said sleepily.

I turned around.

"Did I wake you?"

"Don't you always?"

She rolled over.

"I've got to take a shower," I said.

"Now?"

"Why not?"

"Because the shower makes too much noise. You'll wake everyone. Why not take one in the morning?"

"I don't want to wait until morning," I said. "It's already morning. I need to take one now, alright?"

Victoria went silent.

I took my shower, far longer and hotter than usual, blow-dried my hair, shut off the lights, and crawled into bed.

Victoria was still awake. "Feel better?" she said.

Her tone had softened. I answered politely. "Yes, thank you."

"Oh, good."

"How was your day?" I said, staring up at the dark, hands behind my head.

"Terrible. Jeffrey didn't come home until an hour after dark. I had to ground him. Jessica isn't speaking to me either."

"Again?"

"Just because I wouldn't let her stay overnight at Kim's house. She's been out practically every night for the past week. I'm tired of being her chauffeur."

I yawned. "I don't blame you," I said.

"You know it's her birthday tomorrow?"

"Damn, I forgot."

"I still don't know what to get her," Victoria said. "Any ideas?"

"What does a fifteen year old like besides boys?"

"Not much."

"How about clothes?"

"She doesn't like what I pick out."

"How about a record or a tape."

"I don't choose the right music."

I yawned again. "How about a swift kick in the ass?"

Victoria put her arm on my bare chest. "Good idea," she said. "You do it tomorrow."

"Yeah, sure. Thanks a lot. She hates me enough already."

Victoria let her fingers trace down my stomach. "All teenage girls hate their fathers," she said. "It's normal. Don't worry about it. Just don't allow yourself to drop down to her level. You argue with her too much."

"I can't help it. She pisses me off."

"She'll grow out of it."

"When?"

Victoria grabbed me. I almost jumped out of my skin.

"What's the matter?" she said, taking her hand away quickly. "I thought you liked it when I did that?"

It took a few seconds for the pain to die down, my eyes to clear. I said. "I do, but not tonight."

Victoria reached down again and touched them lightly with her fingertips. "Why not?" she said, her fingers beginning to work. "Have you been fooling around?"

I closed my eyes. "Yeah," I said. "With a Puerto Rican soccer player."

"What?"

"Go to sleep."

"Do you want me to stop?"

"No."

Daybreak.

I heard scratching at the back door. I went into the family room and opened the slider. Marmalade, our giant orange and white cat, bounded past me. He looked up at me with his it's-about-fucking-time look then waddled into the kitchen for his breakfast.

"Where the hell have you been all night?" I said.

I fed him. He purred loudly.

"You stop killing those chipmunks — you hear me? They're friends of mine."

He kept eating.

I liked talking to Marmalade. He was the only one in the house who didn't talk back.

I went back to the newspaper and my cup of coffee.

The headlines spread across the front page of the *Boston Globe* said: **TELEVISION REPORTER DEAD IN BOMB BLAST.** There were three small photographs of the victims inserted into a larger photograph that showed the entire scene. I read a little of the story. As usual the guy who wrote it got it wrong.

I flipped to the Metro section of the paper and two

headlines blared at me **4-YEAR-OLD BRUTALLY RAPED AND MURDERED,** said one. **MATTAPAN TEENAGER KILLED FOR RADIO** said the other. Another headline halfway down the page caught my attention. **YOUNG MAN'S LIFE LOST IN BOTTLE — FOUND DEAD UNDER EXPRESSWAY.** I read Lieutenant Bailey's quote next to the kid's photograph. "I was at the autopsy, and after viewing the body, I was going to guess he was about 40. When I found out he was 17, I was shocked. They must have been 17 hard years."

A small headline in the lower right hand corner said **JAMAICAN POSSE GANG FEUDS TRACED TO NJ KILLING.** I lowered the paper and took a drink of coffee.

These Jamaican punks in Roxbury, Mattapan and Dorchester were slowly becoming a giant pain in the ass. At least for now they're only killing each other. But it's the way that they do it that scares the shirt out of everyone. They throw bullets everywhere. They hit the guy they're after, fine. They hit anyone else, tough shit.

Christ. I'm glad it's Area B's problem, not mine. I went back to the front section at the *Globe* and read a page two feature story about some illegal Irish immigrants hiding in Southie — could be as many as nine hundred the article said. I figured it was more like three thousand.

Across the page, something caught my eye. A photograph of a dead man, an Irish politician killed by a sniper outside his front door while his daughter looked on. There was something familiar about him. Maybe the way he combed his white hair — maybe the long nose or the glasses. The headlines under the photo said his name was Seamus O'Rourke, one of three Roman Catholics from Northern Ireland to be elected to the British Parliament last year. A Marxist splinter faction of the IRA calling itself the Irish National Liberation Army had claimed credit for the assassination saying they were opposed to O'Rourke's idea of unification and nationalism through peaceful means.

I took one more look at the photo, then returned to the Metro section to read Mike Barnicle's column. I loved reading it. Mike was always dumping on somebody — especially politicians and the Red Sox. Tommy and I met him once at the Doughboy's Coffee Shop in Eddie Everett Square, Dorchester. Nice guy. Talked street. Bought us coffee. Hated the Patriots and a lot of other people, too. Tommy loved him because he smoked cigars. I didn't hold it against him because Mike's brother was one of us — a uniform out of Area D in the South End.

I was half way through Barnicle's column about a brain-dead, four year old girl who had been raped and murdered by a thirty-eight year old guy named Muhammed, when my daughter Jessica walked into the kitchen.

I looked at my watch. 8:25 am.

"Well, well," I said. "Look what the cat dragged in? Morning, sweetheart. What gets you up so early?"

Jessica mumbled something that sounded like "morn'n" and opened the refrigerator. Taking out the milk, she put it down on the table, went to the pantry for some Crunch Berries, then sat down across from me.

Pouring the Crunch Berries into a bowl, Jessica said. "Dad? Can I go to a party Friday night?"

Ah, ha! Now I knew what she was doing up. Her mother must have said no.

"What party?" I said, playing dumb, which wasn't difficult when it came to dealing with my daughter.

"Kim's party, Dad," she said, pouring on the milk, and the sweet talk.

"That the girl who lives in Canton?"

"Yes."

"I don't know. What did your mother say?"

"She said to ask you?"

"Is Mom going to drive you?"

"No. She said she was tired of driving."

"Then how are you going to get there?" Jessica fell silent. Here it comes.

"Missy's boyfriend said he'd drive us."

I shook my head. "No way."

"But, Dad..."

"I said, no. You know how I feel about you riding around with boys. I don't trust them. Nor do I like the way they drive."

Jessica stood up. Gone was the softness in her voice. "I'm sixteen years old now," she said, her voice and blood pressure rising. "I'm not a baby anymore. I don't see why I can't ride with him. He's a safe driver."

I tried to remain calm. "Look, Jessica," I said. "We've been through this before. Give me a break. I don't want you riding in cars, alright? End of conversation."

Jessica threw down her spoon; it bounced off the table and hit the cat. Marmalade gave me a dirty look.

"I hate you!" Jessica shouted, teary eyed. "You're a big jerk and I really hate you!" She ran from the kitchen. A couple of seconds later, the door to her room slammed shut.

I looked out the window wondering what the hell had happened.

A moment later, my only real friend in the world appeared in the doorway.

"I told her you would say no," Victoria said.

"You mean, she didn't listen?" I said, letting my eyes roam over my best friend who wasn't wearing much.

"Did you wish her a happy birthday?" Victoria said, putting the kettle on.

I looked at the calendar. August 19th. "Hell, no. I never got a chance."

"You want another cup of coffee?"

"No, thanks."

"What time will you be home? Or is that a stupid question?"

I kissed Victoria long and soft on the lips. "Yes," I said, squeezing one of her breasts. "But I'm used to them."

Victoria slapped my hand away. "You big jerk," she said.

"So everyone keeps telling me," I said, going out the door.

"You're late," Tommy said, getting in.

"Fuck you."

Tommy looked at me. "I see you're in a great mood this morning. Get shut off again?"

"Kiss my ass. Close the door."

"Where we going?"

"Out to Channel Eight."

"I've never been there."

"Me either."

"How's your balls?" Tommy asked with a grin.

"Sore."

"They should be, you stupid bastard. You took your eyes off him. Rookies do that for Chrissakes. You had him down your barrel. How come you didn't shoot the prick?"

I looked out the window. "I couldn't."

"Couldn't, or wouldn't?"

My head snapped back. "What does that mean?"

Tommy looked at me for a second or two. "You're not going soft on me are you?"

I felt blood rush to my face. "If you call shooting an unarmed man in the back soft, then yes. I'm going soft."

"The bastard killed two kids for Chrissakes. Cut off their faces and fucking laughed about it. He's an animal. You don't let animals like that run away."

"Spare me," I said.

We went down Blue Hill Parkway and turned right on Canton Avenue.

Tommy lit a cigar then rolled his window down.

We didn't speak for three miles.

"Any idea who might have planted the bomb?" Tommy said. He spit a huge lunger out the window.

I looked at him in disgust. "Do you have to do that all the time?" I said.

"I've got postnasal drip. You know that."

"Tell that to the kid you just spit on."

"Fuck'im," Tommy said.

We reached Rte. 138, went a few miles then turned on-to Rte. 128 and headed north.

"By the way," I said. "You never answered my question last night?"

"What question?"

"Where were you until eleven-thirty?"

"Checking a few things out I told you. You my mother now?"

"No. Your boss. From now on, don't get lost at night. At least until things settle down. And we'll be putting in some extra hours, so don't cry."

Tommy looked at me hard. "If you say so."

It was ten after nine when we pulled into the Channel Eight parking lot. Security had traffic backed up about a hundred yards. One rent-a-cop checked ID's while two others gave each vehicle a close inspection.

"Think they're panicked out here?" Tommy said.

"Looks that way don't it?"

I pulled the Plymouth left past the row of cars, and drove up to the gate.

One of the guards, a curly-haired kid with a mustache wearing a white shirt, a tin badge, and a Norris Security patch sewn on the sleeve, put up his hand and stopped us.

I held up my badge. So did Tommy.

"Boston police," I said to the kid. "Homicide."

The kid's panicked eyes quieted down.

"I'm Detective Sergeant Knight," I said. "This is Detective Sanders. We've got an appointment to see the news director."

The kid looked in at me. "Okay, Sergeant," he said, pointing. "Pull through the gate and park over there. Mr. Lombardi is right behind you. You just cut him off."

I checked the mirror. So we did.

Mr. Lombardi nodded to me.

We parked and went in.

The lobby was huge. Pinpoint spotlights shined down from the dark ceiling, forming circles on the gray rug, bathing funny looking artwork in assorted yellows, oranges and greens.

Tommy and I followed the news director past the receptionist who buzzed us through a glass door and past two more rent-a-cops who gave us the twice over.

There were a dozen color photographs of Channel Eight personalities encased in glass on the wall.

"Tommy stopped and looked at the photo of Patricia Day, one of the news anchors. "Is she here now?" he asked.

The news director said, "No. She comes in around three."

"Too bad," Tommy said.

The news director continued down the hall.

"I thought you hated the press?" I said to Tommy.

"I do. But I love Patricia. Tell me who doesn't?"

We followed Lombardi into the news room. There were only three people actually working at the first weird-shaped desk we came to: a fat guy with more scalp than hair who kept squinching up his nose like a rabbit; a good looking blonde with heavy makeup who looked pregnant; and a black guy I'd seen many times on the street. A few others stood around wondering who the hell we were. Everyone had on a sad face.

"You're Dave Floyd," I said to the black guy.

Dave Floyd stood up. That's right, and you're — "

"Joe Knight. Homicide." We shook hands.

"You did a story on us once a long time ago," I said. "I was riding a motorcycle for the MDP unit at the time, remember?"

"No, I don't. But nice to see you again." Floyd sat down and put a piece of paper into the typewriter. The expression on his face said he had better things to do than to bullshit with a fat, ex-bike cop.

"I'm sorry," Floyd said. "But we've got a show to write."

"Sure. No problem."

Across the newsroom was the news set, three large television cameras and a zillion lights hanging on metal rods from a high ceiling. Beyond the cameras — behind a glass partition — was a control room that had more television sets stacked along the wall than I'd seen at Lechmere's.

Going up a spiral staircase, I saw Jill Rodney, the assistant news director, sitting in a glass enclosed office. She was on the phone. When she noticed me, she put up a finger, meaning she would join us in a minute.

In the news director's office, we sat down in black clothed chairs in front of Lombardi's desk. Behind us were four television sets turned to different channels. On the shelf next to me, I noticed some gold statues, and some plaques. "Quite a few awards," I said. "They all yours?"

"Yes," Lombardi said. "Some are for individual achievement in television, others are for outstanding station programming."

"I see."

"Nice," Tommy said. "Real nice."

Jill came in.

I was the only one who stood up.

She smiled briefly at me and sat down on the sofa.

"As you have no doubt noticed, Sergeant," Lombardi began, "All of us here are in a severe state of shock."

"I can understand that," I said. "What kind of calls did you get? Any of them claim responsibility?"

"Yes. Quite a few in fact."

"I'm not surprised."

Lomardi handed me a sheet of paper. "This is the list of calls," he said.

I scanned the list then showed it to Tommy.

There were about twenty-five names of radical organizations on the paper. Even a group calling itself the Anti-news of America Society. Christ.

"Any calls from anyone not part of a group?" I said.

"No," Lombardi said. "None."

"I still say it was some sicko," Jill Rodney broke in.

Lombardi said. "Do you have any thoughts of who it might be, Sergeant?"

I sat back. "No. I don't."

"What story was she working on?" Tommy said. "The day she was killed?"

"A nothing feature about the new Latin Academy headmaster," Jill said. "Before that she did an interview at city hall with the mayor on rising housing costs in the city. That's it."

There was a brief silence.

"What about some of your other reporters?" Tommy said. "Any of them receive any threatening phone calls or letters lately?"

Lombardi looked at Jill. Both shook their heads. "Not that we are aware of," Lombardi said. "I'm sure we would have been told if anyone had."

"Could you check on it?" Tommy said.

"Of course," Lombardi said. "I've scheduled a staff meeting later today. I'll ask."

"Can we take a look at Miss Howell's desk?" I said.

"Of course," Lombardi said. "Jill will show you where it is."

We followed Jill to an office down the hall. In it were several metal desks, separated by four-foot-high wall dividers. Every desk had clutter. Susan's desk against the wall was the worst. Above it, pinned to a cork board, was a smiling color photo of Susan and Jack Adams.

Jill, gazing at the photo, said, "Have you talked to Jack yet? Poor guy — he must be devastated. They really loved each other."

"It's our next stop," I said.

"Who sits in these desks?" Tommy said, pointing to the two desks next to Susan's.

"Our state house reporter, Jane Wright, and Marion Heath, our consumer reporter."

We searched Susan's desk and found nothing unusual. Under some papers in the bottom drawer, I found a small notebook that had some phone numbers written in it. Next to two of the numbers were the letters PW and LE, and some others I couldn't make out. I slipped the notebook in my pants pocket, not knowing why I did. Instinct maybe.

We talked to several reporters — most of them in a rush to get out of the building to cover some horseshit assignment. None of them had any idea what Susan had been working on, if anything.

Ten minutes later, we headed up Rte. 128 to Rte. 2, and went east toward Belmont.

It was hot. The temperature was ninety-two and the

humidity so high it was like breathing in syrup through the nostrils.

"You noticed the lieutenant lately?" Tommy said out of the blue. "He looks like shit. You ask me, he ought to see a doctor."

"He has."

"And?"

I hesitated. "He's got cancer," I said.

"Jeeszus. I knew something was wrong. How much time does he have?"

"Six months maybe. A year at the most. But don't say anything. He doesn't want anyone to know."

"He's only forty-six for Chrissakes."

"Yeah. Life's a bitch."

"And then you get fucked."

We turned off Rte. 2 onto Pleasant Street in Belmont. When we reached Stelt Avenue, we turned right up the hill. Susan Howell and Jack Adams lived at number 17. Six or seven cars were in the driveway. We parked in the street.

The house was a huge white colonial with an attached three-car garage. The front lawn was perfectly manicured, the grass cut short like a golf course fairway.

I walked up to the front door and rang the bell.

The door opened. A stunning tall brunette in a white blouse opened wide at the collar and no bra stood in the doorway. "Yes, can I help you?" she said.

I showed her my gold badge. "I'm Sergeant Knight, Boston Police, homicide. This is Detective Sanders. We'd like to talk to Mr. Adams."

Her legs were long, her breasts large. The shorts she wore looked painted on. "Just a moment please," she said. "I'll see if he wants to speak with you. He's very upset right now."

"I'm sorry, Miss — "

"Fredricks," she said. "Janet Fredricks. I work with Jack at Channel Three. I'm a news writer."

"How nice," I said.

Jack Adams came to the door. He was taller than he

looked on TV, and older. "Who is it, Jan?" he asked. His eyes were swollen red; he had been crying.

"Policemen," she replied. "From Boston."

"Oh," Jack Adams said. "It's all right. Let them in."

Janet stepped aside, and Tommy and I went in.

A dozen or so people were in the living room, most of them standing because there wasn't much furniture. Some were crying.

"I'm sorry," said Jack Adams. His voice was soft, almost a whisper, nothing like the wisecracking sports guy I knew and loved. "I'd offer you a seat, but Susan...Susan and I...we just moved in a couple of weeks ago. We..." He stopped.

"That's okay," I said. "We can stand."

We followed Jack into the kitchen.

I looked out the window. The back of the house had a thirty-foot deck overlooking a forty-foot swimming pool and the best view of Boston I ever saw.

I turned around. The kitchen was busy with people making drinks and fixing themselves something to eat.

"Is there someplace we can talk?" I said.

Jack nodded toward the deck. "Out here," he said and opened the glass slider.

It wasn't like my slider at home. This one was made of heavy wood and thick glass, and rolled smooth along the track. Very expensive — eight or nine hundred bucks. The ones I had were cheap metal, bought at Grossman's for a hundred and a half. They still worked. That's all I could say about them.

We sat down on a cedar bench.

"Can I offer you a drink?" Jack Adams said.

"Got any root beer?" Tommy said.

"I believe so." Jack's eyes fell on me. "How about you...I'm sorry. I don't know your names."

I told him.

A couple of minutes later, someone brought us drinks, then left us alone.

Tommy looked around. "If you don't mind me asking,

Mr. Adams . . . ."

"Please. Call me Jack."

Tommy nodded. "How much does a place like this go for these days, Jack?"

Jack Adams looked toward the city. "Susan and I . . . we paid eight hundred thousand for it."

Tommy choked on his root beer. Some of it spilled on his beard; he did his best to wipe it off with the palm of his hand.

"I'm sorry about your wife, Jack." I said. "I know it's been hard on you, but we have to ask you some questions. If you're not up to it, we can — "

"No," Jack said. "It's alright. What would you like to know?"

"When was the last time you saw her alive?" I said.

"Four days ago. I went out to the coast to do a story on one of the Patriots' top draft choices."

"The one who came down with some kind of disease?" Tommy said.

"Yes," Jack said. "Elroy MacMillian from Stanford."

"Leukemia wasn't it?" I said.

Jack looked at his drink. "Yes."

"Too bad," I said. "He's a helluva football player."

"Do you know if your wife was working on any particular story?" Tommy asked. "You know. Like the Revere cop story a couple of years ago?"

"No," Jack said. He finished his scotch. "She never discussed her work with me. It was an agreement we made when we got married. We left everything at work."

"She almost went to jail?" I said. "For protecting a source. I remember you stuck by her. It was on the news every night for weeks."

Jack took a moment. "Susan was a tough woman," he said. "Stubborn as hell. There was absolutely no way she could be intimidated. The Suffolk County DA found that out."

"So you have no idea if she was working on anything like that?" I said.

Jack shook his head. "No. And even if she had, she would never have told me."

"What about threatening phone calls or letters?" Tommy said.

"None," Jack said. "She would have told me if she had."

I glanced into the kitchen. "Is there a place in the house where Susan did her work?"

"Yes," Jack said. "Upstairs in the spare bedroom."

"Do you mind if we take a look?"

"It's a mess. I'm afraid Susan wasn't very neat."

"We've just come from the Channel Eight newsroom," I said. "By the look of things, no one in television is very neat."

Jack smiled weakly. "You're right. We're not."

Upstairs, Jack opened the door to the spare bedroom, and stopped.

I looked past him into the room. The place was beyond not being very neat. It had been trashed. There was a pile of books on the floor below empty shelves; their bindings had been precisely cut and pages torn out. The draweres in the wooden desk had been pulled out and emptied onto the floor.

Tommy leaned over my shoulder. "He said she wasn't very neat, but this is ridiculous."

"My, God," Jack said. "What the hell happened here?"

"You tell us?" Tommy said.

Jack's eyes were a mixture of panic and bewilderment. He couldn't speak.

I said, "This the first time you've seen this?"

"Yes."

"What time did you get home last night?"

Jack leaned against the wall. I thought he was going to collapse. I gave him another moment.

He looked at me. "I think it was around nine," he said. "I. . .I'm not sure."

"You notice anything — like the door open, or a window?"

Jack took in a breath. "No," he said.

"No, you didn't notice, or no, the doors and windows were locked?"

Jack closed his eyes. His face had gone sheet white.

I'd seen the look a zillion times before. Everything had finally caught up with him.

"You going to be sick?" I said.

He nodded and started down the hall toward the bathroom. He didn't make it.

4

Tommy and I agreed it wouldn't do any good to call in our lab people to have the room dusted. Whoever did the trashing was a professional who knew how to look, and pros don't leave prints.

We had spent an hour going over everything in the room. If there had been anything worth taking, it was already took.

Tommy said, breaking the long silence. "Think we should run a check on our friend Jack Adams? See if he really was in California?"

"Wouldn't hurt," I said. "While you're at it, ask around — see how they were getting along. You know how those TV people are. They're not screwing us, they're screwing around on each other."

"I'll get Warren to check it out. He loves TV people."

I glanced at my watch. 10:40 am. "You hungry?" I said.

"I could eat something."

"How about Haymarket Pizza? It's on the way?"

Tommy pulled out a cigar. "For Chrissakes, Joe. Not there again. Don't you ever get tired of eating fucking pizza?"

"No."

Tommy looked at my gut. "It shows."

"What do you want to eat then? Another doughnut?"

"How about Chinese?"

"Had that last night."

Tommy lit his cigar. "I thought you were on a diet?"

"I am. One slice won't hurt."

"One slice my ass."

"Alright. I'll have two."

At the end of Route 2, when we grabbed the circle onto Brooks Parkway, I checked the rearview mirror. Call it paranoia, but there he was again — a thin guy with rimless glasses and shaggy hair, wearing a denim jacket and racing gloves, driving a shiney black Trans Am.

Tommy saw me looking. "What's the matter?" he said, keeping his eyes front.

"I think we've picked up a tail."

"Who?"

"White guy with glasses. Driving a black Trans Am. I don't know. Maybe I'm getting paranoid."

"Not you? Not Mister Perfect?"

"Hey. Just because you're paranoid doesn't mean they're not after you."

"What?"

I watched the Trans Am come around the Route 2 rotary and follow us over the railroad bridge. He was staying well back — hiding behind four other cars. Whoever he was, he was good. But following someone on a divided four-lane highway was easy. On a two-lane, that was something else altogether.

Tommy said, "How do you know he's following us?"

"Instinct," I said.

"Of course."

The Fresh Pond rotary was coming up. I slid the Plymouth into the right lane and slowed down hoping the Trans Am would pass.

It was a mistake. Whoever the guy was obviously knew he had been made. As we went around the rotary toward Fresh Pond, the Trans Am bolted right, fishtailed with screaming tires, and left a trail of blue smoke up Concord Avenue toward Belmont.

I watched the Trans Am turn into a black speck and disappear. "You see a plate?" I asked.

"You shitting me?" Tommy said. "I barely saw the fucking car."

We drove the rest of the way into Boston in silence. Whoever he was, he'd turn up again. Instinct told me that.

Haymarket Pizza Shop used to be called Al Capone's Pizza Shop. It was stuck in the middle of Blackstone Street, a crowded row of run-down buildings adjacent to the Expressway — near the entrance to the Callahan Tunnel — that also served as Boston's weekend, open-air produce and meat market. You had to eat standing up at makeshift tables of plywood perched on saw-horses on floors covered in sawdust. At lunchtime, the lines could get three or four deep at the counter waiting for slices. But it was worth it. It was the best pizza in the city.

I wheeled the Plymouth up on the center curb on Blackstone Street, and we went in. I was glad. We had beaten the noon crowd.

Getting two slices of pepperoni, two plain, and a diet Coke, I went outside and sat next to Tommy on a wooden fruit box left over from the weekend market when the street was wall-to-wall people buying fruit and vegetables from screaming vendors behind decaying wood carts.

Tommy shook his head. "Four slices of pizza and a fucking diet Coke. I can't believe it. How much do you weigh now, fatso?"

I had a tough time balancing the cardboard plates on my lap. "Two twenty-five," I lied.

"More like two fifty."

"Kiss my ass."

I was about to bite into my third slice when a voice cracked out of the portable two-way radio I carried in my back pocket.

"Operations calling the Victor Eight-Six," the dispatcher's voice said.

Reaching back, I took out the portable and held it up to my lips. "Victor Eight-Six," I said, chewing fast.

"Victor Eight-Six," the dispatcher said. "At the Fan Pier next to Anthony's Pier Four, there's a body washed up on the rocks — possible homicide. Your presence is requested. The M.E. has been notified and is on the way. Victor Eight-Six . . . ?"

Tommy looked at me and said, "Shit!"

The traffic on Atlantic Avenue was grid-locked. Nothing moved. At Rowes Wharf, there was construction going on, another hotel-condominium project. Huge trucks full of lumber and bricks moved slowly, along the Surface Road through steel girders that held up the Northern Artery. I found a lane inside and took it. The front tires hit the sidewalk, and we bounced through the Milk Street intersection down to New Congress. Over the Congress Street bridge, we took a left by MacDonald's, out to Northern Avenue. Nothing moved there either; traffic jammed tighter than a well digger's ass. I hit the siren to move an old man in a Caddy who could barely see above the wheel. The old man flashed us the finger and shook his fist.

"You see that?" Tommy said.

I smiled and said, "What's the world coming to?"

I hit the siren again, stepped on the accelerator, wheeled the Chevy right and stopped alongside the Caddy.

Tommy yelled into the guy's open side window. "Hey, you old bastard. Don't you know a police siren when you hear it? Or are you fucking deaf?"

The old man looked at Tommy, slowly raised his hand, and gave him the finger again. It was beautiful. The first time I'd seen Tommy speechless.

Reaching Anthony's Pier Four restaurant, we pulled into the huge parking lot, drove past the front door and went around through an open gate onto the Fan Pier. Driving over clumped patches of tall grass that grew their way out of the decaying field of tarmac, we parked next to three police cars and an ambulance.

I walked through tall grass onto the granite block retaining wall that sloped toward the water and looked down. The corpse, in blue jeans and a black waist-length jacket, was face down on the rocks. His legs were in the water swaying with the tide.

"Sorry to bother you, Sarge," Patrolman Jimmy Hillman said, coming up behind me. Jimmy and I had worked together years ago when I was a rookie at old District 3 in Mattapan. Jimmy was getting past his prime, but still a good cop.

"That's okay, Jimbo," I said. "What've you got?"

"White male about thirty-five," Jimmy said. "Shot twice in the back of the head, execution style. Been in the water maybe ten, fifteen hours."

Tommy climbed down on the rocks to take a closer look. "Any ID?" I asked.

"Don't know. Didn't touch him. I know how you are about things like that, Joe. Preserve the scene. That's what you're always preaching."

"Glad to know you remembered, Jimbo. Who found him?"

"Some kid from Somerville — the valet parking attendant over at Anthony's — he spotted him. First he thought it was a bunch of rags washed up. He got curious and came over."

"What time was that?"

"Around ten-thirty. Billy and I got here shortly after that."

"The kid touch anything?"

"No. Don't think so. I called in the ME."

I watched Tommy go through the dead guy's pockets. "Why us, Jimbo?" I said. "How come you didn't call the day shift?"

Jimmy walked away and beckoned me to follow. "I got something to show yah," he said.

I followed him across the tarmac through a fence behind an old rusted-out railroad passenger car. On the other side of the railroad car was a parking lot and a black Ford Granada with its trunk open. I nodded to Billy Loring, Jimmy's partner, who had been keeping an eye on the car.

"Nice day huh, Joe?" Billy said.

"Yeah," I said. "Great."

"I saw the memo you put out in the locker room during lineup," Jimmy said. "You know — the one about the bombing of that TV truck?" He leaned in the trunk and picked up a stick of dynamite. "I found this. It was stuck down between the fender hollow and the spare tire."

My heart skipped a couple of beats. "Son-of-a-bitch! Great work, Jimbo. Great work."

Jimmy handed me the stick and smiled. "Thanks, Joe."

I leaned down and searched the rest of the trunk. Nothing. I straightened. "You run a check on the car?" I said.

"Yeah. But nothing has come back yet. All the computers are down as usual."

"What about inside the car?"

"I don't know. The doors are locked."

"Who opened the trunk?"

"I don't know. It was open when I got here."

I examined the stick closely. The name MacFarland Industries was stenciled in black letters on the bottom.

"You call in our lab people?" I said.

"They're on the way."

"You and Billy done good, Jimbo."

"Thanks, Joe."

I walked back. Some gawkers had found their way through the six-foot high chain-link fence that surrounded the Fan Pier and had climbed down onto the granite.

"Get those sick bastards out of here." I said to Jimmy. "While you're at it, call in and get some more help. I want this entire area sealed off."

Jimmy said, "You got it," and hurried off.

Tommy climbed back up the rocks. He had dirt on the knees of his tan slacks and a strange look on his face.

"What's the matter?" I said.

Tommy looked down at the corpse. "I found a wallet."

"And?"

"I know the guy."

Surprised, I said, "Oh, yeah? Who is it?"

Tommy showed me the wallet. The silver badge inside said the dead man was a Chelsea cop. "His name's West. Peter West. He's a drug cop — or was. Remember last year when I was assigned to that drug task force? Did a major raid with the state police and the feds."

"Yeah?"

"West was part of it. Nice guy as I remember. Too bad. I better make a call to Chelsea."

"Talk to Charlie Williams, the chief. Don't talk to anyone

else. Not now, anyway."

Tommy nodded.

Reaching back, I took the stick of dynamite out of my blue jeans. "Look what Jimbo found in the trunk of the car over there," I said.

Tommy's eyes widened. Examining the dynamite, he said, "Don't tell me we finally got a fucking break?"

"I don't know. Maybe."

Tommy gave me one of his what-the-fuck-now looks. "Okay. Let's hear it. Tell me what's going on in that fat brain of yours."

"Everything's too convenient, Tommy. You know what I mean?"

"No, I don't."

"The car, the dynamite — the stiff out in plain sight . . ."

"There you go again," Tommy interrupted. Fuckin' complicating things. Take the dynamite to Latina — if it matches what he found at the scene? Bingo. We found our bomber. What could be simpler than that?"

"Okay, asshole. You've got the case solved. So tell me? Who killed your cop friend down there? Slipped two bullets in the back of his head at close range? A pro hit if I ever saw one."

Tommy looked at the corpse. For a few seconds he didn't say anything. "Okay. Maybe West was dirty. Maybe the people who paid him didn't like the way he did it. Maybe he got greedy and demanded more money."

"Maybe it's not even West's car," I broke in. "Maybe he knew who did the bombing and tried to stop it. Maybe you should stop bullshitting and start making some calls?"

Five minutes later, the Medical Examiner arrived in his gray Olds, followed by a white van that said OFFICE OF THE MEDICAL EXAMINER in blue letters on the side.

Ten minutes after that Doctor Katzman told me what I already knew.

"The man appears to have expired from two gunshot wounds to the back of the head, Sergeant. Also, there appear to be several bruises about the face. Perhaps from a fall — perhaps not. I will know more when I examine him.''

The crime lab people showed up and went to work, taking pictures and dusting the car for prints. They took samples of skin, hair and blood from the rocks around the corpse and put them in small glass tubes. When they were done, the M.E. nodded to his two vultures who immediately descended on the body, flipped the dead man over, stuffed him in a green rubber bag, and tossed it on the stretcher.

I went down the rocks and took a last look around. Nothing.

''Don't take him away just yet,'' I said to the vultures carrying the stretcher up the rocks. ''We've got someone coming over to take a look at him.''

''Oh, Sergeant,'' the doctor called down to me from above. ''I forgot to tell you.''

I looked up. A jet took off from Logan across the harbor, so low over us I could feel my teeth vibrate.

The doctor waited until the jet banked left over South Boston before he spoke again. ''I finished the examination of those unfortunates from Channel Eight. I have determined the cause of their deaths.''

''What's to determine, Doc,'' I said, climbing back up the rocks, brushing some dirt off my jeans. ''They got their asses blown off.''

''The two men, yes. But not the woman.''

I stopped slapping my jeans and looked at him. Katzman had that look on his face I hated. Like a guy holding four aces to your four kings. I could already feel the shit rising.

I said, ''What do you mean? Not the woman?''

The ME said. ''I found a projectile in the base of her brain. The cause of death was from acute cerebral hematoma.''

''What the hell are you saying, Doc? You telling me that Susan Howell was shot? That she didn't die from the explosion?''

''That is correct.''

I looked skyward. ''You've got to be shitting me, Doc,'' I said. ''Tell me you're shitting me.''

"As you so crudely put it, Sergeant Knight, I would not dare to shit a shitter."

"Give me some time frame here, Doc. How soon after she was shot did the bomb explode?"

"It is impossible to tell. It is my judgment the woman died from a single gunshot wound to the head — not from the explosion."

It took me a few seconds to catch my breath and balance. I felt hot — no, I felt cold. Christ!

"Where's the bullet, Doc?" I said.

"It is on my desk."

"What about the caliber?"

"It is not my responsibility to determine the caliber. I can tell you the bullet is badly spent."

I shot the Doc a hard look. "How come it took you so long to tell me about this, Doc?" I said.

"I performed the autopsy on the woman only this morning."

"You could have called me?"

"Yes, I could have. I'm sorry."

"How long do I have to wait for this one?"

"I will begin the autopsy as soon as you release him. You will have the results by three."

I looked at my watch. It was twelve-thirty.

Doctor Katzman took out a handkerchief and wiped the sweat from his forehead. "I can understand your impatience, Sergeant," he said. "But you must realize the pressure we medical examiners are going through these days. Not only the sheer volume of work and the lack of support staff, but the absolute deplorable conditions in which we must work. One day it is the breakdown in the elevator we use to bring the bodies to the autopsy room. Another day, it may be problems with the outdated refrigeration system that keeps bodies cool in the vaults downstairs in the morgue. Or the roaches or the mice. Only this morning, I found several mice droppings on my desk." He paused a moment to wipe his brow again. "Did you know that three of the six state medical examiners have resigned in the past week?''

"No, I didn't."

"Do you also realize what their departure means to us? Five years ago, 250 autopsies were performed in Boston. Now we do approximately 950. I dare not count how many you have sent me over the years, Sergeant."

"We all got our problems, Doc."

"And thank you for listening to mine."

"Did I have a choice?"

I watched him walk to his car. "Thanks for the heart attack, Doc," I said.

"You're welcome," he said.

Tommy came back from making the phone call to Chelsea. I didn't like the look on his face; he didn't like the look on mine.

"What's the matter?" he said.

I told him.

Tommy stared at me with a strange pathetic glaze in his eyes, both of us quiet, both feeling it rising over our heads, knowing there was nothing we could do to stop it.

"You get hold of Chief Williams?" I asked.

"Yeah. He's on the way over."

"He say anything?"

"Not much. West worked nights in the drug unit. No one's seen him for a couple of days."

"He say what West was working on?"

"No."

A half hour later, Chief Williams showed up with two detectives. The tall guy with the muscles, hard face, and cold blue eyes was named Hartman. The shorter cop with dark hair and dark eyes was named Mallory. He wore a blue Scally cap tilted forward, the bill almost touching his long pointed nose. Both wore light colored suits; so did the chief. Strange. Neither of them sweated. Tommy noticed it, too.

We small-talked while the chief went to the back of the van, opened the door, unzipped the bag, and positively identified Detective Peter West.

The chief could barely talk when he came back — said

he'd talk to me in his office. I said okay, how about tonight?
He said make it tomorrow, and they left. So did we.

In the car, going across the Northern Avenue bridge, I
shoved the accelerator to the floor. The Plymouth jumped
forward through the intersection at Surface Artery and High
Street, coughed, sputtered, then stalled.

Traffic stopped dead. Horns sounded. People shouted.

Some jerk in a dump truck behind us stuck his head out
the window and yelled. "Hey, asshole! Get that piece of
shit out of the way before I shove it out of the way!"

Before I could stop him, Tommy opened the door and
leaped out. "Fuck you, pal!" he shouted back at the jerk.

The truck door flew open. "You fuck'n talk'n to me,
buddy?" the hairy bare-chested jerk yelled, half out of the
cab.

Tommy stormed toward the truck.

I got out and went after him.

Before I could stop him, Tommy had jumped up on the
running board. He shoved the door against the guy's legs,
drew back his fist, and punched him in the mouth.

"Now, you ugly piece of shit!" Tommy said. "You got
something else smart to say? Huh?" He opened and closed
the door hard on the guy's foot. "C'mon, fatshit. Open your
mouth again!"

Surprise and shock showed on the jerk's face. Blood
trickled down his chin from a giant cut on the lip. "What
the fuck is the matter with you?" he screamed. "You fuck'n
nuts or someth'n?"

"Yeah. I am! I just got out of Mass Mental. What are you
going to do about it?"

"Tommy!" I said. "Cool it. Get down off the goddamn
truck."

Tommy glared at the guy a second longer then stepped
down.

"Fucking asshole!" Tommy screamed.

I led him away from the truck, back to the car.

No horns blew. No one shouted.

Tommy got in, slammed the door. I turned the ignition.

This time it started and the Plymouth bolted forward, careened down the ramp, into the South Station tunnel.

"Classy show you just put on," I said. "Must have been the heat."

Tommy looked at me. "Fuck you!"

I looked straight ahead, trying hard not to laugh. "Okay. Fuck me. Let's get a root beer — maybe a cinnamon doughnut."

The Southern Mortuary on Mass. Ave. was across from Boston City Hospital. I hated going there. Every time I went there, I got nauseated. Just thinking about what was behind those white porcelain doors stacked four high against the wall in the basement gave me the creeps. Seeing them dead in the street was one thing. Smelling them rot like a bunch of dead chickens, that was something else.

I followed Tommy down the ramp through a set of freshly painted red double doors. Smoke from Tommy's cigar came back at me. It was the only time the smoke actually smelled good.

A stout black man wearing a threadbare blue sweater and tan trousers stopped sweeping the floor and looked at us. "Afternoon, Joe," he said to me. "How yah been, Tommy? Ain't seen you two since last week."

"How are you, Leroy?" I said. "Keeping you busy?"

"Oh, can't kick. Can't kick at all."

Leroy was in his sixties, but he looked forty. The only evidence of his age were some little white curls that had snuck into his black hair. He put down the broom, picked up four bottles of pinescent out of a box, and unscrewed the caps.

"Where's your boss?" Tommy said.

"Upstairs cutt'n," Leroy said.

Leroy pulled out the wicks and began placing the bottles around the dimly lit room.

"Take it from us, Leroy," I said, walking back up the ramp toward the elevator. "They don't work."

Leroy went up a step ladder and stretched to put a bottle

on one of the zillion exposed pipes hanging from the ceiling. "The boss thinks it does," he said with a smile, showing a line of brilliant white teeth. "That's all that matters to me."

We took the elevator to the fourth floor. When the doors rumbled open, we turned left and went down the dark hall to the cutting room.

Pushing through the double doors, I went in first.

Detective Pete West from Chelsea — what was left of him — lay naked on a stainless steel table by the window, disembowled. He had a hole in his chest the size of a crater. His genitals, hanging on the edge, looked as though at any second they might fall in.

The sunlight streaming in from the windows did nothing to brighten the room. Fluorescent lights in the ceiling bathed everything in a drab and dreary green haze. The floors were black speckled tile, the walls green and stained.

I held my breath. Tommy was doing the same, breathing through his mouth as he went closer to the corpse. Across the room, working at another table, was one of the ME's vultures. He had on a blue labcoat and was busy sewing up the chest of what looked like a small boy.

"Where's Katzman?" I asked him.

The vulture turned around. He had a long red neck and a zillion black spots on his face. Maybe the mice had gotten to him, too.

"Talking a coffee break," the vulture said. "Said he'd be right back."

Behind us was a glass case containing various instruments, none of which looked particularly clean, much less sterile.

I looked down at the corpse. The scalp had been cut behind the head, skin and hair pulled up over the face. Only West's mouth twisted into a macabre smile, was visible.

"Katzman through with him?" I said to the vulture, looking down into the crater that had an inch-deep pool of blood at the bottom.

The vulture went back to his sewing. "I don't think so," he said. "He hasn't cut the skull yet."

Tommy looked at me. "You want a puff on my cigar?" he said.

I almost said yes.

Katzman walked in.

He had on a white shirt underneath a long blood-stained, black rubber apron. He wore blue rubber gloves, also blood-stained. I wondered if he took them off to drink his coffee.

"Good afternoon, gentlemen," the doctor said. "I am almost through. I have saved the best for last."

Tommy looked down at the corpse. "Looks like Halloween came early, eh Doc?" he said.

I said, "Everyday is Halloween around here. Isn't that right, Doc?"

Doctor Katzman picked up a miniature powersaw with a circular blade. "I am not amused. What we do here is very serious work."

"How many of these have you done over the years, Doc?" I said.

The ME leaned down and examined the back of the dead man's head. He grabbed some hair, hiked the scalp up over the face a little more, and drew a line on the skull where to make the cut. "This will be number three thousand, six hundred, and seven," he said, pride in his voice.

"You're shitting me," I said. "You actually keep count?"

"Yes. Someday I may write a book." The doctor looked up at me. "I keep a journal you know."

"How nice." Then I said. "Where's the bullet you took from Susan Howell?"

The ME turned on the saw. "It is on my desk," he said. "If you will be patient, I will have two more for you in just a moment."

5

The afternoon sun disappeared, the sky now overcast. A steady, humid drizzle threatened to become a downpour.

Tommy turned on the windshield wipers as we went down Albany Street.

"Hold it a minute," I said. "Pull in here."

"The Flower Exchange?" Tommy said, jamming on the brakes, then wheeling right into the parking lot. "What's in here?"

"Have to send my daughter some flowers. It's her birthday today. Sixteen years old — can you believe it?"

"Where's the time go?"

I went inside and saw Geno Cappucci, the owner of Cappucci's Flowers. Nice guy. Owed me a favor for getting his son off the hook on a minor drug possession charge. It was a nothing favor but to hear Geno talk, I got his son out of the electric chair.

We bullshitted for a couple of minutes then I asked Geno for a dozen long-stem red roses to be sent to Jessica Knight, 75 Pleasant Street, Milton. White house with black shutters and two car garage, I said. He said no problem, he'd send two dozen — be there by five. I wrote "Happy Birthday Daughter, Daddy Loves You" on a card and put it in an envelope. I thanked him, even tried to pay him, but Geno said no way. Nice guy, Geno.

As I got back in the car, Tommy said. "Maybe I should send Sue some flowers for her birthday."

"Don't" I said. "You'll give her a heart attack."

"Fuck you."

I glanced back now and then — checking the side streets as we went up Albany Street under the Expressway. No sign of the black Trans Am.

Going over the Fourth Street bridge into South Boston, I gave Tommy a long look then said, "Tell me something, Tommy — and be straight with me. You been screwing around on Sue?"

Tommy took out a cigar and stuck it between his hairy lips but didn't light it. "No," he said. "But if I was it would be none of your business."

"That right?"

"Yeah. That's right."

"Where did you really go last night?"

"None of your business."

The look in Tommy's eyes told me to drop the subject. I did.

Past A Street, we went left onto D across Broadway, and pulled into a lot opposite the firehouse. Homicide was on the second floor of old District Six, a half brick, half cement three-story that should have been condemned twenty years ago.

Upstairs, I stopped by Lieutenant Bailey's office and looked in. He had his feet up on the desk, his eyes closed, his hands behind his head. His skin had that milky look, pale and stretched. He was losing hair fast.

The lieutenant opened his eyes, saw me staring at him.

"What the fuck are you looking at?" he said. "Haven't you ever seen a dying man before?"

I looked at him a second longer. "Come to think of it, no," I said. "Usually when I get to them, they're dead already."

He hoisted his feet off the desk. "Just what I need today. Another fucking smartass. What have you been doing on the bombing?"

I told him. Showed him the bullets taken from Susan Howell and Pete West.

"I'm no expert," the lieutenant said, examining the bullets, but they look like they could match. What do you think?"

John was right. He wasn't an expert. He was just a street-smart cop who'd been around a lot of years — seen a lot of things. Instinct and hunches. Experienced cops have them, rely on them heavily. No one used them better than John Bailey. So when he said he thought the bullets could match, I swallowed hard. I thought the same thing.

"I'm calling Muggsie McMannus over at state police head-quarters," I said. "Best ballistician in the country. If anyone can match them, he can."

Lieutenant Bailey handed me back the bullets. "Anyone else know Susan Howell was shot?"

I slid the bullets into a small manila envelope. "Just Tommy and the medical examiner," I said.

"Good. Keep it that way."

"What about the commissioner?"

"Fuck the commissioner. You keep working. I'll handle him."

"Like you did last night?"

"I had a long talk with him about that. I told him no one reads our reports unless I see it first. Told him if any necks swing, it'll be mine."

I smiled. "What did he say to that?"

"Told me to get my skinny ass out and stop making excuses for shoddy police work."

I lost my smile. "What did you say?"

"We go back a long way — Frankie and me. I told him to go fuck himself."

My smile came back.

Lieutenant Bailey reached in the top drawer of his desk, took out three plastic bottles of pills, flipped off the caps and spilled some onto his desk.

He looked up at me. "You got something else on your mind, fatty?"

"No," I said.

I walked to the door. "You need anything?" I said, looking back.

John Bailey popped two giant pills into his mouth and washed them down with coffee. "No," he said, wiping his lips with the back of his hand. "And stop mothering me.

Stella is driving me fucking crazy — don't you start."

I was getting watery-eyed again. I forced another smile.

"Oh, yeah," Lieutenant Bailey said. "You got court tomorrow. The Melvin Grosset case. Pre-trial conference. Don't forget it this time."

"Sonuvabitch," I said. "I'm not ready."

"What do you mean you're not ready? You've got the murder weapon — two eyewitnesses. What the fuck more do you need?"

"More time."

"You don't have more time. Hearing begins at nine. You be there. Grosset is a no good murdering bastard, Joe. I want him nailed."

"So do I. But . . ."

"But nothing. See yah later. And next time you're out, bring me back a sandwich. You know what I like."

Yeah. Liverwurst with mayo and onions on dark rye — probably wash it down with scotch. Sonuvabitch. No wonder the bastard's dying.

At my desk, I closed my eyes and rubbed my eyelids with the tips of my fingers. I yawned, wishing I were home on the couch napping.

Opening the bottom drawer, I got out the folder that had "Grosset the Puke" written in red marker across the top. Melvin Grosset was a thirty year old, drug-crazed black guy from Roxbury who lived in a dump on Maywood Terrace, a place where the rats ate better than most of the people. He had a record as long as my arm. He loved flashy clothes, flashy cars, stealing, and killing women. In my twenty-five years on the force, I couldn't remember hating anyone more than I hated Melvin Grosset.

Before I opened the folder, I had that flash again of the dead woman Grosset murdered on Joy Street, Beacon Hill. More blood on the walls and carpet than I'd expect to find in a slaughterhouse. The ME had found twenty-two different stab wounds over her body. Three fingers of the right hand had been severed, others mutilated. Between her legs the flesh had been laid back to the pubic bone, the skin around the eyes sliced, the eyeballs cut open.

I opened the folder and flipped through the black and white photographs of the murder scene. As I gazed at the photo of the woman sprawled at the bottom of the staircase, I wondered what she had felt when the knife came down on her. Surprise? Panic? Whatever. She obviously knew her clock had run out — that she was as alone as she had ever been.

If I were going to kill someone deliberately it would be with a Magnum — one shot to the head. Clean. Quick. That would approach a rational murder. But this was something else. Madness. Absolute insanity.

Tommy came in and sat down at his desk. He saw what I was looking at and shook his head. "When's court?" he said.

"Nine o'clock tomorrow."

"Too bad."

I closed the folder and put it in my briefcase on the floor next to my chair. "We got a chance to nail 'im," I said, straightening. "Not much of a one but still a chance. Depends who's on the bench — who the judge believes. Us or Grosset's slime lawyer."

"You want me to go with you?"

"No. You'll be busy."

"Doing what?"

I handed Tommy a piece of paper off my desk. "I called MacFarland Industries in Lynn," I said. "That's the address. See a guy named Martin. He's expecting you. He's got a list of construction companies who've bought dynamite over the last six months."

Tommy looked at his watch. "It's five o'clock. The tunnel will be jammed tighter than a well digger's ass. Can't it wait 'til tomorrow?"

"Why? You going someplace?"

Detective Warren Dolan walked in and started bitching about the traffic. "Took me a fucking hour just to make it through the South Station tunnel for Chrissakes," he said, running a comb through his thinning brown curly hair.

"Shit's getting worse every day. Imagine what it's gonna be like when they start digging the new tunnel?"

Warren Dolan was forty-one, short, clean shaven, and a sharp dresser like his partner, Jake. He had on a crisp white shirt open at the collar under a light brown sports jacket that matched the color of his eyes, and dark tan slacks that matched his skin. Warren was a good cop, only he bitched too much. Even for a cop. To him, everything sucked. The weather. The work. Dead people, who he absolutely hated — even more than his ex-wife.

I said to Warren, "You find out anything at Channel Three?"

"Yeah," he said, taking out his notebook, checking what he had written. "I talked to the news director — a phony prick named Prosner. Should have seen his fucking hair — looked like fluffed up black plastic for Chrissakes. He said Jack Adams and Susan were having some marital problems."

"Who doesn't?" Tommy said.

Warren flashed a brief smile and went on. "Prosner told me Susan Howell filed for divorce two weeks ago. I checked it out. He was right. The grounds were for adultery."

"What a surprise." Tommy said. "Guy buys her an eight hundred thousand dollar house, and she dumps him 'cause he fucks around a little — what a bitch."

"While I was there, I called California," Warren continued. "The Hyatt Regency confirmed Adams was there. Been there a week — checked out at noon day before yesterday. That leaves him out."

Tommy looked at me and said, "Adams could have contracted. It happens."

I nodded. "Run a tail on him for awhile," I said to Warren. "See where he goes. Who he sees. But do it quiet."

Warren said, "Now?"

"No, moron," Tommy said. "Next month. Of course now."

"It's fucking miserable outside," Warren said. "I'll get soaked."

"Wear a raincoat."

"I don't have one with me. I can't sit in my car because the windshield leaks."

"What about the back seat?" Tommy said.

"It leaks back there, too."

Tommy shook his head. "What an asshole."

I said, "Quit bitching, Warren, and get going. Your cute little clothes get wet, send the bill to the city."

Warren gave me one of his disgusted looks. "At least mine are worth cleaning," he said. He opened his jacket and showed me the Milton's label. "Nice, huh? Cost me three hundred bucks."

"For the label?" I said.

Warren let the remark go. He leaned forward and fingered the sleeve of my blue striped shirt. "Nice shirt," he said. "Where'd you get it? Morgan Memorial?"

He had me. All I could think to say was, "Fuck you, Warren. Get out."

He did, with a grin on his face.

So did Tommy.

I called downstairs and asked the desk officer if he had something for me to drive. When I got downstairs, the officer threw me the keys to a beat-up '80 Dodge station wagon that had BOSTON POLICE INVESTIGATIVE SERVICES in giant blue letters across the front.

So much for inconspicuous.

State Police headquarters was at 1010 Commonwealth Avenue in Brookline, down from Boston University's Nickerson Field. I found a parking spot on Babcock Street, went in the building, and took the elevator to the fourth floor. Following the signs that said FIREARMS REGISTRATION AND BALLISTICS, I walked down a narrow hall crowded with metal lockers and cardboard boxes, and turned right into ballistics.

There were a zillion guns hanging on the walls. M-16 rifles, .45 automatics, .9mms, some .38s like mine. Even a grenade launcher.

A young trooper in plain clothes with short dark hair sitting at a desk — a large automatic clipped to his belt —

looked up at me from a microscope, and asked politely, "Can I help you, sir?"

"Is Lieutenant McMannus in?" I said, showing the kid my gold badge. "Sergeant Knight. Boston police homicide."

The kid looked at my badge. "He's in the back room testing a weapon," he said, pointing at a doorway to my left. "Go through there, sir. Back of the room take the door to your left."

I said, "Thank you," and went through the narrow room that had two giant microscopes hooked to television screens, and a zillion glass jars sitting on shelves containing various projectiles labeled "Unsolved Homicides."

Sonuvabitch. And I thought the shit was up over my head.

"Joe," Lieutenant Muggsie McMannus called out as I walked in. He had on a pair of protective eyeglasses and earphones. "Take a seat — be with you in a minute. Have to test this .357. Grab a set of earphones."

I did.

I sat down and put them on. The room was small, made smaller by the giant water barrel sitting on metal legs that McMannus used to test-fire weapons and to recapture projectiles.

Muggsie was a big man with a big voice, a huge face, and huge hairy arms. He was, however, gentle as a lamb, and smart as hell. He knew more about firearms than most manufacturers.

"Hold on to your hat, Joe," Muggsie smiled, opening a tiny metal door at the end of the water barrel, leaning down and placing the .357 magnum on a wooden cradle. "Trying to match this gun with the bullets taken out of that guy in Melrose."

"The one with his hands tied behind his back and heaved into the lake?" I said.

"That's the one."

Muggsie cocked the hammer and fired. There was a massive explosion. Even with the earphones on, I thought the world had come to an end. Instantly, the five-inch square piece of rubber that kept back the water in the barrel erupted and water rushed out. Muggsie closed the small door stopping the water, went around the barrell, and stepped up on the platform. Sticking the .357 magnum in his belt, he raised the door of the barrel and looked in. "There it is," he said proudly. "Take a look."

I took a look — couldn't see a thing.

Muggsie reached in, felt around, then came out with the projectile. "Beats sifting through bales of cotton," he said with a grin.

Drying his hands with a paper towel, Muggsie said, "What can I do for you this time, Joe?"

I took out the manila envelope, opened it and let the mutilated shells drop into my hand.

"Oh, swell," Muggsie said, looking down at them. "Not another one of those? You keep wanting to test me, don't yah?"

I handed him the shells. "Those two were taken from a Chelsea cop named West."

"I heard about him on the radio. Too bad." Muggsie held up the projectile taken from Susan Howell, gazing at it under the fluorescent light. "What about this one?"

"I'd rather not say."

"C'mon, Joe. Who the hell do you think you're talking to here — some dummy? I know you're working on the bombing case that killed Susan Howell." He stopped talking and looked at me. I tried putting on my poker face. It didn't work. "Don't tell me she was shot?" he said, astonished.

"Okay. I won't tell you."

"Holy shit."

"Yeah. Holy shit."

Muggsie put on his bifocals and examined the two good bullets. "Looks like .9mm hollow-point supervells," he said. "Common round. Let's go put them under the scope."

The room with the scopes I went through earlier was narrow and dark. The only source of light came from a tiny lamp below a miniature camera lens under the scope and from a black and white TV. I pulled up a stool and watched

Muggsie place the two bullets taken from Pete West side by side under the scope. Adjusting the focus of the lens, both bullets appeared on the black and white TV. "Now to line them up," Muggsie said.

He did. The grooves matched.

"Just as I thought," Muggsie said. ".9mm hollow-points. Fired from the same gun." He leaned closer to the screen with a puzzled look.

"What's the matter?" I said.

Muggsie took out a pencil from his shirt pocket and used it as a pointer. "Look at the rifling. It goes right to left."

"So?"

"Normal rifling goes left to right."

"What does that mean?"

Muggsie looked at me above his glasses. "It means in a few short seconds, I've narrowed the make of the weapon down from five hundred to about twenty."

"What a genius. Can you take a guess what make it was?"

Muggsie turned his attention back to the screen. "I don't guess," he said.

"What about the one that killed Susan Howell?"

Muggsie put the bullet under the scope. "Hard to tell," he said looking at the screen. "It's too badly damaged. But if I had to guess, I'd say it was a .9mm hollow-point supervell."

My heart skipped a couple of beats. "I thought you didn't guess?" I said.

Muggsie looked at me and smiled. "I lied," he said.

I looked at the TV screen and saw nothing but a mangled piece of jagged lead. "Tell me straight, Muggs. Could all three have been fired from the same gun?"

"I knew you were going to ask that. The answer is, I don't know. At least not until I've made a couple more tests."

"When will you know for sure?"

"Tomorrow maybe. Things like this take some time."

"What about the make? When will you know that?"

"No idea. It could take a few days."

Muggsie put the bullets back into the manila envelope,

labeled it Boston Homicide, and put it in his pocket. "For you, Joe," he said, "I'll put a rush on. That's all I can do."

"More than I could hope for, Muggs. Thanks."

When I hit the street, it was dark. The rain was coming down hard. By the time I made it to the car, I was soaked.

I tried the old Dodge wagon. It wouldn't start. Son-of-a-bitch! I tried it again. Nothing.

I waited a couple of minutes. Nothing but clicks.

I decided to go back in and make a call. When I opened the door, I stopped.

Down the street, parked just outside the spill of a floodlamp on Babcock Street, was a black Trans Am. Closing the door, I rolled the window down a few inches to get a better look. I could have been wrong but instinct told me I wasn't. Maybe it was the grillwork, or the spiked hubcaps. I don't know. But it was the same Trans Am. I was sure of it.

I reached for the two-way. There wasn't any two-way. Shit!

From where I was I couldn't tell if anyone was behind the wheel. I suppressed the urge to walk down and check.

I tried the key again. The engine rolled over once and died. I tried it again. Nothing.

The Trans Am's headlights went on. I heard the roar of its powerful motor all the way up the street. The Dodge only coughed and whined. I jammed the accelerator to the floor and held it there — waited five seconds and turned the key. Goddamn! It started.

I looked down the street. The Trans Am was pulling away from the curb. I threw the Dodge into gear, keeping one foot on the brake, the other on the accelerator. Spinning the wheel hard left, taking my foot off the brake, the Dodge leaped forward across the road up on the sidewalk. The tires hit the curb hard, the impact bounced me to the ceiling.

By the time I got the Dodge turned around, the Trans Am was through the lights on Commonwealth Avenue, heading east toward Boston.

I ran the red light and did my best to keep up. It was hopeless. The Trans Am went out of sight before I reached the second set of lights.

Sonuvabitch!

At the entrance to Boston University's Nickerson Field, I stopped for a red light. The engine quit.

I left the Dodge in the middle of the intersection, took the T to Broadway Station then walked the rest of the way in the rain. It was after nine by the time I got back to the office. When I saw the desk officer, I threw him the keys to the Dodge, and told him where it was. I also told him to shove it up his ass.

Tommy was waiting for me upstairs.

"Where the hell have you been?" he said in a tone I didn't like.

"I went to shit and the hogs ate me," I said in a tone I know he didn't like.

"It looks like it."

I sat down. My shoes and socks were soaked. I took them off.

"Guess what I saw?" I said.

"Two old people fucking on a train," Tommy said.

"Close. You know the Trans Am we saw following us?"

"Yeah. What about it?"

"I saw it again."

"Where?"

"Down from state police headquarters."

"You're shitting me?"

"The creep was parked down the street when I came out. I tried to follow him, but the piece of shit I was driving died on me. I had to take the T for Chrissakes."

"Why didn't you call me?"

"I did. There was no one here."

"You could have called the dispatcher. He would have sent a cruiser."

"When? Next week?"

"Beats walking — any idea who the guy is?"

I pulled my shirt away from my skin. "No."

"Strange."

"Very," I said. "What did you find out up in Lynn?"

"MacFarland Industries sells a lot of dynamite," Tommy said.

"No shit, Mister Holmes. I never would have known that."

"Kiss my ass." Tommy handed me a sheet of paper. Here's a list of construction companies that bought dynamite in the last six months."

I scanned the list. There had to be over a hundred companies, just in Massachusetts alone. Two hundred if you counted all of New England.

I gave Tommy back the list. "Okay," I said. "Start with the names in the immediate Boston area. Get Jake to help you."

"That could take days for Chrissakes."

"So? You need the exercise."

Tommy folded the paper and shoved it in his pocket. "Look who's talking." Then he said. "Don't forget — you got court tomorrow."

"Yeah, yeah. I know."

"The case is gonna be thrown out, you know that don't you? We fucked up, only you won't admit it."

I wrung out my socks and hung them over the back of the chair. "Don't worry about it. The prick is as good as gone."

Disgusted, Tommy turned around at his desk, made some last minute phone calls, rustled a few papers around, then left for the night. He said he had some things to check out. I asked him what. He said it was none of my business. I said if it was police work, it was my business. It wasn't police work he told me. I thought about his lovely wife, Sue, and his three kids. Stupid bastard!

The telephone rang.

I picked it up. "Homicide. Sergeant Knight."

"Excuse me, sir," my lovely wife said. "Is Sergeant Knight there?"

"Very funny," I said.

"Oh, it's you," Victoria said. "I didn't recognize your voice. It's been so long since I've heard it."

I sat back in the chair. "You saying you miss me?"

"Yes, of course I miss you. When are you coming home?"

"In a little while. I've got a few phone calls to make."

"How about bringing some Chinese home?"

"Where are they going to sleep?"

"Very funny. I'm starved. The kids didn't want to eat so I had some fruit. Now I'm famished."

"Am I going to get lucky tonight?"

"You sure your nadds are up to it?"

"What a way for a lady to talk. What's wrong with you?"

"I've been hanging around you too long. My mother warned me not to marry a cop, but I wouldn't listen."

"Don't get me started on your mother."

"I'm sorry. I forgot."

"Make the call and place the order," I said. "I'll be home at ten."

"Thanks, babe. I love you."

"Love you too."

"Oh, by the way," Victoria said. "Jessica loved the flowers — after I told her what they meant. I think she felt guilty for being so fresh with you."

I smiled. "I felt guilty for not wishing her a happy birthday."

After a brief pause, Victoria said. "How come you never send me flowers?"

How did I know that was coming.

6

The incessant singsong chirp of the family's new parakeet pecked at my nerves as I scanned the morning *Globe*. My son Jeff said he found the parakeet while he was playing basketball. He asked if he could keep it and naturally, his mother said yes. Now we have a cat named Marmalade, two hampsters named Scruffy and Muffy — one of whom chewed a giant hole in the new rug we put down in Jeff's room — and a turtle named Speedo.

All I ever had growing up was a little rabbit I caught in the field behind our house. I called him Meatball. Meatball got lost one day and I went looking for him. After about a week, we smelled something bad under the foldout couch. We found Meatball, looking every bit like his name. I remember crying for two days.

"Morning, Dad," Jeff said, walking past me toward the family room. Jeff was twelve years old, short and slender, with straight black hair his mother said was too long, huge dark eyes, and a smile that made all the girls go ga-ga.

"Hi, Jeff," I said. "Got a new pet I see."

Jeff stopped at the cage. "Yeah. Do you like him? Mom named him Tweety."

"That's original," I said.

"It belonged to the Whites. Mr. White didn't like him so he let him go. Mrs. White gave me the cage and said I could keep him."

"How nice of Mrs. White."

"Jess said she couldn't stand it around here anymore. She said the place is turning into a smelly zoo."

"Bless her sensitive heart." I said.

Jeff opened the cage. Tweety flapped his blue and white

feathers over my head and deposited something on my *Globe*. I looked down at the multicolored speck, grateful it didn't go in my coffee.

Sonuvabitch. Maybe Jessica was right.

"Hey, Dad?"

"Yeah, Jeff?"

"What nationality are we?"

"Why?"

"I have to do this report about the family over the summer."

I looked up from the paper. "Well, let's see. Your mother is British. My mother is Italian — born two days after your great-grandmother and grandfather got off the boat. My father is half English and half American Indian."

"Oh, yeah? What tribe?"

"Blackfoot. From South Dakota."

"You mean I've got Indian blood in me?"

"Among other things. But mostly Italian and Indian. Guess that's why they call us Wop-a-hoes."

"What?"

I grinned. "Forget it, Jeff."

The telephone rang.

Jeff answered it.

"Dad," he said, handing me the receiver. "I think it's for you."

"Who is it?"

"I don't know."

I took the phone and said. "Whoever you are, I gave at the office."

Silence.

Then. "Sergeant Knight?" The man's voice was quiet and soft.

"Yeah?"

"My name's Edwards. Larry Edwards."

"Whatever you're selling, Larry," I said. "I don't want any."

Again silence.

Larry Edwards spoke again. "I have to talk to you," he

said. "It's important."

"Okay. Spit it out. You've got twenty seconds."

"Not over the phone."

"Why not?"

Larry Edwards didn't answer.

"Look, Larry," I said. "I'm a busy man. You got something to sell, sell it. You're down to ten seconds."

"For Chrissakes." Larry's tone sharpened. "I'm not selling anything. I'm a Chelsea cop."

I sat back in the chair. All I could say was, "I'm sorry."

"I've got to talk to you," Larry Edwards, the Chelsea cop said. "Can we meet someplace?"

I glanced at my watch — 8:05 am. "I've got court at nine. I'm not sure what time I'll be free."

"What court?"

"Boston Municipal Court."

"Suffolk County Courthouse?"

"Yeah. Fourth floor — Second Session. How about meeting me somewhere around the courthouse?"

"No. I don't want to be seen with you."

"Funny. That's what my wife says all the time."

Larry said after a brief pause, "Name another place."

"How about downtown?" I said. "Somewhere around the Boston Garden — 150 Causeway?"

"Okay. In the parking lot. Say eleven thirty?"

"I'll try to be there. What are you driving?"

"A green Chevy Blazer with a white roof. How about you?"

"You don't want to know," I said.

Boston Municipal Court was in the new courthouse addition in Pemberton Square behind One Center Plaza, which used to be old Scully Square where the Old Howard once stood.

Unlike the old courthouse with its carved stone blocks and sculptured latticework above elongated windows, and marble steps leading up to giant scrolled oak doors, the new twenty-story courthouse with its dirty white bricks and square windows stuck to the old courthouse like a giant tumor. Whoever designed it had to be a mindless ass who decided to play a joke on Boston and got away with it.

I showed my badge and .38 to the court officer in the marble foyer then took the crowded elevator to the fourth floor.

When the doors rumbled open, I was hit immediately by cigarette smoke and loud voices. Everywhere you looked, there were maggots. Hookers and pimps, drug addicts, and pushers. The place was a zoo, only the animals wore clothes.

I had on my best green summer suit jacket, light tan slacks, brown shirt, and tan tie, and carried the new black leather briefcase my kids bought me for my birthday.

I headed toward the doorway that said SECOND SESSION, past a young girl of about sixteen dressed in a white T-shirt and tattered blue jeans, holding a baby. Standing next to her was a greasy-looking Puerto Rican wearing a black short sleeve shirt that said WINNING ISN'T EVERYTHING, BUT LOSING SUCKS. Reading it pissed me off. My wife bought me one like that for father's day, only mine was white and somewhat cleaner.

Just as I was about to go in the courtroom, I noticed three black guys dressed to the nines leaning against the wall. They had enough gold on them to fill a jewelry store, or rob one, which they probably did before they got here. The black guy with the white wide-brimmed hat looked away from his lawyer long enough to give me the finger as I went by. At first, I didn't recognize him.

Then I stopped, and said with a smile. "Good morning, Mr. Grosset. Nice day for a hanging, don't you think?"

"Fuck you, Knight," Melvin Grosset said back.

I walked over to him, looked up and down his purple suit, and said. "Nice. Real nice." I glanced up at his wide-brimmed hat. "Nice lid, too. What's it for, Melvin? To keep the birds from shitting on your lips?"

Melvin Grosset, raper and slayer of young women, had to be restrained by his lawyer, a whimpy looking guy with oily dark hair, no eyebrows, and narrow eyes who wore the standard three-piece striped gray suit, only his was wrinkled.

"Cool it, Knight," the lawyer said to me, holding Melvin Grosset's arm. "You're intimidating my client again, and I won't stand for it."

I walked up to the lawyer. Melvin and his two friends stepped in my way.

"It's all right, gentlemen," the lawyer said. "Even Knight's not dumb enough to try anything here. Isn't that right, Sergeant Knight?"

I elbowed my way through the black guys and went eye to eye with whimpy the puke lawyer. "Don't fuck with me, Prescott," I said quietly through my teeth, sticking my finger in his chest. "I don't like you, but I suppose you know that by now. You're scum, just like these assholes you represent. You can pull out all the mumbo-jumbo lawyer shit your slimey mind can puke out — I don't care. One way or another, I'm going to nail this bastard client of yours. I don't know what chain you yanked to get him out of jail, but he's going back in. Bet on it!"

Melvin Grosset shoved his chest against my arm. "You shut yo mouff, mothafucka. Don't you talk to my man like dat."

I smiled at Melvin. "Back off, asshole," I said. "Touch me again and you'll be drawing back a stump."

A court officer saw us talking and walked over.

"Anything wrong, Joe?" he said.

I kept my eyes on Grosset. "It's okay, Henry," I said. "Just having a little pre-trial conference of our own."

"Could have fooled me," Henry said. He checked his watch. "It's almost nine. Second Session is about to start. Why don't you people go in and grab a seat before it fills up?"

I resisted the urge to take out my .38 and blow Melvin Grosset away. We exchanged glares all the way into court.

I slid into the second wooden bench from the front, directly behind the prosecuting attorney's table, and the fat court officer to my left stood up and said. "Courrrrt! All rise please! Court is now in session."

My heart sank when I saw who the presiding judge was, sauntering in from the anteroom behind the bench. It was Her Worshipness, the never right Honorable Margaret Mac-Cormack, chief bleeding-heart liberal.

Son-of-a-bitch!

Allen Wisner, the assistant district attorney prosecuting the case against Melvin Grosset turned around in his chair and looked at me. Allen had a wide head and wide eyes set far apart, making it difficult to focus on both at the same time, especially when they rolled around like they were doing now, giving me that here-we-go-down-the-shit-shoot look. Allen also wore a hairpiece that looked absolutely ridiculous. Every time I looked at it, I had to pinch myself to keep from laughing my ass off.

I looked up at Margaret MacCormack. She was fifty-two, with tied-back silver hair, large puffy dark eyes, a wrinkled face and a huge wart on her hairy chin. I always wanted to ask her if I could go for a ride on her broom, but I never had the nerve.

After listening to three armed robbery cases, a couple of assault with deadly weapons charges, some B and E's, an arson case, two wife-beatings, and some other assorted horseshit cases, my case against Melvin Grosset was finally called. It was 10:25 am.

The court secretary called me to the witness stand to read the charges. After taking the oath, I opened my briefcase and pulled out Grosset's file.

I began to read from it, but Her Worshipness stopped me.

"Rather than bore the court with mundane details, Sergeant Knight," she said, "Could you please tell the court in your own words what happened on the night of June 20th?"

I smiled briefly. "Sure, your honor. Be glad to." I pointed at Melvin Grosset sitting with his lawyer at the defendant's table. "The defendant, Melvin Grosset, sitting there, did, on the night of June 20th, with malice-afore-thought, run a large knife across the throat of a one, Miss Janet

Winchester, a resident of number five Joy Street, Beacon Hill — the wound allowing substantial amounts of blood to run forth, enough to cause her slow and obviously painful demise. Hence, the charge of murder number one against Melvin Grosset.''

Everyone in court heard the chuckles coming from the row of cops sitting on a bench behind me. Her Worshipness was not amused.

''Quiet in the court!'' she called out. ''Sergeant Knight. This is no joking matter. This is a very serious charge.''

''Oh, indeed it is your honor,'' I said.

''Do you have anything to submit as evidence?''

''Yes, your honor. Two witnesses who will swear under oath that they saw the defendant run from Miss Winchester's apartment. And this.'' I reached dramatically into my briefcase and took out the large serrated-edge hunting knife we had taken off Grosset the morning of his arrest. I held it up and showed it to the court.

Melvin Grosset jumped up from the table. ''That ain't my knife!'' he shouted. ''The pig is fuck'n lie'n! Try'n to frame me!''

Her Worshipness banged her gavel on the block. ''Shut up, Mr. Grosset, and sit down. Anymore outbursts, I'll hold you in contempt.''

Grosset glared at me as he sat back down.

I smiled at him.

Her Worshipness called the attorneys to the bench.

I couldn't hear what was being said, but I had a good idea. Slimey the lawyer was doing most of the talking. I didn't like the glances I was receiving, especially from Her Worshipness and the assistant DA. I could feel myself slowly getting fucked.

It was ten after eleven when I stormed out of court, shoving away anyone who got in my way.

The case against Melvin Grosset had been dropped. The reason — illegal search and seizure without a warrant, and intimidation of an alleged suspect.

Intimidation my ass. Grosset fell down the flight of stairs

on his own. Happens all the time.

Son-of-a-bitch!

It took me ten minutes to break through the traffic on New Sudbury Street, and make my way to the Boston Garden. It was 11:25.

I had five minutes, so I went for a coffee and doughnut at the Whistle Stop Deli up Causeway, across from the Garden ticket office.

Back in the parking lot behind the Garden, the doughnut and coffee I gulped down met the chicken wings, pork strips, egg foo young and fried rice I stuffed myself with last night. It wasn't a pleasant meeting. Listening to my gut bitch, I waited until twelve o'clock. Larry Edwards didn't show.

I needed a phone and some Rolaids.

I called the office. I had received a number of phone calls. Lieutenant Bailey read me the list.

The last call on the list was from someone named Jackie Coggs. Said she was the owner of the Pussycat Lounge on Washington Street in the Combat Zone. "You doing some moonlighting we don't know about, Joe?" the lieutenant said.

"Yeah," I said. "She wants me as a stripper. She says fat is in now."

"No comment."

"She say what she wanted?"

"Just that she had something for you. I didn't dare ask what it was."

"Any calls from a guy named Edwards?" I said.

"No."

"What about Tommy?"

"He stayed in town last night. Said he had a long list of construction firms to check out. Where are you going to be if he calls you?"

"At the Chelsea police station." I paused, then said. "I bet the assistant DA had a lot to say when he called?"

"Damn right he did. You fucked up, Joe. This time, you really fucked up."

"I should have shot the prick when I had the chance,"
I said.

"True."

Traffic going over the Tobin Bridge was light — everyone
was on the other side, jamming their way into the city.

Taking the first Chelsea ramp past the sign that said
Chelsea Produce Center, I drove into Chelsea Square and
parked in front of the police station. I glanced up at the
flag hanging at half-mast from a post over the door, then
went inside. I showed my badge to the desk officer who
buzzed me through a glass door. The chief's office was up
a winding narrow staircase on the second floor.

Charlie Williams stood up from behind his desk as I
walked in. We shook hands. He was short and stout, wearing a white shirt, yellow tie and brown slacks. His eyes were
green, his hair curly and gray, his expression strained, his
smile lopsided, and thin.

"Sit down, Sergeant Knight," he said.

I did.

The chief went for a pack of Camels on his desk. "West
was a good cop," he said. His fingers assaulted the foil,
found a cigarette, and put it in his mouth. Lighting it, he
went on. "Can't understand how it happened. West was
sharp. Don't know how he allowed himself to get trapped
like that."

"You find out what West was working on?" I said.

"Just some routine drug cases. Nothing heavy."

"When was the last time anyone saw him alive?"

"Two days ago — when he came in for his paycheck."

"What was his shift?"

"Nights mostly. I let him make his own hours. As I said,
Pete West was a good cop — knew more about drugs than
anyone on the force."

The chief fell silent. Smoke hung around him.

"Everybody's going to miss him," he added.

"Do you have a cop over here by the name of Edwards?"
I asked.

The chief gave me a puzzled look. "Larry Edwards? Yeah. He works nights in drugs. He was West's partner. Why?"

I don't know what made me lie—instinct maybe.

"Nothing important," I said. "Used to know a guy named Edwards in high school. Thought it might be the same one."

"Not likely," Chief Williams said. "Larry Edwards is twenty-five years old. Anything else, Sergeant Knight?"

"Not now," I said, knowing a brush-off when I hear one.

"If it's alright with you," the chief said, "we'd like to handle the case ourselves. Hope you don't mind?"

"Be my guest," I said. "I've got enough problems."

"If you do come up with something," the chief added, "I'd appreciate a call."

"No problem."

Downstairs, I stopped at the desk and bullshitted the officer into giving me Larry Edwards' home phone number and address. Down Broadway, I found a phone and made the call. No answer. I asked a cab driver where Louise Street was. He said it was off Eastern Ave, near Merritt Park.

It took me ten minutes to find it. Number 13 was a freshly painted white three-decker with red shutters and trim. I went up to the porch and checked the mailboxes. Larry Edwards lived on the second floor.

I looked around for a green Chevy Blazer. Not seeing one, I opened the front door and walked up the stairs. When I knocked on Edwards' door, it opened. Instinct told me to draw out my .38 and keep it ready.

I pushed on the door gently and saw the most blood I'd seen in a long time—not since Beacon Hill, the night of June 20th. It was everywhere. On the walls, the carpet, the furniture, even on the mirror.

I hesitated, not knowing where to step.

Then I saw it. Behind the sofa. A giant German Shepherd, its throat slashed, its insides spread out on the rug like spaghetti.

I grimaced. I didn't like dogs much myself, but this was ridiculous, as if someone had gone completely beserk.

Madness, Absolute madness.

I went downstairs and knocked on the door. A woman of about seventy-five answered. "What do you want?" she said, peeking at me from around the door. Her mouth was wrinkled and drawn in from lack of teeth.

I showed her my gold badge. "Sergeant Knight. Boston police," I said. "You know the man who lives upstairs?"

"The guy with the dog? You bet I do. The fucking thing barks all night. No one can get any sleep around here."

Hearing a little old lady say fuck sounded a little strange. I almost laughed. "I don't think you'll have to worry about that anymore," I said. "Can I use your phone?"

"What for?"

"I have to call the police."

"You said you were the police?"

"I am."

"Then why do you have to call them when you're already here?"

Sonuvabitch!

"Look, lady. Are you going to let me use your phone or not?"

Reluctantly, she undid the chain and stepped aside. "Okay, okay. No need to get your fucking hemorrhoids hot. The phone's in the kitchen."

"Thank you," I said, exhausted.

Fifteen minutes later, two uniforms in a Chelsea cruiser pulled up. So did Chief Williams, and Hartman, the chief's muscleman.

Upstairs, Chief Williams took a look around and got sick. Out in the hall, wiping his mouth with a handkerchief, he said to me, "What the hell were you doing here?"

"Looking for Larry Edwards," I said.

"What for? And don't give me that bullshit about being schoolmates."

I glared at Muscles. Hartman got the message and went across the room.

"Larry Edwards called me this morning," I said. "Said he had to see me."

"What about?"

"He didn't say."

"Why didn't you say so before?"

I didn't answer.

The chief looked inside the living room. "Jesus Christ. Rusty. I can't believe it. He was a great dog. Larry trained him. Best drug sniffer in the business. Won all kinds of awards." He paused and looked at me. "I know what you're going to ask next, and the answer is no. Larry Edwards didn't kill the dog. He couldn't. They loved each other. They were inseparable."

I looked in the room. Someone managed to separate them. I swallowed.

Chief Williams looked at me. "Something's not right here, Knight. I don't like it. First Pete West, now this. What the hell is going on?"

I shook my head. "I don't know," I said, looking in at Rusty.

"Edwards calls you again," the chief said, "You tell him I want to see him. If he's in some sort of trouble, I want to know about it."

An hour later, I headed back to Boston.

Other than a couple of local bars that a cop told me to check out, no one knew where Larry Edwards was. Someone said he had a girlfriend but didn't know who she was, or where she lived. I was sure Edwards would call again, if he was alive, and that prospect didn't look good.

Throwing sixty cents into the box at the toll booth, I went the rest of the way over the Tobin Bridge into Haymarket Square. I thought about stopping for a slice of pizza but settled for another cup of coffee at the Cookie Shack on Cambridge Street by Mass General Hospital.

I made a call to Muggsie MacMannus. I wasn't surprised when he said the bullets taken from Susan Howell and Pete West matched, fired from the same gun. Muggsie said if he had to guess, it was an HK VP70Z .9mm double action recoil with an eighteen round double stacked magazine. Extremely powerful, and deadly accurate. A killer's weapon. I asked Muggsie if he was sure, and he laughed.

Sonuvabitch!

I thanked him and hung up.

As I walked away from the phones, something else entered my mind. I turned back and called Sue Sanders.

"Hi, Sweety," I said. "How yah doing?"

"Fine, Joe," Sue said. "If you're looking for Tommy, he's not home. He stayed at his brother's house last night."

"I'm not looking for Tommy, Sue, I want to talk to you."

"Oh, what about?"

I didn't know how to put it, so I came right out with it. "Are you and Tommy getting along alright?"

"Other than the normal fights we have every other night, yes. Why do you ask?"

"I don't know. He's been acting kind of strange lately."

Susan laughed.

"What's so funny?" I said.

She stopped laughing long enough to tell me she was pregnant again.

"Son-of-a-bitch," I said.

"You've probably been wondering where he's been going at night?" Sue said.

"The thought occurred to me once or twice."

"Please. Don't ever tell him I told you—he'd kill me. But Tommy's been taking a baby-care course. Not just to learn how to change diapers—Lord knows he's done plenty of that already. He's studying baby first aid. He's absolutely panicked about crib death, you know. He said he didn't want anything like that to happen to us. You know how he is about certain things."

I felt the weight of a zillion bricks lift off my shoulders. "Yeah. I do," I said with a wide grin. A baby-care course. I'll be a sonuvabitch.

"Why don't you and Victoria come over some night?" Sue went on. "We haven't seen you in a dog's age. How about Saturday night?"

"I don't know. We'll see. I'll have Victoria call you. Goodbye, Sue. And congratulations."

"Thanks, Joe. Goodbye."

I stood on the sidewalk for a long time watching the traffic go up and down Cambridge Street, not sure what I should do next, where I should go. I felt like a lost traveler in a foreign land who was unable to reach a certain destination by a specific time because of too many wrong turns.

I also felt aware of a dangerous mental state—no longer did I feel capable of repelling the assaults on my mind. The city was throwing up all over me, and I couldn't stop it.

I walked up the street to my car parked in a cross-walk. I watched some dizzy-looking metermaid with bleached-blond hair approach my Plymouth, take one look at the rust and corrosion, shake her head, and move on. Guess she thought the poor slob who drove it must be on welfare, or an escapee out of Mass Mental who couldn't afford the ticket anyway, so why bother.

Things like that could really make your day if you weren't already eyeball deep in shit.

I got in behind the wheel and closed the door.

The hell with everything.

I took a nap.

7

By the time I got to Doughboy's in Eddie Everett Square, Dorchester, it was one o'clock. Tommy was inside reading the paper. He looked up as I came through the door.

"You want a coffee?" Tommy said.

"In this heat?" I said, wiping my forehead with a handkerchief.

"How about a root beer?"

I sat down in the booth next to the window. "Large—plenty of ice."

Sliding the paper toward me as he got up, Tommy said "You see the *Globe* today?"

"No."

"Take a look at the front page."

I did.

The headline said: **Boston Police Kickback Probe Is Widespread.** The article said that maybe thirty to fifty of the city's 290 detectives were involved in a kickback scheme from about 249 restaurants and bars. Internal affairs, along with federal and state law agencies, have been investigating the case for over five years and indictments are expected by the end of next month. Bar owners have told a grand jury that detectives promised to overlook license violations in return for payoffs. FBI agents late last night seized all license records from the Mayor's Office of Consumer Affairs and Licensing Division.

I read the quote from the commissioner.

"The vast majority of Boston police officers, both past and present, have been and will continue to be honest and dedicated to serving you, the citizens of Boston."

The president of our patrolmen's association, Bob Guinnerti, was also quoted. "The press conference was unbelievable. Everyone's been painted with the same brush. We have mechanisms to handle this ourselves," referring to the involvement of the FBI and the New England Organized Crime Strike Force. "Why weren't we allowed to?"

Disgusted, I lowered the paper and said to myself, "Because too many of us are crooks, Bobby. That's why."

Tommy came back with two root beers and sat down. "Nice article, huh Joe? Makes us all look real nice."

I took a long swallow. "Stupid bastards," I muttered.

"What did you find out?" Tommy said.

I told him about Rusty.

Tommy puffed on his cigar. He seemed mildly impressed with my detective work.

I took another long swallow of root beer. "You find out where the dynamite came from?" I said.

"Nope."

"What do you mean, nope? What the hell have you been doing?"

"I've been at the doctor's."

"What's the matter?"

"Nothing."

"Then what were you doing at the doctor's?"

"Taking care of Allison."

"What for? Where was Sue?"

"Seeing the doctor."

"What? She pregnant again?"

Tommy bit off the end of a cigar and spit it out onto the floor. "You know damn well she's pregnant again. She told you."

I smiled. "Yeah. She told me."

"So let's hear it, asshole. C'mon. Tell me what a stupid shit I am for having so many kids. Tell me I should have had it cut off."

"Take it easy, Tommy. I'm not going to bust your balls."

"Bullshit. You can't wait to bust my balls. I know you. I suppose Sue told you about the baby classes I've been going to?"

"She mentioned something about it."

Tommy glanced around the coffee shop, making sure no one overheard us. He said, looking back at me, "Wipe that stupid smirk off your face. I've got one more class tomorrow night then it's back to business. You don't like it — go fuck yourself."

I finished my root beer. For a couple of minutes we didn't talk.

Tommy gazed out the window, took in a long breath, and let it out slow between his teeth.

"C'mon, Tommy," I said, getting up from the stool. "Stop feeling sorry for yourself. What's done is done. So you're going to be a daddy again. It's not the end of the world."

Tommy stood up like a lost man and followed me to the door. "Maybe you're right," he said sadly. "Maybe I should have had it cut off."

I smiled. "I know a cute little blonde who might be able to help you out."

"Fuck you."

It was dark. 9:45 pm.

We took the ramp off the Expressway and went into Chinatown, took Kneeland Street to Washington Street, and turned right into the Combat Zone.

Tommy jerked the Chevy to a stop across from the Pussycat Lounge. "You think she's in there now?" he said, shutting the engine off. "It's still early."

"Jackie said she came in around nine last night with some asshole wearing a cowboy hat. She said the same blonde came in the night before, so she called me."

"What's with you and this Jackie? You tapping something on the side I don't know about?"

"Yeah," I said, watching the broad-shouldered guy guarding the door of the Pussycat pick his nose. "I love fat broads. They're so soft and cuddly."

"I believe it. What do you do? Roll her in flour and fuck the wet spot?"

"You're sick, you know that?"

Disgusted, Tommy opened the door and got out. "C'mon, Needle-Dink the Giant Fucker. Let's make this quick. I'm tired. The last thing I need is to chase some little cock-biter around all night."

The bouncer at the door had the worst case of bad breath I ever smelled. I turned away from him when he said, "Go right in, gentlemen. Enjoy the show."

Maggot-breath must have seen "cop" written across our foreheads because as soon as Tommy and I went by him, he was on the phone to someone inside.

The place was dark and loud. The only source of light spilled down on us from multicolored spotlights above the stage behind the bar, where a stunning naked brunette with long supple legs and huge breasts danced erotically to Bob Seeger's "Night Moves."

I stared at her, feeling my groin tighten.

"Hi, boys," Jackie said to us. "Enjoying the show I see."

I glanced at her and nodded, then my eyes fell back on the naked dancer. Damn, she had smooth skin.

Jackie Coggs, owner and operator of the Pussycat, was a fat woman of about forty-five who looked sixty-five. She wore long false eyelashes and a ton of milk-white makeup that covered her square, brutal face and hard yellow eyes. Her mouth was an oblong hole surrounded by bright red lipstick. There were blisteres at the corners of her mouth which she licked from time to time with the tip of a pale tongue.

Still, Jackie was a good broad with a good heart, and she loved cops. I did a favor for her brother one time, and she'd never forgotten it. Said I could come in for some free ass anytime I wanted. So far, I'd resisted.

Jackie grabbed my arm and led me away from the bar. "This way, sexy," she said. "Perhaps I can find you something out back."

"What would my wife think?" I said.

"Fuck your wife," Jackie said.

Tommy laughed. "He's been trying. Can't you tell by the look in his eyes. Think you better grease up the cat."

Jackie's office was a match box. All that could fit into it was a chair and a tiny desk. Jackie sat down in the chair, I sat on the edge of the desk. Tommy stood by the door and took out a cigar.

"Don't you light that miserable fuck'n cigar in here, you asshole," Jackie said. Her tongue flicked out to lick the blister. "I can't stand cigar smoke."

"Amen to that, sister," I said.

Tommy gave me a disgusted look. I grinned.

The cigar retreated into his shirt pocket.

I said to Jackie. "Has she been in here tonight?"

"No, not yet," Jackie said. "But she will. She's been ask'n around for a job. Says she's some sort of great dancer. You ask me, she'll never make it. Too fuck'n skinny."

"What makes you think she's the one we're looking for?" Tommy said.

Jackie smiled. Her teeth were as yellow as the tight dress she was stuffed into. "I know," she said. Her tongue flicked out again. "I know a piper when I see one. She goes down on it alright. You can bet your sweet asses on that. You don't hang around this business thirty years without learn'n something."

"I'm sure," Tommy said.

"You guys gotta promise me one thing though. She comes in — you don't wreck the place try'n to get her out. Promise me?"

"We'll do our best," I said.

"Don't worry about a thing, Jackie," Tommy chimed in. "We may be fat, but we move like cats. We're trained killers."

"Swell," Jackie said. "That makes me feel a whole lot better."

I checked my watch. 10:20 pm.

I slid from the desk. "Thanks, Jackie," I said.

"Don't mention it, Joe. Like I said, I owe yah one."

I said to Tommy as we left the office, "We'll give her an hour. She don't show by then, we go."

"You boys want a drink?" Jackie said, following us out.

"No, thanks," Tommy said, rubbing his forehead, "But

I could use a couple of aspirins."

"Aspirins," Jackie said. "Fuck no, I ain't got no aspirins. We cause headaches here, pal. We don't fuck'n cure 'em."

As Jackie brushed by us and walked away, Tommy made a face and gave her the finger.

It was quarter to eleven when we spotted the fat guy with the white cowboy hat and short sleeve Hawaiian shirt come through the door and find a stool at the bar.

Tommy and I were in a booth by the front door. It was dark as hell; for a long time, the only way I saw Tommy was when he struck a match to his cigar.

We waited twenty minutes for Miss Cocksucker. She didn't show, so we decided to go up to the bar and query her fat boyfriend as to her whereabouts.

We didn't get off to a good start. The boyfriend took exception to Tommy's first inquiry.

"Hey, fatshit," Tommy said. "Where's your little cocksucking girlfriend tonight?"

The boyfriend turned to Tommy and said. "You talk'n to me, asshole?"

I pushed aside the stool next to the boyfriend and leaned my elbows on the bar. "I believe he is," I said.

The boyfriend's head swiveled around to me. I showed him my gold badge. "Sergeant Knight," I said, having to shout above the music. "Homicide. Step outside. We want to ask you a few questions."

Maybe it was the loud music. Maybe it was the darkness. Either way, the boyfriend didn't pay any attention to my badge. Instead, he leaped from the stool, pulled a knife that looked the size of a bayonet from nowhere, spun around, and stuck it into Tommy's left arm.

I didn't hear Tommy scream because there were screams and shouts of panic everywhere.

Everything froze for a few seconds. Tommy looking down at the knife through his forearm. Me backing away from the bar, reaching for my .38. The boyfriend slipping from the bar stool about to make his break.

The music stopped. The naked dancer stopped dancing.

Everyone in the world heard me yell to the boyfriend, "Hold it right there, asshole! Make a move off that stool, your mother will puke when she sees what we send her in a basket!"

The boyfriend didn't listen.

He came at me hard and fast, the knife raised. All I could see was a giant silhouette against the red lights of the stage beyond. I aimed my .38 somewhere in the middle of the silhouette and fired one shot.

The explosion scared the shit out of me, and everybody else. I thought for a moment I had gone deaf.

The silhouette took another step, staggered, then disappeared into the darkness of the floor. There was a thud — after that, everything went quiet and still. Then the boyfriend moaned. He was still alive. I was glad.

Someone turned on the house lights. Everybody squinted at the sudden brightness.

I heard Jackie shout, "Joe. You stupid bastard! Look what you've done! He's bleeding all over my new rug for Chrissakes — cost me two thousand bucks! I told you I didn't want you messin' up the place!"

Ignoring her, I rushed to Tommy. He was bent over at the bar, holding his arm tight against his chest, his hand pressed against the wound, blood flowing from around his fingers.

"You okay?" I said.

Tommy looked at me. "No, I'm not okay," he said, irritated. "It hurts like hell. What a stupid fucking question."

I smiled, feeling my pulse rate slow down. He was going to live.

It was eleven forty-five by the time Tommy left in one of the city's Health and Hospitals ambulances, his wound not serious but needing stitching.

The boyfriend was still on the floor, surrounded by two paramedics and an EMT. His pretty Hawaiian shirt was torn open, revealing a hairy fat chest and stomach. My bullet had caught him in the fleshy part of his right side.

I said to the stocky paramedic with the mustache and receding hairline, "He going to make it?"

John Ladvine, the senior paramedic on duty, looked up at me and said, "It's a good thing you're a lousy shot, Joe, that's all I can say."

The boyfriend opened his eyes and groaned at me. "I'm . . . gonna sue you . . . you miserable . . . motherfuck'n asshole. You . . . just wait and see if I don't . . . ."

One more time, cowboy," I said. "Where's your girlfriend?"

The boyfriend shut his eyes briefly. "Go . . . fry your ass," he said.

It was then that I realized he needed some prompting.

I took a look around. The lounge was empty except for Jackie, some strippers, and a couple of wide-eyed cops. I said excuse me to the senior paramedic and got down on one knee. Leaning over the boyfriend, I peeled back the bandage, stuck my middle finger deep into the wound and moved it around.

The boyfriend told me what I wanted to know.

I went out the back door and took the alley up to LaGrange Street to avoid the horde of press that had gathered out front. Walking on the darkside of LaGrange, I slow-walked out onto Washington Street. There they were, the maggots, waiting by the front door of the Pussycat, cameras down, everyone bullshitting. None of them noticed me come around the corner behind a couple of Boston police cruisers and go across the street. By the time they spotted me, I was in my car, going up Washington Street.

The boyfriend said her name was Maggie — he didn't know her last name. Lived with two other girls in Bay Village on Fayette Street. He wasn't sure of the number, could be number twelve. He said she was maybe in her late teens or early twenties, blonde hair, blue eyes, slim build and liked tight clothes and heavy makeup.

The hookers were out in Chinatown and along Kneeland Street as I turned left on Tremont, taking the back way into Bay Village. On Fayette Street, I gave number twelve a quick look, saw no lights, drove past, and pulled to the curb in front of number sixteen.

The street was bright with streetlamps, spaced thirty feet apart along bricked sidewalks. Tight rows of freshly painted three and four-deckers lined both sides of the street. Once a run-down neighborhood, Bay Village was now one of *the* places to live in Boston. The cops called it Yuppyville because most of the residents were young business types who drove BMW's, walked tiny hairy dogs, and bitched to the police about hookers and street people littering their sidewalks.

I checked my watch. 12:40 am.

I looked in the rearview mirror. Number twelve was still in darkness; only a hint of light came from a third floor window. I thought about going in, but didn't. I had to know more. Like what floor she lived on? What apartment? I decided to sit and wait.

I began to think of other things I could be doing. Like being home in bed with Victoria after having a quiet dinner someplace, or maybe after going to a ball game with my son.

The job. It was always the job. Just when I think I've a handle on things, the city throws up something else, something more brutal, more shocking.

Seeing a kid senselessly stabbed, or a wino's face blown off does something to you. Carves a hollow out of the heart. Causes the sick-in-the-gut feeling that doesn't want to go away.

Sometimes the world was nothing but grief — suffering the major part of the human condition. The only way to stay sane was to immunize yourself against it. Go the hard-bitten route like Tommy — refuse to be surprised or disgusted by anything. Hide behind cynicism.

I wondered if I was going soft.

I looked up and down the empty street. My eyes were burning, having a hard time staying open.

I told myself, ten more minutes. If she didn't show by then, more than likely she was already in her apartment.

At least I'll know where to look tomorrow.

The sound of high heels echoing off the brick sidewalk caused me to open my eyes. I must have dozed off because for a second or two, I forgot where I was and what I was there for.

There she was, walking toward me. Tall and long-legged, her glistening blonde hair bouncing off her shoulders, a dark red dress pressed firmly against her small but firm breasts.

I held my breath, feeling a tightening in my groin. Seeing her made me wish I was twenty years younger, and a hundred pounds lighter. There was something formidable about her, almost threatening in the way she walked. Was it power? Recklessness? I wondered why I suddenly had that sense of her.

I waited until she was a few feet away from me, then opened my door and stepped out. She stopped walking and looked at me, more curious than frightened.

"Looking for something, handsome?" she said. Her voice was strong, deep-throated and raspy. I could see her hand sliding inside her purse.

I took out my gold badge and showed it to her. "Sergeant Knight. Homicide," I said. "Mind if I ask you a few questions?"

She gazed at my badge. A wall instantly went up between us. "What sort of questions?" she said.

I kept my eye on her handbag. "I understand you've been biting off more than you can chew?" I said.

"What?"

"Nothing. Bad joke."

She took a step back. It looked like she was getting ready to run.

"You know a fat slob named Vinnie?" I said. "Vinnie Black? Wears a cowboy hat and shit-kicker boots?"

She didn't answer, but her face told me she did.

"I saw him tonight at the Pussycat," I said. "Says you go in there with him sometimes. That right?"

Her green eyes darted. "I don't know what you're talking about," she said. "I don't know anyone named Vinnie Black."

"I think you do. Anyway. He's been shot. I shot him."

I could see the anger in her eyes. She was a lousy actress. "So?" she said. "Why should I care about someone I don't even know getting shot?"

"You know a man named Larry Wagner? Or a guy named Jack Fleming?"

"No, I don't."

"You should. You bit their pricks off a couple of weeks ago."

She looked at me for several moments, not saying anything.

I predicted her next move. Before she could pull her hand out of the purse, I grabbed her wrist and squeezed. Slowly, cautiously, I took her hand out. In it was a small caliber pistol with a pearl handle.

"Let go of me," she said. "You're hurting me."

I reached for the gun and pried it from her fingers. She was amazingly strong. I had to use both hands.

"You bastard," she said between clenched teeth.

"Yes. I know."

A shaft of white light shot across us from a doorway to the right. A young, gay-looking guy walked out on the top step with a furry little white dog on a leash. I viced a grip around the blonde's arm, instinctively moving her in front of me, concealing the gun from the fag on the steps.

Holding her close to me, her dress felt silky, her perfume had the enchanting aroma of wild lilacs.

The faggot looked at me, then at the blonde. "Ralphie," he sang. "I see you've found yourself a big one? My goodness. I can't believe all the luck you have."

I looked at the blonde. "Ralphie?" I said, stunned.

Ralphie's eyes were rivited on mine, her lips parted, her breath erratic. I should have known by the strength in her arms. Ralphie wasn't a she.

So much for wild lilacs. Son-of-a-bitch!

I reached up and grabbed Ralphie's hair; it slid off his head.

"Why, Ralphie boy," I said, concealing my shock, holding up the blonde wig. "What greasy, black hair you've got. You flaming faggalet, you. You're under arrest."

Choked laughter came from Ralphie's throat, the veins in his long neck pronounced. "I'll scream," Ralphie sang out.

"I'll shoot," I said, shoving the pistol in Ralphie's back.

"No, you won't," Ralphie sang back. "Because it's not loaded."

Before I could react, Ralphie spun around, raised his dress above his knees, and kicked me hard in the shin. I doubled over and grabbed my leg; as I did, he kneed me in the chest.

I stumbled back, pain spreading through me. I shook my head, trying to catch my breath and balance and regain some focus.

Before I could right myself, the faggot on the porch ran down the steps, jumped on my back, and proceeded to slap me about the head. I must have looked like a complete fucking asshole, dancing around in the street with two faggots hanging on me, one bashing in what brain cells I had left, the other trying to kick my nuts in. Not to mention the little hairy mutt running around me, barking, trying to bite my ankle off.

I spun around wildly, trying to throw off the guy on top of me. No luck. He tried to rake his fingernails across my face. I grabbed his fingers in time.

"You little fag bastard!" I said. "I'll break your fucking neck! Let go of me!"

He did. Long enough for me to get a grip on some skin and hair, and yank him over my head. The faggot's back hit the pavement hard. I heard a wheeze and expulsion of breath. I knew he was hurt but I didn't care — my eyes were on Ralphie with his dress up around his thighs, running like a frightened cat down Fayette, toward Arlington Street.

I chased him a couple of blocks. No luck. All I got for my effort was a burning chest.

Ralphie had gone down an alley and disappeared.

I headed home. I was tired and sore and bullshit for letting myself get so far out of shape. A couple of years ago, I could have taken them both with no problem. Now, I had all I could do to keep from passing out. Anyone would have thought I smoked three packs a day the way I was breathing so heavily. Two skinny fags. Jesus Christ. Glad Tommy wasn't there.

I don't know when I picked up the Trans Am behind me. I was in a fog. I yawned and blinked several times, and checked the rearview mirror. It was still there, three cars back.

Going by Franklin Park down Blue Hill Avenue past American Legion Highway, I reached for the two-way and called the dispatcher. I asked if he had any unmarked cruisers in the area. The Victor Seven-Six car heard my call and broke in.

"The Victor Seven-Six car is coming up Columbia Road, Victor Eight-One."

"That you, Danny?" I said.

"It's me, Joe." Danny said.

Danny Murphy was a detective out of drugs, worked the graveyard — midnight to eight. Tough cop. Hard nosed. Only trouble was, he was starting to look like a druggie — long hair, full beard and mustache, smelly clothes. Drove a brown and maroon '81 Buick that had more rust than my Plymouth.

"What can I do for yah, Joe?" Danny said.

"Where are you?"

"Com'n up on Blue Hill Avenue. How 'bout you?"

"You're close. I just went by American Legion."

"What's the problem."

"Nothing heavy, Danny. I've got a black Trans Am with fancy hubcaps on my ass. Been there a couple of days, off and on."

"You want me to take him out?"

"No. Tail 'im for me. Get a plate number if you can."

"Then what?"

"Call me."

"You got it."

"Thanks, Danny."

8

The last time I saw the Trans Am was when I went through Mattapan Square. I never did see Danny.

I crawled out of my car in the garage, closed the door, and walked up the steps to my house like a man who wanders in deep sleep. Time and place were lost; disorientation had swept over me. I didn't notice it until I walked up onto the porch.

Son-of-a-bitch!

Somebody had toilet-papered our house. It was everywhere. White toilet paper dangled from the trees and the mailbox. Long strands of it ran across the lawn up the steps, and over the porch rail. I had to tear away several strands just to get in the front door.

"You're late," Victoria said in the darkness of our bedroom.

"No shit," I said, taking off my clothes.

"Had another hard day I see," Victoria said.

"No shit," I said. "Did you see our front yard?"

"You noticed."

"I noticed. I'd have to be goddamn blind not to."

"Don't swear."

I yanked off my shirt. "Who the hell did it?"

"No doubt some of Jessica's friends."

"You see them do it?"

"No. We were watching the Red Sox. Can you believe it? They lost again — Yankees got three runs in the ninth. Smith gave up a two-run homer to Mattingly."

"Wow. That's terrible. Someone's out throwing stuff all over our front yard and all you can talk about is the Red Sox. I don't care about the Red Sox. They're going to choke again — same as every year.''

"They're leading the league by eight games. It's their year. I can feel it.''

"It's August. They'll be dead by the middle of September.''

"Pessimist.''

"No. A realist.''

I took a shower, brushed my teeth, took a shit, and went to bed.

It was 2:35 am.

"Sort of looks like Christmas out there doesn't it?'' Victoria said as I got into bed.

I rolled over on my side and punched my pillow. My legs ached, the calves especially. The base of my spine felt sore too. "If you say so,'' I said.

"Jessica and I see it as a status symbol. Having your house toilet-papered usually happens to football heroes before the big game. Jessica was quite proud to have it happen to her — being Milton's number one soccer player of course.''

"I'm thrilled.''

"Don't worry. Jessica is going to clean it up tomorrow.''

"Swell.''

Silence.

"You want to fool around?'' Victoria said, teasingly.

"No.''

"What? I must be hearing things. I can't believe you said that.''

"Neither can I.''

I closed my eyes.

Sleep came. Then the dreams. Then the nightmares.

The relentless ring of the telephone sounded like some demented bird. I opened my eyes, seeing a slit of cruel white light through the drapes from the street lamp across the street.

My eyes found focus on the clock next to the bed — 3:17 am.

I reached for the telephone. Before I could pick it up,

it stopped ringing.

Sonuvabitch!

Ten minutes later, the phone rang again.

I picked it up. "This better be good," I said wearily. I heard someone laugh. A sick, maniacal laugh — the kind you'd hear at the Mass Mental Hospital psycho ward. Then a click.

"Who was that?" Victoria asked, sleepily.

"I don't know," I said, hanging up. "Go back to sleep."

"That happened to me earlier," Victoria said. "All I heard was someone laugh."

My eyes widened. "What time was that?"

"I don't know. Around eleven I think."

"Probably just some whacko," I lied. "Don't worry about it. If it happens again, let me know. I always wanted an unlisted number."

I stared at the ceiling, knowing I had heard that laugh before, but I couldn't remember where.

The lights went out again.

The weather sucked. The skies were muddy again, storm clouds hung across the city like some unnameable doom, shrouding high-rises in a dark mist.

I yawned. At least the air was cooler.

I had slept terrible, dreaming distorted dreams, haunted by unidentifiable shapes. I kept waking up sweaty, my skin sticking to the sheets. I kept hearing that laugh, over and over.

"You look like shit," Tommy said. "You getting enough sleep?"

"Does it look like it?" I said.

Tommy looked at me. "Going to be one of those days, is it?"

I yawned again. "How you feeling by the way?" I said, looking down at Tommy's bandaged left arm.

"It's sore but I'll live. Where'd you hit him?"

"In the side."

"Fatal?"

"No."

"Too bad. What happened after I left?"

Light mist hit the windshield; I turned on the wipers.

"Did fat-shit tell you where little Miss Cocksucker was?" Tommy said.

"Yeah, he did." I hesitated. "Only little Miss Cocksucker turned out to be a little Mister Cocksucker."

"What?"

I told him what happened.

Tommy laughed all the way to Dorchester. When we got to Doughboy's, he said. "Aww, c'mon, Joe. Getting beaten up by two fags isn't the end of the world. Maybe it's the diet. You need some energy. C'mon. Let me buy you a sweet-roll."

"I don't want any sweet-roll," I said.

"How about a doughnut then?"

"Okay," I said. "But you tell anybody what happened, I'll kill you."

Tommy grinned. "My lips are sealed."

"So will your asshole if you so much as open your mouth."

Lucky for Tommy, Doughboy's was empty.

Back at the office, I stopped by the front desk and checked for messages. The dispatcher said I had gotten a call from Detective Danny Murphy. He handed me a piece of paper with a phone number on it — said to call him at home.

I did.

"Danny. It's Joe."

Danny groaned something, then he said. "What time is it?"

"Ten o'clock."

"Don't you ever sleep?"

"No. What have you got for me, Danny?"

"Wait a minute." Danny put down the phone. Twenty seconds later, he came back on the line. "I got a plate number. Wanna take it down?"

I did. New York 223-444.

"You run it through, Danny?"

"No. Everything was down."

"Were you able to follow him?"

"Yeah. Guy's got class — say that much for him. Guess where he took me?"

"Where?"

"Beacon Street. Number 441. The Equador Complex."

"You're shitting me."

"Nope. I followed the bastard around to Back Street — watched him go in."

"Did he spot you?"

"You kidding? Me? The Dog Man? No one spots the Dog Man."

"Sorry. I forgot."

"You're forgiven."

"You know what apartment he went in?"

"Yeah. Apartment 2C. Second floor, the Charles River side."

I thanked Danny and hung up.

Tommy had taken off to Medford. Downstairs, I asked the desk sergeant if he had anything for me to drive. My Plymouth had shit the bed in the parking lot. He threw me the keys to an '88 black Buick Regal parked out back. Getting in behind the wheel, it felt like Christmas. It still had the new-car smell.

I took it to the Back Bay.

Beacon Street was old and new money, especially the lower part, around Dartmouth and Exeter, where condo conversions had been allowed to run rampant, and all you needed was a million bucks to own one.

Heading one-way west toward Mass. Ave., I watched the numbers go by. Neat rows of brick and stone buildings lined both sides of the street. Old stately homes of nineteenth-century architecture with roofs and windows framed in painted metal, wood and concrete. Stone steps and wrought-iron railings leading up to recessed doorways, and illuminated carriage lamps perched on black metal posts spaced evenly along red-bricked sidewalks. As always, I thought it must be nice to live here.

Number 441, the five-story Equador Complex, was at the

corner of Beacon and Exeter. The front was made of glass, polished marble, and black-iron latticework. So was the back that looked out over Storrow Drive and the Charles River.

Going slowly down Back Street, I looked around. No sign of the black Trans Am. Finding a space next to a dumpster, I got out, hiked the collar of my tan jacket up around my neck, watched the rain come down, then tried the back door. I expected it to be locked, and it was.

I stood a few moments wondering what to do next. I was getting soaked. I was about to take out my lock-jimmy when an old lady walking the ugliest black and white dog I'd ever seen at the end of a leash came up behind me with a key in her hand. I smiled at her and tipped my Red Sox cap. "Looks like I forgot my outside key," I said with a smile.

The old lady reached down and picked up the ugly little dog. Holding it protectively under her arms, she gave me the twice-over.

She was a petite, elegant-looking, gray-haired woman with soft aristocratic features and a bearing that bespoke monied gentility.

"Your dog is getting wet, mamm," I said, flashing her the kindest smile I could call up.

I'm not sure if it was the smile or that I was kind to her dog. Whatever, she said. "I don't recall seeing you around here before?"

Her voice confirmed my appraisal; it was typically Boston, refined in the better finishing schools and at polo matches.

"I just moved in," I said.

"Is that so? What apartment?"

"Second floor. Apartment 2C."

"With that other nice young man, Mr. Cole?"

"Yes. I'm his cousin. He's letting me stay with him until I can find a place of my own."

The rain fell harder.

"Mamm, it's getting awfully wet out."

"Oh my, yes. I am terribly sorry."

The woman unlocked the door. We stepped inside. The ugly dog looked even uglier in the soft light of the hall.

I followed the woman to the elevator. "My name is Mrs. White," she said. "I live just down the hall from you. What is your name?"

The doors opened. We got in.

"Mr. Johnson," I said. "Melvin Johnson."

"How do you do, Mr. Johnson. Please, do say hello to Mr. Cole for me won't you? He is a very nice young man. Very nice. You must be very proud to have a cousin such as he?"

"I am." I watched the number two light up. The doors opened. The old woman got out first, the ugly dog looking up at me. At least I had fooled the old woman.

The lighting in the hall was soft and dramatic. She stood in the circle of light that shined down from pinpoint spotlights in the dark brown ceiling.

Taking off her clear plastic head wrap, she said. "Please. Don't repeat this. I wouldn't want to offend dear Mr. Cole. But there is one tiny thing I wish Mr. Cole would do."

"What's that, Mrs. White?"

"I wish he would get a haircut. He is much too handsome a man to wear his hair that long. And another thing — and please don't tell him I said this — I wish he would wear different clothes. He seems to be always dressed in black. I hate black — don't you, Mr. Johnson? It's so depressing."

"I'll be sure to tell him."

"Thank you. But remember, I did not say it."

"My lips are sealed."

She started down the hall.

"By the way, Mrs. White. How long has he lived here? He never told me."

She stopped and looked back. "Not long. Perhaps a month."

"He must be rich. I mean. To live here in a place like this."

She gave me a sly smile. "We are all rich here, Mr. Johnson. Very rich."

"Like I said, Mrs. White. I haven't seen him in a while. Where does he usually go during the day?"

"Oh, heavens. How should I know? He comes and goes

at all hours. Mostly at night. Frankly, I am surprised he is not at home now. He usually is during the day."

She continued down the hall. "Well, good day, Mr. Johnson," she said. "Don't forget to say hello to Mr. Cole for me."

"I won't."

I pretended to search my pockets for the key. I looked down the hall. Mrs. White gave me a final brief smile as she opened her door and disappeared inside.

I reached in my jacket and took out my lock-jimmy, wishing I knew how to work the damn thing. Slipping the hooked end into the key slot, I twisted and turned it for almost a minute. Frustrated, it took everything I had to keep from screaming.

Then I heard something click. I twisted the lock-jimmy gently to the right. Another click. I turned the knob.

Sonuvabitch. The door opened.

I slipped inside and closed the door gently behind me.

I looked around, past the archway that led to a large living room. I'd never seen a room more beautiful. There was a grand piano by the window overlooking the Charles River, and everywhere — on the piano and on the polished tables that glistened under the spill of subdued lamps — were gold-framed photos of past wealth and grace. Sailboats, men and women on the decks of ocean liners, and several military portraits.

I took off my shoes and went across the peach-colored rug to one of the bedrooms. It was the only room in the apartment that looked lived in. Dirty clothes on the floor; some on the king-sized bed. Three leather suitcases opened on the floor, still more clothes dripping over the sides, most of them black.

I went through them. Didn't find anything. I opened all the bureau drawers in all three bedrooms. They were all empty. I thought, whoever this Cole character was, he's all set to make a quick getaway.

The telephone rang on the table next to the bed. It scared the shit out of me. I left in a hurry.

At the office, I was about to go upstairs when the desk sergeant called me over.

"Joe," he said. "I got some bad news. Lieutenant Bailey had to be taken to the hospital."

"Why? What happened?"

"Heart attack. I was sitting here drinking coffee — bullshitin' with Jimmy when I heard this loud thud. I called upstairs and got no answer so we went up. There he was — on the floor, grabbing his heart, gaspin' for air, Jimmy gave him mouth-to-mouth. He looks bad, Joe. Real bad. Has he been sick? Jesus, he's lost a lot of weight. He looked awful."

"Where'd they take him?"

"Mass General."

"Anyone call his wife?"

"Yeah. She's on the way to the hospital."

When I got there, Lieutenant John Bailey was in intensive care. I peered into the ICU through the narrow window in the double doors. John's eyes were closed, a tube protruding from his nose, probes running from his chest to a heart monitor. Everything was quiet. I could hear the machine beeping. I prayed.

Ten minutes later, a Chinese doctor in a white coat wearing black rimmed glasses, and carrying a clipboard, came through the double doors.

He stopped and said in broken English. "Are you friend or relative of Mr. Bailey?"

"Friend," I said, my throat tight. "How is he, Doc?"

"Not good. Not good."

"What does that mean, for Chrissakes? Is he going to make it?"

The doctor shook his head slowly.

"Oh, Christ. . . ."

"Do you know wife?" the doctor said, looking down the hall. "Is she here?"

I blinked several times and glanced toward the waiting room at the end of the corridor. "I don't see her."

"She must hurry."

"They live . . . in Canton. The traffic . . . ." I couldn't talk anymore. I went to the water cooler and took a drink.

A few minutes later Stella showed, eyes glassy and huge. All I could say to her was. "I'm so sorry."

She nodded and we held each other a long time, then she slipped away from me and went through the double doors.

Lieutenant John Bailey died an hour later. And I cried.

None of us could do much of anything the next couple of days except sit around the office, drink coffee, and tell John Bailey stories. Everybody had one. My favorite was when I first joined homicide. John was the senior detective then. I was a transfer from the MOP unit, trading in my motorcycle for a beat-up Ford no one else wanted. My second day in homicide, John sent me over to a Roxbury apartment building off Seaver Street. Some black woman was supposed to have been stabbed to death, only when I got there, the door was locked and there was no one around. When I heard a woman scream behind the door, I broke the door down and barged in with my .38 drawn and ready.

There she was — naked and lying in a pink-laced casket, surrounded by lighted candles, the room smelling of incense and cheap perfume. When I finally got up enough nerve to walk over to the naked woman and find out what the hell it was all about, I saw the sign written in Magic Marker that covered her short-hairs. It said: "Still Warm and Juicy — Happy Birthday and Welcome to Homicide." It was signed, "JB."

John Bailey had paid her twenty bucks, a hundred if she could talk me into the casket with her. She only got the twenty.

Wednesday morning, we gathered at the station for the drive to the funeral home in Canton. Jake Callaghan called me aside and handed me a piece of paper. It was the autopsy report from the medical examiner. It said that Lieutenant John Bailey had died from an overdose of nitroglycerin. Feeling like I had suddenly lost my ability to breathe, I couldn't control my trembling fingers as I read the mumbo-jumbo about what effect an overdose of nitro had on the heart and the rest of John Bailey's withered organs. The bottom line was, his death was ruled an apparent suicide.

I folded the report and put it in my pocket. I told Jake not to say anything about it to anyone. He said he wouldn't. I did tell Tommy. He wasn't surprised.

After the funeral, everybody went back to work. Tommy went off to check on the dynamite and call on some of his song birds. I went to the office to make some phone calls. I was about to go upstairs when the front door flew open and a black kid about nineteen stumbled in gasping for breath and holding his side. Blood flowed from between his fingers. He leaned against the counter, and said to the desk sergeant, "I. . . I've been stabbed."

The desk sergeant immediately picked up the phone and called Health and Hospitals for an ambulance. I went over to the kid, kept him from falling over and said. "What happened?"

"I. . . I was in this poker game," the kid groaned. "They said I fuckin' cheated so they stabbed. . . me. So I stabbed the fucka's back. You. . . better hurry, man. I. . . I think the fucka is dead, man."

The desk sergeant said wait a minute to Health and Hospitals, then cupped the phone and asked the kid. "Where'd this happen?"

"Roxbury," the kid said.

"Where in Roxbury?"

"Humboldt and Warren Ave."

"Humboldt and Warren Ave.? Jesus Christ. What's the number?"

"I don't know. Ten maybe. Or Twelve."

"The Area B police station is a couple of miles down the street," I said to the kid. "You could have gone there to get help. How the hell did you get all the way over here to South Boston?"

The black kid grimaced. "I. . . I was. . . go'n there when I saw. . . saw these two white cops sit'n in a police car. I went up to them and I. . . I jumped in the back seat and told 'em I just stabbed two guys and that I was stabbed myself.''

"Why didn't they take you to the hospital?" I said.

The kid looked at me strangely; he was ready to collapse. "They . . . they said they didn't wanna make out no report 'cause it was time to go home. They wanted to throw my ass out, only I wouldn't fuckin' go. I started fuckin' screamin' and kickn' and holdin' onto the door handle. I kept tellin' them I stabbed these two guys so they said okay — they'd drive me down here where the murder people was because they said that's probably where I'd fuckin' end up anyways."

I exchanged blank looks with the desk sergeant. He shrugged and said to me, "No one's perfect," then uncupped the phone and gave Health and Hospitals the address where the alleged stabbings took place.

Hearing sirens in the distance, growing louder, I went back upstairs wondering what the hell had happened to police ethics. Sure, we all immunized ourselves against the grief and suffering — older cops especially. Everyday the city threw up a ton of shit from its darkest places. A corpse — a young kid brutally stabbed, face mutilated. A drunk under the Expressway, dismembered for a miserable drop of whiskey. A kid shot to death for a radio because he refused to hand it over to a bully. So on and so forth. All of it never stopped giving me that sick-in-the-gut feeling, or carved some hollow out of my heart. Cops who lost that feeling shouldn't be cops.

I sat down at my desk and looked at the clock on the wall, watching the day melt into night, wondering what I should do next. I opened my top drawer and removed a bottle of aspirins. I took five with a gulp of cold coffee. It was going to be a long night.

9

It was that time of night when the city felt clean in its emptiness. Little traffic on the streets, few people on the sidewalks. A gentle rain fell. Everything glistened.

Shortly after midnight, I picked up a pepperoni pizza and a diet Coke at T Anthony's at the corner of Commonwealth Ave. and Babcock Street, walked to my car, drove down to Back Street, and slipped it into the same narrow space behind the dumpster.

Light traffic rolled along Storrow Drive. My eyes searched Back Street. Nothing moved.

No sign of the black Trans Am.

Gulping down a slice of pizza, watching the rain bead up and trickle down the windshield, mottled by the light from the city of Cambridge across the river, I thought about Victoria and the kids. Earlier I had called to see what was doing. Victoria had said everything was fine, except that she had received another strange phone call. I asked if the jerk had laughed. She said he had. I asked if she had heard anything else. She had said yes — some sort of Reggae-type music. I told her not to worry about it. I knew who it was.

I also told her not to wait up for me.

She said don't worry, she wouldn't.

Finishing the Coke and pizza, I tossed the can and empty box on the floor in the back seat, settled back, stifled a yawn, and rubbed my eyes. 12:46 am. Still no sign of the black Trans Am.

I popped a couple of Rolaids in my mouth and chewed. It helped quiet the screams my stomach was making.

I woke up. Son-of-a-bitch! What a stupid shit!

I blinked several times, finding it difficult to find focus

through the rain on the glass. I checked my watch. 1:45 am.

Then I saw it. Parked by the fence, gleaming in the spill from the street lamp overhead, the black Trans Am.

My head spun around like an owl. I was alone.

I reached up and flipped the plastic cap off the dome light, removed the bulb, opened my door slow and easy, took another look around, then walked real nonchalant over to the Trans Am.

The passenger side door was unlocked. I opened the door fast, knowing I had to be quick because of the interior light. It didn't go on. I climbed in the backseat and closed the door gently.

Crouching, I felt around in the darkness, checked everything with my fingertips. Some papers on the backseat, a canvas bag, in it a shirt, socks, a toothbrush, jeans, a pair of boots — some other stuff I couldn't identify. On the floor, a couple of number plates, a long flashlight, and a zillion paper cups and french fry boxes from MacDonald's.

I illuminated the dial on my watch. 1:53 am.

I was about to open the door and get out, but I stopped. A tall figure in dark clothes emerged from the building, ducked the rain, and ran quick-legged toward the car.

I took out my .38 as the guy with rimless glasses and long scraggly hair approached the Trans Am and opened the door. I let him slide behind the wheel and close the door before I pressed the barrel of my .38 into his skull.

"Hello, asshole," I said in my usual calm voice.

The guy went rigid — made no attempt to turn around.

"What do you want?" the guy said flatly.

"Some answers."

"To what?"

"Like who the fuck are you? What were you doing following me and my partner?"

At first he hesitated. "I don't know what you're talking about."

I nudged his skull with the barrel of my .38. He flinched. I know it hurt because I meant for it to hurt. He tried to pull away but I had his collar bunched in my fist.

"Watch the head, pal," the guy said.

"I'm not your pal."

"No shit."

I didn't like the way he talked — something about the accent. New York City maybe, or New Jersey. Same difference. Something told me to shoot the prick now and get it over with.

"You got an ID, Mr. Cole?" I said.

Cole didn't move. "How do you know my name?" he said.

I didn't say anything.

I could sense his eyes looking for an escape. He must not have seen one because he slipped his fingers inside his denim jacket, came out with a leather wallet, and handed it back. Unfolding it, I was barely able to see the guy's photo in the dim light spilling in through the windshield. But I saw the gold badge.

The ID said his name was Cole. Robert Trenton Cole. The badge said he was from New York City. Sergeant. NYPD. Badge number 4442.

Sonuvabitch.

I lowered my .38 but kept it handy.

"Can I turn around now?" Cole said.

"Yeah," I said, "but do it slow."

He did.

"Okay," I said. "You're a New York cop. Start talking."

"Not here," Cole said. "I need a cup of coffee."

"People down in hell need ice water."

"I know a place on Mass. Ave."

"Guido's?"

"You know it?"

"It's my city."

"Thank God."

Cole didn't give me a chance to say anything more. He leaned forward and started the car. I felt the vibration of the Trans Am's powerful motor go through me as we backed up, fishtailed from the parking lot, skidded to a stop at the off-ramp of Storrow Drive, bolted right, and headed up

Beacon toward Mass. Ave."

"You always drive like this?" I said, struggling to right myself in the back seat, watching the world go by the window a zillion miles an hour.

"Only when I'm going for coffee," he said.

I had to admit I liked the feel, the speed, the throated roar of the muffler. I hadn't ridden in anything this fast since I gave up my Harley fifteen years ago. Maybe I wasn't becoming an old fart after all.

Guido's coffee and sweet shop was down an alley off Mass. Ave., across from the Berkeley Performance Center. The place was small — only four tables. We got our coffee at the counter full of gorgeous looking pastries which I avoided and sat at the table against the back wall. Except for the night cook who came out of the kitchen every now and then with a fresh tray of wonderful smelling doughnuts and sweet rolls, we were alone.

Cole took off his denim jacket and draped it over the back of his chair. He wore a black short-sleeve shirt, the veins in his slender, muscular arms pronounced. When he changed positions in the chair, I saw the handle of an automatic sticking out of his belt.

I showed him my gold badge. "The name's Knight," I said. "Joe Knight. Homicide. But I suppose you know that already."

Cole glanced down at my badge then looked at me, dark eyebrows below dark brown hair joined in a frown. Though weary, there was a look of eager confidence about his eyes I'd seen a hundred times. After a while that kind of light was extinguished, and what you saw instead was a glazed weariness.

"So talk," I said. "What's a New York City cop doing in Boston, living in luxury no less?"

"The condo belongs to my parents," Cole said. "You like it?"

I didn't say anything. I looked at him a moment longer, then said, "So why the tail?"

"I'm looking for someone." Cole said.

"Who?"

"A renegade cop."

"You came to the right place. We've got seventeen hundred of them. Take your pick."

"This one is different."

"Aren't we all."

"This one's turned killer. A paid assassin."

"What's his name?"

"Styles, Manfred Styles."

"What makes you think he's here in Boston?"

The cook came over carrying a tray of cinnamon rolls. Both of us fell silent.

"Care for one of these, gentlemen?" the cook said, showing us the tray. "Just baked them. You won't ever taste any better."

They were hot and gooey and smelled heavenly. I couldn't resist any longer — I took two. Cole just asked for more coffee.

After the cook refilled both our cups and walked away, Cole said, "Two weeks ago, Styles met with two guys from Boston. We took some pictures." He reached back and removed a small white envelope from his jacket pocket and handed it to me. I licked my fingers clean of frosting and opened the envelope. In it were a half-dozen black and white photos.

Cole leaned forward and pointed. "That's Styles — the guy with the sunglasses on the right. The guy in the middle is a Boston mobster named Vinnie Torchia — you probably know him."

I did.

"The other guy we don't know. We assume he's from Boston but we've got no ID on him."

I stared at the photograph a long time, my stomach muscles tense, my eyes not believing what they were looking at. I shut them a second and brought my hand up to my forehead in an effort to conceal my astonishment. The third guy in the photo was a friend, a good friend. Brendan O'Hara.

Until a year ago Brendan O'Hara and I were inseparable. We joined the force the same day, walked a beat together, rode motorcycles and horses with the MOP unit together, drank beer together. Even shared the same girl until I got ugly and he didn't. Though the photo was slightly out of focus, I could see Brendan hadn't changed; same curly brown hair, same strong build that belied his forty-seven years. Christ. He was my best man at my wedding.

If Cole noticed the shock on my face, he ignored it. He said, sitting back. "The same thing that's happening now in Boston happened in New York City about a year ago. Hate to tell you, Knight, but you've got some bad cops doing drugs."

I wasn't shocked. "What do you mean, doing drugs?" I said.

"They're ripping off street dealers then reselling the drugs to major dealers — not just in Boston either — all over. This guy Styles was a drug cop assigned to the 77th Precinct in the Bedford-Stuyvesant section of Brooklyn. About a year ago, he and twelve other cops were indicted for stealing drugs and money from low-level street pushers in Brooklyn neighborhoods. They mugged drug dealers, took their money and drugs and resold them to other dealers. The investigation started seventeen months ago when we arrested a guy and he told us that two officers were shaking him down. The guy agreed to wear a bug and a couple of months later, we had enough on the two cops that they agreed to cooperate and record conversations with other cops. Two days before the indictments came down, Styles disappeared.

Cole paused to take a drink of coffee, then went on. "Two weeks ago, a major drug king named Alphonse Dia was blown out of his shoes while starting his car. An eyewitness put Styles at the scene and later identified him in a photo." He paused again and leaned forward, placed his elbows on the table, looked around to make sure he wasn't being overheard, then said quietly, "What was strange about the bombing, the medical examiner found a single bullet in the back of the guy's head. A nine millimeter supervell hollow-point. Sound familiar?"

I didn't say anything. I couldn't.

Cole studied my face. It remained expressionless, my eyes noncommittal. I drained my cup, looked around for the cook, and waved him over to fill it up again.

"Too much coffee's not good for you, Joe," Cole said. "Bad for the heart."

I glared at him, feeling the blood rising to my face.

Cole saw my eyes and changed the subject fast. He leaned toward me and pointed to Brendan O'Hara in the photograph. "You wouldn't happen to know who this guy is would you?" he said.

I shook my head. "No," I said.

I didn't know why I lied. I only knew I had to. It was something I learned over the years. Lying gave me time to think of another lie because the truth — at least this time around — hurt like hell.

Cole said, "There's a better photo of Styles there somewhere."

I shuffled the photos until the one of Styles was on top.

Though Styles wore a cop's uniform, he didn't look like a cop. He could have been a priest, or a choirboy, or a Yuppy stockbroker. He had short dark hair and a thin, neatly groomed mustache. But it was Styles' eyes that betrayed him. They were huge — two dark orbs that bulged slightly. They were animal eyes, not human. Cold.

I looked at the other photos. There was another one of Brendan O'Hara getting into a car with Vinnie Torchia. I felt my blood heat up again.

"Alright, Cole," I said, giving back the photos. "Let's stop playing games. So you know about Howell and West?"

Cole nodded.

"This guy, Styles. You think he killed them?"

"I know he killed them."

"Why?"

"That's what I don't know."

"I think you do."

"That's your problem."

"No. It's yours." I put my elbows on the table. "You're

talking, Cole, but you're not saying much. You got some undercover operation going down? Is that it?"

He didn't answer. He just looked at me through those glasses I wanted to smash and shove through his pukey green eyeballs.

Then Cole said, "Okay. I know Styles hit Howell and West. I've got a pretty good idea who hired him and why. But I can't tell you. At least not right now. I know Styles is still in Boston. He hasn't finished his business."

"What's that?"

"I can't tell you that either."

"Can't or won't?"

"Take your pick."

"I'm conducting a murder investigation for Chrissakes. You got something I can use — you tell me now. Or maybe someone down in New York will."

Cole's face went blank. "That wouldn't be too cool."

"Is that right?"

"No one in New York knows I'm here. And I want to keep it that way. Styles finds out and it's all over. Everything."

Cole finished his coffee. Putting down his cup, he said. "Frankly, Joe. I fucked up. I wasn't supposed to get close to you. They said you were sharp."

"Who's they?"

Cole stayed silent.

Maybe it was the hour, or the cinnamon rolls feeling like two giant bowling balls in the pit of my massive belly, I don't know. But I was starting to get the picture and I didn't like it.

I said, "That's shit about not knowing the third guy in the picture with Styles and Torchia. You know who he is, don't you?"

Cole didn't say anything. He didn't have to. It was in his eyes.

"And you know I know who he is, don't you? That's why you were tailing me. Seeing if I'd lead you to him. Seeing if we were still friends."

Cole looked around. After a few moments staring at the floor, his eyes fell back on mine. "They said you were a smart cop," he said, obviously stalling for some time to think. "They said you had an incredible knack of reading people. Now I believe it."

"Fuck they — and fuck you. Talk straight to me, Cole, or you and I are going to have a little dance right here and now."

Cole wasn't bad at reading eyes either. He saw mine and started to talk. "Okay," he said. "I know who he is."

"You telling me that O'Hara had something to do with the killings?"

"He's connected somewhere."

"So you thought because I was his friend I'd be involved, too?"

"It happens, Joe."

I took a second to gather my thoughts. What I wanted to do was reach across and punch the four-eyed prick in the face. But I resisted.

"When's the last time you talked to him?" Cole said.

"Six months ago. We had lunch."

"Did you know O'Hara has been running with some bad company?"

"So have I. It doesn't make me one of them."

"Okay. I've been tailing you. Not all the time — sometimes. You're a hard guy to follow — don't know how many times I got lost. Guilt by association? I don't know. It was something I had to check out. You were friends with O'Hara. I had to know if you still were. If it means anything, you checked out okay."

"Fuck you."

"You've got a wife, two kids, a beat-up Ford your wife drives and a heavily mortgaged house in Milton. Four hundred dollars in a savings account, two hundred in a checking account. You don't belong to any organizations other than the detective's union. You don't smoke, and you quit drinking. And you're a dedicated work-a-holic who sometimes doesn't go by the book, but no one's held that against you. What I'm saying is, you're clean. Every cop should be as clean. You think for a minute I'd be telling you all of this if you weren't?''

I was getting a miserable headache listening to him talk. I wanted to know more but I was too tired to ask. Besides, I hated his face. If I looked at it another second, I'd punch it for sure.

I gulped the last of my coffee that had gone cold. "I got nothing more to say to you. Not tonight anyway. Take me back to my car."

Cole didn't say anything for a few seconds. "Maybe we could work a deal, Joe," he said.

"I don't make deals," I said.

"Alright, exchange information. I find Styles, I hand him over to you. Your murders are solved. You help me keep an eye on O'Hara."

"Why? What is so fucking important about O'Hara?"

Cole looked away. "I can't tell you that right now, Joe. You'll have to trust me."

"Kiss my ass."

"Joe. I'm telling you. Trust me. There's a lot more involved here than just murder."

I stared at him in disgust. "You know something, Cole?" I said. "I've been around a long time. I've met a dozen cops like you. We've even got a few of them here, too. You're a rogue. Everything's a fucking game with you. No rules, nothing. The more dangerous the better. You crawl down into holes with all the animals — sleep with them, eat with them, even look like them. Pretty soon, you become an animal yourself. What I'm saying, Cole — you sleep with dogs, pretty soon you're bound to get fleas."

Cole looked into his empty cup. "What I do, I do because I love it," he said sharply. "The danger, the excitement, everything. I don't need some jerkwater cop passing judgment on me. You're trying to solve some murders — I'm trying to help bust something bigger than you could even imagine. What's the difference how we do it as long as it gets done. From what I know about you and your partner, you're no saints. Some say you can be downright nasty. So I've done a few things over the years that broke some rules. So I do things a little different than everybody else. I enjoy the game, so what. It keeps me sharp. Like tailing you."

Cole stopped talking and smiled.

"What's so funny?" I said.

"I was just thinking about when I drove into the parking lot tonight and saw you sleeping. I went inside laughing my ass off. The same way I did the night I saw you in that shitbox station wagon at state police headquarters. Thought I'd die seeing you bounce up on the sidewalk — even waited for you down Commonwealth Ave., but you never showed. What happened?"

"Kiss my ass."

I got up and headed for the door. Cole followed me out to the alley.

Cole said, unlocking his car door, looking at me over the roof, "I wish I could tell you more, Joe. I really do."

"Why O'Hara?" I said.

Cole leaned his forearms on the roof, his keys dangling in his fingers. He smiled. "C'mon, Joe. I can't — "

There was a spit of air behind us, somewhere in the distance. I stared at Cole, unable to move.

Cole's mouth had sprung open. A red circle formed over his left eye. He stood for a second, frozen in death. And then his legs gave way and his corpse fell over collapsing to the pavement.

There was another spit and the air shattered above my head. And another; there was a ping. A bullet had ricocheted off the wall behind me.

My mind exploded. What remained of my instincts caused me to move off my feet, take out my .38 and hit the pavement. Two more spits came at me. A fragment of something whipped past my ear; inches closer and I would have been blinded or killed. I rolled onto my back and tried to squeeze under the Trans Am. I was too fat.

The pavement was wet. I hugged it anyway.

I looked at Cole. He gazed back at me, motionless and

dead. Blood ran through his eyes that were glassy and huge.

The shooting stopped. I heard the sounds of racing footsteps. I got to my knees, poked my head above the hood. I could see them, two figures running down the alley toward Hemenway Street. I scrambled to my feet and took off after them, running where instinct directed me, following the footsteps.

Near the end of the alley, I stopped running and checked the sounds. Nothing. Then I heard a car's engine start up, doors slamming shut. Tires screeched.

Wet and breathless, I wandered out to Hemenway. I saw the car careen through the marble arch and disappear into the Fenway.

Heading home down Blue Hill Avenue, street lights danced across the hood of the Buick over my face. It was nearing daybreak.

I looked at myself in the rearview mirror. I was tired and drawn, my skin pale, accentuating the dark hollows under my eyes.

Cole was dead. Killed by unknown assassins. The rogue had obviously slipped up — made one of those mistakes a young bull often makes going too fast down the hill to fuck one of the cows, instead of walking down like us old bulls and fucking them all.

What pissed me off more than anything, the killers were there all the time. Watching us — waiting. Why didn't I know they were there?

I had a zillion questions. But I was too tired to look for any answers.

As I drove through Mattapan Square into Milton, watching the rainy night grow progressively brighter, checking the rearview mirror for the zillionth time, I thought, goddamn you, Brendan O'Hara. Goddamn you.

10

I woke up around nine with a splitting headache, a sore shoulder and a stiff neck. There was some blood on the sheets from a cut on my elbow. I got out of bed, took a long steamy shower, then dressed.

The kids had gone out somewhere. Victoria had left me a note on the kitchen counter. "Went shopping. See you sometime tonight, I hope. And under that she wrote, "P.S. Received another phone call last night. This time he mumbled some profanity. I'm too much of a lady to say what it was but it had something to do with my vagina. I Love You, Stranger."

What a woman.

I called headquarters and talked to Rita Barns, a black policewoman I broke in a few years back when I was at the old District Three station in Mattapan. Great looking woman. Fantastic body. Loved computers — worked her way off the street into Operations. I asked her to do me a favor, to run a check on a Robert Trenton Cole, NYPD, badge number 4442. Everything was confidential. Also a Manfred Styles, same city. Rita said she'd see what she could do.

Hanging up from Rita, I called the office. A strange voice answered. "Homicide. Lieutenant O'Keefe."

Sonuvabitch. Lieutenant Robert O'Keefe. Chief kiss-ass and Southie Mick buddy to the commissioner. What the hell was he doing in our office? I didn't want to ask.

"What the hell are you doing there, O'Keefe?"

"Sergeant Knight. Nice to hear from you. Are we going to do any work today or have you decided to take another day off?"

"Fuck you, O'Keefe. You didn't answer my question?"

"What question?"

"What the hell are you doing in our office?"

"Someone has to keep an eye on you lot. The commissioner thought it should be me."

"Oh, Christ."

O'Keefe was the biggest asshole on the force. Most of us real cops were professional assholes. We worked hard at being assholes — took pride in our accomplishment — but we could change if we wanted to. We could be nice guys sometimes. O'Keefe was one of those born assholes who could never change.

"Where's Tommy Sanders?" I said.

"On the way over to pick you up. At least that's what he told me."

"And a few other things if I know Tommy."

"Get used to it, Knight," O'Keefe said. "Who knows, I might actually grow to like it here and stay."

I hung up. Asshole!

I put some water in a kettle, went over to the stove and turned on the gas. Taking two cups out of the cupboard, I put in some instant coffee. No matter how hard I tried, I couldn't take my mind off what Cole had told me.

Brendan O'Hara. You son-of-a-bitch. What happened? What pushed you over the edge? What the hell are you into?

All I could think about was the time Brendan and I started riding bikes for the MOP Unit. We were in Hyde Park, on Hyde Park Avenue. He was good on the bike — I had some problems, like getting the sonuvabitch started. Every time I stopped, the bike stalled. One day near Cleary Square, some punks went by us in a big Buick. One of them leaned out the window and slapped me on the helmet, which pissed me off. Brendan took exception to it, too, and took off after them while I pounded the starter. Finally when I got the bastard going, I took off in hot pursuit. As I screamed around a corner — to my surprise — there was Brendan with the Buick stopped, the kids spread-eagled on the hood. I panicked because my bike wouldn't stop — no brakes —

at least I couldn't find them quick enough. Anyway, I hit the back of the Buick going forty and found myself flying over the top, bouncing off the hood, and landing in the street. The only thing I hurt getting up and checking myself was my pride. Everybody was laughing, even Brendan, so hard, in fact, he let the kids go if they promised not to tell anyone what happened. They lied. By the time I got back to the barn in Jamaica Plain, everybody knew. And it wasn't the kids who told them either. The next day when I went to the garage to get my bike, there were two giant pillows tied to the handlebars and a bumper sticker that said: Warning — The Driver Of This Bike Is An ASSHOLE.

I heard a knock on the door and saw Tommy's face pressed against the glass. My thoughts broken, I waved him in.

Tommy threw the morning *Herald* on the table and said, "You see the paper?"

"No."

"Read the headlines."

I did.

It said, NEW YORK CITY COP SHOT DEAD.

The kettle whistled. I poured water into the cups, put in some milk, then sat down.

I glanced at the front page. Under the headlines was a dark photograph of the scene. I could barely make out the Trans Am and the body of Sergeant Robert Trenton Cole under a white sheet. I looked for my name. I didn't see it.

I shoved the paper aside, drank some of my coffee, and told Tommy everything.

"Brendan O'Hara," Tommy said. "Jesus Christ. You want me to arrange something with Milton police to keep an eye on your house?"

"What for? It wasn't me they were after."

"How do you know that?"

"For Chrissakes, Tommy. I am not a fucking rookie. The killer used a silencer — took Cole down with one shot to the head. I was standing in the light on the other side of the car. If the bastard wanted me dead, he could have shot me blindfolded. The shots were a warning for me to back off.''

''Think it was this Styles character?''

''I don't know. But it gives us a name to chase. Even a face.''

I showed Tommy the photos I took off Cole's body before the other cops got there. ''That's Styles,'' I said pointing. ''That's Torchia and there's O'Hara.''

Tommy stared at the pictures a long time. Tossing them onto the table he said, ''You hear who headquarters sent us to take Bailey's place?''

''I just got off the phone with him.''

''What the hell are they trying to do to us?''

I finished my coffee and made another. ''Someone wants to keep an eye on us. Ever think of that?''

''Here we go again,'' Tommy said. ''Paranoia runs rampant in Gotham.''

''Yeah, well, I don't like it. Something's going down in this city besides dead people. It stinks big. Cole said so before he got shot. From now on, we keep everything to ourselves.''

''What about Jake and Warren? We can't trust them, who can we?''

''Okay. Jake and Warren. But nobody else.''

Tommy gazed at me. ''Brendan O'Hara. That sonuvabitch.''

I got up from the table and went to the phone.

''Who you calling?'' Tommy said.

''The horse barn in JP,'' I said.

''That's fucking stupid. What if O'Hara answers?''

''I'll disguise my voice.''

Tommy shook his head in disgust.

I dialed.

On the fourth ring, ex-patrolman Wally Leonard answered. ''Horse barn. Leonard,'' he said. Wally had been a cop's cop until he got so fat he couldn't ride a horse anymore, so he retired. Now all he does is shovel horseshit.

I cupped my hand around my mouth and spoke in a high,

squeaky voice. "This is Mortimer Slade in personnel," I said. "I'm looking for an Officer Benton O'Mara?"

"No such animal here by that name," Wally said irritated. "We got a Sergeant Brendan O'Hara. Only he ain't on horses no more. He's riding a bike."

"That's the one. Can I speak with him?"

"No."

"Why not?"

"He's on nights. Won't be in until six or so."

"Oh, darn. It's imperative that I speak with him."

"What for?"

I hesitated, trying to think fast.

"His patrolman's insurance policy has expired," I said finally.

"I never heard of no patrolman's insurance policy," Wally said.

"It's something new this year."

Wally fell silent. I could see his fat little face frozen in a deep frown.

"Would you happen to know where he lives?" I asked.

"You got his records," Wally said. "What are you asking me for?"

Same ole Wally. What an asshole.

Then Wally said, "Look, Sergeant O'Hara comes in around six. Call back then."

He hung up on me.

I called the morgue. Leroy said his boss hadn't showed up yet. Call back later in the afternoon he told me.

It was quarter after nine by the time we went up Blue Hill Avenue in Roxbury. Call it paranoia, whatever, I couldn't helping looking back. There were a dozen cars behind us. As far as I could tell, no one followed us.

The rain had stopped sometime in the night. The sky remained heavy overcast, the air had turned unseasonably cool for late August. I was dressed for it in my waist-length tan jacket, brown corduroy pants and Red Sox baseball cap. Underneath my jacket, I wore a black and green striped shirt. Strapped to my ankle, I had some extra heat — a .9mm Browning.

Tommy had on a blue windbreaker, blue jeans and his tweed Donegal cap.

"You see the report sent down from headquarters?" Tommy asked. "The murder rate is up twenty percent from last year. Drugs the biggest factor."

"No shit. We needed a report from headquarters to tell us that? Who made it up? O'Keefe?"

"Probably."

"Asshole."

"Handguns caused half the homicides last year. Twenty-six by knife and fifteen by blunt force, nine by strangulation, three by fire, and two by motor vehicle. Eighty-two men and twenty-four women. The highest number of murders in eleven years."

"If you're trying to cheer me up, Tommy, it's not working."

"You know the one that pissed me off the most?" Tommy went on. "The four-year-old South End girl who was raped and beaten by her mother's boyfriend."

I nodded in agreement, remembering when Jake and Warren brought the guy in. I wanted to kick his balls in. Tommy wanted to shoot him.

As we went past Columbia Road, Tommy said, "What do you think about this fucking Jamaican Dog Posse gang that's running around Roxbury and Dorchester? Heard they had another shooting on Dudley Street last night. Bastards are really trying to tear up the city."

I looked across at him. "You got anything good to say, Tommy?"

"No."

"Then shut the fuck up."

"Touchy, aren't we?"

Slowing for the lights at Seaver Street, a young woman in a white BMW came up on our tail fast and braked hard. There was a truck to her left preventing her from whizzing by us. The woman was white; the area she was driving through was predominantly black. Any white person in-the-know could walk down Blue Hill and not be bothered.

Obviously she was a first-timer to Roxbury, so I could understand her impatience. But not her driving skills.

I remember reading a report the state police put out on such wild driving habits — tailgating, excessive speeding, erratic operation. The report said, check your rearview mirror anytime on the highway, and eight times out of twelve, there'll be a young woman between the age of eighteen and thirty-five on your ass, either combing her hair, fooling with the radio, or painting on makeup in the mirror, paying absolutely no attention to where the hell she's going.

The woman behind us did everything the report said she'd do, only when the light changed, she did something even I'd never seen before. She swerved right around a bus, darted between two parked cars, went up on the sidewalk — nearly hitting a black kid on a bike — and whizzed down Blue Hill Avenue like a woman possessed.

Funny thing was, at the next set of lights, we pulled up behind her.

Tommy said. "We had more time, I'd like to get out and yank that broad out of the car, kick her ass, and piss on her front seat."

I smiled. "Thank God for dead people. Where're we going?"

"Everett."

"What's over there?"

"Got a call from Medford police," Tommy said, lighting a cigar. "Some guy called and reported some missing dynamite. Some Mexican named Santana. Works for Petrelli Construction."

"How come he waited so long to report it?"

"I didn't ask."

"Did Medford talk to him?"

"No. I said we wanted to. They said okay."

I looked back again. Didn't notice anyone. I said to Tommy, "Do me a favor. Take a left down Warren Avenue."

"What for?"

"I've got to take care of something that's been on my mind."

"What?"

"Tell you when I get there."

Before the light changed, the woman in the BMW bolted. Maybe there already was piss on her seat.

We went down Warren Avenue, took a right on Maywood, then another right onto Maywood Terrace.

"What are we doing here?" Tommy said. "That's Melvin Grosset's house."

"You're right. Pull over behind that red Camaro."

He did.

I got out.

"We were told to stay away from him," Tommy said.

"So?"

"So we've got enough problems."

"The bastard's been making some phone calls to my house. I want him to stop."

"How do you know it was him?"

"Trust me."

"What are you going to do?"

I looked at Tommy. "Ask him to stop making the calls. What else?"

"Yeah, well. Make sure you ask him nicely."

"Oh, I plan on it."

I looked around. A cat scurried from beneath a burned-out car across the street. Everywhere was the acrid smell of feces and urine, some of it human.

"Open the trunk," I said to Tommy.

"What for?"

"I might need to use some persuasion."

"Oh, shit. Not again."

Tommy reached in the glove compartment and hit the trunk-release button.

I leaned in and took out my heavy oak, pickaxe handle.

"Think I'll stay in the car," Tommy said.

Melvin Grosset, the killer of young women, lived on the second floor of a decaying brown three-decker with pea-green shutters and a crooked front porch. Most of the steps leading up were broken; so were most of the windows. The dirt front yard was littered with trash and broken glass. An old washing machine and refrigerator lay battered in the middle of the yard.

I walked around Grosset's new red Camaro. It was time to wake Melvin up.

With as much strength as I could call up, I raised the pickaxe handle, took a baseball swing, and shattered the driver's side window. Reaching in, I leaned on the horn until Melvin Grosset appeared with his whore girlfriend at the bedroom window.

"Hey!" Melvin Grosset yelled down to me. "What the fuck you doin', man? You fuckin' crazy wakin' everybody up like dat."

"Melvin," I called up to him. "I realize that stealing cars and killing people is a tiresome business, but hey — it's nearly eleven o'clock. Time to rise and shine."

Melvin Grosset took a long look at me and his Camaro. "How'd you get in my car, man?" he said.

I held up my pickaxe handle. "I used my key. Had a little trouble with the lock, but I finally managed."

Melvin Grosset must have seen the look in my eyes because he made no attempt to leave the window. "You get the fuck away from my car, man. You hear me? Get the fuck away!"

"You going to stop making those phone calls to my wife, Melvin?"

"What fuckin' phone calls?"

I walked slowly and deliberately around the front of the car and crashed in one of the headlights.

"Hey! Stop! Dat's my car, man!"

"I'll ask you again. You going to stop making those obscene phone calls to my wife?"

"Don't know what the fuck you talkin' about, man. You fuckin' crazy! I'm gonna call my lawyer. You just wait and see if I don't, muddafucka!"

I broke the other headlight with so much force it dented in the entire left front of the car. I smiled thinking Wade Boggs would have been proud of my swing.

"I'm not sure that I appreciate your language, Melvin,"
I said. "I know I don't appreciate the phone calls." I smashed in the entire windshield with one solid blow.

"Alright! Alright!" Melvin shouted. "I'll stop! Jesus
Christ!"

"Stop what, Melvin?"

He hesitated.

I annihilated the passenger side window.

Some kids on bikes showed up and an old couple came
out onto the porch next door — all curious onlookers. The
old man nodded to me. He had a wide grin on his face. I
nodded back.

"Okay!" Melvin Grosset said, leaning out the window,
waving his arms. "I'll stop makin' the phone calls!"

"You promise, Melvin?" I said.

"Yeah. I promise! I fuckin' promise! Now leave my car
alone! I just got it, man! Jesus Christ! Look what you did!"

"I know you just got it, Melvin. I've been keeping an eye
on you. But you know that don't you?"

Melvin nodded.

"Don't mess with me again, Melvin," I said holding up
the handle. "If you ever make another phone call to my
house again, I'll come back and pound your shithead right
down into your asshole! Do your hear me, Melvin?"

Melvin nodded. "I hear yah, man."

"Good. Then there's nothing more to be said. Thank you
for your attention, Melvin. Have a nice day."

On the way back to the car, I tapped one of Melvin's
taillights. It broke. Sonuvabitch. They don't make plastic like
they used to.

Heading down Blue Hill Avenue toward the Expressway,
Tommy said, "Who fed you the ugly pill this morning?"

"Fuck you," I said. "Drive."

Tommy looked at me and smiled.

It took us forty minutes to get to Everett. Traffic on the
Expressway was brutal; we got off at the North Station, went
over the Charlestown Bridge, around the circle past the old
District 15 police station, and out Route 99.

Juan Santana lived on Baldwin Avenue, on the second floor of a two-family with green shutters and yellow vinyl siding.

A dark haired woman of about thirty with large dark eyes and huge breasts opened the door.

Tommy held up his badge. "Detective Sanders. Boston police. This is Sergeant Knight."

She looked at the badge. "Come in," she said, stepping aside. She had on a thin yellow dress with nothing on underneath. I could see her nipples clearly. "I am Juan's sister," she said in soft broken English. "He will be right out. He is dressing."

She looked at me — saw me staring at her breasts. The top three buttons were undone; she made no attempt to cover up. I smiled.

Juan Santana came out of the bedroom. He was in his late thirties, early forties. Tall and thin with dark hair and a mustache, he had a scar over his left eye, another on his right cheek. He looked nervous as hell.

"Which of you is Detective Sanders?" he said.

Tommy said, "I am. This is Sergeant Knight." He looked at the woman. "Can we talk to you alone?"

"Of course." Juan nodded his sister out of the room, then sat down on the sofa.

"I am not sure I should be speaking with you," Juan said.

"Why not?" Tommy said.

"Because I am afraid."

"Afraid of what?" Tommy said.

"The people who stole the dynamite — they might find out I talked to the police. They could come here and kill me."

"No one's going to kill you, Juan," Tommy said.

"If you're so afraid," I said, "why did you give the police your name?"

Juan shook his head. "I am not sure why. I read the papers — saw the news on television. I kept thinking about that poor woman being blown up like that. It was just the right thing to do."

"You done good, Juan," Tommy said. "Now tell us about the dynamite. Who took it?"

Juan looked at the floor, toying with his fingers. He had on a red Patriots' football jersey with the number 20. I tried to think who on the Patriots wore that number. I couldn't come up with a name.

"Santana," Tommy said, sitting down in one of those wicker chairs with chrome arms. "Don't go south on us now. Who stole the dynamite?"

Juan looked up. I could see the fright in his eyes. "I only saw them briefly," he said finally, his voice soft but steady.

"Them?" I said.

Juan looked at me. "Yes. There were two of them. It was dark — I couldn't see them clearly."

"Did you know them? Did they work for Petrelli Construction?"

"No." Juan looked out the window. "I remember one was tall, the other man much shorter. That is all I remember about them." Juan's eyes wandered back to us. "I was on a break so I went outside in the yard to get some air. I heard some noises coming from one of the storage sheds — where we keep the dynamite. I went around the building and that's when I saw them — carrying two boxes to a van."

"What sort of a van?" Tommy asked.

"One of those four-wheel type vans," Juan said, looking back at us. "Like a Bronco or a Chevy Blazer."

I looked at Tommy, then at Juan. "What color was it?" I said.

"I'm not sure exactly," Juan said. "It had a white roof."

"Was it light green?" I said.

Juan's eyes widened. "Yes, light green. And I saw a little bit of the license plate. The first three numbers were 663. I remember that 'cause it's the number of our house."

11

It was ten after one in the afternoon when we stopped at the Registry on Causeway Street in Boston. Tommy got two hot dogs and a root beer from a vendor while I went in the building and checked on the Chevy Blazer.

Ten minutes later, what I knew already had become fact. The Blazer was registered to a Lawrence Edwards, address of 213 Woodlawn Avenue, Chelsea.

In Chelsea, when we knocked on the first floor door of the gray three-family, a blonde-haired woman carrying a fat-faced baby, opened the door and said, "If you're looking for Larry, I ain't seen him."

I showed her my gold badge.

"You don't have to show me that," she said. "I know you're cops. How many times I gotta tell you people? I don't know where he is and I don't give a shit either. The bastard walked out on us six months ago. Left us with no money — nothing. I hope the bastard is dead somewhere."

I said. "I'm sorry, Mrs...."

"Ruth," she said. "Just plain Ruth."

"Okay, plain Ruth. I'm Sergeant Knight. This is Detective Sanders. We're from Boston. We'd like to come in and ask you a few questions if it's alright?"

Ruth was thin and pale with a zillion pimples on her chalk face. She had cloudy-blue eyes with dark circles underneath. Her teeth were yellow and she reeked of alcohol. She could have been twenty-five years old but she looked fifty. "I don't know," she said. "I'm tired of the questions."

"It won't take long," I said.

"That's what they all say."

Reluctantly, she stepped aside. "Okay. You got five minutes."

We went in. The place was filthy, the furniture old and tattered. Clutter everywhere; difficult to find a place to sit. Pushing aside some dirty dishes, I sat down at the kitchen table.

"Who's been asking questions about Larry?" I said.

"Everybody for Chrissakes," Ruth said.

"Who's everybody?" Tommy asked.

"Chelsea cops mostly. Some of 'em friends of Larry I recognized, some of 'em I didn't. The chief came to see me a couple of times."

"Anyone else?" I said.

"Some other guys I never seen before."

I took out the photo of Styles and showed it to her. "This guy one of them?" I said.

She looked at the photo. "No," she said.

I glanced at Tommy leaning against the refrigerator. "You sure," I said, looking back at her.

"Course I'm sure. Eyes like that? Who'd ever forget them."

I took back the photo. "When was the last time you saw your husband?" I said.

"He's not my husband." Ruth pulled a chair beneath her. As she sat down, I got a whiff of her breath. I almost gagged.

"Your boyfriend then," I said.

"He's not my boyfriend anymore."

I glanced at Tommy again. He grinned.

"Alright. Larry," I said. "When did you see him last?"

"Six months ago." Ruth changed the position of the baby on her lap.

The kid was beautiful. Wavy blonde hair, bright blue eyes, big red cheeks. Nothing like his mother.

"When he walked out on us," Ruth went on. "We had a fight. Christ, we were always fighting."

"Did you ever go to his apartment on Louise Street?" I asked.

"I told you. I ain't seen him in six months — him and

that damn dog of his. The filthy mutt ate us out of house and home for Chrissakes. He treated the dog better'n he treated us."

I looked at the kid again. Didn't look like he had skipped any meals.

Tommy asked, "Larry got any family you know of?"

Ruth looked up at him. "Yeah. Lots of 'em."

"They live around here?" I said.

"Most of 'em do."

"Which ones?" Tommy said.

"There's eight of 'em," Ruth said. "Five sisters and two brothers."

"Who is he close to?" Tommy said.

"His brothers. Billy and Buzzy. Buzzy is the mouthy one. Billy is the oldest — little chubby guy. Quiet ballbuster type. You know what I mean?"

I nodded. "Where do Billy and Buzzy live?"

"Billy lives a little ways from here — on Grandview Road. Don't know the number. Buzzy lives in Revere. Somewhere in the Point of Pines section. Bateman Avenue, I think."

"Do you have any photographs of Larry?" I said.

"No," Ruth said. "I burned them all."

I stood up.

"Not that I really give a shit," Ruth said. "But what's Larry done? No one seems to want to tell me."

Tommy followed me to the door. "Neither do we," he said.

We left.

Billy Edwards lived in a single family house with a two car garage out back. Tommy followed me up the brick steps onto the porch. We had checked the driveway and the garage. No sign of a green and white Chevy Blazer.

I rang the doorbell. A tall woman with dyed auburn hair wearing a red robe opened the door. "Yes," she said curtly.

I gave her the once-over. She wore a ton of makeup. Her eyes were deep-set, surrounded in heavy blue eye-shadow. I could see her legs beneath the robe; they were spindly.

I wondered how they could support such a large upper frame.

I showed her my badge. "I'm Sergeant Knight. This is my partner, Detective Sanders."

She took a hard look at us. "What do you want?" she said.

"We'd like to ask you a few questions. Is your husband home?"

"No. He's at work. What sort of questions?"

"Can we come in?" Tommy asked.

"No," the woman said. Her eyes darted away.

"Look, Mrs. Edwards. It is Mrs. Edwards?"

"It is."

"Yes. Well, we're investigating the disappearance of your husband's brother, Larry Edwards."

"Billy and I have already said all we are going to say. We don't know where he is. And personally, I don't care."

"We heard the family was close?" Tommy said.

"Who did you hear that from? That tramp, Ruth? She's a filthy little slut. I wouldn't believe anything she says."

"What time does your husband get home from work? We'd like to talk with him."

"It won't do any good," Mrs. Edwards said. "Billy is fed up with Larry's act. So's the entire family" She stepped back, closing the door. "Do us all a favor. Look somewhere else." The door slammed in our faces.

Tommy looked at me. "Nice lady," he said.

"How would you like to wake up every morning looking at that?" I said.

"No, thanks."

We walked down the steps to the car.

"You notice anything strange about her act?" Tommy said, getting in behind the wheel.

I looked toward the house. The sheer window drape was pulled back; I could see her peering out at us. "Yeah, I did," I said.

Tommy started the car. "She's lying through her fucking teeth."

As I closed the door, I saw the drapes fall back into place.

"I know," I said.

We drove off.

"You think he was in the house?" Tommy said.

"She was hiding something."

I watched a young kid whizz by us on his bike. I checked my watch — 2:45 pm.

I thought about Jessica and Jeff, and wondered when it
was I last saw them, and how much I missed them.

We turned onto Route C-1 north.

It took us a half hour to find Buzzy Edward's house on
Bateman Ave. It was on the water overlooking the Saugus
River, just down from the General Edwards Bridge that went
into Lynn.

No one was home.

"What now?" Tommy asked.

I watched a sailboat go under the bridge on its side.
Though the sun was bright, the wind was up and chilly.

"How about getting something to eat?" I said.

"Thought you'd never ask," Tommy said.

After we ate, we went back to the office.

Tommy hung up the phone, lit his cigar then quickly
made another call.

I shuffled through some papers on my desk.

Lieutenant O'Keefe came in. Tommy hung up quickly and
left, leaving me alone.

O'Keefe was a short guy with a huge head that looked
twice the normal size. His skin was pale, almost white, like
the skin of a week-old corpse in the river. He was hairless,
except for some grey-brown fluff above the ears, no
eyebrows to speak of, and no eyelashes. When he sat down
on the edge of my desk I could smell cheap cologne.

"Where have you been?" O'Keefe said.

"You writing a book?"

"Look, Knight. Let's cut out all the bullshit between us
right now. I don't like you and you don't like me."

"Sonuvabitch. Maybe there is hope."

Lieutenant O'Keefe slid off my desk. "I don't know how

it was around here before — "

"It was wonderful, believe me. There were no assholes."

"Well things are going to change around here, Knight. You and your partner had better get used to it. The commissioner sent me down here to get some answers. From now on, everything goes through me. You got it? Everything."

I looked at him a second, then said. "You got anything more to say, say it fast. If not, get the fuck out of my office."

O'Keefe looked at me hard. He walked to the door, turned and said, "Don't fuck with me, Knight. You won't win."

"Kiss my ass."

He left and Tommy came back in.

"What a prick," Tommy said, sitting down at his desk.

I went back to shuffling papers.

I called the morgue again. Leroy said the ME still hadn't showed. I checked my watch — 4:25 pm. Call back in an hour Leroy told me.

I called Rita Barns at headquarters to see what she had for me. Nothing yet, she told me, but she was working on it.

Tommy picked up the phone and dialed. A little while later I stopped what I was doing and listened to his conversation.

"Look, " Tommy said into the phone, pen in hand, writing fast on a yellow notepad. "I am not a fucking brain surgeon. Give it to me slow again. What do I do after I run the microphone up the steering column? Yeah . . . yeah, then what? Connect the transmitter to the battery. Then what? Don't you have anything simple — like one of those miniature bugs I see on television you stick in a phone or under a lamp? Yeah . . . yeah. Okay. So I'm fuckin' stupid. I'll be there in an hour."

He hung up, read over his notes briefly, puffed on his cigar, and said confidently, "This is going to be a piece of cake. Any moron could do this."

"Who were you talking to?" I said.

"A friend of mine at Allied Radio. Best electronic bug-man in the business. He's letting me borrow everything —

the transmitter and receiver, two microphones, two sets of earphones. Even a tape deck to record what's being said." He showed me his notes. "All I have to do is run this wire up the steering column and tape down the mini microphone, run a wire from the battery to the transmitter then hook the transmitter to the radio antenna by using a splitter. Hook up the receiver to the tape deck, and bingo."

I knew what he was up to but I played dumb.

"What's it for?" I said.

"I'm gonna bug O'Hara's car. What the hell do you think it's for?"

"It's illegal."

"Since when did you give a shit about that?"

"Okay, Sherlock. What's the range of the transmitter?"

"Five hundred yards — depending on line of sight. Give or take a few feet." Tommy folded the piece of paper and put it in his jacket pocket. "What time you going back to Chelsea?"

"Nine o'clock," I said.

Tommy glanced at his watch. "It's seven now," he said. "I better get moving. I'll call you when I got something going."

"Take it slow," I said. "If it isn't right, back off. Don't be a hero. O'Hara's a smart bastard."

Tommy smiled at me. "This your way of saying you love me?"

I waved him away, reached for the phone, and punched in my home number.

On the fourth ring, Victoria answered.

"Hi, it's me," I said.

"Me who?" Victoria said dryly.

I smiled and said, "A tall dark, handsome stranger who wants to talk about your vagina."

"Oh, you sweet-talker, you."

"Had any more phone calls?"

"No, come to think of it."

"Good. It's been taken care of. How are the kids?"

"Driving me crazy as usual."

Here it comes.

Victoria went on. "Jessica is in one of her moods. Jeffrey is upset because I wouldn't allow him to have a friend over. Getting them to do any work around the house takes an act of Congress. I have to feed all the animals — you think Jeffrey would do it? Nooooo. Too busy playing. Hasn't cleaned his room in a month. I'm afraid to go in there for fear something might attack me. Other than that, everything is wonderful."

"I'm glad."

"Oh, yes. How could I forget. Your darling little daughter came home last night sick as a dog. Vomited all night."

I frowned. "She sick?"

"You could say that."

"From what?"

"From drinking wine coolers."

"What?"

"Sixteen years old and she's out drinking. Can you imagine? I've grounded her, of course. No more weekend parties."

"I'll have a talk with her," I said, feeling the blood heat up my face.

"Yes. I wish you would."

"I've got to go," I said.

"Don't tell me," Victoria said after a brief pause. "You'll be home late, right?"

"Yeah. Don't bother to wait up," I said.

"I never do," Victoria said.

"I've noticed."

Parked on Kimball Road in Chelsea, I had a clear view of Billy Edwards' house across a trashy vacant lot on Grandview Avenue. It was dark, the neighborhood quiet except for an occasional barking dog, and the distant roar of traffic moving along Route One a few blocks away.

Sitting low, I kept my eyes on the house. There was a light on in the front room — one more in the hall, another upstairs. Nothing moved.

An hour later, at 10:37 pm, a short figure came out of a back door and walked to the garage. He stood in the shadows for a few seconds looking around, then disappeared.

I sat up and started the car.

Two minutes later, the garage door opened, and a blue Ford came out, went backwards out the drive, then peeled off in the direction of Route One. I followed.

Billy Edwards wasted no time going up the Revere Beach Parkway in Revere, heading north towards Wonderland Dog Track. The Buick LeSabre I was driving had no trouble keeping up.

Up Route 1-A before the bridge going into Lynn, Billy Edwards turned off at Point of Pines. As I suspected, he was headed for Buzzy's house.

I slowed the Buick to a crawl and shut off the lights at Rice Avenue.

Billy Edwards pulled into the driveway and sounded his horn. A minute later, Buzzy Edwards came out carrying a shopping bag and a suitcase. Throwing it in the back seat, he got in the passenger side and closed the door.

The Ford wheeled out of the driveway and came straight at me. I ducked down. Switching on the headlights, I caught up with them over the bridge on the way to Lynn. I stayed four cars back.

Entering Lynn, the Ford took several back streets, stopped twice, once at a Shell station, then at a 7-Eleven store. Going down more back streets away from the center of town, they swerved onto Route 129, and headed north toward Swampscott, following the coast road past Blocksidge Field and Phillips Park.

The Ford turned right onto Bates Road, up Littles Point Road, down a dirt road that led to a quiet stone house on the rocky coast of Massachusetts Bay.

I shut off my lights, parked the Buick in some foliage off to the side of the road, and went the rest of the way on foot.

It was 11:15 pm, the night chilly, the sky clear. I was the chameleon dressed for the occasion — black gloves, black baseball cap and black jacket. I even had on my favorite pair of jeans — the ones with the holes in the knees.

I crept through the grass toward the house thinking the last thing I needed was to get an ass full of buckshot from a panicked cop on the run.

Thirty feet from the house, I craned my neck, looking above the grass at the windows, looking for a face, a figure. There was no one. Suddenly the front door opened. I crouched, thrusting my hand under my jacket for my gun.

I could see them clearly; Billy and Buzzy on the porch, carrying the suitcase and paper bag, talking to someone. I couldn't see who that someone was, but instinct told me it was their younger brother, Larry Edwards.

I heard someone say, "It's about time. Where the hell have you been?"

There was some laughter, then Billy and Buzzy disappeared inside.

Considering Larry Edwards was panicked and on the run, standing in the doorway like that told me he was either arrogant to the point of carelessness, or a damn fool.

I went around back. The wind was harsh off the water; I could hear the waves crashing against the rocks below me. To my left was a long set of stairs winding down to the bay. At the bottom was a dock and a huge powerboat.

I heard more laughter from inside.

I moved onto the back porch and peered in the window.

There they were. The three brothers — Larry, Curly and Moe drinking beer and carrying on as if they hadn't a care in the world. Billy Edwards was on the sofa with his feet up on a glass coffee table. He had straight black hair with some gray on the sides, a high forehead, and a double chin. Buzzy was next to him. He had red curly hair, small eyes, and a lot of muscles under a white Red Sox T-shirt. Larry Edwards stood by the fireplace with a Coors Light in his hand. He was slender and taller than his brothers. Strapped to his chest over a green Celtics T-shirt was a .357 magnum. Leaning against the rock fireplace was a twelve-gauge shotgun.

I moved away from the window and tried the door. It was locked.

I took out my lock-jimmy and inserted it in the lock. I couldn't unlock the door. Shit!

Reluctantly, I did the next best thing. I went around front and rang the doorbell.

There was a rush of movement inside. I could hear muffled shouts and rumbling footsteps. Lights went off. Then quiet.

I raised my .38 and rang the doorbell again.

I said in a loud voice, "Larry Edwards. This is Sergeant Joe Knight. You said you wanted to talk. So here I am."

Silence.

Again I rang the doorbell.

Again silence.

"Okay, Edwards," I said irritated. "One more time or I walk."

The outside light went on over my head. I squinted.

"Alright," said a voice from the window to my left. "Show me something."

I took out my gold badge and held it close to the black window.

The voice said, "Put your gun down and come in slow. Make a mistake — it'll be your last."

I put my .38 down on the step, straightened and opened the door. My ankle still held the .9mm if I needed it.

The hall light went on. Billy Edwards stood to my right, a shotgun aimed at my face. Buzzy Edwards was to my left, an automatic aimed at my gut.

I closed the door behind me. "I think you've got me covered," I said. "Hope you boys know what you're doing with those?"

Buzzy said. "Why don't you try somethin' and find out, asshole?"

Billy said. "Yeah. Try somethin'."

Jesus Christ. What morons.

Larry Edwards came out of the shadows. "Alright, you guys, back off before you hurt yourselves."

Billy and Buzzy gave me a long hard look, then reluctantly lowered their weapons.

Larry was in his late thirties, his bearded face angular, his features sharp. His recessed blue eyes, though weary, were engaging, apprehensive yet steady. "I was wondering how long it would take you to find me," he said. "Now that you're here, I'm not sure I want you to be."

"That makes two of us," I said. "All you had to do was call. Save us both a helluva lot of aggravation."

"I couldn't take the chance." He took a step back and turned. "Let's go sit. You want a beer?"

"No, thanks," I said, following Larry down the hall to the living room. "I don't drink."

Larry Edwards looked back at me. "A cop that doesn't drink? You've got to be shitting me? They say never trust a cop who doesn't drink."

"I don't smoke either," I said, lowering myself to the sofa.

Buzzy said, "Don't tell us, you diddle little boys?"

I glared at him. "Why you little devil," I said. "You've been peeking."

Larry said, "Okay, Buzz. Why don't you and Billy take a walk someplace and let us talk? But stay close and keep your eyes open for Chrissakes."

Buzzy shot me a look; so did Billy. Both grabbed a beer and went out the back door.

I looked around. The richly furnished living room smelled of money. A large rock fireplace, a grand piano, oriental rugs, polished tables and chairs that glistened under the spill of subdued table lamps.

Larry waited for them to close the door before he spoke. "I owe them my life," he said. "They saved my ass — just when I thought it was all over."

I sat back. "That the day your dog was butchered?"

Larry's eyes filled. "Yeah. Poor Rusty. Best dog I ever had. The bastards made me watch while they slit his throat."

"Who's they?" I said.

"Two guys I never seen before. Both of 'em big pricks. I hit one of 'em over the head with a nightstick and the bastard never flinched.''

I showed Edwards the photo of Styles. "This one of them?"

Edwards looked at it. "No," he said. "These guys were huge."

I pocketed the photo. "Why do they want you dead?"

Larry sat down in the high-backed chair by the fireplace, took a gulp of Coors, and wiped his mouth with the back of his hand. He looked at me for several long moments. "Me and Pete," he began finally. "We made a mistake."

"That before or after you ripped off the dynamite from Petrelli Construction?"

"You get around," he said, eyebrows up.

I didn't say anything.

"It wasn't my idea," Edwards said. "Pete told me a friend needed it. Couldn't believe how easy it was. We made a quick grand a piece. Pete said there was a lot more bread to be had — just stick with him. So I did — like a fuckin' jerk."

I shifted my position in the chair and let him talk. His eyes swept over the walls and ceiling. "Pete gave the dynamite to this Boston cop — you might know him. Big Irish bastard named O'Hara. I gotta tell yah, Joe. The bastard's no good. He's pushing. You can't believe how much."

I was too disturbed to speak, but I did. "Pushing what?" I said.

"Cocaine, man. And not just shit — the stuff is eighty to ninety pure. Never been stepped on. You just don't come across shit like that every day."

"Where's this guy O'Hara getting it?"

"He's been ripping off dealers, man. All over the place. Providence, Connecticut, Maine. A lot of places."

"So where did you and West fit in?"

"We pushed a few kay up the line, that's all. We slid what bread we made back to O'Hara."

"By kay you mean kilo?"

"Yeah. Kilo. Like I said — it was easy pushing it. Dealers

up north loved it. All of 'em paid some heavy bread and wanted lots more.''

"How much did you and West make?"

"Not enough."

I looked around. "Looks to me you did okay."

Edwards didn't say anything.

"So what went wrong?" I said.

Edwards looked at the floor a second, then at me. "I fucked up — that's what went wrong. I didn't like what was goin' down — never really did. Didn't like what was happening to me and Pete either. He changed, man. I mean, he really changed. He got greedy and started skimming. Started out as a couple of hundred, then a grand, then two and three. He tried to get me to cover for him. I told him it was dangerous, that we ought to get out while we still had the chance. But he wouldn't listen.''

"So you contacted Susan Howell?"

"Yeah. And what a fucking mistake that was. The next thing I know, Pete was found with two bullet holes in the back of his head, Susan Howell's blown out of her fucking shoes, and I'm on the run.''

Larry looked away a second. Blinking several times, he said, ''That's when I called you. I had to tell someone what was going down. That day I was supposed to meet you at Boston Garden, I panicked — saw someone I recognized so I bolted. I was mixed up. Didn't know who I could trust anymore. O'Hara's got a lot of cops on the take doing his dirty work — some of them from Chelsea. I had to go someplace and sort things out. My brothers and I bounced around different places then ended up here. Place cost me three hundred grand — all drug money. I'd like to burn the fucking place down, all that it really cost me.''

"Why didn't you go to the DA? Or tell Chief Williams. They could have protected you.''

"Like I said. I couldn't trust anybody."

"What makes you think you can trust me?"

"Your partner, Tommy. We worked together once. I remember him telling me what a great guy you are.

Straightest cop there was. When I saw you on the news, I decided to call."

"Why did you tell Susan Howell?" I said. "Talk about running a knife across your own throat."

"I know. It was stupid. But she did me and Pete a favor once. Kept our names out of that convenience store scandal a couple of years back. We owed her one."

"How did they find out you talked to her?"

"Who the fuck knows. Maybe she said something to someone she worked with, another reporter maybe — I don't know. I sure as shit didn't tell anybody."

"How much money did you deliver to this cop, O'Hara?"

"Oh, hell. Had to be over a million."

Son-of-a-bitch.

I looked away, feeling something tight in my throat — probably my heart. It felt as if it had just been ripped from my chest and shoved up my ass.

I said, "Ever hear of a New York City cop named Cole? Robert Cole?"

"No."

"What about a Manfred Styles?"

"Never heard of him either, why?"

I stood up. "No reason."

Larry Edwards looked at me. "I'm really sorry for what I did, Joe. Despite what I've told you, I'm still a good cop. I know where the shit is going — who's buying and when. We could make a fucking bust that would blow the entire East Coast apart. You want to turn me in — that's okay, too. You tell me what you want me to do and I'll do it."

His eyes conveyed the tension he'd been living with. "For now," I said, heading for the door, "Stay put and stay alive. After that, we'll see."

12

Midnight. I was hungry and there was no place open except a MacDonald's over the bridge into Revere. Reluctantly, I pulled in and picked up two cheeseburgers, large fries and a root beer. The fries were cold and soggy, the cheeseburgers tasted like shoe leather, and the root beer was watery.

Sonuvabitch. I threw everything back in the bag and tossed it in the back seat.

As I approached Wonderland Dog Track, the races were letting out. A Revere cop wearing an orange slicker and white gloves put up his hand and stopped me to allow people to cross the road to the parking lot. I studied the faces. Some smiled and talked; most didn't. Some were going home broke, others happy to come away even or down a few bucks.

I thought of the time a bunch of us guys went down to the Raynham track in Taunton a few years back. Tommy, me, and Brendan O'Hara bet a straight trifecta in the first race and won it. Eleven hundred bucks. We couldn't believe it. They had to carry us out of the place that night. Brendan singing Irish songs at the top of his lungs across the parking lot. Tommy on top of the car pissing on the roof, me laughing like a goddamn fool, drunk on three lousy beers. All of us ended up in a motel someplace in Brockton. I never did figure out how I got home.

We did a lot of crazy things like that together — Tommy, me and Brendan. I wondered for a brief moment, as the cop waved me on, if there would ever be another time like that. I knew there couldn't be.

Going around Bell Circle toward the Sumner Tunnel, I

reached for the microphone. "Victor Eight-Six to Opera-tions," I said.

"Operations answering, Victor Eight-Six," the dispatcher said.

"Any calls from the Victor Seven-Five?"

"Hold on one."

After a few seconds, the dispatcher said, "Only one message, Victor Eight-Six. Victor Seven-Five says — go to location number two and wait for his call."

"That it?"

"Yes sir. That's it."

"Thank you, dispatcher."

"Operations clear at twelve forty-one in the AM."

Traffic through the Sumner Tunnel was heavy because of the track letting out, but it moved. I made it to Jack's All-Nite coffee shop off Congress Street a little before one. Making a quick trip inside for a coffee and sweet-roll, I waited in the car next to the bank of phones at the corner of State and Congress.

One o'clock came and went.

Sitting in the warmth of the car, I struggled to stay awake. There had to be a string running from my eyelids to my stomach. Everytime I ate lately, my eyes went heavy and wanted to close. Someone said it was the pressure on the heart slowing it down caused by an over-inflated stomach. Maybe there was something to it. I thought about getting another checkup. Maybe next week.

The telephone in the third booth rang.

I got out in the chill, waited for the fifth ring, picked up the receiver, and gave Tommy our special code. "You suck — we all suck. Everybody sucks."

Tommy said, "Get over here right away."

"Where's here?"

"Cooper Street in the North End. Bring me some coffee and a couple of cinnamon doughnuts. And hurry up."

"You watching O'Hara?"

"No, moron. Al Capone. Of course I'm watching O'Hara."

"I'll be right there."

"Come in off Salem Street and go down Jerusalem Place. Take the alley before you get to North Margin. And don't forget the doughnuts."

Twenty minutes later I crammed the Buick into a space on Salem Street and walked down Jerusalem Place. Turning into the dark alley, following it out to Cooper, my nostrils flared. Everywhere was the wonderful aroma of garlic and the magnificent smell of spaghetti sauce. Tomorrow was Wednesday — Prince Spaghetti Day. It reminded me of home a long time ago. Damn, my mother could cook.

I could see Tommy's shadow sitting low in the Chevy Nova parked across the narrow street. I waited in the alley until a young couple passed by, then went across and opened the passenger side door.

Tommy said in a low voice, "It's about time. Where's the doughnuts?"

Getting in, I tossed him the bag.

"Where's O'Hara?" I said.

Tommy opened the bag, pulled out a doughnut, took two quick bites, then gulped down some coffee. "Over there on North Margin," he mumbled. "Number 21. Second floor."

I looked up. There was a light on in one of the front rooms. "Who's he with?" I said.

"Vinnie Torchia."

"What about the other two guys with O'Hara?"

"Too dark. Couldn't see them."

"Who owns the house?"

"Don't know."

Tommy inhaled the second doughnut and finished the coffee. "Should have had you bring me two more," he said, wiping his beard with a napkin, brushing the sugar off his dark brown jacket. "You find Edwards?"

"Yeah. Alive and well in Swampscott of all places. Staying in a mansion on the water."

"What'd he have to say?"

I told Tommy everything.

"Stupid prick," Tommy said.

"Right now he's our only link to O'Hara — if he stays alive long enough." I looked toward the five-story. "They been in there long?"

"Almost two hours."

"Did you install the bug?"

"Yeah."

"Anyone see you do it?"

"Nope."

I looked down the street. "Which car is his?"

"The white Olds over there under the light."

"You're shitting me?"

"Always thought he had more class than that. You should see the back, you think the front looks bad. The smell inside will gag you. All I could think of was dried puke."

"Wonderful."

I looked at the Olds and said, "Does the bug work?"

Tommy flashed me his shit-eating grin. "Thought you'd never ask," he said, reaching down for the cassette tape recorder under his seat. Putting on a set of earphones, he handed me a pair. "Here. Put these on."

I did.

Tommy pressed the rewind button on the recorder, and said proudly, "You won't believe the quality. I was a long way back — sounds like the assholes were in my back seat."

"They say anything?"

Tommy stopped the tape and pressed play. "Listen," he said. "It's O'Hara talking to Vinnie Torchia."

I did.

The first thing I heard was a car door slam. Then Vinnie. "Where the fuck yah been? I been wait'n here almost a fuck'n hour."

"Tough," O'Hara said.

"You got some good shit for me?"

"It's not shit."

"After you stepped on it how many times? Two maybe three? That's shit."

"You don't like it, don't buy it. Get the fuck out of the car. There's always someone else."

"Where is it? I wanna check it."

"I don't have it. Not with me anyway."

"How we gonna check it?"

"I brought a sample."

Hearing Brendan O'Hara say the things he was saying made my jaws lock so bad, my teeth hurt.

Vinnie Torchia said, "Where you gettin' the shit anyway?"

"None of your business," O'Hara said.

"Mister Angellini says I should make it my business."

"Fuck Mister Angellini."

"I'll tell him you said that."

"I'm scared to death."

"He don't trust you."

"That's his problem."

"I don't either."

"That's your problem."

"No. It's yours, asshole. The people Mister Angellini told me to take you to — they want to know what they're gettin' up front. They ain't gonna like it — they already think you're jerkin' us around."

"I'll deliver. I always do."

"We gave you some heavy fuckin' bread up front, man. You ain't think'n of tryin' somethin funny are yah?"

"Fuck you, Vinnie," O'Hara said. "Your fucking Mob is down in this city — remember that. After what happened to the Angellinis, no Family is the country wants to deal with you. Now that Iazanno is gone, who you got left?"

"We still got Jocko Gambrialli, asshole," Torchia said. "And he hears the way you're talkin', he's gonna stuff you in a box and drop you in the harbor."

In the brief silence, someone rolled down a window. The sounds of the city rushed in. Some cars went by, then a truck. Someone rolled up the window.

"Okay," Torchia said, "You get your money when we get the shit."

"You'll have it all by Saturday," O'Hara said.

"Don't convince me, pal. Convince Mister Angellini."

"I'm not your pal."

"And I ain't yours," Torchia said.

Again silence.

I looked at Tommy and shook my head in disbelief. Shifting my concentration back to the tape, I listened as Vinnie Torchia spoke again. "You sure about gettin' the shit Saturday night? I gotta know. My partners gotta know. You call me, okay? When you know for sure."

"Don't worry about it," O'Hara said.

"I do worry about it. That's what Mister Angellini pays me to do. Worry about things."

There was another long silence. A truck or bus must have gone by, something loud that drowned out their voices momentarily. I did a slow burn waiting to hear them speak again.

Gerry Angellini. Jesus Christ. He and his brothers are serving eighty years in the federal pen for extortion and loansharking. Wouldn't the Feds like to hear this tape. He's still running things from the inside.

Someone turned on the car radio to the Red Sox game. Ken Coleman said it was the ninth inning in California, Sox tied with the Angels three to three. Smith was in for Clemens and had just struck out the side. Wade Boggs was leading off the tenth.

I closed my eyes for a moment, and wondered when it was everything had gone wrong for Brendan. He saved my life, for Chrissakes, in Charlestown near the old high school across from the Bunker Hill Monument. It seemed so long ago, another life. We were both on bikes at the time, crusing the city. Some crazy, pissed-off-at-the-world drunk had come out of a house with a shotgun and started blowing away everything in sight. Brendan was the first one on the scene. I came second, storming up Monument Avenue like the young hell-bent-for-leather cowboy I was in those days. I didn't even see the guy standing on the corner, but he saw me and aimed his shotgun at me, point-blank. Brendan had no choice but to shoot the drunk dead. I remember it took Brendan months to get over it. Until that time, he hadn't even drawn his revolver against anyone, much less used it.

He was a cop's cop. Everything had to be done by book. He had it made in the department. Made lieutenant over me, then deputy superintendent. Then all of a sudden he gave it all up — the stars, his soft job at headquarters — and went back to the street. That was two years ago. He never did tell me why.

I switched my concentration back to the tape. The Sox went up four to three on a homer by Mike Greenwell. No one talked for nearly a minute.

Then O'Hara said, "Where we going?"

"You'll know when you get there," Torchia told him. "Take a right here. Now park over there. You're gonna have to do some fast talkin'. Jocko has gotten the word from Mister Angellini. He wants more of the action."

"What?"

"Mister Angellini wants more. He thinks you're holdin' out."

"Fuck you. No way. You tell him that. No fucking way."

The radio cut off with the engine, but the transmitter remained alive. I heard doors open and close; footsteps walking away.

Tommy shut off the tape and looked at me. "What do you think?" he said with a smile. "Great quality, huh?"

I looked at him. "Yeah. Great quality. You done good, Tommy. You done good."

Ten minutes later, the door of the apartment building opened. Four men came out and stood on the sidewalk. It was dark as hell — I couldn't see a thing, only shadows.

Tommy slumped low again. So did I.

"That's O'Hara," Tommy said, his eyes peeking above the steering wheel. "I think the guy on the right is Torchia. Can you see the other two guys?"

"No." I whispered.

"What we need is one of those fucking cameras," Tommy

said. "One of those surveillance types. You know what I mean?"

"I know what you mean. And people down in hell need ice water."

"Vice has one. They use it in the Zone all the time. Maybe we could steal it from them?"

"That's a thought."

O'Hara gestured, said something to Torchia, then went down the steps across the street to his Olds. Torchia went back inside with the others.

Tommy waited until O'Hara was headed down North Margin before he started the car.

"Hurry up for Chrissakes," I said. "You're going to lose him."

Tommy started the car, put the Nova in gear and was about to turn on the headlights when he stopped. "Shit," he said, looking down the street. "We got company."

Headlights shot out of the darkness ahead of us. A red late model Chevy Impala pulled out of a space a short distance from where we were parked, turned left and disappeared up North Margin.

Tommy didn't hesitate. He snapped on the headlights, shoved the accelerator to the floor, and sent the Nova careening over the sidewalk between two parked cars. Screeching to a halt at a stop sign, Tommy turned right down North Margin.

"What are you doing, you asshole?" I said. "They went left."

"I know what the hell I'm doing. I'm heading them off. North Margin goes around to Endicott. Endicott is one way to Thatcher."

I sat back. "Oh, yeah."

Tommy looked at me. "Asshole," he muttered.

I put the earphones on. I don't know why I did. O'Hara wasn't going to talk to himself, but you never know.

The Sox were in the bottom of the thirteenth now. Stanley was in for Lee Smith. Score tied four to four. I didn't know the Sox could stay awake that long.

The North End streets were narrow, and the cars parked on both sides made it difficult to maneuver. It made no difference to Tommy; he drove the Nova like a madman, swerving right and then left.

We reached Thatcher Street and stopped. Tommy couldn't have timed it better. The Olds crossed in front of our headlights. Twenty or so seconds later, so did the red Impala.

"Who the fuck are they?" Tommy said.

I only caught a glimpse of them; two men, both in dark clothes. The passenger had a hairy face and wore a stocking cap. I couldn't see much of the driver — only that he was huge.

Tommy turned right and joined the parade. "Whoever they are," he said, "they're assholes. Any closer, they'd be in O'Hara's trunk for Chrissakes."

The Olds and the Chevy went straight down Endicott heading toward Prince Street.

We were close enough to the Chevy to get a number off the plate. New York 771-333.

Sonuvabitch.

We went left out to Washington Street. Running the red light at Washington and Commercial, we swerved right by Polcari's Restaurant and hurried to Prince Street. Pulling to the curb, Tommy shut off the lights.

A minute later, the Olds came down Prince the wrong way on a one way street. We ducked down.

I looked at Tommy. "How the hell did you know he'd do that?" I said, amazed.

Tommy grinned. "Skill, pal. Pure skill. If you knew the city like I do, you'd know everyone in Italianville goes the wrong way down Prince. You don't, you go back deep into the North End. You could get lost forever in that maze, you're not careful."

The Olds turned right down Commercial and headed toward Hanover Street. Thirty seconds went by; no sign of the Chevy.

Tommy said. "See? I told you. Those assholes got lost."

We waited another ten seconds. Still no sign of the Chevy. "Move it," I said. "We don't want to lose O'Hara."

The Olds went right onto Hanover, past the firehouse and St. Leonard's Church, turned left down Fleet Street, and headed back to Commercial. A few minutes later, the Olds was on the Expressway heading south.

Over the Broadway Bridge into Southie, staying three cars behind, we followed the Olds up Broadway, past Dorchester Street to Farragut Road by Marion Park. Turning right past Pleasure Bay and Castle Island, we made it around the corner to East Fourth Street in time to see O'Hara lock his car and go up the steps of a three-decker.

We turned right onto P Street and stopped.

"Sonuvabitch," I said, looking around. "I've been here."

"When?"

"Long time ago. The apartment belongs to O'Hara's ex-girlfriend. Lives on the first floor."

"Yeah. I remember now. A knockout named Sherry something."

"Sherry Condon."

"That's the one. Great set of tits."

I looked up and down the street. No sign of the Chevy.

Tommy said, "Everything's dark. Let's go. He must have gone to bed. At least we know now where he drops his underwear."

I checked my watch — 2:13 am.

I said, "I wonder how the Sox did?"

"Who gives a shit," Tommy said.

I let the cold water run in the basin, leaned against the sink, and looked into the mirror. My eyes were bloodshot, the stubble of my beard pronounced. I hadn't shaved in nearly three days, my cumulative hours of sleep were not much more than eight hours. It was half past three in the morning and no time to consider shaving.

Across the hall, Victoria and the kids slept peacefully.

I thought, what would happen if someday I didn't come home? What if I was found dead somewhere with a bullet hole in the back of my head? How would they react? Would they cry? Maybe they'd wonder who the stranger was in the casket. What was all the fuss about, my kids would say? Why were so many policemen marching at the funeral? Who was that guy, Mom?

He was your father, for Chrissakes. Your father!

The alarm went off at 6:30 am.

I was already up, shaved, showered, dressed, and in the kitchen. I heard Victoria's footsteps on the stairs.

Sleepily, she wandered in.

I said cheerfully, a dishtowel wrapped around my waist, protecting my jeans from splashing bacon grease. "Good morning, sweetheart. Just in time for breakfast. Take a seat."

Victoria looked at the breakfast table, complete with eggs, bacon, toast, juice and coffee. "What's all this?" she said with a smile. "I must be dreaming."

Marmalade the cat rubbed up against my leg. "I've fed you, cat," I said. "Don't say I didn't."

I pulled out a chair. "Here. Take a seat. It's getting cold."

Victoria sat down.

Jessica and Jeff stumbled in.

"Morning, Dad," Jeff said. "What's all this?"

"Don't tell me it's Sunday already," Jessica said.

I poured myself some coffee and sat down. "C'mon, kids. Eat before everything gets cold."

Jessica sat down, grabbed a piece of bacon and took a bite. "You cook all this, Mom?" she said.

"No," Victoria said, looking at me. "Your father did."

"Why?" Jeff said. "I mean, it's great but how come, Dad?"

"Can't a guy make breakfast for his family without getting the third degree for crying out loud? I miss you guys."

"We miss you too, Dad," Jeff said, chomping down a slice of toast.

"Me too," Jessica said. "Nice going, Dad. This sure beats cold cereal. How are you at making pancakes?"

"Not bad," I said.

Victoria smiled. "It's very nice, hon. We love you, too."

I returned her smile. "I'm glad."

Jeff checked the clock on the wall above the sink. "It's seven o'clock. C'mon, Jess. Hurry up. We're going to miss the bus."

"What bus?" I said.

"The school bus, Dad," Jeff said. "We're going on an end of summer camping trip to Maine. Camp Squantum. Great place. You remember it, don't you, Dad? You took us there a long time ago."

"I remember." I looked at my daughter.

"What's the matter, Dad?" Jessica said. "Why you staring at me like that?"

I said, "I can't believe it. You? Going on a camping trip?"

"Don't be stupid, Dad," Jessica said. "I'm going to soccer camp with the girls. And I can't wait. Mom's been driving me crazy. So's this idiot brother of mine."

Jessica and Jeff exchanged faces, sticking out their tongues.

"Forget the bus," I said. "I'll drive you."

"You will?" Jeff said. "Gee, Dad. That's wicked nice. Thanks."

"Oh, no," Jessica said. "You're not going to drive us to the school in that smelly old Plymouth are you? My friends will freak if they see me. I'll die."

I looked at Victoria. "Can you believe this? Should I tell them the story about when I was a kid?"

"I think they've heard it."

"Yeah, well. Don't panic, Jessica. I'm driving a new Buick now — picked it up just for you."

Jessica got up from the table and hurried off. "Okay," she said over her shoulder. "I'll ride with you, but only if you drop us off out back of the school. I don't want anyone to know I got a ride from my father. That would be gross."

"Oh, heavens," I said. "We couldn't have that. Everyone knows fathers have a zillion severe disorders."

"Don't worry about it, hon," Victoria said. "If it makes you feel any better, she hates riding with me as well."

We held hands. I said, "You know? Maybe Jessica should move out now while she still knows everything."

At the office I called Tommy, Jake and Warren into the room and closed the door. Lieutenant O'Keefe was out of the building. That made it easy for us to talk. Warren sat down at his desk and put his feet up, Jake sat on the corner and fingered some papers. Tommy rocked a chair back against the wall.

I took out a piece of chalk and wrote on the wall. It didn't bother me because the walls hadn't been painted yet — and probably never would be.

I wrote down the names Susan Howell, Pete West and Larry Edwards. Also Robert Cole. Next, I wrote down the names Styles, Vinnie Torchia, the Mob and Brendan O'Hara.

"Brendan O'Hara?" Warren said.

Tommy said, "Yeah. Brendan O'Hara."

I added a couple of other things, then turned around.

"Alright," I said. "What we talk about stays in this room."

Everyone nodded.

"Okay," I said. "Susan Howell and Pete West. Dead. Howell — shot once in the back of the head before the explosion. The bullet taken from the skull was .9mm supervell, fired from a VP70Z."

Jake and Warren looked at each other, then at me. "You're shitting us," Jake said. "She was shot?"

"Seconds before the explosion."

"How come you didn't tell us this before?" Warren said.

"I'm telling you now."

"A VP70Z," Jake said. "Powerful weapon. Any idea who it was?"

"I'm coming to that." I turned back to the wall and wrote down the name Cole. "The late Detective Sergeant Robert Trenton Cole," I said. "NYPD. He said he was here looking for a hit man named Manfred Styles. I've got a photo of Styles — I'll get some duplicates made up for you guys. Cole said Styles was hired to kill Howell and West."

"Hired by who?" Warren said.

"For Chrissakes, Warren," Tommy said. "Let the man talk."

Warren gave Tommy the finger.

I went on. "Larry Edwards was West's partner. I found him hiding out in a house in Swampscott."

I told Jake and Warren everything Edwards told me.

"Prick," Warren said.

"Yeah," Jake said. "Fuck 'im."

"We can't. He's our only link to O'Hara."

"Someone's going to have to watch Edwards," Tommy said.

Warren looked at Tommy then at me. "Oh, no. Not me, Joe," he said. "I don't like baby-sitting. Remember what happened the last time."

I did. Warren was supposed to watch this guy who we thought set his dog on an infant girl next door. The dog — a rottweiler — had knocked over the bassinet and tore the kid to shreds, killing her. I had sent Warren to check on complaints by other neighbors who said the guy was crazy, that he might have sicced the dog on the kid because the parents had complained to the police about the dogs he kept in the back yard. Warren got tired of watching the guy and decided it was time to get some answers to some questions that had bothered him. Knowing Warren's affection for young children, I should have known not to send him. But I did. So Warren went into the back yard and knocked on the guy's door. That's when the rottweilers came after him. One of the dogs had taken a serious chunk out of Warren's leg before he had a chance to pull out his .357 magnum. Warren shot the three dogs dead. The case has been in the civil courts ever since.

"Okay, Warren," I said. "You're right. I'll send Larry and Jack."

"Good," Warren said. "They deserve each other."

I waited for Warren to shut up, then I told the rest.

"Brendan O'Hara was a friend of yours wasn't he, Joe?" Jake said.

"Yeah," I said. "Was."

Warren said, "All I can remember about the guy was how clean his hands were all the time."

"You would," Tommy said.

"No. I mean it," Warren went on. "I keep my hands clean, but O'Hara. Christ. I remember watching him wash his hands six times in a row one time. We were working a detail at the auto show in the old Hynes Auditorium. All he did was open a couple of doors and let some cars in the back garage. After that he spent ten minutes washing his hands. Dry 'em, then wash 'em — dry 'em, then wash 'em. Strange guy."

Warren was right. Brendan O'Hara was obsessed with clean hands. And checking the stove at night to make sure it was off — a zillion times. Those facts reminded me there was another phone call I had to make.

"From now on," I said, "I want to know what O'Hara does. Where he goes and who he sees. I want his bank account checked. I want his girlfriend checked. Most of all I want to know where the hell he's getting all the drugs he's been selling. And what he's been doing with the money."

"It's not going to be easy," Jake said. "He knows all of us. Not me as much. But you, Tommy and Warren."

"We'll switch cars as much as we have to. We'll stay back and give the bastard room. I know someone I can call to get some surveillance equipment — someone who'll keep his mouth shut, which is what we need right now. Everybody keeping their mouths shut."

13

After everybody left, I called the Mass General Hospital and talked to a psychiatrist I met a few years ago, a doctor named William Minch. He had treated Brendan O'Hara for this disorder called OCD—Obsessive Compulsive Disorder. Because I was a friend and had demanded to know what was wrong, the doctor had told me O'Hara's disorder afflicted about three million people. Some were called "checkers" who can't get to work in the morning or sleep at night without reassuring themselves every five minutes that the stove was turned off. Others were "ritualizers" who compulsively open and close the refrigerator door a zillion times before they take anything out to eat.

O'Hara was known as a "washer." Sometimes he'd shower nine or ten times a day—even wash his hair one strand at a time. If he wasn't in the shower, he'd be in the bathroom washing his hands. One time the doctor called it the "Lady Macbeth Syndrome" because Lady Macbeth was a compulsive hand washer. Weird.

I asked the doctor to keep my inquiry quiet. He told me he hadn't seen O'Hara since last October. He had given O'Hara a drug called clomipramine and some final behavior therapy. It must have worked, the doctor told me; O'Hara hadn't been back since.

I wrote down on a piece of paper everything I could remember about O'Hara. His habits. His likes and dislikes. Where we used to go together. Who he hung around with. He was an Irish-Catholic from South Boston and hated everyone who wasn't—Italians, Blacks, but especially the British.

O'Hara loved "the Mother Land" as he called it. *Erin go*

Bragh and all that nonsense. Ireland forever. Every St. Patrick's Day he'd march in the parade through South Boston—drunk on his ass—wearing a stupid looking green leprechaun hat. I don't know how many times I heard him say that someday the British would all be blown out of Northern Ireland. He knew my wife was British, so whenever he had brought the subject up around me, he had tried to make a joke out of it, but I knew he was dead serious.

Everyday he had to eat at the Eire Pub in Dorchester—nowhere else. Even had his picture taken with the President when Reagan made a surprise visit there a few years back. The picture is still hanging over the bar. "To my friend Brendan O'Hara" the President had written. "Ireland Forever."

Jesus Christ.

It was almost noon by the time I got to the morgue. Upstairs, I met Leroy, wet-mopping the hall outside the cutting room. "How you doing, Leroy?" I said.

"Oh, can't kick, Sergeant Joe," Leroy said. "Can't kick at all."

"Your boss in there?" I said, nodding toward the double doors of the autopsy room.

"No sir, Sergeant Joe. He's gone home for the day."

"Gone home? You know if he finished the post on that New York cop they brought in yesterday?"

Leroy looked at me as if I had spoken in some foreign language. "What New York cop?" he said.

"Don't bust 'em, Leroy. I'm not in the mood for jokes."

"Who's joke'n, Sergeant Joe? We ain't got no New York cop's body here. Never did."

My pulse quickened.

Leroy said, "You don't believe me, Sergeant Joe? Comes downstairs and see for yourself."

I did—opened all the porcelain doors, held my breath as I unzipped each white bag, and checked every body. Leroy was right.

I checked the log. No one named Cole was on the list. I got to a phone fast, called the Area D police station, and asked for Jenkins and Macmillan. The desk officer said they were out on patrol. I said I needed to talk to them immediately and gave him the number I was calling from. He said he'd contact them right away.

Ten minutes later, Marty Jenkins called me back. "What's up, Joe?" he said.

"Marty," I said, "yesterday morning, who picked up the body of that New York Cop?"

"Why?"

"Never mind why. Just tell me who picked it up?"

"The medical examiner."

"You sure?"

"Yeah, I'm sure. The van said medical examiner on it. The two guys had on white coats."

"Anything else you remember about them?"

"Who notices faces? It was raining. You told us to clean up the scene fast."

"Tell me something, Marty. Who called the medical examiner?"

"Didn't you?"

"No, I didn't."

Marty fell silent.

"What about the Trans Am?" I said.

"It got towed away," Marty said.

"Who called the tow truck?"

Again Marty fell silent a few seconds. Then he said, "Not us."

"Oh, Christ."

"What is this, Joe?" Marty said. "You said keep your name off the report so we did—now you're trying to nail us."

"I'm not trying to nail you, Marty. You know me better that that."

"Could have fooled me the way you're talking."

I paused to gather my thoughts. "Forget this conversation ever happened, Marty. Okay? As another favor to me."

"It's forgotten." Then Marty said, "I didn't know you so good, Joe. I'd say you're losing it. What's the matter? You got so many people dropping dead around you can't keep track of 'em?''

"Something like that, Marty."

I thanked him and hung up.

Someone opened the double doors leading to the morgue storage room. Where I was sitting in the office across the hall, I got a whiff of rotting meat wafting up from the basement. I wanted to puke from what I had just found out and this smell didn't help.

I called Tommy at the office and told him to meet me downtown.

At Police Headquarters, I took the elevator to the basement and walked through a maze of file cabinets, suspended pipes, and stacked cardboard boxes, to the computer room.

My friend Rita Barns was black and gorgeous. Smooth skin. Great body. Her hair was braided in a zillion strands that ran over her head with multicolored beads dangling from each end.

"Nice do," I said with a smirk, pulling a chair beneath me and sitting down next to her at the computer terminal.

"Thank you, Joe," she said, showing me a brilliant line of straight white teeth. "Nice of you to notice."

She wore huge red-rimmed glasses that kept falling to the end of her nose. Pushing them back, she said, "I got something for you, Joe."

"Make it good, Rita babe. I need it."

"I can tell. I saw the way you were staring at my tits."

"Nice talk."

"Sorry."

"You should be. Besides, I wasn't staring. I was ogling."

"There's a difference?"

"I think so."

Rita punched some keys. I waited.

"Not sure you're gonna like it, Joe," Rita said.

Green words started moving across the black screen. Rita was right. I didn't like it.

The screen said: ROBERT TRENTON COLE. NO SUCH NAME ON FILE WITH THE NEW YORK CITY POLICE DEPARTMENT. BADGE

NUMBER 4442 REPORTED STOLEN BY NYPD, JULY 3RD, THIS YEAR.

"Jesus Christ," I said. It took me a few seconds to gather myself. Then, "You try the Feds?"

"There's no way to gain access to their computers," Rita said.

"You try?"

"Of course I tried, turkey."

"Try again."

Rita rolled her eyes at me. "You think all I got to do is sit here and run checks for you, blood? You know how many federal agencies this turkey could belong to?"

"Rita, honey child, I don't give a shit if it takes you all week. I have to know who this guy was. Stop making excuses and get your ass in gear."

Rita looked at me a long time. "You know, you're kinda cute for a honky. I could go for you if it wasn't for the fact you've been eating too much of that honky food."

"What the hell are you talking about?"

"Honky food. You know, doughnuts—sweet rolls. You people eat shit like that all the time. Look at what it's doing to your belly."

"Kiss my ass, Rita," I said, standing up. I planted a kiss on her forehead. "You find out anything on Styles?"

"New York is sending me his file. Should be here in a few days."

"Thanks, babe," I said.

The telephone rang. Rita answered. "It's your partner," she said, handing me the phone.

"Joe," Tommy said.

I didn't say anything. Whenever he said my name like that it meant trouble.

"I'm upstairs." Tommy said. "Just got a call from Jake. He said our pal Juilo Pasquez is holed up in a three-decker on Linwood Street in Hyde Park. Jake's waiting for us on River Street."

Son-of-a-bitch. Chasing Julio Pasquez was the last thing I wanted to do right now. But I still wanted him bad. Tommy said, "I'll be out in the car. Hurry up."

On the way over to Hyde Park, going up Columbus Ave to Washington Street, Tommy said, "Guess what? You know that New York plate number you told me to run through the registry—the one on the Chevy we saw following O'Hara? Well it came back. So did the plate number I ran on the Trans Am."

"Don't tell me. There's no such plates."

"How'd you guess? I had the registry run them both through LEAPS and NCIC twice. New York says there's no such plate numbers on file. They're phony."

As we went down Washington Street, I told Tommy that the New York City police had said the same thing about Cole. I also told him Cole's body never made it to the morgue—his Trans Am never made it to the pound.

Tommy looked at me. "The shit is rising, Joe. How in hell are we ever going to stop it?" was all he could say.

I had no answer.

Watching the world go by, a thought struck me.

"Stop," I said.

"What for?"

"Turn around and head for state police headquarters."

"What for?"

I took out the envelope containing the photos of Styles. I don't know why I gripped the edges with my fingertips but I did, holding each one up to my eyes, examing them like it was the first time I ever saw them. If Cole's fingerprints were still on them, they were smudged by now. But they were all I had, the only chance to identify Cole—if that was his real name, which I'd bet a week's pay it wasn't.

Sergeant Billy Andrews was the best fingerprint man in the country. Anyone could lift a print off paper, he could. Maybe we'd get lucky.

The state police fingerprint lab was on the same floor as ballistics. When we went in, I showed the civilian girl at the desk my gold badge.

"Sergeant Andrews around?" I asked. "Sergeant Knight, Boston police. This is Detective Sanders."

Billy Andrews called out to me from behind a frosted glass

partition. "Hey, Joe. Back here."

We went around back.

Billy was tall, in his mid-forties with light brown thinning hair, mischievous blue eyes, and the biggest ballbuster you'd ever want to meet. But he could afford to be. He was the best at what he did.

I introduced him to Tommy. Between the two of them, I wondered who was going to be the first to take a shot at me.

It was Billy. "How's the diet, Joe? Geezus, are you putting it on or what?"

I didn't say anything—only looked at him, waiting for the next one. I didn't have to wait long.

"Isn't that the same striped shirt you had on the last time I saw you? I recognize the stains."

I looked at Tommy. The bastard was grinning, enjoying every word of it.

I said to Billy, "You through, asshole?"

My voice said I wasn't serious, but my eyes did. Billy was as good as anyone at reading them. "What can I do for you, Joe?" he said.

"I got some pictures I want you to look at."

"Your wife already gave me some. Great body."

I tried to smile, but it wouldn't come.

I slowly removed each photo from the envelope. Billy took a pair of tweezers, plucked them one by one out of my fingertips, and carefully placed them down on the desk. He slid the one of Styles under a microscope. Lowering his head to the scope, adjusting the focus knob, Billy said, "Holy shit. There's so many prints here I can hardly see the guy's face. Who is it by the way? Got to be a sicko. Look at the eyes."

"Can you weed out the prints?"

"That depends."

"On what?"

"How many of the prints I can match up. Any idea how many people handled them?"

"Only three I know of for sure. Myself, Tommy here. And

the guy whose prints we need to get."

"Looks like you showed them to all of Boston."

"C'mon, Billy. Can you do it or not?"

Billy looked up from the scope. "Of course I can do it," he said, sliding another photo under the scope. "If I can lift a latent from a dead broad's tit like I did a few weeks ago that nailed the prick who killed her, I sure as shit can sort through this mess."

"Okay," I said. "When?"

"Soon."

"How soon?"

"Maybe tomorrow."

Five minutes later, Tommy and I were back on the way to Hyde Park.

Jake Callaghan saw us coming down River Street and got out of his green Ford looking like he had just stepped out of the window of a men's store. Three-piece light blue summer suit, neat haircut, clean shave, crisp white shirt, and maroon tie. I had on my Red Sox cap, a tan jacket over my green striped shirt, and my favorite faded blue jeans. Tommy had on his Celtics jacket and tan slacks.

I pulled to the curb behind the Ford. The wind had strengthened; trash littered the sidewalk, flat and soggy from the rain.

Jake said, poking his head in the side window, "Where the hell have you guys been? I've been waiting almost two hours for Chrissakes."

"I thought you were supposed to be checking on O'Hara's bank account?" I said to Jake.

"I was until I got a call from this guy I know. Ex-cop private dick doing some free-lance work for the family of one of Julio's victims."

"Where's Julio now?" I said.

"Up the street," Jake said. "Ten Linwood—back apartment, third floor."

"Who's with him?" Tommy said.

"Two, maybe three guys. Shacking with a couple of broads. Think we should call in more help, Joe? These bastards are probably armed to the fucking ceiling.''

"Wouldn't hurt," I said.

I called the Area E dispatcher—told him to send in some marked units. Come in slow—no sirens or lights, I told him. While we waited, Tommy and I took a ride by the three-decker. There were two burned out shells of cars in the driveway and four more scattered in pieces around the yard. Everything was quiet.

Ten minutes later, two rapid response units showed. I sent one two-man unit up to Valencia Road. Told them to come in through the back. The other went in with us.

Jake and two uniforms took the back stairs to the third floor; Tommy and I shouldered our way through the front door and climbed the narrow staircase. The place smelled of cat piss. On the second floor landing, we stopped and listened. No sounds. A radio played softly in the apartment behind us.

We went up to the third floor. With my back against the door, my .38 raised, I checked my watch. One minute to ten. At ten straight up, Jake was to hit the back door. Tommy and I would bust in the front.

We waited. Ten o'clock.

I whispered to Tommy. "You ready?"

He nodded.

We hit the door, knocking it off its hinges.

Inside, we started screaming. "Police! Everybody up! Everybody up!"

Jake and the uniforms did the same coming in the back.

Breaking in the door to one of the bedrooms, I shouted to the naked guy reaching for a shotgun beside the bed. "Don't do it!"

He froze, his arm outstretched, his eyes locked on mine, wide open and panicked. "Don't shoot!" he screamed. "Please, don't shoot!"

"Get the fuck out of that bed!" Tommy said, tearing off the covers, revealing a naked teenage girl hiding under them. "You too, Queenie!"

Jake came into the room. "Julio isn't here!" he said, out

of breath.

"What do you mean, he isn't here," I said. "Where the hell is he?"

"I don't know. Maybe in one of the other apartments. Maybe he heard us coming."

"Take your people and go downstairs. Break in all the doors if you have to."

Tommy grabbed the guy's hair and yanked him out of bed. "Where's Julio?" he said, his face inches from the Puerto Rican's.

"I don't know! I...ain't seen him. He...never was here, man."

Tommy slapped the guy in the face. "Lying bastard!"

The girl screamed.

"Tell me," Tommy continued, "or your cunt here plays with herself the rest of her life because you won't have a prick!"

"I told you. I—"

Tommy kneed the guy in the balls. He groaned, folded up, and crumbled to the floor. Tommy grabbed him by the hair again.

"That's enough, Tommy," I said, waiting for the right moment to play the good guy.

Tommy gave the guy a final slap, winked at me, then backed off.

I knelt down. "Look, pal," I said, my voice soft. "Don't make—"

"Joe!" Jake shouted from downstairs. "Down here! He's down here!"

I straightened and said to the two uniforms, "Stay with this asshole. He moves, kick him in the nuts."

Running toward the window at the end of the hall, Tommy said, "I'll take the fire escape."

I went down the stairs two at a time.

Jake met me on the first floor landing, his back pressed against the wall, gun in hand, barrel pointed toward the ceiling. "He went out the back, Joe!"

"He armed?"

"Think so. All I saw was his back."

I ran down the hall, and stopped at the back door. It was a good thing I did. The explosion from Julio's sawed-off shotgun was deafening; the entire wooden door next to me shattered, sending splinters whipping into the air by my face. Jake had hold of my jacket and pulled me back away from the door.

"Jesus Christ! You alright, Joe?"

I nodded. My breath was gone.

Jake said, "What the fuck's he got? A cannon?"

I said, "Go around front. I don't want him reaching the street. And for Christsakes, Jake, Stay low."

"Don't worry."

Jake darted down the hall and out the front door.

I took a step toward the door—inched my face around the frame. "Julio!" I said. "You there, Julio?"

No answer.

I got down on my knees and elbows, took off my Sox cap and peeked out. Julio was crouched in tall grass behind a rusted car frame. All I could see was the top of his head. Then I saw his face. His eyes were the eyes of a terrified animal, darting in all directions.

I saw one of the uniforms go behind a parked car out in the street and another go behind a tree. I knew Tommy and Jake were somewhere out back but I couldn't see them.

"Julio!" I called out again. "You can't win, Julio! Give it up before someone gets hurt."

"Fuck you, man!" Julio said

Four gunshots came at me in rapid succession.

I buried my face in my arms.

The bullets exploded the wood inches above my head; wood fragments erupted, danced in the air, then sprinkled over me. The bullets had been fired from a high-powered handgun—a .357 or a .45.

Son-of-a-bitch!

I raised my eyes and I looked out. Julio was crawling away through the grass. I stood up, paused to catch my breath and balance, then sprinted out onto the back porch. Raising my .38 with both hands, I yelled, "Hold it right there, Julio! Don't make us kill you!"

He didn't listen.

Julio spun around, shotgun raised in his right hand, a .45 in his left.

I fired twice. So did everyone else.

For a few seconds, it was war. Bullets flying everywhere.

The shotgun and .45 flew out of Julio's hands as he catapulted back and disappeared in the high grass.

"He's hit!" I shouted. "Hold your fire! Hold your fire!"

The sudden silence was deafening. My ears rang. The acrid smell of gunpowder sickened me.

I waited a couple of seconds, saw no movement in the grass, then cautiously went down the steps, and walked haltingly toward Julio.

Tommy came in from behind a fence to my left, Jake and two uniforms circled in from the right. I held up my hand and cautioned them to stay back. They did.

As I neared the tall grass, my shock was replaced by a shudder of fear and revulsion. Julio was on his back; blood soaked his purple T-shirt. He was staring up at me, his eyes huge, his thin lips parted and quivering.

I stepped closer, feeling a hollowness in my stomach. Julio had been hit—where I couldn't tell from all the blood.

"Julio," I said softly. "For Chrissakes, why didn't you listen?"

"Bastard!" Julio screamed at me. "You...fucking bastard!"

From somewhere beneath him, Julio pulled a knife, a thin stiletto.

He was on me before I had a chance to react, the thin knife plunging straight forward. I leaped backwards, crashing my gun down on Julio's forearm. He withdrew it quickly in pain, but kept coming.

"Stop, you crazy bastard"' I shouted, leveling my .38 directly at his face. "Don't do it!" For an instant I couldn't catch my breath. It was as if my lungs had become constricted, shrivelled, useless sacs in my rib cage.

Julio wouldn't stop.

I fired one shot.

The pain in my temples made me want to drop to the ground and smash my head on the cement steps, but I knew it wouldn't help.

Instead, I went inside, up the stairs to the office, slammed the door and searched my desk for some aspirins. Finding the bottle, I took out five, popped them in my mouth and went to the water cooler.

"What happened?" Lieutenant O'Keefe said, coming out of his office.

I crushed the paper cup and threw it in the wastebasket. "I don't want to talk about it," I said.

"You'll have to," O'Keefe said. "The Stress Unit is on the way over."

I shot the lieutenant a hard glare. "Who called them?"

"I did."

"What the hell did you do that for?"

"It's procedure."

"Fuck procedure."

The lieutenant followed me to my desk.

"Look at you," he said. "Your hands are shaking."

"Bullshit." I sat down. "Leave me alone."

"Look. Finish your report and leave it on my desk. When the Stress Unit gets here, you talk to them—understand? After that, go home and get some rest. That's an order."

"Fuck you."

O'Keefe looked at me a second longer then stormed out.

A minute later Tommy came in with some coffee. "How you doing?" he said, handing me a sweet roll.

I didn't answer. Nor did I touch the coffee and roll.

"Now I know you're sick," Tommy said.

"Leave me alone."

"Hey, partner. It couldn't be helped. You did the only thing you could do. Think of it this way. You saved the taxpayers a lot of money—not to mention the joy you gave the parents of Julio's victims. Anyway, fuck Julio. He got what he deserved."

I brought my hands up to my forehead and rubbed my temples. "You through?" I said.

Tommy finally got the message and left me alone.

A half hour later, the Stress Unit showed up. Sergeant Jack Halloran and Officer Jimmy Hill found some chairs and sat down. They were cops as well as counselors, two of the nicest guys you'd ever want to meet. Nothing phony about them. They cared.

Sergeant Jack Halloran said in a soft voice, "Oddly enough, Joe, you've become a victim yourself. You took a human life—something you'll have to live with for the rest of your life. Scum or no, it was still a human life."

"How do you feel right now?" Jimmy Hill asked me, his tone equally soft.

I looked out the window. It was raining quietly. Not like the storm that was raging inside my head. "Pissed off," I said. "Guilty. I can't help thinking there was something else I could have done."

"What?" Jack said.

"I don't know."

"Have you ever shot anyone before today?" Jimmy asked.

"No."

"Ever come close?"

"Lots of times."

"What went through your mind when he came at you with the knife?"

"Panic mostly."

"That's natural," Jack said.

"Maybe he wanted to die," Jimmy Hill said. "Ever think of that?"

I closed my eyes briefly. I could still see the look in Julio's eyes; two dark orbs reflecting primitive fear, and something else—maybe some satisfying realization that it was finally over. Maybe it was what he wanted all along.

We talked for over an hour. In that time, an odd passivity passed over me. I found my sanity again. I knew what had happened would remain with me always, but now—talking about it—I felt more capable of dealing with it.

Before he left, Jack said, "We don't go out every day and blow people away, Joe. None of us are Dirty Harry. We're people. We have feelings—emotions. We care. The trauma you're going through now tells us that you care. That you have feelings—good feelings towards others. You're a good cop, Joe. Take some time off. It will help."

I did. The rest of the day and night.

Slumped in my overstuffed leather chair, my feet up on the glass coffee table, I opened my eyes and looked at the clock on the wall over the fireplace. It was eight twenty-five in the evening, and still raining.

Victoria was sitting under a lamp on the sofa across from me, crocheting a table cloth, her feet tucked beneath her.

"Haven't you finished that damn thing yet?" I asked.

Victoria looked up at me. "Pretty hard to concentrate when someone is snoring," she said.

"I wasn't snoring."

"Not much you weren't."

"I wonder how the kids are making out at camp?"

"I'm sure they're having a good time."

"When they coming home?"

"Next Sunday."

Victoria put down her needle. "How's your headache?" she said, looking at me, concerned.

I rolled my neck around. "Gone I think."

"You want to talk about it?"

"No."

"Why not?"

"Because I've already talked about it."

Victoria went back to her crocheting, obviously hurt.

"I'm sorry," I said, feeling like a jerk.

"That's okay."

"It's not okay. It's just hard to talk about."

Victoria looked at me, her eyes soft. "There's no one home, big guy. You want to come up and lie on the bed together?"

I smiled. "Thought you'd never ask."

Upstairs, Victoria slipped into a pink nightgown. I put my arms around her and held her against me. She kissed me for a long time. And she touched my hair and rubbed the back of my neck, touched my cheek quietly and kissed me again.

Victoria held me as I held her. We kissed and she patted me. There was love and need.

14

I hit the horn twice. Tommy appeared at the window and flashed me the finger. I wasn't sure if it meant he'd be out in a minute, or he was telling me to go fuck myself. Whatever, I waited.

Tommy's house on Elliot Street in Milton was a mile from mine. It had four bedrooms; mine had three. His had two and half baths; mine had one and a half. His had white vinyl siding and black shutters; mine was the same color but with clapboards and wooden shingles.

But my lawn was better than his — neater, greener and thicker. His had a lot of weeds and a zillion bare spots. Tommy didn't give a shit; he hated yard work. So did I, but someone had to do it.

Tommy came out of the house wearing his Donegal cap, a tan jacket, blue jeans, and a long face.

"What's the matter with you?" I said as he got in. "Get shit on your fingers from changing diapers?"

Tommy looked at me. "You know Lieutenant Tony Walker?" he said quietly.

"The night commander of the General Investigations Unit?" I said.

"Yeah."

"What about him?"

"They found him dead this morning. Shot his wife, then killed himself."

I couldn't say anything.

"Manny Starano called me a little while ago," Tommy said. "He said he's got something to show us, only we better hurry before he takes it downtown."

"What is it?"

"He wouldn't tell me over the phone."

I checked my watch. 9:30 am.

"Who's watching O'Hara?" I said.

"Warren," Tommy said. "I said I'd relieve him at noon."

I backed the Buick out of the driveway, avoiding Tommy Junior's ten speed bike. Going up Brook Road toward Blue Hill Avenue, I said, "Where's Walker's house?"

"West Roxbury," Tommy said. "On Maplewood Street."

We took River Street out of Mattapan Square to Turtle Pond Parkway and headed north. Maplewood was across Washington Street, down from the Roxbury Latin School.

Tommy's eyes were locked on the road ahead. "Jesus Christ," he said. "What makes someone all of sudden blow his brains out? It doesn't make sense."

"What does?"

Walker's house was a small single family on a corner lot, surrounded by tall oak trees. A half dozen police cruisers lined both sides of the dead-end street. We parked the car and walked up to the house.

Inside, Tommy said to Superintendent Manny Starano, head of the General Investigations Unit, "Thanks for the call, Manny. What have you got?"

"A suicide note," Manny said. He reached back, took the note from his back pocket and handed it to Tommy.

Manny and I said hello. I loved the way he wore his uniform — small blue tie resting on a huge gut, the skin of his chubby neck dripping over the edge of a tight blue collar, white matted hair shooting out from under a gold braided service cap. Manny was normally a happy-go-lucky guy. This was the first time I'd seen him without his infectious smile.

I looked down at the chalked outline showing where Tony had fallen; a rambling bloodstain soaked the gray carpet in the area of the head. "Too bad," I said. "He was a damn nice guy. A good cop."

Tommy handed me the note sealed in a plastic bag to prevent fingerprints. "He used to be," he said.

I read the note. The words were blurred through the

plastic but I could read them: I'M SORRY FOR WHAT I DID. THERE IS ONLY ONE WAY OUT. FOR BOTH OF US. BRENDAN O'HARA — YOU BASTARD. YOU DON'T OWN ME ANY MORE.

The note was unsigned.

Another hollow was carved out of my heart. I handed the note back to Superintendent Starano.

"What was Tony's problem, Manny?" Tommy said. "Heard he was out on disability."

"Yeah," the superintendent said. "The last seven or eight months. Bad luck, I think."

"How's his finances been?" I said.

"I don't know," Manny said. "I could check."

"Thanks," I said. "We'd appreciate it."

No one said anything for a few moments. Then Manny said, "Hard to believe Tony was into something."

Kneeling down, I glanced at Tommy, inspecting the blood on the rug.

"Anyone else see the note, Manny?" Tommy said, straightening.

"Don't worry, Tommy," the superintendent said. "We know when to keep our mouths shut. Thought you guys would be interested that's all. See'ns how O'Hara is your friend."

"Was," I said.

We headed for the door.

"Oh, by the way," the superindendent said. "We got divers down at Pier Three pulling a car out of the water. Hate to break the bad news to you guys but there's a corpse in the trunk. I told them to hold the scene 'til you got there."

Tommy said, "Wonderful. Well, the bastard will just have to take a number and go to the bottom of the pile. Jesus Christ!"

"That bad, huh?" Manny said to me.

"Yeah. That bad."

We drove down to the fish pier. Pier Three was a hundred yards past Jimmy's Harborside restaurant, across from a fish processing factory. When we got there, police divers had a muddy '86 black Caddy dangling nose down at the end of a steel cable, half the hood still in the water. It took fifteen minutes or so for the crane to right the Caddy on the pier and another five to get the trunk open.

There it was. Stiff number three zillion; wide-eyed, wrinkle-skinned and dead. The body was bent back, a rope around the neck tied to the feet. Been in the water two, maybe three days. If I had to guess, the guy was alive in the trunk a long time until his legs got tired and he slowly straightened them, choking himself to death.

Looking at him, I didn't know what made me sicker, the smell of dead fish on the pier, or the way his tongue was hanging out of his wrinkled white face, long and purple.

Ten minutes later, we had an ID on him. Vincent Michael Torchia.

The next morning, shortly after nine, I met Bobby Dunn at Doughboy's. I had called him the night before — told him I had an exclusive for him. Something about the press I've discovered over the years — mention the word "exclusive" and no wall is high enough to keep them away.

Over the years, I only gave out one other exclusive, and that backfired right up my ass — so bad I had to go in front of the mayor. There had been a series of murders, five black women between the ages of sixteen and twenty-five. They were all hookers, and they were all viciously attacked and raped, then hacked to death. Everybody thought there was a serial killer running loose. The entire black community was in an uproar. I had to stop the rumors before all hell broke loose, so I had called this reporter from Channel Three — Rick Sanders. I had thought he would give me a fair shake, but I was wrong. The bastard stiffed me; said on the news I was lying to the public, that there was a serial killer because his horseshit sources had sworn to him there was, that I had tried to cover it up. We had nearly come to blows at the mayor's news conference. Even today, I'm pissed at myself for not decking the prick.

Bobby Dunn was different. Most news photographers were. You could tell them something without worrying about it getting back to a reporter. A lot of dimes have been dropped on them — never has there been a problem. They go in behind you on a raid, and you do something to a suspect you don't want showing up on the six o'clock news, all you have to do with guys like Bobby is turn around and hold out your hand. He gives you the tape he shot — no questions asked. That's the way it should be.

At Doughboy's I pulled in and parked. Bobby Dunn was driving a black Ford van with tinted windows all around. A half dozen radio antennas stuck out of the roof.

When I got in the van, he put down his half-eaten doughnut, leaned over and turned down the police scanners so we could talk.

"What's up, Joe?" he said, folding up the morning *Globe,* tossing it on the back seat. "You find out who killed Susan Howell?"

I didn't answer the question. "I need a favor," I said.

"Name it."

"I need a nightscope."

"What sort of nightscope?"

"You tell me. You're the cameraman."

"Tell me how you want to use it — under what light conditions. Maybe I can come up with something. How dark is the area you want to see?"

"I don't know."

"Real dark, or are there some lights around?"

"I don't know that either."

Bobby said, "I think you need a True Star."

"What's that?"

"It's for extreme dark conditions. I mean, pitch black. You won't believe what it can see."

"Sounds good. Can I borrow it?"

"That depends."

"On what?"

"If I can go along with it."

"No way."

"You'll never be able to figure out how it works."

"What's to figure out?"

"Nightscopes are tricky little bastards. In total blackness they're great. Let some light in the lens and poof — there goes the tube if you're not careful. End of surveillance."

"I can't let you go, Bobby. It could get dangerous."

"So was bussing in Southie. I know what I'm doing."

"I know you know. I just can't be responsible for you."

"I'm a big boy, Joe. I can take care of myself. Besides, I don't go, the nightscope don't go. Get what I mean?"

"You prick."

"Aren't we all."

Bobby stopped talking. Reaching down, he turned up one of his scanners and listened.

"Hear something?" I said.

"Yeah. There's a house fire somewhere. It came out over Metro fire. Think they said Winthrop."

He listened for another twenty or thirty seconds. Metro fire finally came on calling in a second alarm in Winthrop.

"Shit," Bobby said. "It never fails. Everybody wants to burn themselves up these days." He looked at me. "Well, you make up your mind yet?"

"Okay. You go tonight. You got a problem with that, let me know now."

"Tonight's fine with me. What time?"

"I don't know."

"Where we going?"

"I don't know that either. Be here around six — just to be safe."

"What else do you need besides a scope? You'll need a camera to put it on plus some adapters. You got one?"

"No."

"I'll bring mine. What about a tape deck?"

I shook my head.

"You're a pisser, Joe. Leave everything to me."

Bobby picked up a book of street maps and flipped the pages, stopping when he found Winthrop. "One more thing," he said. "When everything goes down, I want Channel Eight to have the exclusive. I'll get Ron Gold to do the story. He's the best — he won't do a hatchet job."

"Pushy bastard, aren't you?" I said.

Bobby grinned. "It's how we make our living," he said.

It was quarter past ten in the evening when we went over the Tobin Bridge toward Revere. Tommy was behind the wheel of the van, Bobby Dunn in the seat behind him. I was in the passenger seat up front.

Several cars ahead of us, Brendan O'Hara was alone in his white Olds listening to classical music. It was something we had shared in common. Many nights we'd sit in my living room, not saying anything — just listening with our eyes closed. It was something we needed to do often. A number of times I'd go to bed with O'Hara still on the sofa. When I'd gotten up the next morning, he'd still be there, asleep, headphones dangling from his head, music still blaring.

"Where do you think we're headed?" Bobby asked, breaking the brief silence.

"I don't know," I said.

Tommy adjusted his headset, turning down the volume of the wireless receiver. "What the hell is that shit he's listening to?" he said.

I pressed my headphones tight against my ears. "It's the Overture to William Tell," I said.

Tommy looked at me. "Doesn't sound like the Lone Ranger to me."

"It's the beginning of the first section," I said.

"Oh, really?"

I let my fingers dance as if I were conducting the Boston Symphony, which had always been one of my dreams. "Listen, Tommy," I said. "Close your eyes. You can almost see the grandeur and glistening beauty of the Swiss countryside at sunrise. Rossini's score called for only five cellos. This lovely andante has been given magnificent new richness — perhaps by as many as sixteen cellos. I'm not sure which orchestra is playing but they are awfully good."

"I'm thrilled."

"Shhhh. Soon the pastoral tranquillity of the opening yields to the sudden fury of an alpine storm in the second section. But the storm spends itself and a second andante offers a shepherd's song of thanksgiving.''

"Be still my foolish fucking heart."

"Now the English horn solo based on the traditional Ranz des Vaches, or Dance of the Cows.'' I contorted my fingers and moved them faster. "Now the finale which progressively builds to a peak of momentum, volume and intensity. The trumpets. It's the call to arms of the Swiss cantons against the Austrian invaders. Listen to that, Tommy. Son-of-a-bitch! The Lone Ranger rides again!''

The overture ended. Tommy took off his earphones and tossed them down on the seat. "Jesus Christ,'' he said. "It's finally happened. We get back, I'm taking you to Mass Mental.''

"What do you mean? It was Rossini's last great work. Magnificent. Absolutely magnificent. Surely you agree?''

Tommy looked at me. "I've heard of faggots coming out of the closet, but this is ridiculous. You never told me you liked that shit.''

"Shit? You call Rossini's masterpiece shit?''

Tommy rolled his eyes. "Sorry I brought it up.''

"You should be.''

Silence.

"Anyone want an apple?'' Bobby Dunn said.

Twenty minutes later, the Olds made it to Route 128 and headed north. It took another forty-five minutes to reach Gloucester. At the end of Route 128, we went around the rotary and along the inner harbor until we reached Eastern Point heading toward the Atlantic Ocean. Traffic had fallen off to three cars, then two, so we dropped back a half mile. The road followed the coastline. There was a three-quarter moon passing in and out of thick clouds. At times through the trees, we could see waves breaking over rocks, but nothing else.

"Aren't we too far back?'' Bobby Dunn said. "I can't see the taillights anymore.''

I switched on my miniature flashlight and checked the road map again. "There's only two places O'Hara could be heading," I said. "Lighthouse Cove or Brace Cove. My guess is Brace Cove. I've been there. Plenty of trees around. Very little beach. The map says there's a narrow road going off to the right before the Cove. It goes down to the water. Maybe there's a path." I looked back. "Bobby, how close do we have to get with that nightscope?"

"Depends on what you wanna see. Full figures — about a hundred yards. Close-up of faces, maybe fifty or sixty yards. I got to tell yah, Joe. I've got a lotta heavy equipment with me. Camera, tripod, recorder, lens and adapters. We have to walk anyplace, it won't be far. The best thing for us to do is find a break in the trees someplace and shoot out the side window."

The road took a sharp turn to the left. There was a brief flash of taillights ahead, then blackness. I adjusted my headset. I could still hear classical music coming from O'Hara's stereo.

"Slow down, Tommy," I said. "There's the road on the right."

"Where? That's not a road for Chrissakes."

"Take it anyway."

Turning, we bounced along the path toward the rocky shore, branches scraping the side of the van.

Bobby Dunn said, "Watch the wax job."

"Send us the bill," Tommy said.

Near the end of the path I said, "Stop here, Tommy. Shut off the headlights."

He did.

I opened the door and got out. "Wait here. I'll see if there's another path."

I headed toward the water. The air was crisp. Everywhere was the scent of pine and the smell of the sea. The land was pitch black, yet I could see the white spray of waves crashing over the jagged rocks below. Closer to the water, I found a path. I followed it for nearly a hundred yards until I came to a clearing. Across it, silhouetted against the sea beyond, I could see the faint outline of the Olds.

I leaned against a tree. For several moments I let my body

196 — Fat Guys

sag and rolled my neck back and forth, trying to ease the tension, reduce the exhaustion. I checked my watch. 11:20 pm. I pushed myself away from the tree, breathing deeply, forcing thoughts of sleep from my mind. Whoever O'Hara was meeting had not yet arrived. There was still time to set up.

I walked along side as Tommy inched the van, headlights off, down the gravel path and stopped at the edge of the clearing. Any noise the van made was lost in the sounds of the sea.

Through the trees, the Olds was now seventy to eighty yards away.

"You need to go any closer?" I said to Bobby Dunn, keeping my voice low. "If you do, we walk."

"This will do," he said quietly, sitting on a box next to the tripod in the space behind the back seat.

Picking up his camera — an Ikegami 95 — Bobby snapped it in place on the tripod. "Now hand me the nightscope, Joe. The silver case on the floor behind you."

I snapped on my mini flashlight, holding it below the windows. The beam was narrow, the diameter of a pencil. But in the blackness, it became a searchlight, tracking along the floor until it found the silver case.

Bobby had showed it to me and Tommy before we left. It was long like a telescope, about three inches in diameter. It had an eyepiece the size of a miniature TV screen, and a black hood that Bobby put over his head. "So no one can see the light from the green screen shinning in my face," he'd told us.

The lens now in place, Bobby connected the cable from the tape recorder to the back of the camera. Taking out some black tape, he covered some of the blinking lights on the recorder, then turned it on.

"You've done this before," I said.

"Like I said, Joe. I've been around."

Adjusting the hood over his head, Bobby switched on the nightscope. "It will take a couple of minutes for the tubes to warm up," he said.

We waited.

"Anything yet?" Tommy said.

"I see something now," Bobby said.

"What?" I said, anxious.

"He's sitting in the car by himself."

"What kind of a picture you got?"

Bobby came out from under the hood. "Wait a second," he said. "There's a Sony Watch-man in my bag — and some cables. Hand me the bag."

I did.

A couple of minutes later, Bobby had a video cable running from the recorder to the Watch-man. Another black cloth draped over us, Tommy and I were now able to see everything the camera saw.

"You're a genius, Bobby," I said from under the cloth, staring at the miniature black and white screen on my lap.

"Yeah," Tommy said. "I take back all the shit things I said about you."

"Thanks."

"Can't believe the quality," I said.

"Now you know what a fifty-thousand dollar rig can do for you," Bobby said.

"Fifty-thousand dollars?" I said. "You're shitting me."

The picture was incredible; we could see O'Hara clearly, sitting quietly behind the wheel. I adjusted my earphones and listened.

"He's shut off the stereo," I said.

"Thank God," Tommy said.

We waited.

Ten minutes to midnight. Still no one showed.

"I've got to take a squirt," Tommy said. "The overhead light dead?"

"Yeah," I said.

Tommy opened the door and stood beside the van. As he pissed, a car pulled into the parking lot, its headlights darting through the trees spilling over him.

"Shit!" Tommy said, spinning away from the light, jumping back in the van. Struggling with his zipper, he said,

"I think I pissed myself."

The headlights went out.

Bobby panned the camera left. The scope picked up two men sitting in a dark Mercedes. The driver was black and bald but had a full beard. The passenger was white, wore rimless glasses and a New York Yankees baseball cap.

"Recognize them?" I said to Tommy.

"No. Do you?"

"No."

The two men stayed in the car.

The camera panned right and followed O'Hara. He was out of his car, walking slowly toward the Mercedes, hands in his leather jacket pockets, looking around.

"Go back to the Mercedes, Bobby," I said. "See if there's a plate."

There was. A New York plate, number 445-131.

"Here we go again," Tommy said.

"Go back to O'Hara," I said.

The camera tilted up. O'Hara had his hands on the driver's side door, leaning down, talking to the black guy.

Tommy said, "I wish we could read lips."

They talked for about two minutes, then the driver got out and followed O'Hara to the Olds. Opening the trunk, O'Hara took out a giant stuffed gorilla wearing a white sailor's hat, and handed it to the black guy.

"What the fuck is that?" Tommy said.

"Sonuvabitch," I said. "I've seen stuffed animals before but that's ridiculous."

"I wonder what it's stuffed with?" Tommy said.

"Yeah. I wonder."

Silence.

Staring at the TV screen, Tommy said, "Know what I'd like to do right now? Take that bastard O'Hara down — right fucking now. One shot. Right in the fucking head."

I didn't say anything.

O'Hara followed the driver back to the Mercedes, watched the guy open the trunk and stuff the gorilla in. It barely fit.

Go back inside the Mercedes,'' I said to Bobby. "Show us the guy with the glasses again.''

He did.

The guy said something to O'Hara, then reached down and hoisted a briefcase, passed it to the black guy who handed it to O'Hara.

A few more words were exchanged. Five minutes later, they left. So did we.

Monday at noon I awoke exhausted and threw open the curtains to see an overcast sky with a heavy blank grey that meant rain again. The wind had got up and was blowing in sharp, threatening gusts. As the sheers slipped from my fingers back into place, I wondered if the sun would ever shine again.

I went to the bathroom and looked at myself in the mirror. Moved closer, picked up the scissors and snipped at the hairs in my nostrils, aware of myself in the silence, seeing how old I was getting. I showered, put on a pair of fresh khakis, a blue striped shirt and my linen sport coat that cost me a hundred bucks at Filene's Basement. It matched my khakis but was lighter. I went downstairs.

Making us coffee, I sat down with Victoria at the kitchen table and listened to her bitch about my kids.

Last night, no sooner had Jessica got home from soccer camp, than she had wanted to go to a dance with her friend Bonnie, only Victoria was late getting home from a dinner date with some girlfriends. So when Victoria walked in the door, Jessica began blasting away with her viper's tongue. Victoria couldn't stand it any more so she took her to the dance just to get rid of her. Even had to give her ten bucks.

All the while Victoria talked, I kept thinking how foolish she was for letting Jessica get away with it all. I would have slapped her on the head, dragged her upstairs and thrown her in her room. Dads have a way of dealing with things like that. Daughters don't usually like it much, but tough shit. Should have seen what it was like growing up with my father.

Anyway, Victoria went on to say Jessica came home late like always, that I should have a talk with her before I went off again.

I drank the last of my coffee. "Okay," I said. "Where is she?"

"Still in bed," Victoria said. "Where else."

"Where's Jeff?"

"Cleaning his room."

"Great boy that Jeff. Never any trouble."

"Is that so? I've grounded him again."

Here we go.

Victoria called Jeff out of his room.

"Yeah, Mom?" Coming down the stairs, he saw me and said. "Hi, Dad."

"Hi, Son."

"Tell your father about that computer game he bought you." Victoria said.

"What's the matter with it?" I said. "Cost me fifty bucks."

"You obviously didn't read the fine print on the box. The game was for adults only. It has a few hidden examples to help create characters."

"It does?"

"Go ahead, Jeffrey. Tell your father."

Jeff was reluctant, then he said matter-of-factly, "Well, first I went north — you know, Dad — with the arrows."

I nodded.

"And I got this hooker to sit on my lap," Jeff went on.

My eyelids went up.

"Then I went west and had some difficulty unbuttoning her blouse. Then I went south to discover beads of perspiration running down her ample breasts."

I swallowed a laugh, glanced at Victoria who saw no humor in it all, then said to my son, "Oh? And what did you do next, Jeff?"

"I went east."

"Good."

"Can I go now, Dad?"

"Okay. But don't erase the game."

"No sweat, Dad. Neat game. Thanks."

He left.

Victoria said, "I thought that's how you would react. Animal. You want some breakfast?"

"No thanks."

"Where were you last night until four?"

"Gloucester."

"What were you doing in Gloucester?"

"Police work."

"What sort of police work?"

"You writing a book?"

"Yeah."

"Well leave this chapter out and make it a mystery."

Victoria made me another coffee. "You look tired, Joseph," she said. It was never Joe. Always Joseph.

"I'm doing alright."

She was staring at me again, those blue eyes patient, waiting. When I didn't say anything, she said, "I've seen that look in your eyes before, Joseph. Something's bothering you. I don't mean just your work. It's something else isn't it?"

I never could lie to Victoria — something I tried hard not to do over the years. It wouldn't do any good anyway. She read me better than anyone.

I told her everything.

For a long time, Victoria looked at me with sympathetic eyes. "Joseph, I'm sorry. Brendan O'Hara was your best friend. It must be terrible for you." She put her hand in mine and I squeezed it gently.

"You'll do the right thing when the time comes, Joseph," Victoria said. "You always do."

15

We watched O'Hara closely for five days, mostly at night; Jake, Tommy, Warren and me taking turns in different vehicles, keeping well back, not taking any chances of being spotted.

In that time, O'Hara made another trip to Gloucester, one to Providence, Rhode Island, another to Hartford, Connecticut. Each time, he had come out of his apartment in Southie carrying a stuffed gorilla with the same stupid looking sailor hat pinned to its head.

On the times Tommy and I had tailed O'Hara, we took Bobby Dunn with us.

In Gloucester O'Hara had met with the same Mercedes. In Rhode Island, Jake said that O'Hara had met a Ford Thunderbird from New York; some fat guy with a lot of gold chains hanging from a fat neck. Warren said in Hartford, O'Hara met a blue station wagon — maybe a Pontiac — with Florida plates. It was too dark for Warren to see who was driving. Each time O'Hara had delivered a stuffed animal and came away with a briefcase — no doubt, full of money.

Jake and Warren had taken a still camera loaded with high-speed black and white film; but the pictures they brought back sucked. Most of them were out of focus or under exposed.

At my desk, flipping through the photos, I threw them aside disgustedly, picked up the phone, and called the medical examiner.

"Good afternoon, Sergeant Knight," Doctor Katzman said. "It is nearly five o'clock. You are late. I had expected to hear from you much earlier than this. I understand from

Leroy you are missing something. A corpse perhaps?"

Not only was the doctor good with a scalpel, he wasn't bad with the needle either. But I was in no mood for any humor.

"You finish the post on Vinnie Torchia yet?" I said.

"Yes."

"And?"

"The cause of death was acute compression of the trachea."

"He was strangled."

"If you must put it so crudely, yes. Strangled."

"He wasn't shot?"

"No, he was not."

"Tell me something, Doc. You wouldn't have any idea how two guys dressed up as morgue technicians could steal one of your vans and rip off a corpse would you?"

"Is that what happened?"

"Yeah. That's what happened."

"If one of our vans had been misappropriated, my technicians would have certainly reported it to me."

"At two in the morning?"

"There is a guard on duty."

"Then he had his fucking head up his ass, Doc. Either that, or he was paid off. Check it out for me, Doc. Or I will."

"There is no need to shout, Joseph."

"I'm sorry. It's been a long day."

"Yes, it has."

Hanging up the phone, I looked up at the cardboard sign on the wall over my desk. It said: STRESS. THE CONFUSION CREATED WHEN ONE'S MIND OVERRIDES THE BODY'S BASIC DESIRE TO CHOKE THE LIVING SHIT OUT OF SOME ASSHOLE WHO DESPERATELY NEEDS IT!

I smiled remembering the day I had hung it up — the same day a telephone repairman had found an electronic eavesdropping device in one of Lieutenant John Bailey's telephones, tucked inside the mouthpiece. The device had turned out to be nothing more than a cheap voice amplifier and not a wiretap. After a semi-horseshit investigation, the commissioner's office had said it was the work of a prankster. Maybe it was, but with all the federal and departmental probes going on at the time, every cop in the city had unscrewed the caps to mouth and ear pieces and checked their phones. None of us had bought that crap about it being a joke, especially John Bailey. He was bullshit about it for days, and had wanted to choke the living shit out of everybody.

I spent the next few hours going over some papers. I stretched and yawned and looked around. Everybody had gone home. The office pressed in on me — the shadowy desks, the pale light from the lamp on Tommy's desk throwing a faint glow everywhere. It was quarter after midnight. Where the hell did the night go?

I put my hand up to my forehead. Perspiration. A touch of pain. But I still had one more thing to do before I could go home.

It was ten minutes to one in the morning as I drove down Broadway through Southie. Before I had left the office, I had called the horse barn in Jamaica Plain. Some cop said O'Hara was still there. I knew I had plenty of time to get in and out. I didn't know exactly what I'd be looking for, but knowing O'Hara's penchant for bookkeeping and writing notes to himself, I might just get lucky.

As I approached O'Hara's front door, everything was quiet except for the rain. The September night was cold, the sky black.

I was dressed for it. I had on a black stocking cap, my neck concealed under the collar of my dark blue jacket.

O'Hara's girlfriend, Sherry, worked nights as a bartender at Halloran's Drinking and Eatery, a Yuppie joint across from Faneuil Hall Marketplace downtown. She was never home before two or three.

I climbed up on the porch and waited in the darkness a few minutes, listening to the rain and for anything else.

I glanced around. No one.

A door opened across the street. Someone came out onto the porch. I crouched, thrusting my hand under my jacket for my .38. I thought for sure I'd been spotted. But what I heard the guy say told me I hadn't.

"You sure you don't want me to stay tonight?"

The guy moved away from the door. Standing under the spill of light inside the doorway, I could see a young woman wearing a pink terry cloth bathrobe. "I'm sure," the woman said.

"You said your parents won't be home 'til tomorrow night," the guy begged. "Please can I stay?"

"I said no, Shawn. It's late. Now go home."

I wanted to go across the street and kick Shawn square in the ass. I let go of the .38's handle, wondering what I'd do if it were my daughter doing what that young woman had obviously done. What could I do? The night suddenly got a little colder.

Shawn finally gave up, pulled up his collar, said good-night, went down the steps, and disappeared around the corner. The door closed and silence returned to the quiet street.

I thought about going around back, but I knew the door would be bolted. The front door was still my best chance.

I took out my lock jimmy, knelt down and inserted the hooked end in the lock. That's when I saw the blade of light dart across the floor underneath the drawn shade.

I stopped breathing, withdrew the lock jimmy, and took out my .38. Holding it barrel up, I pressed my back against the wall next to the front window. Someone was inside.

I listened. No sounds. Just the rain.

I got off the porch and checked all the windows as I ran around back. I crept up the stairs and tried the back door. Locked. I went back down the steps, and waited beside the porch.

Two minutes later, I heard a window slide up. I lifted my head above the porch, my .38 gripped tight. In the twisted darkness, I could see a faint outline of someone climbing out the window. First legs, then hands — in the left, the shadow of a huge automatic with a large perforated cylinder attached to the barrel. I tensed.

Something made me turn.

The last thing I saw was this huge hand raised high that looked like a giant claw in the night sky, a curved hand that held an object in it coming down on me from the right. And then nothing. Only a huge chasm filled with wind.

And darkness.

I felt the cold first. It made me shiver. Dampness everywhere. I opened my eyes to distorted images of grass and stairs. I rolled over, grateful to see the night sky, lighter to the left, darker to the right.

My head ached, and my face felt like someone had jumped on it with two huge feet. Slowly, I raised myself and looked at my watch. 3:15 am. Christ!

I felt my head. A bump had formed, the skin unbroken. Must have been a padded blackjack or pipe that hit me.

I turned and took a couple of awkward steps, then stopped. Somewhere in the distance, I heard a door slam. Lights from the window above went on, spilling light out onto the grass. I moved to avoid the light. A radio went on.

Sherry had returned home. Or was it O'Hara. I didn't wait around long enough to find out.

The next morning, after spending an hour wearing an ice pack on my head and consuming a zillion aspirins, I called Tommy and told him what had happened to me. I didn't get a lot of sympathy.

"What a stupid shit," he said. "Everytime I leave you alone, you fuck up. You okay?"

"I'll live."

"Any idea who they were?"

"Could have been the same guys we saw in the North End the night you put the bug in O'Hara's car. The guy had a beard."

"Think they got what they were after?"

"Maybe," I said. "Only one way to find out. I got to go back."

"Not without me, asshole," Tommy said.

"You're right," I said. "I'll need someone to lift me up to the window."

"How about we rent a crane?"

"Kiss my ass."

We bullshitted a few more minutes then I hung up and called Brighton. The guy I wanted to see had been out of town the past week and a half, and was heading out of town again. His secretary said it was either now or wait two more weeks. I couldn't wait.

Up Brighton Avenue past the lights at Harvard Street, I pulled into a tiny parking lot reserved for employees of the New England Council for the Deaf.

Inside, a tall woman with heavy-framed glasses, made taller with all her blond hair pulled up, escorted me to Vance LaBelle's office.

Vance LaBelle was deaf, but in no way was he dumb. His blue eyes sparkled as I walked in carrying my video tapes. He had thin brown hair and a shiney red face. He smiled and said something I couldn't understand — maybe it was hello. Anyway, I put the tapes on the desk and we shook hands.

Using some fucked-up hand signals, I managed to say to him, "Where is your signer?"

After a few puzzled looks, Vance finally understood and pressed a buzzer on his desk. A few seconds later, a short guy with black-rimmed glasses and pock-marked face came into the room.

"Hi," the guy said warmly holding out his hand. "I'm George Thatcher, Vance's partner."

We shook hands. "Sergeant Joe Knight," I said. "Boston police."

"Nice to know you. Are you a friend of Vance?"

"We go back a long way. Best lip-reader in the business."

Thatcher looked at Vance. "Yes, I know. All of us here have to watch where we say anything. Especially when we are talking behind his back. Isn't that right, Vance?"

Vance nodded in agreement, still with that perpetual smile frozen on his face.

Signals flashed between them.

"Vance says he's pleased to see his good friend," Thatcher said to me. "It's been a long time. Much too long."

"I've been busy, tell him," I said to Thatcher.

"Tell him yourself. Simply turn around so he can see your lips."

"Oh, yeah."

I did.

"Vance," I said, slow and deliberate, each word carefully delivered. "I want you to take a look at some tapes. Do you have some time?"

Hand signals flashed again.

"Speak normally," Thatcher said. "There is no need to speak so deliberately. Remember, Vance reads lips faster than most of us can talk — if you can believe that."

"I can believe it." Picking up the tapes, I said. "These are surveillance tapes, Vance. What you find out about them remains absolutely with you. And you too, Mr. Thatcher."

"George, please," Thatcher said.

"Okay, George. The same goes for you."

"Our lips are sealed," George said.

Vance grunted something, brought his fingers up to his lips and pinched them together.

"Good. These are three-quarter inch tapes. I know you've got a three-quarter machine here somewhere."

"Yes, we do," George said. "It's in the office next to mine."

I gathered up the tapes and followed Vance and George into an office filled with books stacked to the ceiling on metal shelves. The tape machine and a small color monitor were on a table, the only piece of furniture in the room.

George brought in three metal chairs and positioned them around.

Vance flashed some signs to George.

"What did he say?" I asked.

"He said, let's get started."

I smiled, turned on the monitor, and put in the first tape.

All it cost me for Vance's service was a promise to speak

to his students at the School for the Deaf in Randolph about what it's like being a cop in Boston. I told him his students really didn't want to know, but I agreed. Small price to pay for what I had found out.

It was ten o'clock by the time I got back to the office. Tommy was checking on something, I didn't know what. Jake was watching O'Hara. Warren was chasing something down — more than likely another broad. Lieutenant O'Keefe was on the phone in his office, kissing someone's ass at headquarters.

I got myself some coffee, shoved some papers out of the way on my desk and sat down with my notebook. Carefully, I went back over what I had written.

Tape 1 of 3. Electronic video surveillance. Gloucester, Mass. Brace Cove. Thursday. August 28th. 1:17 am. Witnesses: Robert Dunn, Cameraman from Channel Eight; Thomas Sanders, Detective, Boston police, homicide; Joseph Knight, Sergeant, Boston police, homicide. Tapes interpreted by Vance LaBelle and George Thatcher. Both expert lip-readers.

Conversation between Brendan O'Hara, Boston police officer — suspect in murder investigation and drug trafficking and two men in a black Mercedes. Both unidentified. Brendan O'Hara is man with leather jacket standing on driver's side.

O'Hara looks in car. Talks to black man behind the wheel. "Who the fuck is he? You were supposed to come alone."

Driver, facing suspect O'Hara. Response unknown.

O'Hara looks around. Head reappears in window.

O'Hara. "What the fuck took you so long? You got the money?"

Driver. Response unknown.

O'Hara. "You trying to give me the runaround or something? You said you were bringing me buyers."

Driver. Response unknown.

Driver gets out, follows O'Hara to Olds. O'Hara opens trunk, takes out giant stuffed gorilla.

Driver. "This some sort of fucking joke, O'Hara?"

O'Hara. "Ten kilos. Take it or leave it."

Driver, holding up gorilla. "Dude's cute, man. Where'd you get 'im?"

O'Hara. "What difference does it make?"

Driver takes gorilla, goes to trunk of Mercedes and stuffs it in.

Driver. "My kids's gonna really get a kick outta this."

O'Hara. "I'm sure."

Driver. "Where you gettin' the shit anyway? Shit's prime, man. Only two people I know handles pure like this. And you ain't one of 'em."

O'Hara looks away. Response unknown.

Driver gets back in car.

O'Hara leans in window. "Next time. You come alone. Understand."

Passenger reaches down and hands O'Hara a briefcase.

O'Hara takes briefcase to car and drives off.

I sat back, put my hands behind my head, and watched the rain hit the window.

After a few minutes of gazing, I leaned forward and checked my notes from tape two.

Sunday. August 31st. Midnight. O'Hara in telephone booth, back to camera. Corner of Arlington and Stuart Streets. Conversation unknown.

Monday. September 1st. 2:35 am. O'Hara in telephone booth. Corner of Mass. Ave. and Beacon Street. O'Hara, after three minutes on the phone. "I think I'm being watched. Someone's been in my apartment. Yeah. I'm being careful. Yeah, well, I'll be there. You just make sure your man knows what to do. What? No. I'm not taking all of it . . . it's too risky."

O'Hara's back turns to camera — rest of conversation unknown.

Tape 3. Tuesday. September 3rd. 1:55 am. O'Hara goes to South Boston office of City Councillor, Shawn O'Malley. One hour later comes back out carrying a large brown paper bag under his arm.

3:25 am, same date. O'Hara in telephone booth. Corner

of Broadway and Dorchester Street, South Boston. O'Hara, at times looking directly at our van. "It's a go. I'm leaving Wednesday night — nine o'clock flight. No. I don't need any help. Alright. Don't get excited. No problem. What? No . . ."

Back turns to camera — rest of conversation unknown.

At eleven-twenty I headed back to headquarters, first stopping at Amrhein's on Broadway for one of their hot pastrami sandwiches on pumpernickel. Sitting at the end of the bar, Jimmy the Nose put a draft in front of me. Wiping up the spill around the glass he said, "You look like you could use this, Joe."

I nodded.

"Where the hell have you been lately? Ain't seen you around much. What's the matter? You look like shit."

"Thanks."

"I mean it. You look like you ain't slept in weeks. Why don't you go home and get some sleep before you keel over for Chrissakes. Don't need no heart cases in here."

"You're all heart, Jimmy. All heart."

Jimmy the Nose was a big guy with a big mouth, but everybody loved him. You wanted to know what was going on in the city, you asked Jimmy the Nose. He was Irish Catholic, like everyone else who lived in Southie. He had red hair combed straight back, a round fleshy red face, and a zillion blue veins popping through his huge red nose. He wasn't called Jimmy the Nose for nothing — and not only because he had a big nose. More like he was always sticking it in other people's business. But no one seemed to mind. It was the way he did it. Like it was his right. Jimmy the Nose was actually a funny guy. A little aggravating at times, but who isn't.

I looked around. The place was empty. No cops. Just an old couple sitting at a table opposite the bar. "Where's everybody?" I said, looking for someone other than the Nose to bullshit with.

"It's only eleven-thirty."

"Oh, yeah."

"Too bad about Tony Walker," Jimmy the Nose said. "Got to be really fucked up to shoot yourself like that. Heard you was there after it happened?"

I sipped the draft. It tasted good.

"How did the bodies look?" Jimmy the Nose asked wide-eyed.

"Sorry to disappoint you, Jimmy. The bodies were gone before I got there. You'll have to get your gore stories from someone else."

Jimmy the Nose went down the bar mumbling, "Too bad."

A minute later he came back with my pastrami sandwich. Dropping the plate in front of me, he said, "What was Walker into?"

I put some mustard on the pumpernickel. "Don't know, Jimmy."

"Had to be something. Maybe it had to do with the probe that's going on. You know. The police corruption thing. The one the Feds are moving in on. Don't you remember — they seized records from the General Investigations Unit? That's where Tony Walker worked."

"That so?"

"C'mon, Joe. You can tell me. You're supposed to be Joe Super Cop."

I took a couple of bites of the sandwich, washed it down with the rest of the beer, then took another bite.

"I also heard Tony had a lot of money stashed away," Jimmy the Nose went on, his elbows on the bar in front of me, his huge honker practically hanging over my sandwich. "Hear he's been seen with some bad company."

"Who?"

"Who knows? I don't ask those kind of questions. The less you know about things like that the better off you are. Anyway, he's been throwing some heavy money around. Even bought himself a new Lincoln. Money had to come from somewhere."

Something came out of Jimmy's mouth and fell on my

sandwich. Jesus Christ. I pushed the plate away, slipped off the stool, threw ten bucks on the counter and walked out.

"Nice talking to yah, Joe," Jimmy the Nose said sarcastically.

"It's been a pleasure," I said over my shoulder.

At headquarters, going up the granite steps through the double doors, I ran into the commissioner coming out of the elevator. I turned away as soon as I saw him, but it was too late.

"Knight!" Frankie called out. "Where the hell have you been? Why haven't you kept me informed about the investigation? You know how many phone calls I've gotten from reporters — not to mention the news director from Channel Eight. That sonuvabitch hasn't left me alone since the explosion. Look at me when I'm talking to you."

I glanced at the young cadet behind the front desk. He was red-faced, looking for a place to hide. So was I.

"I've been busy, commissioner," I said. "Anyway, you've got that asshole O'Keefe telling you everything. You don't need me."

"Don't get smart, Knight. I want to know right now what you've got. Come up to my office."

We took the elevator to the sixth floor.

In his office, I sat down in the high-backed leather chair. The commissioner threw his umbrella down on the desk and stood behind it, arms akimbo.

"Okay, Knight. Start talking."

I did. Lying like a bastard. I even made up a story about a suspected South African terrorist plotting to blow up Roxbury because they voted not to secede from Boston. Sounded great. Even I was begnning to believe it. I'm not sure the commissioner did, however. I tried to change the subject.

"What's going on with this federal kickback probe, Frankie?" I said.

"I can't talk about it."

"Can't or won't."

"Take your pick."

"Was Tony Walker a target of the investigation?"

The commissioner's face went ashen. I watched him swallow hard. "Get out, Knight," he said. "Go tell your horseshit story to someone else. But remember this — I'm watching you."

I went to the door. Before I left, I decided to plant one more seed. "Oh yeah, commissioner," I said, opening the door. "Did you know you've got some Boston cops running around ripping off drug dealers, reselling it themselves to other dealers?"

"What?"

I loved watching people squirm. Especially assholes like the commissioner.

16

There was a call waiting for me when I went upstairs. Sitting down at my desk, I picked up the phone. "Sergeant Knight." I said.

It was Larry, one of the detectives I sent up to Swampscott to keep an eye on Edwards.

"Joe—I'm sorry," Larry said.

I leaned forward, my elbows on the desk. "Don't be sorry. Just tell me what's the matter?"

"Edwards is gone."

"Gone? Where?"

"We don't know. We were watching the house like you told us. Jack noticed the back door open. When we went inside, no one was there."

"Jesus Christ! When was this?"

"When we went inside? About ten minutes ago. Before that the last time we saw Edwards was when his brothers arrived—when he let 'em in. That was four or five hours ago."

"Any signs of a struggle?"

"None."

"What about suitcases or clothes? Edwards take anything with him?"

"I don't know. We didn't look."

"Go back there and look for Chrissakes. What the hell do I have to do—come up there and hold your fucking hands? Call me back when you find out. And look down at the dock. See if the boat is still there."

"We looked already. It's gone."

"Wonderful."

Ten minutes later, Larry called me back. Edwards' clothes

218 — Fat Guys

were still there, so were his suitcases.

I made a call to Buzzy Edwards. His wife said he was at work.

I called Billy Edwards. Same thing.

The wives gave me the phone numbers where they worked. I called. Both had called in sick.

Hanging up, I called the Chelsea police station. The chief wasn't in. I left a message to return my call.

Lieutenant O'Keefe stormed in. I ignored him and dialed another number.

"Put the phone down," O'Keefe said. "I want to talk to you."

I kept dialing. "I'm busy. What do you want?"

"I just got off the phone with the commissioner."

"I know. Your lips are still puckered."

"Cut the wise stuff, Knight. The commissioner want to know what you meant about Boston cops going around ripping off drug dealers? Where do you get off saying things like that to the commissioner without a shread of evidence to back it up?"

"Kiss off, O'Keefe. Can't you see I'm busy?"

"And another thing. The commissioner wants everything you've got on the killings on his desk in an hour. No bullshit. Every fucking-thing. One hour. You got it?"

"Impossible."

"What do you mean, impossible?"

"Just what I said."

"It's a direct order."

"I don't give a shit."

"I know you don't Knight. That's your problem. You come and go out of here all hours. No one knows where the hell you are or what you're doing. That may be the way it was with Bailey in charge but that's all going to change. I mean, look at this place, It's a mess. And where the hell is everybody?"

"Out in the street where they belong. Doing what they're being paid to do. Maybe you should try it instead of sitting on your ass all day behind a desk, getting shit on your lips from all that ass kissing you've been doing."

O'Keefe's face puffed up. "That's it, Knight. I'm writing you up for insubordination. Consider yourself on report."

Outside in the hall, two uniforms came around the corner from traffic and poked their heads through the doorway, curious who was doing all the yelling. One of them was an old friend, Harry Killery, the other cop was Hammond— didn't know his first name.

O'Keefe wasn't aware they were there. He kept on. "That report is not on my desk in an hour," he said, "go home. Because that's where you'll be after your suspension."

Harry Killery made a face at O'Keefe's back.

I grinned.

"You think it's funny, Knight," O'Keefe said. "We'll see who has the last laugh." He spun around, shouldered his way through Killery and Hammond, stormed to his office, and slammed the door.

Harry Killery smiled at me. "Think you struck a nerve, Joe."

I smiled back. "More than one it seems, Harry."

"As long as it makes you happy, Joe."

"It does, Harry. Believe me."

Harry gave me a wave and left. So did Hammond.

I got tired of holding the phone to my ear. I put it down for a minute knowing it always took three to four minutes of ringing before anyone at the State Police Major Crime Unit would answer. I let another minute pass then picked up the receiver. Thirty seconds later, someone answered.

"Major Crime. Trooper Carlson."

"Trooper Carlson, this is Sergeant Knight. Homicide. Boston Police. Is Lieutenant Kneffly around?"

Silence. More than I cared to hear.
"You there Trooper Carlson?"

"Just a minute, Sergeant Knight."

Another thirty seconds of uneasy silence. I smelled something and I didn't like it. A few seconds later, Lieutenant Kneffly came on the line.

"Joe," he said. I was right. It did smell. Of what I wasn't

sure. The way Kneffly said "Joe" was different, like I was the last guy on earth he wanted to hear from. Usually he was glad when I called. He loved talking street with me— loved swapping war stories. But not this time. "What's up?"

"You tell me, Bobby," I said.

"What do you mean?"

"I think you know exactly what I mean. We've been friends too long, Bobby. Don't bullshit me. I want to know what's going on."

Joe. For Chrissakes." He was stalling, thinking up some lie. I could always tell. Maybe he forgot who he was talking to. "Nothing's going on. Just the same old shit. You know how it is."

I decided it was time to play one of my aces. "There was a New York cop killed the other night. I was with him. His name was Cole. Robert Trenton Cole. Only I don't believe that was his real name. He sure as hell wasn't a New York cop. I checked. The badge he showed me was stolen. Before he was shot, he told me he was looking for a New York cop turned hit man. A creep named Manfred Styles. He said Styles was the one who iced Susan Howell and Pete West. Cole snowed me good—not many people can. Who was he Bobby? I got this feeling you know what I'm talking about. You got some operation going on with the Feds, Bobby?"

It was as if a bomb had suddenly dropped on the other end of the line—a neutron bomb, the kind that kills all the people but leaves everything else. I said, "Bobby? I know you're still there. I can hear your two brain cells clicking together."

Breaking the long silence Bobby said, "Not over the phone, Joe."

"Where?"

"Brookline, Jamaica Pond. Perkins Street side. Eleven o'clock tonight."

I reacted with a brief rush of anger. "Why so late?"

"No more questions, Joe."

He hung up.

Tipping my chair back, I closed my eyes and rubbed my

eyelids with the tips of my fingers. The afternoon sun streamed in on me through the window, filling the drab office with shafts of yellow-orange light. The brightness was overwhelming; hadn't seen the sun in over a week. I rose, went to the window and looked down. Some firefighters were washing a ladder truck across the street at the firehouse. I could hear them talking and laughing; something about flames shooting a hundred feet in the air. Those bastards loved fires; most of them got their rocks off running in and out of burning buildings. They loved their work; couldn't wait for the next fire. The bigger the better.

I wondered as I watched them squirt each other with hoses why I didn't feel the same about my job. Maybe I'd seen too many people with their throats slit or their heads blown off. I don't know. I guess there's a limit to the horror which the human mind can experience. I know I passed that limit years ago. Maybe it was time to move on to something else.

Turning from the window, I felt everything we had investigated so far was leading us down the proverbial shithouse path. So many paths to take. Whatever one we took, we were damned sure to run smack into another shithouse.

I didn't like sitting alone in my car at night, especially on a deserted street next to a pond. Maybe I've seen too many movies. I mean, how many times have you seen sickos creep out of the woods, sneak up on their victims who always seem to be sitting in a car on a lonely road, then whamo, the poor sucker gets it. Trouble was that happened in real life, too. Like last night at O'Hara's. I decided to take a walk.

I followed the path around Jamaica Pond for about a hundred yards, keeping my car in sight. There was a three-quarter moon so the visibility was fair. I heard voices ahead; two teenage kids holding hands and kissing coming toward me. They saw me and hesitated, looked for another path, and took it. I couldn't blame them. Meeting a man my size out here alone could scare the shit out of anybody. Me included.

I walked back toward the car, found a cement bench and sat down. I hiked the collar of my corduroy jacket up around my neck and folded my arms. The sky was clear, the September night cool.

Where the hell did summer go?

I thought about my kids going shopping for school clothes. How fussy Jessica was—everything had to match, right down to her underwear. Jeff—he didn't give a shit what he wore. What a boy. Just like his Dad.

The minutes went by, the air grew progressively colder. I illuminated the dial of my watch. Red numbers flashed eleven-thirty-one. Kneffly was a half hour late.

Or had the lieutenant decided not to show up at all?

"Joe."

I turned, startled by the whisper. Instinctively I slipped my hand inside my jacket, brought out my .38, and held it close to my side.

The figure of Lieutenant Bobby Kneffley came out of the shadows from a clump of bushes to my right. The .38 went back.

"Kneffly? How long have you been there for Chrissakes?"

"About forty-five minutes." Kneffly walked toward me. We shook hands.

Lieutenant Robert Kneffly was an Ivy Leaguer. He was slender and tall, his face thin, the features clean, hair cut short and neatly parted. He had brown eyes that were a little distant but never vacant. His uniform, as always, was a single-breasted dark suit, crisp white shirt and tie.

"What the hell were you doing hiding?" I said.

"Making sure no one followed you," Kneffly said.

"And I thought I was paranoid. Sit down. Let's talk."

"Not here. Let's walk. You could use the exercise."

"So everybody keeps telling me." We started down the path and walked along the water. "Okay, who starts?"

"No how aׁe yah doing, Bobby? How's the family, Bobby?"

"Later. Now talk."

Some traffic moved along the Jamaica Way fifty yards over the hill to our left. The muffled hum of tires, loud at first, echoed into silence.

I stopped walking and faced Kneffly. "What about this guy Cole?" I said. "Or whatever his name was?"

"He was a federal agent."

"I guessed that much."

We started walking again. I said, "Who was Cole working for? The FBI?"

"I don't know."

"That's horseshit, Bobby. It's me, Joe, you're talking to here."

"Don't remind me. I forgot what a relentless bastard you are."

I didn't say anything.

"I'm telling you straight, Joe. I honestly don't know where the hell this Cole character came from or why he was here. All I know is, one night I got this call from the Colonel."

"Pasely?" I said.

"Yeah. But don't bother, Joe."

"What do you mean?"

"I can see that sick mind of yours working. You don't like what I tell you, you'll go to Pasely. Well, forget it. He won't tell you anything. I'm only telling you because we're friends. I owe you."

"Yes, you do. Now what about this Cole?"

"Like I said. I don't know anything about him. Pasely said I would be contacted by this federal agent named Cole. I was ordered to cooperate with him. Don't ask questions—just do what he instructed."

"What was that?"

"Nothing. We never talked—he never called."

"So why the panic when I called?"

"I don't panic."

"Bullshit. What do you call what you're doing now?"

Lieutenant Kneffly hunched his shoulders against the chill. We walked a little more.

I said, "How come you didn't call me after Cole got shot? You must have known I was with him."

"I didn't know. Not until later."

"What do you mean? Later?"

Kneffly stopped and looked toward the water. "Soon after the shooting," he said, "I got this call."

"From who?"

"I don't know exactly. He gave me the code word."

"code word?"

"Yeah. 'Iron Hammer'—that was the code word Cole was supposed to use when he called. I was told if anyone called and said 'Iron Hammer', I was to do exactly what the caller said to do."

"What was that?"

Kneffly turned and faced me, then said. "Pick up Cole's body and get rid of it."

I went silent for a couple of seconds, too stunned to speak. "That was you?" I said.

He nodded.

"Sonuvabitch."

We started to walk again.

"What did you do with the body?" I said.

"Took it to Logan Airport like I was told. Put it on a private jet at Butler Aviation." He stopped walking again. "I know what you're thinking, but I was only following orders. That sounds strange to you, I know. You fucking guys in Boston don't know the meaning of the word."

We had walked nearly two hundred yards around the pond. We turned and headed back. I said, "That it? That all you can tell me about what's going on?"

Lieutenant Kneffly looked at me. Even in the dark I could see the strain. "Joe," he said. "Can you see my lips? Watch me talk. I don't know anything. I don't want to know anything. Now, if you don't mind, I'd like to get the hell away from you. I love yah, Joe. But you're bad news—yah know what I mean? You have this knack for pissing people off. You want some advice, Joe? Back off a little bit. You're a goodie-two-shoes cop who doesn't know the meaning of easy. Balls to the wall—that's you. You asked me a while ago why I was panicked. Okay, I'll tell you why. Someone's got you in their gun sights, Joe. Maybe the other night you got lucky—I don't know. But you keep on like you're doing—sooner or later your luck's going to run out.''

I felt the wolf in me pulse up again. I didn't know when it was my friend Bobby Kneffly went chicken-shit, but hearing him talk like that, I knew he had. There was nothing more to discuss.

When we reached my car, I said. ''How's the family, Bobby? Everybody okay?''

''Yeah, Joe. Everybody's okay. Thanks. How about yours?''

''I think they're beginning to wonder who that stranger is who keeps sneaking in at night.''

Bobby nodded. ''Don't remain a stranger too long, Joe. You know what I mean?''

I nodded.

Lieutenant Kneffly lifted the collar of his suit jacket, hunched his shoulders and disappeared into the shadows.

''Stay in touch, Bobby,'' I said.

He didn't say anything.

The following morning, I called Colonel Pasely's office at State Police Headquarters. As I suspected, his secretary told me he was out of town. Wouldn't be back for a couple of days. I said I'd call back.

Ten minutes later, I got a call from Sergeant Billy Andrews. He told me I was one lucky bastard. Using a special process I didn't give a shit hearing about, Billy had lifted two thumb prints from the photographs, neither of them mine or Tommy's. I told him I'd be right over.

An hour later, after bullshiting with Billy for twenty minutes or so, I was on my way back to Boston when I got a call on the two-way radio. The dispatcher said to meet Detective Dolan at the Coast Guard station. Make it in a hurry. I did.

Using my siren, I made it from Kenmore Square to the

North End in eight minutes. The Coast Guard station was off Commercial Street, at the end of Hanover Street. Driving up to the gate, flashing my gold badge, the young Coast Guardsman gave me a quick look and waved me through. I slowed down long enough for him to tell me everybody was waiting for me over on the pier to the right, behind the cutter *Chase,* moored in the fore-dock.

I went right, then left, and drove to the end of the long cement pier. I stopped behind a Health and Hospitals ambulance and got out.

Warren spotted me. "Joe," he said, waving. "Over here."

I made my way to the edge of the dock, shouldering my way past a herd of Coast Guardsmen. As I stepped over a rope, one of the Guardsmen stopped me. Instead of a lollipop, the kid was carrying an M-16 rifle at port arms. That in itself scared the shit out of me. The thought of him having real bullets frightened me to death.

I showed him my gold badge. "Easy kid," I said. I thought of saying something smart, but I resisted.

"Take a look at this, Joe," Warren said, pointing down to the dark green canvas tarp. Stepping around the kid with the rifle, I had already noticed the six legs sticking out from under the tarp. Warren couldn't wait to show me the rest.

Lifting the tarp, he did.

Though it was warm out, an instant chill ran up my spine and settled in the pit of my stomach. Lying face up, eyes open, hands and feet tied, looking very wet and dead, were the Edwards boys. Larry, Buzzy, and Billy. Each with two small bloodless holes centered in a milky forehead.

Jesus Christ.

"The Coast Guard found them a mile out of the harbor," Warren said, looking down. "Tied to the bottom of a boat. The ME was here—he said the bodies were only in the water a few hours. Poor bastards."

I put my hands in my pockets. "Yeah," I said. "Poor bastards."

I looked out across the harbor at a jet taking off from Logan, thundering overhead, and banking over the city, and wishing I was on it. I didn't give a shit where it was going—just to be on it—kissing all this madness goodbye.

I said, my eyes falling back down on the Edwards brothers, "Better call their wives."

On the way back to South Boston, I stopped off at headquarters and went downstairs to the computer room.

Rita Barns was at her console, eating an apple.

I handed her the thumbprints enhanced in black ink under clear tape, attached to a white four-by-five card. "What do you think, Babe?" I said. "Can you do anything for me?"

Rita studied the prints, then looked up at me and smiled. "I can't," she said, swallowing what she chewed, "I might as well go back to the streets. It might take a little while though."

"Take your time, Babe. Just make it good news when you call me."

"I'll try."

"Can't ask for more than that."

"Yes, you can. All the time."

Before I left, I asked Rita to make me a printout of Sergeant Brendan O'Hara's personnel file. As always, everything was confidential. She said she would, but after all the favors, I owed her a dinner. I said okay. Where would she like to go? Locke-ober's, she told me. I said, there goes the neighborhood—not to mention my paycheck. She said, your mamma.

It was a little after one in the afternoon when I got back to the office. I made myself coffee, stuffed a day-old sweetroll down my gut and went over some papers on my desk. Five minutes later I got a phone call.

"Homicide," I said. "Sergeant Knight."

"Listen to me, Knight," the voice said. "I'm only going to say this once."

"Who is this?"

"Never mind that." The voice was high-pitched and squeaky, like someone trying to make his voice sound like some cartoon character. "You want Styles?"

I leaned forward, too stunned to speak.

"You there, Knight?"

I swallowed. "I'm here."

"You want Styles?"

"Okay. I'll play your silly fucking game. Yeah, I want Styles."

"Go to 121 Homestead, in Roxbury. Guy named Willis Boyd lives there with some of his cousins. They're bad asses, Knight—and heavily armed. So you better bring an army."

"How do you know all this?"

"I know. Trust me."

"How many guns are there?"

No answer.

"Hello?"

There was a click and the line went dead.

I called everybody into the office and closed the door.

"What's up, Joe?" Tommy said. "What's with the vest and shotgun?"

"We're going on a hunt," I said, buttoning my shirt over my bulletproof vest that seemed a lot smaller than the last time I wore it.

"Where?" Jake said.

"Roxbury."

"What happened?" Warren said. "They finally secede from Boston?"

I put on my jacket. I couldn't zip that up either. Not even after I sucked in. "You guys got vests," I said, "wear 'em. We're going after Manfred Styles."

"You're shitting us?" Warren said.

"You know where he is?" Jake said.

"Yeah. I just got a phone call. Someone tipped me."

"Oh, yeah?" Warren said. "Who?"

"I don't know," I said, heading for the door. "Trust me."

Warren took out his .45 automatic he kept in his top drawer, popped the clip, checked it, then slipped it back in the handle. Following me to the door, he said, "Trust me. Isn't that what the cannibal said when he had his teeth wrapped around this guy's balls? Trust me?"

17

Warren and Jake grabbed their shotguns out of the trunk and ran down the alley off Homestead Street behind three uniforms from the Special Operations Division, wearing dark blue baseball caps and bulletproof vests. Tommy was waiting for me at the end of Humboldt Ave.

I ducked behind his Chevy, looked up Homestead at the yellow and brown three-decker. "You see anybody?" I said.

"No," Tommy said.

I looked down Humboldt. The SOD unit had the street blocked at Crawford, diverting traffic out to Elm Hill Ave. Across the vacant lot on Ruthven Street, I could see the SOD communications van — Superintendent Matt Doyle beside it, directing some of his men into place.

"What about Styles, Joe?" Tommy said. "We're gonna look like fucking fools if he's not in there."

"Since when did that bother you?"

"Hey, I don't give a shit about being wrong. I just don't like not being right?"

I pushed five rounds into my shotgun and threw the lever forward. "Don't worry, Tommy. He's in there. I can smell the sonuvabitch. Wish we knew how many are in there?"

"Only one way to find out," Tommy said.

I checked my watch. "Two minutes," I said. "We hit the door in two minutes."

We waited.

Three teenagers wandered across Humboldt. One of them had a ghetto-blaster on his shoulder screaming Bon Jovi all over the neighborhood. I recognized the song — the same one that screamed out of my daughter's bedroom every morning.

Two helmeted cops came out from behind a car and led them away. One of the cops was black. Everybody on the street heard the kid with the ghetto-blaster yell. "Watch what you do'n, mudda-fucka! Keep yo' Goddamn hands off me, honky mudda-fucka! Same goes for you, Uncle Tom!"

Uncle Tom took out his nightstick and shoved it up the kid's ass, helping the kid along. I smiled. My kinda guy.

The place went quiet again, as quiet as it gets in this part of the city.

I looked at my watch again. One minute.

I took out my portable and checked with Superintendent Dole. Everything was set. His men would take the back. Me, Tommy, Warren, Jake and the other uniforms would rush the front.

One of the uniforms was a big kid, no more than twenty-five, I'd never seen before. He had upper arm muscles the size of cantaloupes and held a huge sledgehammer in his hands. He was the sledge-man, and it was his job to knock down the door to the house, then step back so the other uniforms — all of them with shields — could rush into the place. The hammer looked like a good idea to me, and the shields looked even better.

Everybody knew who we were after, who he was and what he did. Manfred Styles was to be considered armed and the most dangerous prick you'd ever want to meet. Everybody knew I wanted Styles alive. Any others in there, I didn't give a shit about.

I heard the superintendent say "Thirty seconds" over the portable.

We moved closer. The front door was only a few yards away beyond a badly weathered picket fence.

Warren and Jake came out of the alley and darted across the street. Warren knelt down next to me, his back against the parked car we were crouched behind.

"I hate this shit, Joe," he said. "I really do. Scares the shit out of me every time."

No one said anything.

Ten seconds, five seconds.

We stormed the door running. The big kid hit the door with two terrific blows, and knocked it spinning off its hinges. In all my twenty-five years on the force, I've never seen it done that quick.

Inside, Warren and Jake took the stairs behind two uniforms with shields. The other uniforms took the basement. The big kid, then me, then Tommy, thundered into the front room. There was no one.

Then to our right, the kitchen door flew open. A brilliant flash accompanied the explosions from the black guy's shotgun. The big kid from the SOD unit went down in front of me, flesh and hair from his head went everywhere.

The fabric of my jacket was blown away, blood matting what remained of my shirt. I spun around, hot, searing pain spread through my right side. I went down. As I did, an explosion came from behind me. I looked up in time to see the black man catapult back with no chest and half a face.

Tommy knelt down beside me. "Geeszus Christ, Joe!" he said, holding my arm tight. "You okay! Jesus Christ! Didn't you see the fucking guy!"

I gripped my side, blood slipped between my fingers. Strange there was no pain now, only numbness.

I heard gunshots from somewhere out back, or upstairs — I couldn't tell which — some thunderous, others staccato.

Tommy dragged me across the floor and tried to lift me on to the sofa. He was about to raise my feet up when two figures came at us from nowhere. One had an automatic, the other a knife.

Tommy brought his shotgun up and hit the guy with the automatic in the cops with the butt. The second guy was on me before I had a chance to move.

Pain or no, I had to reach up and grab the black guy's arm to keep the knife from going into my gut. Jesus Christ did that hurt.

I spun to my right, my arm arcing up and crashing down over the black guy's elbow. I jabbed the fingers of my left hand in the guy's throat. The knife fell to the floor.

The bastard was huge — I couldn't hold him off any longer. An enormous weight was crushing my chest, a forearm — like a heavy iron bar, was across my throat, choking me.

The last thing I saw was a hand raised high like some dark claw. And then nothing.

I opened my eyes to distorted images of intravenous bottles, plastic tubes, and Richie Scarvino's smiling face looking down at me, dabbing my forehead with a cold cloth.

I heard sirens. Motion swayed me in circles. I was drifting again, the currents gentler now.

"Hey, big guy," Richie the paramedic said. "Glad to have you back among the living. Thought we lost you back there. Had us all scared."

Richie's puffy face was going in and out of focus. "Just another fucked up day at Black Rock," I said wearily. "Where the hell am I?"

"In the back of an ambulance," Richie said. "On the way to Boston City Hospital."

"Son-of-a-bitch."

The pain in my side wasn't that bad. It was my face that hurt like hell. I tried to raise myself but the strength wasn't there. "What...happened?" I said.

"You got shot," Richie said.

"No shit...really?"

"Your partner, Tommy, said some big black guy knocked you out."

"Did we get him?"

"Who? The black guy?"

"No. Styles?"

"I don't know. They arrested a bunch of guys. Most of them had to be taken away in ambulances. Three of them are on the way to the morgue."

"What...color were they?" It was getting hard to talk because my face felt like it was being squeezed in a vice.

"What do you mean, what color?" Richie said.

"Were the dead guys white or black?" I said.

"Black. There was one white guy arrested — if that's what you want to know."

"Did you see the guy?"

"No."

The lights went out again. Somewhere in the darkness of my mind, I heard Richie say to his partner who was up front driving, "Pick it up, Kevin. He's out again."

I didn't know where I was when I woke up. Shapes slowly came into focus, lit by the fluorescent light overhead. There were voices in the distance across the room. I was in a large room on a narrow bed, a sheet covering me. Across the room were two people. I couldn't tell who they were, then I saw Victoria look my way.

She smiled and came cautiously toward the bed.

"You're awake," she said softly, taking my hand. I could see the relief in her eyes, but there was tension in her voice. "How do you feel, darling?"

"Where's Tommy," I said.

"Right here," Tommy said, appearing over Victoria's shoulder.

"Did we get him?"

Tommy smiled. "We got 'im."

I closed my eyes. "Thank you God." I opened my eyes again. "The others?"

"Three bought the proverbial shit house."

"How much did it cost us?"

"Only one," Tommy said. "The kid that went in ahead of you. Name's Jones. Been on the force four years. Too bad. He never knew what hit him."

"What happened after I blacked out?"

"I busted the guy's skull and dragged him off you. But never mind that now. I'll fill you in on everything later. Talk to Victoria. She's been worried sick."

Before Tommy left, I said, "Where's Styles?"

"Downstairs," Tommy said. "Warren put two bullet holes through his legs. The doctors are sewing him up now. Can't believe it? Warren actually hit what he was aiming at."

"So Styles is going to be okay?"

"Unfortunately."

Tommy reached down and squeezed my shoulder, kissed Victoria gently on the forehead, then left.

Victoria stood motionless, looking down at me, her tone controlled. "The doctor said you should be back on your feet in a day or so." She allowed herself a tentative smile. "It was just a flesh wound. But you do have a cracked cheekbone."

I could tell. The right side of my face felt the size of a basketball.

"Where are the kids?" I said.

"Home. They send their love. I bring you mine."

Already I could feel myself gaining strength. Victoria could always do that for me somehow.

I switched off the remote to the TV after the late news. Everything went dark in the room, except for some light spilling in from the corridor outside. I closed my eyes, trying to remember what the hell had happened. What had gone wrong? How could I have been so stupid — worse yet — been so damn slow to react? I was losing it. Slowly maybe. But steadily losing it.

I stared out the window, consciously trying to bring everything back into some sort of focus. I couldn't. Losing focus again. Feeling dizzy. My sense of survival nearly gone. If only the pain would disappear. The numbness.

The telephone rang on the table next to the bed.

Shit!

I reached for it instinctively but stopped.

The pain in my side under the bandage immobilized me, and blurred my vision. I drew my hand back, only able to reach a few inches.

Finally, I was able to slide myself to the edge of the bed and grab the phone.

"Whoever this is," I said, picking up the receiver, wiping away some pain-tears, "it better be important."

"What's more important than your life?" the squeaky

cartoon voice said.

"You again?" I said.

"Yes, me again."

"Doesn't it hurt your throat trying to talk like that?" I said.

He didn't answer my question.

"Congratulations on capturing Styles," the voice said.

"You sound disappointed," I said.

No reply.

"What do you want?" I said.

Silence again.

"You got three seconds," I said.

The seconds went by.

Then.

"I'm sorry you were wounded," the cartoon voice said. "You were careless. I warned you."

"Yeah. You warned me."

"Leave it alone, Knight."

"What are you talking about? Leave what alone?"

"Your investigation of Brendan O'Hara."

"What do you know about it?"

"Enough."

"Is this you, O'Hara? It's really you, isn't it?"

I knew it wasn't. O'Hara could talk through tin cans tied to strings and I'd recognize his voice. I just wanted to piss off whoever it was. It didn't work.

"You're a fool, Knight," Cartoon Voice said. "Drop it while you still can. I'm not sure how long I can keep you alive."

"Kiss my ass."

Again silence.

Then Cartoon Voice said. "You're good, Joe. But you're not in our league. Whatever happens, remember. You were warned. Goodbye, Sergeant Knight."

Three days later, I was out of bed and at a news conference on the fourth floor of police headquarters. Styles was recovering from his wounds at the Charles Street Jail.

Sitting at a long table in front of a zillion microphones were the police commissioner, Superintendent Doyle, Deputy Superintendent Jimmy Hatcher, and Lieutenant Ass-Kisser O'Keefe.

Tommy, Jake and Warren were standing in the back of the room, eyeing everyone who walked in. Ever since I told them about the phone call I got from Cartoon Voice, they'd been hovering over me like mother hens. The only time they left me alone it seemed was when I took a shit.

Watching from a chair away from the lights and TV cameras that lined the front of the table, I couldn't help but smile every time the commissioner made a gesture with his hands. Each time he did, the zillion still photographers on their knees surrounding the table would fire their Nikons, sending motor-drives whirring into a fucking frenzy. I couldn't imagine for the life of me why they shot so many pictures when all they ever used was one — if that.

The Nikons took off again when the commissioner reached in his suit jacket pocket for the sheet of paper containing a prepared statement.

"To begin this press conference," the commissioner said, "I would like to take this opportunity to express the city's sincere gratitude to the men of the Special Operations Division — under the command of Superintendent Matthew Doyle siting here to my right — for the truly professional and speedy execution of the operation that resulted in the capture of one of the nation's most sought after hired killers — Manfred Styles."

For once I agreed with the commissioner.

"Regretfully," the commissioner continued, "all such operations carry with it the danger of fatality, as in the case of Officer Richard Jones — shot to death in the line of duty. There will be a full ceremonial funeral mass for Officer Jones tomorrow morning at ten o'clock, followed by his burial at Forest Hills Cemetery. All police personnel not on duty will be required to attend. All of you in the press are encouraged to attend. Nancy Black, our PR director, will give you the details after this press conference."

As I sat there listening, flashes of that day came back to me. Explosions. Screams. Jones' face everywhere.

I knew I had some praying to do at his grave side. It had been only a matter of inches keeping me from going down six feet with him. All I could imagine was looking up from the casket and seeing my family, hearing my kids saying, "Daddy? What Daddy? Who's that guy down there, Mom?"

"Also," the commissioner went on, bringing my mind back, "I would like at this time to extend my thanks to the homicide unit, headed by Lieutenant O'Keefe, here on my left, for the fine job his squad did assisting in Styles' apprehension."

I looked to the back of the room. I saw Tommy flash O'Keefe the finger. So did Warren and Jake. I grinned.

The commissioner read the statement. It said that on Saturday, September 4th, at approximately one forty-five in the afternoon, members of the Boston Police Special Operations Division, assisted by members of the homicide unit, entered the dwelling at 121 Homestead Street in Roxbury — owned by a one Christa Boyd, cousin to Willis Boyd, a known drug dealer from New York City. Intensive and exhaustive investigation by the homicide unit revealed that Manfred Styles, friend of Willis Boyd, was in residence there.

Manfred Styles — an ex New York City police officer alleged to have been hired by a person or persons unknown — did on the morning of August 17th murder television reporter Susan Howell and two television technicians. Styles is also alleged to have murdered Peter West, a Chelsea police officer.

The commissioner hadn't even finished the last few words of the statement before the zillion questions from the press started flying. What pissed off the commissioner the most, the questions were directed at me. All of a sudden, I felt a zillion eyes on me. The question I heard loudest came from a reporter I knew could be a real ballbuster.

"Sergeant Knight?" Ron Gold from Channel Eight said. "Can you tell us the connection between Susan Howell and

Peter West?''

I looked at Gold. He wore gold-rimmed glasses and had curly blonde hair. I'd seen him around a number of times. I remembered Bobby Dunn talking about him. The guy was good. I could tell by the question. It was one I had asked myself a zillion times.

The commissioner broke in. ''Sergeant Knight, are you feeling well enough to respond?''

I could see in his eyes he was bullshit but he was locked in to a no-win. Reluctantly, I got up and walked behind the table. Superintendent Matt Doyle rose and gave me his seat behind the microphones. I nodded to him and sat down. Even through the glaring lights, I could see Tommy, Jake and Warren up back, snickering to each other like three little kids.

Ron Gold repeated his question. I thought about it a second then said, ''No comment. The matter is still under investigation.''

''What about the Edwards brothers?'' shouted some broad I recognized from the *Globe*. ''Lawrence Edwards was also a Chelsea cop. He was Peter West's partner. Is that correct?''

''That's correct,'' I said.

''Do you suspect Manfred Styles of those murders?'' some goofy-looking, four-eyed prick from Channel Three said.

I looked at him. ''Yes. We do.''

''Has Styles been charged for those murders?'' someone near the back said.

''Not yet,'' I said.

''Are you telling us you've got no idea who hired him?''

The question came from someplace in the middle of the pack. My eyes went cold, my face expressionless.

''Did you hear the question, Sergeant Knight?'' the voice said again.

''I heard it,'' I said.

''And?''

''No comment.''

''What?''

''I said, no comment.'' You miserable fucking prick.

"What led you to the house on Homestead Street?" a frail female reporter with horned-rimmed glasses said.

"Superior police work," I said smugly.

Everybody laughed except the commissioner and O'Keefe. They didn't know what that meant.

Before the news conference ended, the press threw a few more questions at the commissioner about the ongoing police kickback investigation being conducted by the Feds. They also had heard rumors of a police drug scandal involving several members of the Boston police department.

I left the commissioner squirming in his seat and walked to the back of the room. I almost tossed up my lunch when I saw who was standing in front of me near the doors. Brendan O'Hara.

"Nice work, Joe," O'Hara said. "Glad to see you still got it."

I didn't say anything. I couldn't. I just looked up at him, desperately trying to bring some warmth to my eyes.

"Brendan," I said, finally managing a smile. "Nice to see you again. Where the hell have you been lately?"

I extended my hand, trying to play it square, letting it come to me naturally.

O'Hara's eyes played over my face, a hint of a smile crossing his lips. He looked tired. Much older then his forty-seven years. His face was like hard, wrinkled leather — pronounced lines of strain at the edges of his mouth, thinner ones running away from sacks under blue eyes that seemed devoid of the flair and intensity I remembered. No curiosity or mischievous sparkle in them now.

Reluctantly it seemed, he shook my hand but kept his black leather gloves on. If he suspected I knew anything, he didn't show it. Neither did I.

"It's been a long time, Joe," O'Hara said.

"Too long," I said.

He looked sharp in his uniform. Always did. Holding his helmet, he had on a black leather waist-length jacket and knee-high black, highly polished boots. In his side holster was the same mahogany handled .357 magnum he had when we were riding together.

Both of us stayed silent for a few seconds, waiting for the other to speak.

"You never told me why you went back to special operations." I said. "How come you gave up the superintendent's job? Thought that's what you wanted?"

"It's a long story, Joe."

"I've got some time. I'd like to hear it. What do you say we talk over a coffee and doughnut?"

"Some other time, Joe. I've gotta run. By the way, heard you took some pellets? You okay?"

"Yeah. Tough to take down us old dogs. How come I didn't see you there? You're the best shot on the squad."

"I was on a day off."

"Don't they normally call you guys in when something that big is going down?"

"I guess they couldn't reach me."

"Too bad."

"Yeah."

It took everything I had to keep a smile on my face. I resisted the urge to grab him by the throat, rip his head off his shoulders, and shit down his neck. Maybe I should just blow his fucking head off and get it over with.

"Sorry to hear about you and Doris," I said.

"Yeah," O'Hara said. "We couldn't get along. It happens. How are you and Victoria doing?"

"Not bad considering we hardly see each other."

"The kids must be big?"

"Getting there. Where are you living now?"

"I've got an apartment in Southie — moved in with a girl named Sherry. You remember her? I dated her before I met Doris."

I looked away briefly. "I remember her," I said.

Bright red hair. Green eyes. Soft milky-white skin. Best blow job this side of Route 128, I thought.

"Maybe some day I could come over and bullshit old times?" I said. "I still owe you one. Remember Charlestown?"

"Forget it. You don't owe me anything. Like you said, it was a long time ago."

O'Hara checked his watch. "I gotta run, Joe." He made a sudden move away from the wall and headed for the stairs. "Nice talking to you. See yah around."

Sooner than you think asshole, I thought, watching him start down the stairs, remembering that he never did trust elevators.

I took the elevator to the basement and saw Rita. She had sent a message up to the news conference saying she had to see me before I left the building.

"You got something for me, kid?" I said, walking up to her.

She frowned and shook her head at me to keep quiet. Looking around to see if there was anyone paying attention to us, she hit some keys and put something on the computer screen. "Take a look at this, Joe," she said. "The fingerprints you gave me — they came back."

I sat down.

The screen said they belonged to a SAMUEL DAVID MORRIS. CURRENT STATUS: FIELD AGENT, CENTRAL INTELLIGENCE AGENCY. HEIGHT: 5′ 11″. WEIGHT: 180 POUNDS. COLOR EYES: BROWN. DOB: JULY 12, 1956. POB: LONG ISLAND, NY. CURRENT ASSIGNMENT: OPERATION IRON HAMMER.

UPDATED STATUS: DECEASED.

18

Charles Street Jail is across from Storrow Drive out of Charles Circle at the end of Cambridge Street, just down from Mass. General Hospital. Coming off Storrow, Tommy wheeled through the circle and pulled to the curb in front of the entrance.

The jail was a landmark in a city of landmarks, yet its medieval, grey stone walls and barbed wire remained an eyesore to the modern high-rises around it. Because none of the police stations in the city had any kind of adequate lock-up facility, Charles Street Jail was overcrowded like all of the prisons in Massachusetts. Mostly the jail was used as a holding area for people awaiting trial.

The liberals in the city say the cells are small and badly in need of repair, the sanitary conditions absolutely deplorable. We cops say, tough shit. Don't like the time — don't do the crime. Something like that.

Checking our weapons with the guard behind a glass partition, we went through the two checkpoints into the main area.

Manfred Styles was manacled with handcuffs hooked to a wide belt fastened around his waist, and escorted into a private room away from the main jail. Sitting down at the table, I got my first look at him in person.

His shoulders were broad and thick and stretched the cloth of his blue denim shirt. His hair was dark with some streaks of gray, his mustache thicker than I'd remembered seeing in the photographs. His face was smooth and clean shaven, pleasant looking. In fact, almost gentle. Yet there was something menacing about him. Had to be the eyes. Though Styles looked tired, his face pale, his eyes still had that cold, distant look of an animal.

"Do you smoke?" I said, sitting down across from him at the table.

Styles looked at me. "You got any?" he said.

"I can get some."

Styles nodded.

"What kind?" Tommy said.

"Camels," Styles said.

Tommy went out and closed the door.

We looked at each other in silence for almost a minute. I said finally, "My name's Knight. Sergeant Joe Knight. Homicide."

"So what?" Styles said.

"You want your lawyer present?"

"What for? I'm not saying anything."

"So I've heard. But you will."

"Bullshit."

"We've got you, Styles. Your gun. Your silencer. Everything. We can prove you hit Howell and West. When we get the results back from ballistics, we'll nail you to the Edwards murders as well. Who knows — maybe we'll pin the Vinnie Torchia job on you, too."

"Go fuck yourself, Knight. You've got nothing."

"You know, Styles. For a smart guy, you're stupid. You know what I mean?"

Styles didn't say anything.

I said, "New York is looking for you about some murders you committed down there. Frankly, I don't give a shit what you did in New York. Here in Massachusetts, you get life. Two, maybe five times over. No parole. You go to prison and rot away. Maybe you'll survive, then again maybe you won't. You know as well as I do what cons think of ex-cops in prison. Think about it."

"Get out of my face, man. I've said and heard it all before."

"Oh, yeah, I forgot. You were a cop once."

Styles looked away, his face showing the strain of being locked up. I recognized the look.

"Who paid you to hit Cole?" I said.

"Don't know what you're talking about."

"I think you do."

"Who gives a shit what you think?"

"C'mon, Styles. You're balls are strung out and you know it. You talk to me — maybe I can swing a deal."

Styles laughed in my face. "Give me a fucking break, Knight."

"I'm trying."

"Fuck you."

I was holding all the cards. Choosing which one to play was another matter. I decided on one of my aces. "Did Brendan O'Hara hire you to make the hits?"

Styles stared at me long and hard, his eyes not betraying him. "Fuck you," he said. "I'm through talk'n. Where's that asshole with my cigarettes?"

Tommy came in like we rehearsed a zillion times before. It was going to be tough playing good cop, bad cop with an ex-cop, but maybe we'd get lucky. We still had ways .

"Who you calling an asshole?" Tommy said, closing and locking the door behind him, making sure Styles saw him do it.

"Screw you," Styles said. "Open the pack and light me a cigarette. I haven't had one since they arrested me."

Tommy looked at me. I nodded — my eyes telling him to do what Styles wanted, then go into his act.

He did.

Tommy took out a Camel and stuck it between Styles lips. "I suppose you want me to light it for you?" he said.

"Can't smoke dry air, pal."

"I'm not your pal."

"No shit."

Tommy struck a wooden match but instead of lighting the end of the cigarette, he grabbed Styles by the hair and yanked his head back. Surprised by the sudden move, Styles' mouth opened, the cigarette dropped from his lips to the floor.

Holding the match close to the face, Tommy brought the

tip of the flame to Styles' nostrils.

Styles was able to blow out the flame, but he got the message in a hurry.

He laughed nervously. "What are you two bastards try'n to prove, huh?" Styles said. "That bad-cop shit won't work on me. So forget it."

I got up slowly and walked over to Styles. "How stupid of us, Tommy," I said. "Styles is an ex-cop." Standing above him now, looking directly down at his face, I added, "Why, he must have done the bad-cop routine a zillion times himself? Isn't that right, Styles?"

"Fuck you."

Tommy lit another wooden match. This time, I cupped my hand over Styles' mouth so he couldn't blow it out, at the same time gripping the back of his head so he couldn't move it.

"Okay, Styles," I said. "Now allow me to let you in on a little secret. My partner, Tommy, here. Well, he's not all there — you know what I mean. The lights are on but there's nobody home? You know. He's one sandwich short of a picnic? I'm sure you had those kind of cops in New York City when you were there?"

Tommy brought the flame up to Styles' nose. I had all I could do to keep his head still.

"Let me tell you another secret, Styles," I said. "I'm fucking crazy, too. And you know what we hate more than child molesters? Hit men. You are a hit man, aren't you Styles? Someone paid you. All we want to know is who it was? It was Brendan O'Hara, wasn't it?"

The flame flicked against the side of the left nostril. Styles' head jolted back. I knew he wanted to scream, but he couldn't. My hand was cupped tight over his mouth.

I said, "One more time, Styles. Did O'Hara hire you? You can nod. I'll let you."

He didn't.

I winked at Tommy. He lowered the tip of the flame to Styles' left earlobe. Styles nearly bolted to the ceiling. I had to bring my knee up and jamb it down on his wrist to keep him from flying out of the chair.

It took three more hits of the flame against the ear to make Styles nod.

"Good, Styles," I said. "Very good. So O'Hara did hire you."

Styles nodded.

"How many besides Howell and West and the Edwards brothers?"

Styles shook his head.

Tommy struck another match.

Styles jerked in the chair.

"Okay," I said. "I'm going to take my hand away from your mouth. You open it — you scream — it will be your last. I've got a nine millimeter Browning strapped to my leg I forgot to check in at the front desk. You grabbed it. We tried to take it away. You got shot in the face. Do you get my meaning?"

Styles nodded.

I took my hand away.

"Jesus Christ!" Styles said, gasping, bringing his left shoulder up, rubbing his charcoal broiled earlobe against it. "You guys are fucking nuts!"

"We told you we were," Tommy said with a grin. "You should have listened."

"What about Vinnie Torchia?"

Styles looked away. "No. That wasn't me," he said.

"Bullshit. You tied a rope around his neck so he'd choke to death and dumped him in the harbor. Why?"

"Okay, so I killed him. He was scum anyway."

"What about Cole?" I said.

"Who?"

"Robert Cole. Morris. Whatever. He was a federal agent. You hit him."

Styles looked away. "I didn't know he was a Fed."

"But you hit him."

"Yeah, I hit him. I thought he was a New York cop coming after me. He was following me. A friend called me — told me the guy was in New York asking a lot of questions about me.''

"You shot at me.''

Styles gave me a sick grin but didn't say anything.

I sat down. "How come you missed?'' I said.

Styles stayed silent.

I let it go for now.

"I need a cigarette,'' Styles said.

Tommy gave him one and lit it.

Styles inhaled the smoke deeply, then let it go into the air.

I turned away from the cloud and went to the other side of the table.

I said, "So what was going down?''

"What do you mean?'' Styles said, the cigarette dangling from his lips. "What was going down? I don't know what was going down. I got paid to do some clips — that's all I know. All I wanted to know.''

"Who paid you?'' I said.

"Vinnie Torchia.''

"Not O'Hara?'' Tommy said.

"Vinnie was a friend of mine. I knew him in New York.''

"When he hung with the Castilano mob?''

"Yeah. O'Hara wanted the job down and asked Vinnie to get somebody. Vinnie gave him my name.''

"How much did O'Hara pay you?''

"Fifty grand.''

"That's a lot of cash.''

"No shit.''

"He didn't say why he wanted them hit?''

"I told you already for Chrissakes. How many times I gotta tell yah. He paid me — I hit 'em. That's all. Business is business.''

"Who's sick idea was it to blow Susan Howell out of her shoes?'' Tommy said.

"Mine,'' Styles said, matter-of-factly.

"What was it,'' I said. "Some sort of game with you? One finger on the trigger, the other on the detonator? See how close you could time it?''

Styles smiled. "Something like that.''

"You're a sick son-of-a-bitch, Styles," Tommy said.

Styles looked at Tommy. "Aren't we all."

"You were a stupid bastard to shoot her," I said. "You should have known we'd dig the bullet out of her head."

Styles shrugged. "So I fucked up. So what."

"How come you didn't take the wind, Styles?" I said. "What kept you in Boston?"

Styles looked up at me. For a long moment he didn't say anything. Just looked at me with those cold eyes. Then he said, "Because O'Hara paid me fifteen grand to make one more hit," he said.

"Oh, yeah? Who?" I said.

A cruel smile spread across his lips. "You, asshole."

The next morning, Wednesday, we followed O'Hara back to his apartment in Southie where he stayed until seven o'clock in the evening.

The sun was below the trees. A stiff, cool breeze blew in off the harbor causing me to close the side window. Parked on Farragut Road across from Day Boulevard, we still had a clear view of O'Hara's front door two hundred yards away.

Tommy cracked his window and lit another cigar. "I don't like it, Joe," he said. "The prick is probably watching us out the window right now."

"Maybe."

"He knows we're on to him. Why else would he want you taken down?"

I didn't answer. I wasn't sure myself. Whatever, I thought I was worth more than fifteen grand. Maybe not.

Tommy drew on his cigar, blew smoke out the window. He looked at me the way he did sometimes, trying to read my face. Sometimes he was good at it, like now. He said, "Okay, Joe. Spit it out. You know something. What is it?"

I shrugged. "It's only a guess, Tommy," I said.

"That's always been good enough for me."

I thought another second, then said, "Last night, I kept asking myself — why would a guy like O'Hara give up so much for so little. I mean, look at the car he's driving? The guy is making a bundle ripping off drugs from dealers, right? What's he doing with all the money? He's not exactly living in the fast lane. Look where he's living. You checked his bank account. What's he got in it — a couple hundred bucks? Strange for a guy who's moving money around faster than he can count it. He's been running around like a crazy man, seeing people all hours of the night, making strange phone calls.''

"Okay," Tommy said. "So what's your guess?"

"I think he's working for the Irish Republican Army," I said. "He's an IRA supporter. Has been for years."

"You're shitting me?" Tommy said.

"You got a better guess? Think back all the times we hung out together, Tommy. What'd O'Hara talk about every time he got a few drinks in him? Northern Ireland. How the British shouldn't be there. How someday the IRA was going to kick all the Limeys out. He told me once he had relatives in Northern Ireland. Somewhere around Armagh I think it was. I think he's become an operative.''

"You sure know how to cheer up a day?"

"You asked me."

"I'm sorry I did."

I checked my watch: 7:15 pm.

Five minutes later, a blue and white Bay State cab pulled to the curb and hit the horn. O'Hara came out carrying two large blue suitcases and walked down the steps to the cab.

We followed the cab through the Callahan Tunnel to Logan Airport.

As usual, traffic approaching the tunnel was brutal. Everything crawled over the Northern Artery. But once we made it down the ramp to the tunnel, traffic began to move.

Out of the tunnel, I slipped the Buick into the right lane and followed the cab onto Airport Road, all the way around to the international terminal.

When the cab double-parked opposite Air France, we drove past and pulled to the curb next to a ten-foot high cement wall that separated the airplanes from the parking lot. Looking back, we watched O'Hara grab his bags, pay the taxi driver, then go into the terminal.

Getting out, we walked up to the floor-to-ceiling window and watched O'Hara get in line at the British Airways ticket counter.

Tommy looked at me, frowning. "British Airways?" he said. "Thought you figured he was going to Ireland?"

I kept my eyes on O'Hara. "That's what I figured."

Neither of us said anything for a couple of minutes.

It was dark out by the time O'Hara reached the ticket agent, checked his bags and got his ticket. A couple of minutes later, after he bought a croissant from one of those vendors wearing a funny looking baker's hat, we watched him go upstairs to the gate. When he was out of sight, we went into the terminal; Tommy went to the bottom of the escalators, keeping an eye out for O'Hara, while I went to the ticket counter.

At the first class check-in, I waved over a blonde ticket agent in a tight blue suit. The woman was in her late forties and looked like she was wearing a mask with all that makeup she had caked on. Bright red cheeks, dark blue eye shadow, dark red lips. If she smiled, I was certain the mask would crack.

As if her face wasn't bad enough, she had a thick and pompous British accent. She said, "If you wish to check in, sir, you will have to go to the end of the line and wait your turn."

I showed her my gold badge and said in a low voice, "You have a passenger named Brendan O'Hara booked on a flight tonight. I want to know what flight."

"I am afraid I cannot give out that information, sir," she said.

"It's police business."

"Yes, I am sure. I am still not allowed to give that information, sir."

I looked around, struggling to keep myself in control. "Then let me speak to your supervisor."

"I am the supervisor."

I took in a slow breath, then let it out even slower. "Alright, Miss . . ."

"Harvey. Josephine Harvey."

"Okay. Josephine. Let me put it to you another way. I'm a Boston police homicide detective. This is my city and you're in it. If you don't tell me what I want to know in the next twenty seconds, I'm going to take off my clothes and do a dance on the top of your fucking counter."

The woman took a quick look around, making sure no one had overheard. "Heaven forbid," she said. "Such language."

"Consider yourself lucky I don't whip my prick out and piss on your computers. Your down to ten seconds."

"Well, I never."

"Tell you the truth, lady, neither have I. But there's a first time for everything. Five seconds."

"Oh, alright."

Disgustedly, she went to the computer and punched some keys. I turned around and looked for Tommy. He saw me and shook his head, which meant O'Hara was nowhere in sight.

My watch said 8:35 pm.

Josephine stopped whacking the keys, looked at the screen, then said, "Yes. Mister Brendan O'Hara is booked on British Airways flight fifty-four."

"Where's it going?" I said.

"To London, of course."

"Of course."

"Flight departs from gate six at nine o'clock. Now, will there be anything else, Sergeant? I have passengers to attend to."

"What time does it arrive in London?"

Josephine glanced at the screen. "Eight-fifteen in the morning," she said.

"Josephine?"

"What is it now?"

"Keep what you told me to yourself, alright?"

She rolled her eyes back, and went down the counter.

I joined Tommy at the escalators. After I told him what Josephine had told me, we went up to the gate, careful not to let O'Hara spot us.

Gate six was half way down the terminal. O'Hara was sitting on the other side of a glass partition in a section reserved for passengers only. He was reading the *Globe*. He was wearing gloves.

The terminal was wide open. It was difficult to find a place where we could observe him without being spotted. We finally did — inside the coffee shop across from the gate. It was nearly quarter to nine — they were late boarding. We ordered coffee.

As I drank, my eyes went over the faces in the gate area. It was something I loved to do at airports — watch the people. Just when you think you've seen everything, something else goes by to make you smile even more. A teenager with spiked orange and red hair dressed in black leather with silver studs forming the letters F.U. on the cheeks of her ass. Holding her hand, a gangly kid with gold earrings and pockmarks on his face the size of craters, and rainbow-colored spiked hair. Jesus Christ. I wouldn't know what I'd do if Jessica dragged anything like that home.

I looked at O'Hara. He was holding a bottle of medicine — my guess it was clomipramine. He struggled with the cap. Finally, he gave up and took off one of his driving gloves. Removing the cap, taking the medicine, he couldn't get his glove back on fast enough. The look on his face said his hand was corroding. Too bad it wasn't.

My eyes wandered right. They stopped at the guy with the washed-out face and white hair with weird looking pink eyes, reading the *Herald*.

"Tommy," I said.

"What?"

"Take a look at the guy three rows to the right of O'Hara. The guy with the white face and blonde hair."

"The Albino in the blue pin-striped suit?"

"Yeah."

"What about him?"

"I don't like the way he keeps looking at O'Hara."

"What makes you think he's looking at O'Hara."

"Instinct."

"Of course. He's an ugly bastard that's for sure."

I watched the guy closely. There was something primitive about him as he sat there, reading deliberately, every now and then stretching to make sure his quarry was still in sight. It struck me that I was watching a predator, his eyes moving in all directions, cold and alert, more than often falling on O'Hara.

At five to nine, they started boarding.

O'Hara was the third one through the door. I watched him disappear down the ramp.

White-face got up slow and took his time. No need to rush. The back of the plane was going to the same place as the front.

"What now?" Tommy said.

I hoisted my bulk out of the tight booth and put on my jacket. "We go to headquarters and make a call."

"Where to?"

"Interpol, in London."

At headquarters I took the elevator to the communications turret on the top floor. An old friend of mine, a black guy named Sergeant Andrew Davis, was on duty. His glass enclosed office was quiet, unlike out on the floor where all the police and ambulance dispatchers were sitting at their consoles, dispatching.

"Hey, Joe," Andy said. "What brings you 'round?"

I told him.

"Can't do that, Joe," Andy said. "Not without authorization. You know that."

I did know that. I was hoping he didn't.

It took me five minutes of crying before Andy finally gave in.

"Alright, Joe," he said. "Use the phone in here. Anyone finds out, you did it on your own. You got it?"

"I got it. Thanks, Andy."

Andy left me alone and closed the door.

Two minutes later, the phone was ringing three thousand miles across the water. That and flying always amazed the hell out of me.

On the fourth ring, some British guy answered, and said, "Mayfair 212127?"

I said, "Is this Interpol?"

"How may I help you?"

The guy was polite. I liked that.

"My name is Joe Knight," I said. "Sergeant Joe Knight. I'm a homicide detective for the Boston police department. I'm calling from the United States."

"One moment please."

After hearing a series of beeps, the guy said, "May I have the number from which you are calling, sir?"

"What for?"

"So we may verify your call. Please give me the number, then ring off and wait for my call."

I did.

Five minutes later, the phone rang. I picked it up.

"Sergeant Knight?" the guy said.

"Yes?"

"Your department is verified."

"Oh, good."

"My name is Inspector Grayson. How may we help you?"

"I wonder if you people could do us a favor?"

"If it is feasible, of course."

"There's a guy on his way to London. His name's O'Hara. Brendan O'Hara. He's on British Airways flight fifty-four that arrives Heathrow at eight-fifteen your time tomorrow morning."

The inspector fell silent, long and uneasy. Then he said, "What do you wish us to do?"

"Put a tail on him," I said.

"I assume you have good reason, Sergeant? We are extremely busy."

"Yes, I do. I believe he's an IRA operative. I'm sure he's carrying a great deal of money. Money he intends to pass on to a contact from the Irish Republican Army somewhere in London.''

The line went silent again. Inspector Grayson had cupped the phone. I could hear some mumbling, but couldn't make out what was being said. I heard a click. Someone else was on another phone, listening in. A few seconds later, Grayson came back on the line.

"Are you quite sure of this, Sergeant Knight?" he said.

"I am."

"This chap — what is the name again?"

"Brendan O'Hara."

"Yes. O'Hara. Can you give us a description?"

"He's tall — maybe six-three. Curly brown hair with some gray on the sides. Deep set blue eyes. Clean shaven. Strong build — wide shoulders, trim waist. He's wearing a waist-length brown leather jacket, tan slacks, white shirt and brown tie."

"He sounds rather formidable?"

"If you mean can he kick ass? Yes, he can."

"Thank you, Sergeant. We will take proper precautions."

"I hope so."

"You say this chap O'Hara is carrying a great deal of money? How much is a great deal?"

"I don't know exactly. Could be a million dollars."

Silence again.

Then, "Yes. That is a great deal. Are you certain about the money?"

"Yes, I am."

"All right, Sergeant. We will be waiting for him."

"One more thing, Inspector. I think there's a guy following O'Hara."

"Oh?"

"The guy has long blonde hair, pink eyes, and a white face — looks like it's covered in baby powder. He's maybe six feet, a hundred and seventy pounds — wearing a blue pin-striped suit, light blue shirt and maroon tie. You'll have no trouble spotting him, that's for sure."

"We will take proper precautions, Sergeant. Thank you."

"Do me a favor, Inspector."

"If it is possible."

"Don't arrest O'Hara. Let him come back to Boston."

"I cannot do that, Sergeant."

"Why not?"

"If, indeed, this O'Hara is in possession of money and does pass it on to the Irish Republican Army, he will be in violation of international law. We will have no other alternative but to place him under arrest."

"Look, Inspector, I'm sure you're smart enough to know O'Hara's only a delivery boy. So's the guy O'Hara hands the money to. You British have a major problem going on in Northern Ireland, right?"

"Very well understated, Sergeant Knight."

"You know what I mean. You want to stop the flow of cash and weapons into Northern Ireland — we can help sever that connection here in New England. We work together, we can do it — at least put a major dent in their operation. Like I said, you grab O'Hara now, all you'll get is a minnow. The bigger fish will slip away."

"Perhaps."

"I'll be straight with you, Inspector. I want this guy back. I want him bad. Let him go. Let him think he's getting away with something. He passes the money — okay. Grab the guy he passes it to. Better yet, throw a tail on the guy. See where he takes you. Maybe you'll get lucky. Meanwhile, O'Hara comes back to Boston — sees how easy it was, and tries it again. Maybe we'll both get lucky."

After a moment, the Inspector said, "I will do what I can, Sergeant. I will pass along what you have said to my superiors. I am sure they will give it every consideration."

"Thanks for your time, Inspector. Good luck."

"Is there a number where we may reach you, Sergeant Knight? I suspect you will want a full report of his travels."

"I would."

I gave him my home and office numbers.

"Like I said, Inspector. Maybe we'll both get lucky."

"Yes. Lucky indeed."

19

That night, around eleven, we drove over to O'Hara's apartment in Southie to take a look around. When we got there, a light was burning in the front window. Shit!

She was home.

"What now, super sleuth?" Tommy said, taking out a cigar.

I thought a second or two, then said, "Maybe it's time to have a talk with her. After all, going through the front door seems to me a helluva lot easier than climbing our fat asses through the kitchen window."

Tommy lit his cigar. "Finally you make sense," he said. "Let's go."

It took Sherry Condon ten minutes to answer our knock.

"What do you guys want?" she said, disgusted, standing in the doorway with nothing on but a man's T-shirt. Her breasts were large and round, the nipples hard, penetrating the soft white material. She was maybe in her late thirties or early forties, with long dark red hair that she brushed back with her long fingers. When she did, I could see ugly spidery veins of red and black spreading away from a large bruise on her forehead over her right eye.

I showed her my gold badge because I wasn't sure if she remembered me from that night in the backseat of O'Hara's beat-up Ford so many years ago. "We met a couple of times — you probably don't remember," I said. "I'm Sergeant Joe Knight. This is Detective Sanders."

Her huge green eyes told me she remembered.

"You're Sherry Condon, right?" I said.

"Yeah. Now what do you want?"

"This won't take long."

"We want to talk to you about your roommate, Brendan O'Hara," Tommy said.

Her eyes darted from me to Tommy and back to me. Then she said, "I don't know where he is."

I looked past her into the hall. "When did you last talk to him?"

"I can't remember."

Tommy placed his hand on the door and leaned against it, gazed at her breasts a moment, then said, "Maybe you'd remember better downtown?"

"Fuck off," she said.

Tommy wanted to smack her. I could see it in his eyes.

I said, "Listen, Sherry, nothing's going to be gained by being an asshole, alright? Just tell us what he's been up to and we'll be out of your hair."

Sherry folded her arms. One of her thighs was quivering from the night chill. "Alright," she said reluctantly. "Sit in the living room. I have to put something on."

"Too bad," Tommy whispered, following me in.

I shot him an elbow to the chest.

Three minutes later, Sherry came in wearing a short black silk dressing gown. Her skin was soft and milky — no makeup. She sat down on the sofa, and wrapped her legs under her. The gown had risen — she made no attempt to cover up her supple thighs.

Looking at her, I couldn't help thinking back to that summer night — before I met Victoria. The night O'Hara had introduced me. Christ. What was it? Twenty years ago?

It had been Sherry's choice. She didn't want to risk getting pregnant. I could still remember her stroking me. Feeling her hands at my belt — the zipper move. Feeling myself strain against her hand. Seeing her brilliant hair in my lap. Feeling her mouth around me. The warmth. Her teeth against me. Gently pulling. Then sucking hard. Moving her mouth up and down until I was slick with her juices. Until I felt it coming.

Jesus Christ!

"Where did you get that bump on your forehead?"

Tommy said.

I came back. Too bad.

Sherry picked up a pack of Benson and Hedges, took one out, lit it, drew on it hard, and blew smoke into the air.

"O'Hara give it to you?" Tommy said.

Sherry glared at him. "No. I slipped in the bathtub."

"That's terrible," Tommy said. "Got to be careful where you stick that soap."

Ignoring Tommy, she took another puff on the cigarette and crushed it in the ashtray. Smoke spiraled up.

"Look," Sherry said. "I don't know what this is all about, and frankly I could care less. If Brendan is in some sort of trouble, too bad. He's caused me enough. So why don't you two get the hell out of here and leave me alone."

Sherry picked another cigarette from the pack on the coffee table and lit it. As she did, her eyes wandered. So did mine. I kept getting this feeling we weren't alone. But I had had that feeling a lot lately. Paranoia — ain't it wonderful?

"Mind if we take a look around?" I said.

"I do mind," Sherry said, her eyes coming back to mine, panicked.

"We could get a warrant?" Tommy said.

Sherry didn't answer.

I stood up, took one of my business cards from my wallet and handed it to her. "Thank you for your time, Sherry," I said. "Sorry to bother."

Sherry nodded wearily.

We went to the door.

I stopped and looked at her. "Can I give you some advice?" I said. "Get out of this. Go home if you have to."

Sherry didn't say anything. She just looked at me with that same strange pathetic panic I noticed in her eyes earlier.

We left, and the door bolted behind us.

The following morning, we came back with the search warrant. It was then that we discovered Sherry Condon had disappeared.

After searching the apartment and coming up empty, we

called the bar where she worked. Her boss said he had given her the night off if she'd agree to work the day shift. She never showed.

We checked with the neighbors. No one remembered hearing or seeing anything unusual, but that didn't mean a thing in Southie. A bomb could explode killing all the illegal Irish immigrants they've got hidden over there and no one would hear or see anything.

Back at the office I sent out some flyers and alerted all districts to keep an eye out for her. I ran a check on her through the computers and came up with her home town. Windsor, Connecticut. Her parents owned a quaint twelve room mansion on the river. Mr. Condon was a big-time lawyer, Mrs. Condon a successful dress designer. I called them and made a subtle inquiry as to their daughter's whereabouts — told them I was a college friend of Sherry's, gathering names for a class reunion. Mr. Condon told me she was living somewhere in Boston and hadn't seen his daughter in six months. If I find her, please have her call.

I hung up thinking it was time I had a long talk with my daughter. Maybe take her to a ball game — or Bloomingdales. Daddys and daughters — not a great combination when it comes to talking man-to-man, but it was worth a try. If nothing else, at least to show her I cared.

I sat back, put my feet up on my desk and went over everything in my mind.

O'Hara. The drug money. The IRA. The hits.

Christ, the CIA. Morris was CIA. Which means the Feds know about O'Hara. They've got an operation going. Operation Iron Hammer. What kind of operation? Who's running it? Couldn't have been Morris. Too much of a rogue. Has to be someone else. White-face maybe? Whatever, the game plan had changed dramatically. Do I let it go? Do I let the Feds grab O'Hara? Do I have a choice? Do I have enough to grab him before they do?

I took my feet off the desk and picked up the phone. It was time to get some answers.

I called the District Attorney. Told him what I had. He

said to bring everything to his office and we'd talk. I did.

The DA's office was downtown in the Suffolk County Courthouse on the sixth floor. When I got there, the only one in the office was the DA's right-hand flunky, Charlie Hamilton, an ex over-the-hill TV reporter who could be a real pain in the ass without really trying. I must have caught him on a good day; he was actually civil for a change.

"Joe," he said. "Nice to see you. He's in the shitter — be out in a minute. Have a seat."

I placed the cardboard box I was carrying down on his desk and took a seat.

Charlie put on his blue suit coat and straightened his pink tie. "You look like hell, Joe," he said, eyeing me.

"Thanks."

"No, I mean it. You look like you haven't slept in weeks."

I sighed.

Charlie glanced in the box. "What's all this, Joe?" he said.

"Evidence."

"Against whom?"

"You writing a book?"

"C'mon, Joe. Let's not get into that again. You know how it works around here."

"Yeah. That's the problem."

"What does that mean?"

I shut my eyes briefly. "Forget it, Charlie. Where's Barrow? I've got a lot of things to do."

Two minutes later, the district attorney came out of the shitter.

Herman Barrow was fifty-two, short, stocky, and slovenly. Looking at him, you'd never know he was the state's leading district attorney. Electrified white hair, hazy blue eyes, sleeves rolled up, with one of his horseshit multicolored ties loosened at the collar.

Appearance aside, Barrow was good. Damn good. A wheeler-dealer who'd plea bargain his mother down to a misdemeanor if he thought he could nail his old man for murder one. The thing I liked about him — you tell him anything, it stayed with him.

"Joe," he said, shaking my hand. "How yah been? You look like shit."

"So I've been told."

Barrow went into his office. So did Charlie. I picked up the box from the desk and followed them in. Charlie shut the door.

"What can I do for you, Joe?" the DA said, sitting down behind his oak desk, flanked by the American and state flags.

I opened the box, showed him what I had, and told him everything.

For a long time, Barrow looked over the evidence. He listened to audio tapes recorded from the bug in O'Hara's car. Even looked at a couple of surveillance tapes.

Nodding to Charlie to shut off the tape machine, Barrow leaned back in the leather chair, put his hands behind his head, and said, "Sorry, Joe. We can't use them."

How did I know that was coming.

"You've got to be shitting me, Herman," I said.

"I wish I were, Joe."

"Jesus Christ. What sort of horseshit ruling you going to throw at me now?"

"The latest one."

"Here we go."

"Blame the Supreme Judicial Court for this one. They've put a restriction on taped conversations recorded surreptitiously. No secretly tape-recorded conversations without a warrant. Pure and simple. Anything else is an unconstitutional invasion of privacy. The SJC says that unlawful surveillance techniques 'threaten the privacy of our most cherished possession, our thoughts and emotions.' The only exception the SJC will make is for organized crime. Even then, it'll take some doing. What it means, Joe, the next time, apply for a warrant. You'll have to submit affidavits detailing why the evidence could not be gathered without taping, how organized crime is involved and the subject matter of the proposed conversation."

"Wonderful. What if it isn't organized crime?"

"Then I can't help you."

"Swell."

Absently, I picked up the tapes and put them back in the box. "So, Herman. What you're telling me is, I can take all of this and shove it up my ass, right?"

The DA smiled. "Something like that, Joe. But try not to hurt yourself."

"Too late."

"Why don't you let the Feds have him?" Charlie said.

"What? So he can sit around in one of those luxury fucking federal pens carving fucking furniture? No way." I picked up the box and tucked it under my arm. "O'Hara's mine. One way or another, the bastard's mine. So fuck you all."

I slammed the door on my way out.

Back at the office, I sat behind my desk listening to the wind, watching the rain, wondering where the hell everybody was.

The telephone rang. I stared at it a few seconds, then picked it up.

"Homicide," I said. "Sergeant Knight."

"Good afternoon, Sergeant Knight." It was Inspector Grayson from Interpol. "Or should I say, good morning?"

I leaned forward, my elbows on the desk. "Inspector. Thanks for the call. You got something for me?"

"I do. However, I am not sure it is what you want to hear, old man."

"You arrested O'Hara."

"On the contrary, Sergeant. We saw no reason to arrest him."

"What?"

"Mister O'Hara gave us no cause."

"What do you mean, no cause? Didn't you follow him?"

"We did."

"He passed on the money didn't he?"

"No, he did not."

"What about his suitcases? The money was in his suitcases."

"Our people searched his hotel room at the Strand Palace Hotel. They found nothing. In fact, O'Hara met with no one. Made no phone calls. Instead, he visited London as any American tourist would. Buckingham Palace. Tower Bridge. The Houses of Parliament. Westminster Abbey. Each time he would return to the hotel, dine and retire for the night."

"You sure you tailed the right guy?"

Silence.

"Of course," the Inspector said.

"What about that white-faced guy I told you about?"

"We never saw him."

"What?"

"No one fitting his description left the plane."

"He got off the plane alright — only you didn't see him."

After some silence I said to the Inspector, "O'Hara had the money with him. You can bet your ass on that. What about customs? Didn't they check his bags?"

"No. We asked them not to. They cooperated."

"When your people searched his bags in the hotel, did they look for a phony compartment?"

"We are not amateurs, Sergeant Knight."

"I know that. But even pros can overlook the obvious sometimes."

"I assure you we didn't."

"Then he must have switched bags."

"How? Our people watched him from the moment he exited the plane and baggage claim. There is no possible way he could have switched bags."

"Then he had a connection in baggage claim. Someone from the IRA waiting with the same kind of bags. Whoever it was switched bags and took off with the money."

"I suppose that is possible, Sergeant," the Inspector said.

"Don't suppose, Inspector. Bet your ass on it. Where's O'Hara now?"

"At Heathrow, booked on a flight back to the United States. British Airways flight fifty-three, arriving Boston at four forty-five in the afternoon, your time."

I checked my watch: 11:15 am.

"Thanks for the help, Inspector," I said. "Sorry to bother you."

"Perhaps another time," the Inspector said.

"Yeah."

After a few seconds of silence, the Inspector said, "Be careful, Sergeant Knight."

I didn't like the sound of that. "What do you mean, be careful," I said. "You trying to tell me something, Inspector?"

Again silence. I didn't like that either.

"Goodbye, Sergeant," the Inspector said.

The line went dead.

I hung up the receiver, picked it up again, and called downstairs to the desk sergeant.

"Jimmy. It's Joe. Where the hell are all my people?"

"Wait a minute," Jimmy said. "Tommy left a message." I heard some papers rustling. Then, "Here it is. He says they're going to a warehouse in Charlestown. Down near the Mystic Wharf someplace. Something about hitting a drug factory. He took Jake and Warren with him. Says here he'll call if they get lucky."

"That it?"

"That's it, Joe."

"Thanks, Jimmy. What about O'Keefe?"

"He went with them."

Sonuvabitch. Will wonders ever cease.

At Logan I stood by the window on the upper level of the international terminal and watched British Airways flight fifty-three taxi across the enormous field of concrete. I craned my neck and looked down. The state troopers were in position, keeping well out of sight. I could only see the boots of one and the cap of a second. There were at least five more waiting further down the ramp.

Earlier I had stopped at the state police desk and talked with an old friend of mine, Lieutenant Bob Short who used to be in charge of homicide investigations at the Middlesex County DA's office in Cambridge until his transfer to

Massport two months ago. I told Bob I needed some troopers to keep an eye on a ramp. It was possible the white-faced guy I wanted apprehended might try to escape customs. Bob had said that was impossible, but he'd humor me anyway.

As the 747 taxied to the ramp, I went downstairs and found a seat opposite the double doors where the passengers came through after clearing customs. A large noisy crowd had gathered to greet relatives and friends. I looked at the faces. As usual, my mind slipped into the game of finding the ugliest one. It didn't take long. A toothless woman of about twenty-five with long straight black hair, thick glasses, and more craters in her skin than the moon turned around and looked my way. She was barefoot, saggy breasted and bra-less under a stained green T-shirt. When she walked, her filthy dark toes darted from under soiled army fatigues.

Sonuvabitch.

Bringing the newspaper up to my face, I kept my eyes on the passengers straggling three and four at a time through the doors, listening to the excited screams of people being reunited. Each time the doors swung open I could see into the customs area. No sign of O'Hara, or White Face.

For the zillionth time I looked around wondering who else was there waiting. I didn't notice anyone looking like CIA, but then again, what do they look like? For all I know, crater-face could be one of them. God help us.

Ten minutes later, O'Hara came through the doors.

I tensed as I watched him weave his way through the thinning crowd, carrying the same two bags he left with, heading toward the automated doors and the street.

My eyes darted back to the doorway. No sign of White Face.

It was time to make my move. I had my hand gripped to my .38 and was about to pull it out and make the arrest when someone else caught my eye. A woman in her late thirties, with long dark hair, stylishly cut, framing a face bronzed by the sun, walking slowly, pulling a suitcase toward the exit.

There was something about her that made me take a second and third look. Maybe it was her eyes — the way they surveyed everything.

She was a tall woman, statuesque, her figure tapered, the swell of her breasts accentuated by the sheer, close-fitting fabric of a long white dress that heightened the tan of her skin.

I let her go by, took a last look at the doors for White Face, then walked down the wall of glass to the last exit. Call it instinct, I don't know. But I had to let O'Hara go.

I turned away, wondering if he'd seen me. He hadn't.

From where I stood with my face against the glass, I could see O'Hara in line for a cab, the tall woman a couple of people behind him, paying O'Hara more than casual attention.

Traffic was a nightmare. Cars triple-parked, people rushing, cramming a zillion bags into trunks and back seats. Car rental buses were stacked three deep and trying to squeeze closer to the curb. There were few cabs. The ones that managed to snake through the madness were already taken. O'Hara whistled and waved at all of them with no luck. He was starting to boil. I could tell by the way he tugged at his leather driving gloves, slipping his fingers together and jabbing them like some spastic.

Behind him, the woman put on sunglasses and waited patiently.

I looked left down the terminal. Three of the troopers who had been watching the ramp were making their way through the crowd, looking for me. One of the troopers was Walter Buttner, a barrel-chested guy with more muscles than Hulk Hogan. Walter was the most laid-back guy I ever met, so when I saw the expression on his face, I knew it was bad news. I waved him over anyway.

"Joe," he said, his voice tight. "That guy you was looking for. The white-faced guy with blonde hair and funny looking eyes?"

"Yeah?" I said, noncommittal.

"Hate to break it to you," Walter said, "but a flight attendant just found him on the floor in the back of the plane with a bullet in his head.''

It was quarter to six when I cleared the airport.

White Face was dead alright — shot once in the back of the head with a small caliber bullet, maybe a .25mm. Whoever shot him had gotten close, real close. The British passport he carried said his name was Martin Fox. He had a London address. The troopers also found a wallet with a thousand dollars in cash in it, but nothing else. No other identification. They also found a Baretta M/84 .380 caliber pistol, fully loaded, in the crotch of his pants below a thick, metal belt buckle which he obviously had on to fool security.   I called Tommy, told him what had happened, and sent him to O'Hara's apartment. I told him about the woman — said it was possible she was following O'Hara.

It took the usual half hour to squeeze my way through the tunnel. I met Tommy at ten minutes to seven. Brought him some coffee and three cinnamon doughnuts.

''It's about time,'' he said, as I got in. ''What happened over there? You fuck up again?''

''Kiss my ass,'' I said. ''O'Hara show yet?''

''Nope.''

''Shit!''

''You should have nailed him when you had the chance. You had an army of troopers with you for Chrissakes. How could you miss?''

''Give me a break, alright? I'm not in the mood.''

I looked up and down the street. Just some kids on bikes. An old lady pushing a kid in a stroller

''Did I tell you I went to see the DA this morning?'' I said.

Tommy looked at me. ''No, you didn't.''

''Well, guess what? Your fucking tapes are no good. Not admissible as evidence in a court of law according to the SJC.''

''You're shitting me?''

''That's what I said.''

''Now what?''

I looked toward the house. "Simple. He comes back, we nail him," I said.

"Then shoot the prick between the eyes," Tommy said.

I smiled. "Something like that," I said.

We were silent for a few minutes.

"By the way," I said. "What about this horseshit drug factory bust you went on this afternoon in Charlestown?"

"Thought you'd never ask," Tommy said, biting the tip off another cigar. "O'Keefe got a tip. I was on another phone listening in. Should have seen his face when the guy mentioned the plant belonged to O'Hara. Thought O'Keefe was going to jump out of his skin. The caller had a high, squeaky voice. Tried to make himself sound like some cartoon character — something like that."

"Sounds familiar."

"What do you mean?"

"Sounds like the same voice that tipped me where to find Styles."

"You didn't tell me that?"

"I don't have to tell you everything, do I?"

"No, you don't, but you usually do."

I yawned and stretched. "Looks like someone's trying to help us out, Tommy," I said.

"I wouldn't look a gift horse up the ass, Joe."

"I'm not. But I can't help feeling someone's trying to hand us peanuts while he's running away with the elephants."

Tommy closed his eyes and sat back. "Anything's possible," he said.

"What did you find in the warehouse?" I said.

Tommy grinned. "One hundred kilos of eighty percent pure cocaine," he said. "Give or take a few ounces. Made seventeen arrests — most of them Columbians. When we busted down the door, we found them shoving the coke inside those stupid looking stuffed gorillas O'Hara keeps handing out. Warren and Jake have got some of the Columbians singing their asses off already. By the looks of it, we hit O'Hara hard. Who knows — we might have put him out of business completely."

"Maybe."

"What do you mean, maybe?"

"Just what I said. Maybe O'Hara doesn't give a shit anymore. He's dumb but he's not stupid. He knows the heat is on. He's made all the money he can make now. We know he didn't take all the cash with him to London. So maybe he came back for the rest of it — booked himself on a flight back to London and there you go. He disappears. Clean as a whistle back home to Northern Ireland."

Tommy shrugged. "Save us the trouble of putting a bullet through his skull, wouldn't it?"

I didn't say anything.

Tommy let his unlit cigar dance between his hairy lips. I couldn't watch.

"Wait 'til the drug boys downtown find out we pulled that raid without them," Tommy said, wiping saliva from his lips with the back of his hand. "Will they ever be bullshit."

"We'll hear about it I'm sure," I said.

Silence again.

Then I said, "Wonder what the street value of one hundred kilos of coke is?"

"I don't know," Tommy said. "Four, maybe five million. Give or take."

"Holy shit."

"Aren't you going to say nice work, Tommy?"

"Nice work, Tommy."

"Thank you. Of course we have to give O'Keefe some of the credit."

"Why?"

"At least he had brains enough not to hang up the phone."

"Wonderful. I'll be sure to call the commissioner and tell him."

"That would be nice."

We watched O'Hara's apartment for four more hours. He never showed.

20

Back at the office, I got a call from Rita Barns. She told me the file I had asked for on Manfred Styles had come up from New York City. It was on the way over to me via Mickey the Finn Douglas.

Mickey the Finn Douglas was a vice cop out of Area A downtown. We'd worked together a few years back in the Combat Zone, the time some sicko was going around slicing hookers' vaginas. When we finally nailed him, he was in the backseat of a car on LaGrange Street, getting ready to play doctor again. Three days after his arraignment, the guy hung himself in the Charles Street Jail. He'd turned out to be an accountant from Duxbury, a gentrified affluent town on the South Shore, twenty-five minutes out of Boston. Big house. Fancy car. Good looking wife and two kids.

Mickey the Finn bullshitted with me and Tommy a while, drank some coffee, then left. We had given him the name Mickey the Finn not because he was a zillion feet tall, with more muscles than the Incredible Hulk and could knock out an elephant with a quick jab, but simply because he was a big stupid Finn whose parents had immigrated from Finland. Made sense to me.

I got some more coffee and opened Styles' folder.

Everything I read confirmed what Cole — Morris — had told me the night he was shot. Ex-New York City cop indicted on drug charges. Prime suspect in four drug-related murders in Manhattan. That was page one. I skipped over the part about his personal life, and went on to page two.

Page two said Styles was an expert marksman. He'd won the New York City police pistol sharpshooter competition three consecutive years, the state championship twice, and was fifth in the '86 nationals.

Shit. I had to scramble like hell just to qualify for the annual Boston Police Patrolmen's Turkey Shoot on Moon Island in with a shotgun no less.

What surprised me was page three: Styles had been awarded the city's Legion of Merit in 1986 for bravery; saved two young boys from drowning in a pond in Central Park — jumped through thin ice in the middle of January without regard for his own safety. In '85 he received a mayor's commendation for single-handedly preventing a bank holdup.

Christ, how does it figure?

I went back to page one. Stapled to the bottom of the police report were some 4 × 5 black and white photographs of Styles' alleged victims taken at the scene. The photos of the couple — the ones reported to have been dealing drugs — were disgusting. The woman's face was mutilated. The man's eyes gouged out. Blood everywhere. Madness. Absolute madness.

I flipped to the photos of the two men the police report had listed as innocent victims. Timothy O'Grady and James Michael Patrick. Both had been shot once — O'Grady in the forehead, Patrick in the right temple.

Something bothered me. One of those pain-in-the-ass details that gets caught between your brain cells sometimes — put there just to piss you off. I studied the photo of Timothy O'Grady. Something about the face. The beard, the hair. The eyes — wide open and dead.

Letting go of the photo, I looked for the name of the cop who investigated the homicides. His name was Scavonni. Detective Lieutenant Anthony Scavonni. NYPD. Manhattan.

I called New York. Detective Americas Sinqtrigrana of homicide told me Scavonni was out of the office investigating the murder of a priest. I left my name and telephone number, told Detective Americas it had to do with Manfred Styles, and to have Scavonni call me back, ASAP.

Scavonni did, an hour and half later.

"Sergeant Knight?" he said. "Lieutenant Tony Scavonni.

How yah do'n?''

Scavonni's accent was New York City alright. Christ. And they say Bostonians talk funny.

"Thanks for returning my call, Lieutenant," I said.

"No problem," Scavonni said. "I was gonna call yah when I heard yah nailed the Frog Man."

"Frog Man?"

"Styles."

"Why Frog Man?"

"That's the name everybody called 'im in the Bronx 'cause he always had his head up his ass."

"Sounds reasonable."

"Sorry it took me so long to get back to you," Scavonni said. "A priest got hit last night. Right in the fucking confessional booth. Shot twice in the side of the head — mob style. No witnesses. No one even heard the gunshots." He paused, then went on. "The killer left a note. I got it here someplace. Here it is — listen to this. 'May the worms of mother Ireland crawl through the bastard's bullet holes.' Scavonni let out a nervous laugh. "Think maybe someone got bullshit about the penance he was given? Too many Our Fathers and Hail Marys — yah know what I mean?"

I did, but I wasn't in the mood for sick humor. Scavonni obviously got the message by my silence. He quickly changed the subject.

"So you nailed Styles?" he said. "Nice go'n. We've been try'n to do that for years. Too bad you didn't blow his fuck'n head off, though."

"Yeah. Too bad. I've got his file in front of me. What can you tell me about two of his victims? Timothy O'Grady and James Patrick?"

"Alleged victims."

"Whatever."

"What do you want to know?"

"Your report said they were innocent victims."

Scavonni laughed. "Had to put something down in the report."

"Did you ever run a check on them?"

"Course I ran a check on 'em. Fuck you think?"

I wanted to tell him but thought better of it.

Scavonni said, "Why do yah wanna know about O'Grady and Patrick?"

"Just grabbing at some straws," I said. "You know how that goes."

Scavonni laughed again. "Do that every day down here," he said. "Only when I draw my arm back and open my hand, I seem to have someth'n a little more browner than hay in it."

That made me chuckle.

"Hold on a second," Scavonni said.

I heard a metal file cabinet rattle open, the rustle of some papers. A couple of seconds later, Scavonni came back on the line and said, "Patrick was liv'n in the apartment next door to the Mitchells'. He was a runner in the diamond district. You know. One of those guys that carries wholesale jewelry from one store to another. According to neighbors, O'Grady was a cousin. Came for a visit a couple of weeks earlier. Way we saw it, O'Grady and Patrick must have heard the gunshots and went out in the hall to investigate. That's when they got it."

I flipped through the photos again. "Almost looks like there were two different killers," I said. "Know what I mean?"

"Yeah," Scavonni said. "I thought the same thing. A sicko and a pro. But Styles was both. Good with a knife and a gun."

"Where was O'Grady from?" I said.

"His passport said Ireland."

"Where in Ireland?"

"I don't remember offhand. I'd have to check."

"What about the priest?"

"What about him?"

"What was his name?"

"Father Edward Coogan, why?"

"Where was he from?"

"Brooklyn."

"Before Brooklyn."

Scavonni fell silent. Again I heard the rustle of some papers. "Northern Ireland," Scavonni said.

I stared out the window. The clouds were pressing down on the city again, the walls in the room pressing in on me.

"Could I trouble you to send me a photo of Father Coogan?" I said.

"Why?"

"Like I said, just grabbing at straws."

Scavonni laughed. "Watch out for the brown stuff."

It was five after noon. Jake and Warren were keeping an eye on O'Hara's apartment. Tommy was on the phone placing an order for Chinese food. I had my feet up on the desk, watching another gray day go by my window.

The telephone rang.

I picked it up wishing Alexander Graham Bell had taken up plumbing.

"Joe," Jimmy Murphy said.

"Elephant Man," I said. "How's it hanging?"

"Kiss my ass."

I smiled.

Boston Police Detective Sergeant Jimmy Patrick Murphy out of Area A downtown, aka — the Elephant Man. Everybody called him that, ever since his penile implant operation a couple of years ago. Some doctors shoved these plastic rods up his ass to make his prick eight inches long, giving him the perpetual hard-on he begged for because he thought his wife was going to leave him. I nearly choked to death from laughter the day he told us how it worked. It was the "pump-a-prick" type. His wife had to tickle his balls to make it go. Once up, it stayed — forever and ever.

Some of us should be so lucky.

"You through, asshole?" Sergeant Murphy said.

"Sorry."

"Yeah, I bet you are." Murphy was silent for a couple of seconds. "Got some bad news for you, Joe."

"Wonderful. Just what I need."

278 — Fat Guys

"Your boy, Styles?"

My heartbeat quickened. "What about him?"

"He's gone, Joe."

"What?"

"He's dead."

"Jesus Christ. I thought you meant he escaped. Don't scare me like that."

"Sorry."

"What happened? He kill himself?"

"It would have been cleaner if he did. We're holding the scene for you down here. You wanna take a look or do you want me to handle it?"

I took in a long breath, then let it out slow. "You can handle it, Murph. Just send me the usual bullshit."

"You don't sound surprised about this, Joe. How come?"

"Instinct, Murph. Call it instinct. How'd he get it?"

"His throat was slit. Looks like they got him from behind. I counted twenty to thirty stab wounds to the back."

"Any suspects?"

"None."

"Witnesses?"

"Are you kidding? In here?"

"Right."

"There's some mumblings going around saying it could have been a payback by the mob for the hit Styles made on Vinnie Torchia. Could be something to that, Joe. My gut tells me the order came from outside. Someone in here set him up."

"You could be right, Murph. Keep working on it. And thanks for handling it for me. I owe you one."

"Yeah. And I won't let you forget it either."

"I know, Murph. You're that kind of guy."

He hung up.

Twenty minutes later, Tommy came back with lunch. I decided to wait until he was well into his pork chow mein before I told him what had happened to Styles.

"Someone whacked Styles at Charles Street early this morning," I said.

Tommy kept on eating. "Oh, yeah," he said, his mouth stuffed with egg roll. "He dead?"

"Yeah."

"Tough shit. We knew it was going to happen sooner or later."

I opened the carton of chicken wings and took one out.

"Not that I really give a shit," Tommy said, "but how'd he buy it?"

"Someone slit his throat."

"That's nice," Tommy said, licking his fingers.

"Stabbed him twenty or thirty times in the back," I said.

"Want some more chow mein?" Tommy said.

"No," I said.

Tommy dumped the rest of the chow mein onto his paper plate over three chicken wings, two pork strips and some fried rice.

I wasn't hungry. Not for Chinese food anyway.

"What's the matter?" Tommy said. "You mad because I wouldn't get you a pepperoni pizza?"

"No. I'm just not hungry."

"You? Not hungry? You must be sick."

"I'm not sick. There's just something bugging me, that's all."

"Styles?"

"Yeah. Styles."

"You should be happy the asshole finally got what he deserved."

"It's too soon, Tommy. Styles wasn't there long enough to make any enemies. Murphy thinks the order came from outside. He thinks Styles was set up. So do I. And it wasn't because the mob thought he iced Torchia."

Tommy dropped his fork on the plate. "Jesus Christ, Joe," he said. "Can't you ever fucking leave things the way they fall. Why do you always have to dig so fucking deep your eyeballs swim in shit all the time?"

I shrugged. "So that's why they're brown?"

Tommy picked up his fork. "Asshole," he mumbled, continuing to stuff his face, dripping pieces of egg roll on his beard.

I looked out the window again. The flag on top of the firehouse across the street was straight out and flapping in the wind. To the right, the only patch of blue sky I'd seen in days was disappearing to the east. Coming at us out of the west was more gray doom. Fucking rain. I'll be glad when it snows. At least it will be something different to bitch about.

"Now if you really want a puzzle to solve," Tommy said, making short work of a pork strip. "There's something that's been bugging me for years."

"What's that, Tommy?" I said.

"How come a thermos jug knows whether to keep something hot or cold?"

"What?"

"You put something cold in a thermos jug — it stays cold, right?"

"I suppose."

"You put something hot in it — it stays hot."

"Sounds reasonable."

"There you are. How does the thermos jug know what you just put in it is hot or cold? How does it know what to do? Keep it hot or keep it cold? Got to be one of life's more complicated questions."

"Why don't I check you into Mass Mental. Maybe someone up there has the answer."

"Maybe. Pass me the sweet and sour."

I walked into the bedroom at quarter past eleven, kicked off my shoes, and unbottoned my shirt. Victoria spun her head off the pillow and sat up.

"Who are you?" she said, pretending to be startled.

"Don't get cute," I said.

"Get out of this bedroom right now. I have a husband — he has a gun."

I let my pants slip down my legs. "A long, powerful gun, you hastened to add."

"Is that right? Show me."

I slid down my undershorts.

"Oh, my," Victoria said, extending her arms. "To hell with my husband. He's never home this early anyway. Come to me, big boy."

I did. Jumping on her like the animal I was.

She turned partially away from me and brought her right hand to her throat. In one move she tore her nightgown away. Our flesh met.

Her breasts were soft and sloping, the nipples taut awakened.

My mouth roamed over her skin.

We kissed, and hugged, and touched, and caressed, and kissed again.

Everything was wonderful again.

Spent, I rolled onto my back, exhausted.

"That was nice," Victoria said.

"Yes, it was," I said. "By the way, how are your husband's children?"

"Fine. Except they both hate being back in school. They really enjoyed the summer."

"I'm glad someone did. The Sox in town this weekend?"

"Those bums? Yes, they're back."

"Maybe Jeff might like to go."

"What about me?"

"Okay. But promise me you won't be a jerk like the last time."

"I wasn't being a jerk. Rice is a bum. An overpaid, under-talented, worse-than-mediocre bum. I was just letting him know it."

"I'm sorry I mentioned it."

"So am I. Now I won't be able to sleep thinking about it. Imagine, here it is the middle of September and they're fifteen games back. Out of it. And after such a great season last year. I can't understand it."

"Like you said, hon. They're bums."

"I guess."

Silence.

"When I heard you come in," Victoria said, "I thought

something was wrong with the clock."

I stared at the shadows dancing across the ceiling. "Want me to go out again?" I said.

Victoria clutched my arm. "No way," she said. "I love having you home early. I was just wondering why, that's all."

"Why what?"

"Why you're home so early. Things not going very well?"

"You could say that."

"What about O'Hara?"

"What about him?"

"Have you made up your mind what to do?"

"I think someone's trying to make up my mind for me."

"What do you mean?"

"I don't know what I mean."

"From what you've told me, you've got enough evidence to arrest him. Why don't you?"

"I would if I could find him?"

"He take to the wind on you?"

I looked at her and smiled. "Take to the wind?"

"You know. Blow town. Fly away. Screw."

"I think you've been hanging around too many cops, lady."

"Funny. That's what my mother said to me today."

"Oh, God, no. Your mother?"

"Don't worry. She's not staying for long this time."

I lost my smile. "What? She's staying here again?"

"Only for a couple of days. She's having her house painted. You know how she hates the smell of paint."

"Of course."

"Don't be mean, Joseph. She said she was going to make you a nice breakfast."

"Not like the last time I hope? Eggs were so damn hard, I had to cut them with a hacksaw."

Disgusted, I rolled onto my side.

Victoria rubbed her fingers gently across the back of my head. After a few moments of silence, she said, "Poor baby. How's your head?"

"Still there, I think. I'm not too sure these days."

"Come on, babe. It can't be as bad as all that. You've had worse problems to solve. O'Hara was a friend I know. But you can't let that interfere with what you have to do."

"I'm not. I just can't seem to put it all together. Christ. Nothing's ever simple anymore. Bodies are dropping faster than we can sweep them up. Did you know someone clipped Styles this morning?"

"Yes. I saw it on the news before I went to bed."

"Sliced him up like a Christmas pie. Murphy thinks it was a revenge job by the mob."

"Was it?"

"No. Vinnie Torchia was a giant ugly wart on the mob's proverbial ass. Tried to make a name for himself ever since the Angellinis went up river. O'Hara was selling him drugs. Nothing more than that."

"Who do you think killed Styles?"

"I don't know. But someone obviously wanted to shut him up."

"I thought he talked to you?"

"He did, but he didn't say anything. Not really. Someone made sure he wouldn't again."

"What are you going to do now?"

"I don't know. Go to the commissioner I guess. Tell him what I got. Throw everything in his lap. Let him deal with the whole fucking mess."

"Joseph!"

"Sorry."

"You should be."

"I'm tired, hon, okay?" I said. "Can we get some sleep."

Victoria's fingertips continued across the back of my head. It felt great.

"Thanks, Doctor Freud," I said. "You're great therapy for me, as always."

"You're welcome," Victoria said. "Anything else on your mind I can help you with, you let me know?"

My head sank deep into the pillow.

"There is one thing," I said, drifting.

"What's that?"

"What do you know about thermos jugs?"

We sat in silence in front of the commissioner's desk, Lieutenant O'Keefe to my right, Tommy to my left.

The commissioner closed the yellow folder I had given him along with the audio and video tapes, took off his glasses and dropped them on the desk.

"This is incredible, Knight," the commissioner said, rubbing his eyes. "Why did you wait so long to come to me with it?"

I shrugged.

The commissioner leaned back in his leather chair and looked at the ceiling, thinking everything through. "Who else knows about all of this?" he said.

"Us four," I said. "And Detectives Jake Callahan and Warren Dolan."

"What about the photographer who shot these tapes?"

"Bobby Dunn? All he knows, O'Hara is a suspect in a murder case. Nothing else."

"You trust him?"

"I wouldn't have taken him on the surveillance if I didn't."

"Good. When the time comes, we could use some good press for a change."

"I'll make sure to call him."

The commissioner put his glasses back on. "I'll give all of this a closer look," he said. "You keep looking for O'Hara. You find him, arrest him. I don't care how you do it. Just get him."

"We'll do what we can," I said. "We've got the airport under surveillance. I've talked to Interpol. They're watching Heathrow and Gatwick. And Shannon, in Ireland."

"What about his girlfriend?"

"Like I said, commissioner. She's among the missing."

"Maybe they took off together," Lieutenant O'Keefe said to me.

I looked at him. "Anything's possible," I said. "But I

doubt it.''

The next morning, shortly after nine, what I had guessed all along became fact.

"That broad you were looking for, Joe?" Detective Boots Mallon said over the phone. "Sherry Condon?"

I leaned forward, my elbows on the desk. "You find her for me, Boots?" I said.

"You could say that."

"Where?"

"In Charlestown," Boots said. "Off Chelsea Street under the Tobin Bridge. Hurry it up, Joe. It's wet out here."

"She dead, Boots?"

"As a fucking proverbial doornail, Joe."

It took us about twenty minutes to get to Charlestown. As I walked towards him, Boots Mallon said, "This is not a pretty sight, Joe." He was right.

It was the flesh of the exposed parts of Sherry Condon's body that made me swallow in revulsion. There were cigarette burns — little round charred circles — running in a line down from the small red nipple of her right breast, across the flat of her stomach, to her pelvic area.

I held my breath and knelt down in the tall grass. Behind Sherry's left ear was a small bullet hole, crusted over with dried blood.

"Had to be one sick bastard who did that, Joe," Boots said over my shoulder.

I straightened and looked at Tommy. He was breathing through his mouth like I was.

"She's certainly ripe," Boots went on. "ME says she's been here a couple of days — maybe three. Says the bullet put her out of her misery. Small caliber, possibly a .25mm. Shot at close range — maybe two to three inches from the head."

"Who found her?"

"Some kids from the Bunker Hill Project noticed the stink and decided to investigate. They said they found her like you see her. Even turned over her purse."

"In Charlestown?" Tommy said. "That's a switch."

"I know," Boots said, rain dripping from the visor of his red baseball cap. "Couldn't believe it myself. Not all the kids in Charlestown are assholes."

"They touch anything?" I said.

"Doubt it," Boots said. "They were too busy puking."

"How about your people?"

"C'mon, Joe. Who the hell you think you're dealing with? What you see is what you got, pal."

"What was in the purse?"

"Usual female shit. Makeup, lipstick, wallet, keys."

"Where is it? I want to take a look."

"In my car. I'll get it."

I switched my gaze back to the corpse.

"I don't see any signs of a struggle," Tommy said to me. "Looks like she was dumped."

I nodded my agreement.

Partially clothed, Sherry stared straight up at me, eyes attentive, mouth agape. In the wet grass, her twisted body looked like something dredged from a cold, wet hell. I shuddered.

"Whoever did this had to be one sadistic son-of-a-bitch," Tommy said, staring down.

"Know what I think, Tommy?"

"No, Joe. What do you think?"

"I think who ever did this was there that night."

"There where what night?"

"At O'Hara's apartment — the night we were going to break in — the night we talked to her."

"What do you mean they were there?"

"I could see it in her eyes. Whoever was there was hiding somewhere — must have told her to let us in. We would have come back if she didn't. They were there all the time — watching us."

Tommy kept his eyes on the corpse. "You think it was O'Hara who did this?"

"No. He's a lot of things maybe, but he'd never do this. I'm sure of that."

"You said the same thing about him dealing drugs."

"That's different."

Boots came back with the purse and handed it to me. I searched it and found nothing.

Handing it back to Boots, I stepped aside as the vultures from the ME's office moved in with a green rubber bag and spread it out next to Sherry.

Boots said he had some paperwork to complete and took off.

Tommy nudged me in the side. "You coming?" he said, turning toward the car.

I watched the vultures stuff the remaining strands of Sherry's once bright and soft red hair into the bag. "O'Hara's in trouble, Tommy," I said.

"No shit."

"No. I mean it. He might even be dead."

"Good. Case closed. End of story."

The bag was zipped up, Sherry's body placed on a litter, and carried through the tall grass to a white and blue van.

We walked back to the car in the steady drizzle. I stopped and watched the van pull away.

"Hate to be the one to piss on your parade, Tommy," I said. "If O'Hara is dead — and my gut tells me he is — who killed him? Who killed Sherry Condon? And that Albino at the airport? What about Vinnie Torchia? And Samuel Morris? Who killed them? It wasn't Styles. He would have told us. What did he have to lose? He admitted killing Howell, West and the Edwards brothers. What's two more? No. It wasn't Styles. Somebody else."

Tommy opened the door and got in behind the wheel. Rolling down the window, he coughed up a lunger and spit it out. Christ.

I slumped into the passenger side, exhausted.

"Get me back to the office," I said, closing the door. "I've got to call Sherry's parents in Connecticut."

"Better you than me. All that crying and wailing gives me the creeps."

"I'm surprised it bothers you, seeing how you've got the

288 — *Fat Guys*

sensitivity of a bull moose in heat.''

Tommy smiled. ''What are you talking about? I like cats.''

''You like pussy.''

''That too.''

A couple of minutes later, we were heading over the Charlestown Bridge. Going by Polcari's restaurant, I said, ''Want to know what I've been kicking around?''

Tommy looked at me, his cigar dancing between his hairy lips. ''No,'' he said.

I watched the wipers slap across the windshield. ''I got a hunch O'Hara isn't who he's supposed to be,'' I said.

Tommy's cigar quit dancing. ''What the hell does that mean?'' he said, frowning.

''It means that O'Hara might not be his real name.''

''Fuck me. Here we go again.''

21

I called state police headquarters and talked to Colonel Pasely's secretary. She said the Colonel was in but wasn't taking any calls — he was in a meeting with the Public Safety Director.

I said it was urgent. I told her to go in the meeting and whisper the words Operation Iron Hammer in Pasely's ear and see what happens.

It didn't take long.

"Colonel Pasely," he said, anxious.

I told him who I was.

"What do you want, Knight?" Pasely said.

"Some answers."

"I don't have any."

"I think you do."

"I don't give a shit what you think, Knight."

"What do you know about Operation Iron Hammer?"

"I never heard of it."

"Don't bullshit me, Colonel. I'm tired of the games. I've been shot at, whacked over the head, threatened. I've got bodies falling around me like fucking flies." I took in a breath to keep the blood from exploding my face. "You got five seconds to start talking, Colonel. Or the next call I make is to the press. I'm not bullshitting."

Silence. About ten seconds worth. Then, "Alright," Pasely said. "But not over the phone."

"Where then?" I said.

"You pick it. Someplace quiet."

"How about Franklin Park — across from the golf course?"

"Fine. Give me an hour."

"I'll be in a black Buick in the parking lot down from the zoo. Don't stiff me, Colonel. I'm out of patience."

"I'll be there. Don't worry."

Through the spray of mist hitting my windshield, I watched three black guys with golf bags slung over their shoulders trudge down the fairway. One of them popped open a bright red and white umbrella and headed toward the road which separated the golf course from the Franklin Park Zoo.

Watching the guy pick up his golf ball from the gutter and drop it in the fairway, I couldn't help thinking what a fool he was. Hitting a little white ball around in the rain — chasing it, losing it, finding it, hitting it again, then losing the sonuvabitch again.

Despite the absurdity of it all, the guy looked happy — out in the fresh air, taking a mindless stroll with his friends, maybe suck down a couple of beers after the round.

Sitting behind the wheel, I wondered when it was I had relaxed and enjoyed anything like that. Think the last time was on vacation, which seemed a zillion years ago. Jeff and I went fishing on the *Captain John* out of Plymouth Harbor. Jeff had caught a big one — a five pound Cod. I caught five Miller Lite's, three hot dogs, two Snickers bars, and a giant dose of sea sickness. Worse than I got at Lincoln Amusement Park in Dighton, when Jessica dragged me on the tilt-a-whirl after I ate two slices of pepperoni pizza. Fatherhood. Nothing like it.

I leaned forward, turned on the radio to WCRB FM, sat back and closed my eyes and let Beethoven's 1805 *Piano Concerto No. 4 in G Major* slip softly through my brain.

Half way through Brahms' *Symphony No. 2 in D Major,* I heard the sound of a car approaching. Gravel crunched beneath wheels. I opened my eyes and looked around. I ducked in time to avoid the shards of flying glass, and the sickening thuds of spraying bullets slapping into the door.

"What a fucking mess," Tommy said, shaking his head,

walking slowly around the Buick, sticking his little finger into one of the zillion bullet holes in the door.

Lieutenant O'Keefe and the commissioner had already come and gone, so had the zillion police cruisers, ambulances, and news maggots.

Commissioner Roberts had been genuinely concerned. He didn't like anyone shooting up his police cars, or his cops. Before he left, he told me the department was behind me a hundred percent. Do what you have to do, but find out who's responsible.

"How the hell did you ever get out without being hit?" Tommy said, peering inside the car.

I gazed at Marty the lab man, digging out a slug in the frame above the door. "Wasn't easy," I said, still a little shaken, my clothes wet from the rain and sweat, sticking to me like fly paper.

A flash of the car went across my mind's eye. Everything had happened so fast. The Firebird — candy apple red. The two figures dressed in black. Spits of light from the barrel of what looked like an Uzi 9mm.

"I've got Jake and Warren watching your house," Tommy said. "And don't give me any shit about it either."

"Thanks, Tommy. I appreciate it," I said.

I moved to the side of the Buick, knelt down and examined the bullet holes. None of them fell below the window line.

I breathed in deep, then let some air slip between my teeth in a quiet hiss, "Someone's playing games with me, Tommy," I said, running my fingertips over the holes. "Look at the pattern. It's tight. Whoever did the shooting either had a bad fucking sight problem, or was a damn good marksman. My guess it wasn't no sight problem."

"Here we go again," Tommy said, biting off and spitting out the end of a cigar.

I stuck my head through the window and picked some fragments of glass from the back of the seat. Backing out of the window, I looked at my partner. "It was a warning, Tommy," I said. "They were waiting for me to look at them.

They were giving me time to react.''

Tommy shook his head, jammed the cigar between his lips and flamed it. Smoke billowed around him. ''Okay, Mister Paranoia,'' he said. ''What now?''

''I go home and change clothes,'' I said. ''Then we go to state police headquarters and have a talk with that fucking scumbag, Pasely.''

As we suspected, Colonel Pasely wasn't in his office.

''Where is he?'' I said to his civilian secretary, a plain looking woman with dark hair framing a pale-skinned face and no lipstick who said her name was Mrs. Fisher.

''He left an hour ago,'' Mrs. Fisher said.

''Left for where?'' Tommy said.

''He didn't say.''

''What's his home address?'' I said.

''I'm sorry,'' Mrs. Fisher said. ''I cannot give out that information without the Colonel's permission.''

''What's his home phone number then?'' Tommy said. ''We'll call him and get it.''

''I cannot give that out either.''

''Then you call him.''

Mrs. Fisher didn't say anything.

I went around behind her and leaned down. ''Look, Mrs. Fisher. I want that home address. Are you going to give it to us or does my partner here have to whip out his prick and piss on your desk.''

''Hey!'' The voice came from across the room. ''Who the hell are you talking to like that?''

We turned around.

The biggest uniformed trooper I ever saw was standing in the doorway, his fingers wrapped around the handle of a giant .357 magnum.

I held up my badge.

''I don't care who you are Mister,'' the trooper said. ''You don't come in here and talk to a woman like that. Or anyone else in here for that matter. You heard the lady. No addresses or phone numbers are to be given out to anyone

for any reason. Now if you two alleged police officers are
smart — and I think you are — you'll back off real slow
and get the hell out of here right now while you can still
walk.''

Tommy looked at me. "So much for state police hos-
pitality. Thought these people were your pals?''

I shrugged and didn't say anything.

Coming up the hall behind the trooper, I saw a familiar
face. It was Lieutenant Kneffly.

Approaching the trooper, Kneffly put his hand on the
giant's back and said, "It's okay, Gerry. I'll handle it.''

The trooper turned. "You sure, lieutenant? I can stand
by?''

"It won't be necessary,'' Kneffly said. I could see the
panic. It was in his voice; in his eyes. He did his best to
hide it but it was neon. "Wait outside. I'll call if I need you.''

Reluctantly, the trooper backed out of the room, but not
before he shot me and Tommy some menacing glares.

"Mrs. Fisher,'' Kneffly said. "Why don't you get some
coffee? I'll take care of this.''

Without comment, Mrs. Fisher got up, straightened her
plain blue dress, shot us some cool glares of her own, then
left.

Kneffly made sure the door was locked before he went
back behind the desk and sat down.

"Jesus Christ, Joe,'' he said. "I heard what happened to
you on the news. You were one lucky bastard.''

I placed my hands palm down on the desk. "Don't hand
me that shit, Bobby,'' I said. "Where's your fucking boss?''

"Joe,'' Kneffly said, keeping his voice quieter than mine.
"I know what you're thinking — ''

"No you don't, Bobby. If you did, you'd get up right now
and draw your gun to keep me from putting a hole between
your fuckin eyes.''

A nervous smile pursed his lips. "C'mon, Joe. I'm your
friend for Chrissakes. You don't have to talk to me like
that.''

"Okay. We're friends. So tell me what the fuck's going

on. Where's Pasely?''

"He went out somewhere. He didn't say where.''

"I want his home address, Bobby. Give it to me.''

Kneffly looked away briefly. "Alright,'' he said, "but promise you won't do anything stupid.''

"Too late, Bobby. I've gone past stupid. I'm all the way into fucking insanity. Give me the address.''

Kneffly drew a pad and pencil toward him, wrote down Pasely's address and phone number, tore off the piece of paper and handed it to me. I looked at it briefly then stuffed it in my leather jacket pocket.

"Think he's there now?'' I said.

"I don't know,'' Kneffly said.

"We leave here, Bobby, you make sure that broad out there doesn't drop a dime on him. Understand?''

"I'll make sure.''

"Tell me something,'' I said. "Why would the CIA involve the state police in one of their horseshit operations?''

"I don't know,'' Kneffly said. "It's never happened before. At least not to my knowledge anyway.''

"Why now?''

"Jesus Christ, Joe. How many times do I have to tell you? I don't know. Who the hell knows anything about the CIA? Pasely's the only one who's had contact with them. Ask him.''

"We will,'' Tommy said.

"Where did Pasely come from?'' I said. "What's his background?''

"The military,'' Kneffly said. "The army.''

"What was his job in the army?''

"I don't know. He never talked about it much. All I know is he retired in October of '86. Worked on the governor's campaign staff the last election. Came to us the spring of '87 as head of the state police — by appointment of the governor.''

After a few seconds of silence, Kneffly said. "Joe. You've got to believe me when I tell you I don't know anything about this Operation Iron Hammer. The orders came down from Pasely. All I did was carry them out."

"Like the good little soldier you've always been."

"That's right. I follow orders. Something you've never done."

"That's not true. Ask my wife."

"Anyone ever tell you you're a giant pain in the ass?"

I smiled. "Everyday," I said.

Colonel Richard Pasely lived in a large half-brick half-wood framed house on a tree-studded two acre lot in Dover, a ritzy town over the Route 128 border, twenty-two miles west of Boston. The house had to be worth four, maybe five hundred grand. I counted two huge chimneys, and a three car garage at the end of a long blacktopped driveway. A huge pressure-treated wooden deck overlooked a forty foot swimming pool out back. Christ.

Standing in the driveway, the only thing we could hear besides the wind, the rain, and some demented birds, was this dog barking down the street a hundred yards at the next house.

So much for inconspicuous.

Tommy went around back. I got up on my toes and peered through a window into the garage. Seeing no cars, I went up the stone steps and tried the double oak doors. Both were locked.

I stuck my face against the long window that ran the length of the door. I saw Tommy walking across the living room rug toward me, a shit-eating grin on his face.

Opening the door, he said, "Sorry. I don't need any bibles today, Mister. I left mine at the office with one of my hookers."

I stepped inside quickly and closed the door. "How the hell did you get in?" I said, looking around.

"Call it superior police work. I tested the slider — it was open so I walked in."

"Cut the shit. Let's take a quick look around."

We did, but found nothing out of the ordinary.

Pasely had good taste, I could say that much for him.

Expensive furniture in every room. Dolby stereo component system in the study downstairs. King-size water bed in the master bedroom. Pool and ping-pong table in the game room, complete with full wet bar. Even the closets were neat.

"What do you think?" Tommy said.

"I think we should get the hell out of here."

"Good idea."

Tommy drove down the street and backed the Chevy into a tunnel of foiliage up to a weathered wooden gate that opened into a pasture full of cows.

"Guess it's going to rain all day," I said, looking back at them.

Tommy lit a cigar. "What are you, a weather man now?"

"Not me. Them."

Tommy turned around. "Who?"

"The cows. They're laying down. Everytime they do that, it means rain."

Tommy rolled down his window and blew out smoke. "Jesus Christ," he said. "No wonder I'm losing my fucking mind — hanging around a nut like you."

"I used to work on a farm, you know?" I said, gazing at the fawn and white guernsey standing under a tree away from the rest of the herd. "In Williamstown, Vermont when I was fifteen. My father's cousin owned it. Know what we used to do for excitement at night?"

"Grease up the cats?"

"Close. We used to go Cow-tipping."

"What?"

"Cow-tipping. Cows can sleep standing up you know."

"No shit. Really?"

"Yeah, they can. Anyway, we used to sneak up on them and push them over. It was easy — like pushing over statues. You should have seen the expression on their faces when they hit the ground."

"Sorry I missed it."

I let my eyes roam over the pasture reflectively. "Those were some good days," I said.

"Sounds wonderful. Farm-ass juvenile delinquents. No wonder the milk tastes the way it does."

"Fuck you."

From where we were parked, hidden by underbrush, we had a good view of Pasely's driveway. It was twenty after one, Friday afternoon.

We kept our eyes open for any surprises — like the one this morning. If Pasely was tipped, he knew we were coming, and our asses could be hanging out further than a couple of babboons'. My guess was he wasn't. We would have had the surprise by now — we'd been here over an hour.

Two hours later, someone showed.

It was a woman in a blue Volvo station wagon. We watched her get out, search her handbag for some keys, walk up the steps, and unlock the door. Couple of minutes later she reappeared, went to the back of the wagon, dropped the gate, picked up a couple of bags of groceries, and carried them into the house.

She was tall and slender in a white dress and pink sweater. Her hair was gray and she walked with a slight limp, favoring her right leg. We guessed it was Pasely's wife.

Forty-five minutes after his wife put the station wagon in the garage, Colonel Richard Pasely drove his black, unmarked Chrysler state police cruiser into the garage and closed the door.

Sonuvabitch.

When we rang the doorbell, we had our weapons drawn — my .38 down by my side, Tommy's .9mm at his chest, barrel up. Pasely's face was expressionless when he saw me standing in the doorway. "How did you know where to find me?" he asked. Then he said, "Never mind. Get in here before any body sees you."

We stepped cautiously inside and closed the door behind us.

"You can put the guns away," Pasely said. "There's no one here but me. I've sent my wife next door."

We checked anyway.

Satisfied we were alone, we followed Pasely into the den,

keeping my eyes open for anyone hidden in the walls, or under a rug. Call it paranoia — whatever — I wasn't taking any chances. I had a feeling the rules, as I knew them, were about to change and I wanted to be ready. So did Tommy. He refused the offer to sit down and stayed by the door, his .9mm at the ready.

"Mind if I have a drink?" Pasely said to me, walking over to the bar next to the floor-to-ceiling bookcase.

I shrugged. "As long as it isn't arsenic," I said.

He smiled. "You've been watching too much television, Joe," he said.

I didn't say anything.

Pasely was medium height, with narrow shoulders and slim build. His hair was almost white, his eyes almost blue except for some specks of green. He had on blue jeans and a white shirt, open at the collar. He had the face of a professional soldier; taut skin, wrinkles deeply etched, eyes noncommittal. Still, as he poured himself two fingers of Johnny Walker Black over ice, I thought I saw some fear in his eyes.

"Sit down," he said. It was a command, not a request.

I never was any good at commands. "No." I said. "You sit. I'll stand."

He did.

The room was smaller than the rest. Dark leather chairs, a solid oak desk, mementos of the colonel's military career on the dark paneled walls.

"Someone tried to kill me this morning, Colonel," I said.

There was no reaction from Pasely whatsoever. "How do you know it wasn't me?" he said, spinning the ice around in his glass.

"If it was, you'd be dead now."

It *was* fear. The eyes darted briefly toward Tommy, then back at me.

"I can't tell you anything," Pasely said.

"Can't or won't?" Tommy said.

"Both."

"After you talked to me," I said, "who'd you call? Your

friends with the CIA?''

"I don't have any friends with the CIA."

"Cut the bullshit, Colonel. You set me up."

"I don't know what you're talking about. I was coming to meet you — I heard what had happened on the radio, and turned back."

"You miserable prick. You lying miserable prick. You can't even lie straight. What time did you leave head-quarters?"

"Nine-thirty — something like that."

"The shooting started at nine-fifteen. No one got to the scene until twenty of ten. The press didn't get there until ten-fifteen. That's almost an hour after the shooting. Unless I'm mistaken, it takes ten minutes — maybe twelve — to get from state police headquarters to Franklin Park. Unless of course you went by way of fucking Alaska. What did you do? Stop and meet the boys in the red Firebird? They tell you what a good job they did scaring the living shit out of me. Because that's all they did. That's all they were told to do, wasn't it, Colonel? What were you doing? Playing Mister Nice Guy? No need to shoot holes in the fat guy. He doesn't know that much. Just scare him a little. Maybe he'll dry up and blow away. That what your plan was, Colonel? Because if it was, you're sadly mistaken. I got to tell you, Colonel, I'm one miserable son-of-a-bitch when someone pisses me off. And you've pissed me off."

I stopped a second and glanced up at the walls.

"I see a great military career up there, Colonel," I went on. "The Pentagon. The State Department. Maybe that's where you met your CIA pals, I don't know. But all that up there tells me three things. Discipline. Organization. Dedication." I took a step toward Pasely, leaned down, and bunched the front of his white shirt in my fist. Lifting him half out of the chair, I said, "Well, guess what? I've got no discipline, and my organization sucks. But I've got one thing going for me, Colonel. I'm one dedicated son-of-a-bitch." I let him go — he settled back and glared at me.

"So, knowing that," I carried on, "you have to believe

me when I tell you, you got exactly ten seconds to start telling me what I want to know."

For a few seconds, Pasely sat quietly, frozen into position, his eyes a strange mixture of hatred and fright. When he spoke, his voice was tight.

"You miserable bastard," he said. The contempt in his voice was absolute. "You think you can waltz into my home and intimidate me? Who in hell do you think you are?"

I met his eyes. "Your fucking executioner if you don't start talking."

Pasely stood up, downed what was left of his scotch, turned, and placed the glass on the bar. "Okay, Knight," he said, meeting my glare. His face began to discolor with rage; the veins in his neck came to the surface of his flesh. "I think I've had just about enough of your bullshit. What the hell is it going to take to make you believe me? Alright. You want to shoot me? Go ahead. Blow my brains out. It doesn't matter. You still won't know anything because I don't know anything. It was the way I wanted it — the way they wanted it?"

"Who's they? The CIA?"

"Yes. The CIA."

I swallowed involuntarily as a knot of pain formed in my stomach. Finally I was getting somewhere, but where that somewhere was, I wasn't sure. Nor was I sure I wanted to get there.

I walked over to the window.

Tommy kept his eye on the street, and said to me in a low voice Pasely couldn't hear, "Know what I think, Joe? I think we should get the fuck out of here right now. I smell something. And I don't like it."

I parted the drapes and looked out. "So do I," I said.

One thing was for sure. From now on, I had to go one step at a time. Each move I made had to be considered carefully; yet that caution couldn't slow me down. I'd been given a warning — a deadly warning. Fear, I knew, would make me careful. The rage I felt welling up inside me would give me strength. It had to. I was depending on it.

I let go of the drapes and walked back across the room. Pasely was pouring another two fingers of scotch over some fresh ice. His face was crimson now, so were his fingers. His hand trembled; the neck of the bottle rattled off the top of the glass. Putting the bottle down, he picked up the glass and threw back the scotch in one gulp.

"What do you know about this Operation Iron Hammer?" I said.

Wiping his lips with the back of his hand, he turned slowly and said in a subdued tone, "Iron Hammer is a CIA code name for clandestine operations conducted within the continental limits of the United States. Iron Hammer's primary mission is to monitor and report the activities of foreign agents operating inside these limits. That's all I can tell you. That's all I'm going to tell you."

I looked at Tommy. He said. "Foreign agents? What foreign agents?"

Pasely didn't answer.

My head was swirling. I felt a filmy sheet of sweat across my brow and wiped it with the palm of my hand. So many questions — so many facts buzzing between my brain cells. Too many holes to fill.

"Then Samuel Morris was Iron Hammer?" I said.

No answer.

"Iron Hammer is a person," I said. "Not just a code name?"

Still no answer.

"Morris is dead. That means there's another Iron Hammer. Who is it?"

Pasely gazed into his empty glass.

Something slight, vague, moved across his face. I wasn't sure what it was. Maybe nothing. Maybe it was guilt. Maybe I read too much sometimes into an expression.

Pasely poured another two fingers.

"I'll make a deal with you, Colonel," I said. "You call this Iron Hammer, whoever he is. He convinces me I'm fucking up his operation — he's willing to give up the guy I'm after — I'll back off. No questions asked. If he can't buy that, you tell him this. If he thinks I'm a giant pain in the ass now — just wait. I'll make being a pain in the ass turn into the biggest case of fucking bleeding hemorrhoids he ever saw. You call him and tell him that."

Pasely didn't waver. Eyeing me pensively, he lifted his glass again, took a long swallow, and lowered the glass. "I'm not saying anything more," he said. "I can't get involved."

"But you are involved," I said. "Right up to your fucking eyeballs, Colonel. You called Iron Hammer this morning. You told him where I was."

"Get out."

"Not until you tell me what I want to know."

Tommy moved away from the window. "Joe," he said, alarm in his voice.

"What?"

"We've got company."

"Who?"

"Three state police cruisers just pulled into the driveway."

I looked at Pasely. "You sent out a silent alarm," I said, stupidly.

Pasely walked to the door like some dilapidated prizefighter. "Very good, Sergeant Knight," he said with a crooked grin, half in the bag. "Have a nice day. And please, don't let the door hit you in the ass on the way out."

22

Jake and Warren were in an unmarked Boston police cruiser parked across the street from my house. Seeing me approach, they followed me into my driveway.

I got out and walked up to them.

Jake rolled his window all the way down.

"Who's watching O'Hara's apartment?" I said.

"Danner and Marks," Warren said.

"You tell them why?"

"No," Jake said. "All we said was for them to call us if O'Hara showed."

I looked toward the house. It needed painting, the lawn needed mowing.

"Anyone been around?" I said.

"No." Jake said. "It's been quiet. Just your daughter and a couple of her friends getting off the school bus. Jessica's really grown up since the last time I saw her. She's gorgeous. You better keep a baseball bat handy."

"I do. You guys want some coffee?"

They declined.

"We'll stay out here," Warren said. "You know what's good for you, Joe, you should, too. Victoria looks really pissed off."

I went inside anyway.

Entering the living room, I wasn't sure how I'd begin, sure only that I had to. Victoria was on the sofa with her head back and eyes closed. At the sound of me, she opened her eyes as if startled, and for a time she stared at the wall behind me. It was the look I hated. And she knew it.

"Hello," I said gently.

Victoria didn't say anything, she just looked away, a

practiced move that told me she was angry.

I sat down next to her. "Everything's alright," I said.

"Is it?" she said. "Then why are Jake and Warren watching our house?"

I thought of bullshitting her, but it was no good.

"You want it straight?" I said.

Victoria looked at me. Her wide blue eyes searching mine. "I want you to quit," she said.

"Not this again."

"I mean it, Joseph. Don't tell me what it is — I don't want to know. I'm sick and tired of staying awake nights wondering when or if you'll ever come home. It's not fair to me or the children. God knows what we would do if we ever lost you. Please, Joseph."

I held her face with both hands. "I can't quit, sweetheart. You know I can't. I don't know how to quit. I'm a cop. I don't know anything else."

"You could learn. Lots of men do."

"Maybe, maybe not. But do you remember why you married me? You said I was different. I was my own man. You knew I was a cop — you knew it was dangerous."

"And I've lived with that danger — for eighteen years." She looked away again. Tears formed in her eyes. "I'm not sure I can anymore."

Victoria began to cry and fell on her side, her whole body convulsing, her face ashen. I reached for her and held her, rocking her back and forth.

"C'mon, sweetheart," I said. "Everything's going to be alright. Have I ever let you down before? No, I haven't. Trust me one more time."

Victoria pushed herself away from me, her eyes shut tight, her face wet with tears. But the crying had stopped as quickly as it had begun. "Trust has nothing to do with it, Joseph," she said.

"Then bare with me on this one just a little longer. When it's over, we'll sit and talk about it. Maybe it is time for a change. Who knows?"

Victoria raised her eyes to the ceiling. "Don't lie to me,

Joseph. You're not good at it."

"What can I say?"

"Nothing."

She rose and headed for the kitchen.

I followed her like a whipped dog.

Pouring some coffee into a cup, I said. "I want you and your mother to take the kids and go to her house for a while."

"What?"

"It's just temporary. At least until this thing blows over."

Victoria studied me, her hand to her mouth, curiosity and fear intermingled. "You really are in trouble," she said.

"Not really. Someone's made some threats that's all. But it's just talk. I just don't want to take any chances."

"It isn't just talk, Joseph. I can see it in your eyes. You're frightened."

"Okay. I'm frightened. There. Now I've said it — you satisfied? So start packing. Jake and Warren will drive you. Where're the kids?"

"I don't know."

"Find them."

"Alright. You don't have to shout."

"You're making me shout. Now get moving."

"Alright. I'm moving."

"Faster."

"Shove it."

"I'd love to, but there isn't time."

Pouring some milk in my coffee, I read the note Jessica had scribbled on the pad next to the telephone. All I could make out was the name, Condon.

"What's this?" I said.

"It's a note pad?" Victoria said.

"I know that. What's it say?"

I showed Victoria the note.

"What's the matter?" she said, sarcastically, "Can't you read your daughter's writing?"

"No, I can't. What does it say?"

"It says, 'Mister Condon called. It's important. Please

return call.' ''

She handed me back the note. "How long will I have to stay at mother's — or is that a surprise too?"

"Don't get cute," I said. "Just get packing." I crumpled the note and tossed it in the wastebasket. "Besides," I went on, "you deserve some r and r."

"Not at my mother's, Joseph," she said.

I headed for the door.

"Where are you going?" Victoria said.

"Back to the office to make some calls."

"Aren't you going to kiss me goodbye?"

"Oh, yeah. I forgot."

"Typical."

I kissed her — long and soft, and held her close to me.

"I love you," I said.

Her lips trembled. "I love you, too," she said. "Sometimes."

"Sometimes is good enough for me. Say hello to your mother."

The phone was answered almost immediately.

"Mister Condon," I said. "Sergeant Knight. You wanted to talk to me?"

"Yes, Sergeant Knight," Mr. Condon said. "You said to call if I came up with anything regarding my daughter's death. I'm not sure how important this is."

"Everything's important until we check it out and prove it's not," I said. "What do you have, Mister Condon?"

"Perhaps it's nothing, Sergeant, but I just received a letter from a bank in Massachusetts — the Concord Savings and Loan. It seems my daughter is three months behind in mortgage payments."

"I don't understand?"

"Neither did I until yesterday. My wife had neglected to inform me she had agreed to co-sign Sherry's mortgage application — that she had given Sherry ten thousand dollars as a down payment to buy the property."

"What property?"

"The letter doesn't say. Just that she was behind three months in payments. I hope I'm not being presumptuous, Sergeant. I thought it was something you should know."

"It's worth checking out, Mister Condon."

"Should I make a call to the bank, Sergeant? Both my wife and I agree, we should make restitution. It was, after all, my daughter's debt. It should be paid."

"Why don't you let me check it out first, Mister Condon. I find out anything, I'll call you."

"Thank you, Sergeant. You've been most kind. It must be very difficult to call a parent and inform them their child is dead. My wife and I appreciated your concern and thoughtfulness."

"I have children of my own, Mister Condon."

"Yes, I could tell."

Hanging up, I called the Concord Savings and Loan. A sweet-talking female told me she couldn't give out mortgage information over the phone, especially when it wasn't mine. I told her I was a cop. She said it didn't matter — if I wanted information, I would have to speak to her boss, in person.

I went upstairs looking for Tommy. I found him bullshitting with Jimmy the Nose, the bartender from Amrhein's, who had come for his daily dose of gossip. Tommy loved him. It was a game he played often. He'd feed Jimmy the Nose a ton of made-up horseshit information about someone or something going down. Or he'd make up some lie about a federal probe being conducted on this unit or that squad, then Tommy would laugh like a bastard when someone downtown fed him back the information, telling him it came from sources deep within the department who were in the know. Usually, the twisted story turned out so good, Tommy almost believed it himself, and many times had tried to bullshit me into believing it. But I knew better and that pissed him off.

Tommy saw me coming and turned his back on me, pretending that the conversation he was having with Jimmy the Nose shouldn't be overheard.

As I approached, I saw Jimmy the Nose peering at me over

Tommy's shoulder. Stupid sonuvabitch.

"Tommy," I said, "I've got to talk to you."

He turned around. "Wait a minute," he said, pretending to look around, knowing there wasn't anyone in the room close enough to overhear his horseshit conversation. "I'm talking to my friend, Jimmy, here. Can't it wait?"

"No. It can't."

He said excuse me to Jimmy the Nose and joined me at the day-room table. "What's up?" Tommy said.

"Get your coat," I said. "We're taking a ride."

"Where to?"

"Concord."

"Concord? What for?"

"I think we just got lucky. I'll fill you in on the way. Grab your shotgun."

We drove out Route 2, past the state police barracks and the Concord Prison, and took Route 2A into Concord Center.

At the Concord Savings and Loan, I talked to the woman in charge of mortgages, a thin, pale looking woman of about forty with buck teeth and pimples who fit the mold of a mortgage loan officer perfectly — dry and boring. Even the way she walked in her ankle-length black dress was boring.

It took some bullshitting, but I finally got her to show me the deed to the property. The first thing I noticed was the address. RR #2 Lakeview Drive, Lower Naukeag Lake, Winchendon, Massachusetts. The second thing I noticed was the name of the co-borrower of the note. Brendan O'Hara.

Bingo!

We got in the car and headed north along Route 2 to Route 12. Winchendon was north of Fitchburg by nineteen miles, close to the New Hampshire border. Lower Naukeag Lake was out of Winchendon Center some five miles.

Tommy threw another lunger out the window and rolled it up. "What if he's there, Joe? He might not be alone. We could use a backup."

I folded the road map so I could read it. My fingers were trembling so much I had a hard time tracing the route to

Lower Naukeag Lake. "If he's alone," I said, "we'll take him. He's not alone, it's not of his choosing. Who knows. He might even be dead. Whatever, we'll have to go in slow."

It was growing dark by the time we got to Winchendon, the sun falling behind the distant hills, the shadows lengthening. Out of Winchendon Center, we followed the signs to Naukeag Lake.

The road was narrow and hilly, winding through thick forest. At the bottom of a steep grade was a fork — dirt road to the right, paved to the left. No arrows.

Sonuvabitch!

We took a guess and went right down the dirt road, the Buick bouncing along like a wounded beachball over rocks and craters, sending both of us to the roof more than once.

By the time we realized we were on the right road, having seen the sign that said Lakeshore Drive, it was too dark to drive. We needed the headlights, but couldn't risk being seen. We decided to get out and walk.

It was past eight o'clock when we reached the flat stretch of grassland that fronted what appeared to be a large lake. The low flying clouds had thinned out and moonlight washed over everything. After nearly forty minutes of walking — Tommy loaded down with his shotgun and bulletproof vest, me with my Mossberg riot gun, vest and extra ammo — we were almost ready to drop from exhaustion when we saw the bridge and the yellow glow of lights coming from a house a zillion yards beyond.

I felt my pulse leap abruptly, as if something impossibly bright had lit up in the dark of my head. O'Hara! You sonuvabitch — you're here and we got you.

We kept walking in silence over the bridge and down the gravel road, the only sounds coming from our boots making harsh contact with the profusion of rocks as we ducked through tunnels of foliage, sometimes too thick for both of us to go through together. If a car had passed by here recently, it had to be a four-wheeler. Nothing else could possibly get through.

The house was isolated, no other houses within two to

three hundred yards in any direction, accessible only by the primitive dirt road we were on. We hid in a cluster of fir trees fifty yards from the house, checking for sounds, for any signs of life. Nothing. No sounds. Just some bird and animal noises I couldn't identify.

Crouching, we ran zigzag toward the house. Going up on the porch, I motioned Tommy to keep his eyes on our backs while I peeked in the windows.

Inside, the decor was rustic; heavy beams and furniture covered with quilted cushions, white walls and yellow-checked curtains. A stone fireplace and two floor-to-ceiling bookcases, filled to capacity with books of varying sizes.

We waited. Nothing. No signs of life.

There was a sudden crack from behind us, the sound echoing through the trees. We spun around, hidden in the dark shadows of the porch, braced and tense, peering with weapons raised into the dense foliage. A foot had stepped on a fallen branch. What I saw caused me to lose my breath.

A man was silhouetted in the shadows between two trees, the silhouette familiar, last seen leaving Logan Airport four and a half days ago. Unmistakably, the silhouette of Brendan O'Hara.

What was he doing out there alone? Had he seen us?

We knew he hadn't when he left the shadows and walked briskly toward the house. I waited until he reached the top of the porch.

"Hello, asshole," I said, stepping into the spill of light, the barrel of my Mossberg aimed at O'Hara's chest.

O'Hara froze. "Jesus Christ!" he said, "Joe! Tommy! You stupid bastards. You scared the living shit out of me!"

"That isn't all I'd like to do to you," I said.

"Still wearing those stupid gloves, O'Hara?" Tommy said. "Got to be a bitch jacking off."

"Fuck you, Sanders," O'Hara said.

"Shut up and get inside," I said to O'Hara.

Inside, O'Hara turned to me, his face still flushed from the cold outside, his eyes wide, questioning and afraid. "How did you find me?" he said.

"Does it matter?" I said. "We're here — that's all that concerns you. Get your coat. You're under arrest."

"Just like that, Joe? No hellos. No small talk for old time sake. What happened to reading me my rights?"

"Fuck your rights," Tommy said. "You heard the man. Get your fucking coat."

"You'll never get me back to Boston alive — you know that, don't you?"

"Who's going to stop us?"

O'Hara didn't say anything.

"Ease off, Tommy." Then I said to O'Hara, "What makes you think we won't make it back?"

"C'mon, Joe," O'Hara said. "Don't play dumb-shit with me. It's me, remember? You know damn well what's been going down. You've been on my ass for two weeks straight. Watching every move I've made. I knew you were there. I also knew you wouldn't make a move on me until you were absolutely sure you had me cold. How'd you get to me, Joe? What did you do — pull some shit on Sherry? Make her tell you where to find me? That why she hasn't shown here?"

I looked at Tommy, both of us silent.

"What is it?" O'Hara said, switching his look from Tommy to me. "Something happen to Sherry? Tell me."

"Yeah," Tommy said. "Something's happened."

O'Hara looked at Tommy. "What?"

"She's dead," Tommy said matter-of-factly, intending for it to hurt, which it did. "Someone burned cigarette holes up and down her chest then shot her head full of fucking holes."

O'Hara reacted with a rush of anger. "You bastard!"

He made a move toward Tommy, his fists ready to strike. I had all I could do to stop him.

"Hold it, Brendan," I said, grabbing his arms. "Take it easy."

O'Hara stopped. I could feel the muscles in his arms tremble. "Oh, Christ," he said. His eyes filled with tears. Turning away from me, he collapsed in the chair next to the fireplace. His head fell back, his breathing fast and erratic as if he could not get enough air into his lungs. He buried his face in his white gloves and sobbed uncontrollably. "My God . . . what have I done?"

For an instant, I felt a rush of compassion for him, but it quickly died.

"She was tortured, Brendan," I said. "Obviously by someone who was trying to get to you. Why, Brendan? Who are they? What do they want?"

O'Hara slowly lifted his head, his face wet with tears, his dead eyes staring at me a moment then looking away. He didn't appear strong to me anymore. He looked beaten, almost frail. "Damn, Joe," he said finally. "I loved her. We were going to get married. This was going to be our dream house. We bought it a year ago. Everything was going to be so perfect. It wasn't supposed to happen this way."

I sat down on the sofa across from him.

I was cold suddenly, as if some invisible draft had rushed through the room from an open window. For some odd reason, I felt lost in this place, disoriented. Maybe it was my brain swirling — trying to shove a zillion questions out of my mouth all at once.

Tommy had found O'Hara's jacket. Walking in from the bedroom, he tossed it at O'Hara. "Here," he said. "Put it on. It's almost nine. Let's move."

"Wait a minute," O'Hara said. "Don't you want to know why I did it, Joe? The drugs. The money."

"The murders."

"Yes . . . the murders. I had no choice. That reporter . . . Susan Howell. She would have ruined everything. She had to be stopped."

"What about West and Edwards — his brothers? And Vinnie Torchia. You killed them, too."

"Styles killed them."

"You hired him — same difference. You're guilty."

"Torchia was a bum. He was trying to squeeze me — trying to make a name for himself and impress his scumbag boss, Angellini. West and Edwards were skimming. They had to be taught a lesson. Tough shit about the brothers — they got in the wrong place at the wrong time."

"What about Tony Walker and his wife?"

"I had nothing to do with that. He killed himself."

"He was dealing drugs for you."

"Tony was weak."

"You owned him."

"Yeah, I owned him. Like I owned all the cops who worked for me. Worse than crooks some of them. Greedy fucks."

"Who shot Morris?"

"Who?"

"Morris. The guy I was with that night in the alley."

"Was that his name?"

"Did you know he was a CIA agent?"

O'Hara looked surprised. "Styles said he was a New York cop."

"Styles said you paid him fifteen grand to hit me."

"Styles was full of shit. He was the one who wanted you taken out. I wouldn't let him."

"So you had him killed?"

"I couldn't trust him. He was getting out of hand. Wanted a bigger share of my profits. A couple of guys at Charles Street owed me a favor. I slipped them some cash and it was done."

"That simple?"

"Yeah. That simple."

"You said we wouldn't make it back to Boston. That means you know there's someone after you. I think you know who and why?"

O'Hara looked at me. Anger, surprise and sadness came together in his eyes. He had slipped his right gloved hand over his left wrist, gripping it, his fingers pressed into the flesh with such force I thought his skin might break. "You're the smart cop," he said, strength returning to his voice. "You tell me. You probably know more than I do — it's written all over your face."

I hesitated, then said, "Your name's not O'Hara, is it?"

He gazed at me, his body rigid, as if some sort of paralysis had suddenly set in, rendering him speechless.

"There were three men murdered in New York City recently," I went on. "One was a priest named Coogan. The others were named O'Grady and Patrick. You knew them, didn't you? In fact, if I had to guess, I'd say you were close to them. Who were they, Brendan? Cousins? Brothers? What?"

O'Hara shook his head in bewilderment. "I forgot what a relentless bastard you really are, Joe," he said. "How the hell did you find out?"

"Lucky guess. Now stop bullshitting me, Brendan. Who were they? Who the hell are you?"

He smiled sadly. "They were my brothers, Joe," he said, his voice wavering. "Edward, James and Timothy. All my brothers. All Muldoons. All fighting for one common cause — a free Ireland."

"Why did you change your name?" I said.

"If you knew anything about the struggle in Northern Ireland, Joe, you wouldn't have to ask that."

"I don't, so I'm asking."

"The Muldoons, Joe. The Dungannon Muldoons. Everyone in Northern Ireland knows the name. We're famous people, Joe. We're Irish history. My father, my grandfather. My great grandfather — a friend of Tom Clarke, one of the seven signers of the Declaration of the Republic — a true Irish patriot who was executed for his role in the 1916 Dublin rebellion."

Brendan Muldoon paused, his head down, toying with a strand of thread hanging from one of his gloves. "There were six of us, Joe," he went on. "Six brothers. James was the oldest, I was second, then Edward and Timothy. Then Seamus."

"The one elected to the British Parliament," I said, interrupting. "Murdered outside his house in Armagh a couple of weeks ago."

Brendan Muldoon looked up at me. "How did you know that?" he said.

"I read the papers."

Brendan Muldoon's eyes drifted to the fireplace. "Seamus was a good man," he said. "I loved him dearly, but he had no guts for fighting. He tried to do it another way. Fight the Brits from the inside. Join them in the political process within the Paliament and work toward a peaceful unification of Northern Ireland with the Republic. The IRA violently opposes any peaceful unification. There can never be peace in Northern Ireland as long as those fucking Brits occupy our land."

"We grew up in a household where fighting, being imprisoned or dying for the cause of Irish republicanism was considered worthy and noble. We were Catholics — Dungannon was predominantly Protestant. We saw the wrong, the repression, the discrimination, being Catholic, being an Irishman in that town. Dungannon is to militant Irish nationalism what Cooperstown is to baseball. By the time I was fourteen, every time I went out of the house, I was stopped, searched and harassed by the police and British soldiers. Once I put up a fight and was beaten viciously about the head by a Brit. That's when I decided to join the active service of the IRA, along with my brothers."

"Get off the soap box, Brendan," I said. "Just tell me one thing. Why does someone want the Muldoons dead?"

Brendan Muldoon's expression turned cold, so did his voice. "The bastards will never kill us," he said. "Not all of us. Not Paddy."

"The sixth brother?"

"Yes. Paddy Muldoon. The sixth brother."

"Where have I heard that name before?" I said.

Brendan Muldoon looked away. "Maybe you read about it," he said. "It was in all the papers and on the news. The Brits called it a victory against the terrorists — they said the IRA got what they deserved. We called it murder. In Loughall, in County Armagh a few months ago. My brother, Paddy, led a group of eight IRA men on an assualt of a police station. Some British soldiers and Royal Ulster Constabulary were waiting for them. After my brother and his men dumped explosives on the police station, the Brits opened fire. All of the IRA men were caught in a crossfire and killed. All except Paddy. Somehow he managed to get away.''

"And the British are looking for him," I said.

"Yes."

"And they think you know where he is. They know you're a Muldoon."

Brendan Muldoon fell silent.

I got up from the sofa. Fatigue coursed through me suddenly. The room pressed in on me — the shadowy bookshelves, the pale light from the lamp.

I said, staring down at the ashes in the fireplace, "So the money you got from the drugs went to your brother."

Brendan Muldoon nodded. "No matter what happens, Joe," he said, "I am and always will be a Muldoon — and damn proud of it. You remember that. I have no regrets for — "

A pane in one of the front windows exploded. A crack behind me, the splitting of wood as the bullet imbedded itself somewhere in a molding. Then another pane shattered and glass fragments danced through the air, cracks of plaster sliced the wall like black lightning.

My body had difficulty accepting what my two brain cells were telling it to do.

Move! For Chrissakes, move!

I did, finally, diving to the floor, crawling on all fours behind the sofa like some frightened insect about to lose its insignificant life.

Another pane exploded, another bullet cracked plaster. Then another, this one ricocheting off metal someplace, smashing the glass of a photograph on the wall above me.

"Tommy!" I shouted out. "You alright?"

"Yeah."

"What about Brendan?"

"I think he's hit."

"How bad?"

"I don't know. I can't see him."

I called out. "Brendan! Can you hear me, Brendan!"

No answer.

Slowly, I rose and peered above the sofa. The pain in my temples was so bad, I could barely focus my eyes, the crush of fear I felt so bad I thought I would vomit. Tommy must have been kissing the floor because I couldn't see him.

The door opened. A man in a tan jacket stood holding a sawed-off shotgun waist high.

I saw it coming this time.

The roar of the shotgun was deafening, the blast tearing a hole the size of a basketball in the top of the sofa, causing tiny balls of white fluff to dance in the air and sprinkle down on me. Another blast, this one blowing out the entire window above me.

Silence. Only the ringing in my ears.

I heard footsteps race across the room toward me. Then I heard something else — something that sickened me. The muted sound of an object pulled out of rubber. I looked up. Silouhetted against the light across the room was the man in the tan jacket; the barrel of the shotgun he pointed at my face looked the size of twin civil war cannons. There was a second man next to him, holding up a vial of serum. A needle!

"Wait a minute, pal," I said. "Don't do that! Jesus Christ! I hate needles!"

The two men held me face down. I felt their weight shift above me, the needle puncturing my jacket.

The last thing I heard before the lights went out was Tommy screaming, "You fucking bastards."

23

I felt the cold first. It made me shiver. I opened my eyes to blackness. At first I thought I had gone blind but realized my eyes were open. Soon I was able to see distorted images. A chair. A table. Someone on the floor next to me. Tommy!

"Tommy," I whispered. My mouth was dry, my throat sore. Whatever the drug was, it was wearing off slowly. My head was spinning so bad I thought I was on a tilt-a-whirl with my kids.

Oh, God. My kids. Victoria.

"Joe."

The voice was barely a whisper. It came from across the room.

"Tommy?" I said, unsure where the voice came from.

"No," the voice said. "It's...me. Brendan."

My eyes strained to see him in the darkness across the room. "Muldoon," I said. "You sonuvabitch! What the hell is going on? Where are we?"

Muldoon choked a laugh. "We're...fucked, Joe. That's where we are."

I tested the floor with the palms of my hands. The wood was warped and slick, and smelled of oil and grease. We were in a factory or warehouse — I couldn't tell which.

I pushed myself up to one knee. I could see Tommy's outline; he was on his back, still unconcious, arms outstretched. I felt for his throat. The pulse was strong, so was his breathing. He was alive, thank God.

I illuminated the dial of my watch: 4:10 am. Christ!

Wherever we were, we'd been here over seven hours.

I rose unsteadily to my feet, ran my hands along the wall

trying to find a window. I did, but it was locked. I peered outside. Nothing but black.

I continued along the wall and found a door.

"Joe . . ."

"What?"

"I told them . . ."

I gripped the latch and tried to lift it. No good.

"I . . . told them everything, Joe. The bitch. The fucking . . . bitch. She spit on my hands, Joe. Tore my gloves off and fucking spit on my hands."

"What a shame. Too bad she didn't piss down your throat."

"For Chrissakes, Joe. You don't understand what I'm telling you. I betrayed him. Paddy. My brother. I betrayed him."

Silence.

I stood still a moment and peered into the darkness across the room. "What do you mean you betrayed him?" I said.

"I . . . told her everything." Muldoon's voice was weak. I could barely hear it. "About the . . . raid. Everything."

"What raid?"

"I . . . I don't know where it's going to happen exactly. Somewhere in London, I know that. I couldn't help it, Joe. The bitch . . . she filled me full of drugs. They beat the shit out of me. I was never . . . never any good with pain, Joe. You know that. Christ. She spit on my hands."

"When? Last night?"

"Yeah, after all hell broke loose. A bullet must have grazed my head and knocked me out. When I woke up, I was in the back of a truck with my hands tied to my feet — the bitch looking down at me. I'd never seen so much hate in anyone's eyes like there was in hers."

"She the same woman who followed you off the plane at Logan?"

"Yeah. She must have followed you last night."

"No one followed me."

"Christ, Joe . . . always so sure of yourself. She was there — you just didn't see her."

"Who is she, Brendan? The CIA? A British agent?"

Brendan Muldoon coughed, then swallowed hard. "She's a fuckin Brit, Joe. She killed Sherry. She tortured her...and shot her...trying to get to me. The bitch told me. Laughed about it in my fucking face, Joe. She laughed...in my fucking face. That day I came back from London — you were there — I saw you. She followed me. She killed one of our best people."

"The Albino?"

"Yeah." His words continued to emerge slowly, barely above a whisper. "Billy the Fox. That's what he went by. His name was Billy Dwyer. He was my brother Paddy's best friend. He helped me get the money through British customs. He has a friend in baggage — someone from the IRA who helped him switch bags. I went to the hotel and checked in while Billy delivered the money to Paddy."

"So Paddy's got a million bucks to buy more explosives."

"It wan't a million."

"Whatever. The raid. Where's it going to happen? Parliament? Westminster Abbey? Tower Bridge? Buckingham Palace?"

"It's...one of those. I just don't...don't know which one. Paddy told me it will be something the Brits will never forget."

Muldoon fell silent, then he said, "Paddy is the only one left, Joe. You have to understand...I love him. He has to be stopped before they kill him." He hesitated, his voice weaker still, choked with emotion. "I know what you're... thinking, Joe."

"No. You don't."

Silence.

"I'm hurt, Joe," Muldoon said. "I...I'm...hurt bad."

I stared into the twisted blackness across the room. "Tough shit." I said.

"Whatever you do, Joe. Don't come near me."

"Why not?"

"I'm tied to...a chair." Muldoon coughed. "There's a...wire...tied around my throat. It's connected to . . . plastic explosives under the . . . chair."

I didn't say anything. I couldn't.

I reached inside my jacket pocket and took out my penlight. Making my way across the room from shadows to darker shadows, I raised the light, cupped my hands around the tiny beam and aimed it in the direction of Muldoon's voice. The beam took on the glow of a spotlight as it tracked along the wall until it found what it was looking for.

I shuddered when I saw Muldoon's face. His eyes, nose and mouth were swollen and bruised. Between the swells were a half dozen charred round holes the size of a cigarette, crusted over in dried blood. Each one had been precisely placed to cause maximum pain. Gone were Muldoon's chiseled handsome features. Instead, what was left was a pathetic white mask of panic.

I let the beam trace down his bloodied neck. Around his throat, cut into the skin, was a thin copper wire. There was another wire attached, one end going into a tiny metal box taped to his shoulder, which looked to be some sort of remote control detonator, the other end disappearing over his shoulder down his back. His hands were bound with wire to the chair. So were his legs.

"Things . . . haven't worked out the way it was planned, Joe," Muldoon said. He coughed. When he spoke again, his voice was tight, sullen. "We're dead, Joe. And there's nothing . . . anybody can do about it."

I shut off the light, moved my neck back and forth several times to ease the tension, lessen the strain. I gripped the back of my right shoulder; the skin still hurt where the needle had gone in.

"Joe?"

"What?"

"Tell me something. Are my hands . . . dirty? Could you see . . . my hands?"

"Fuck your hands. And fuck you. I hope they rot off."

"Jesus . . . Christ. Always . . . the fucking . . . hard-ass. Balls to the wall. That's . . . you. Nothing ever changes.

Look . . . where it's got . . . you.''

"Shut up.''

I found the window again, tried it. No good. I listened for sounds. I could hear in the distance a droning sound of tires rolling along pavement. We were close to a highway. But where?

My mind raced back to that night in the alley. Morris' head splitting open — blood rushing. Anger welled inside me.

"That night you and Styles hit Morris," I said. "How come you didn't shoot me? I know Goddamn well you had me in your sights. What was it, Muldoon? Some sort of game with you? Keep me around? See how many times you could make me look like a fucking moron? Prove to yourself you were as good as me?''

"I am as good as you. Better.''

I didn't say anything.

I heard him swallow again.

I glanced at my watch. It was 5:04 am. The sky outside the window was growing faintly brighter. Across an alley — three or four feet away — I could see a red brick wall. I pressed my face against the glass. Looking up, gray daylight, down, the wall disappeared into darkness.

Inside, images came slowly into focus. The room was large, maybe forty or fifty feet long, twenty-five feet wide. Nothing in the room except Muldoon in the chair, hands and feet bound, and Tommy on the floor, still unconcious. And me.

I leaned against the wall, shut my eyes, and brought my hand up to my forehead. For a long moment I stood silently. It was insane. Everything. Absolute madness. Listening to Muldoon talk, I found it difficult to believe he was once my closest friend. What the hell had happened? How could I have been so wrong about someone?

"Jesus Christ, Brendan," I said. "I loved you like a brother. We were best friends.''

"We still are, Joe," Muldoon said. "Despite everything — I still love you. But you never learned when to quit, Joe. Ever since I've known you, that's been your problem. Look where it's gotten you." He paused. "I was going to let you in on it. I needed your connections. You could have sold a lot of drugs for me, Joe. You would have made a lot of money. Greed. . . isn't just for the bad guys, Joe. Everyone's got a price."

"No, not everyone."

"Oh, yeah. I forgot. Joe the Super Cop — the uncorruptible. Clean and pure." Muldoon fell silent a few seconds. "Tell you what, Joe. As a last favor — I'll give you all the names. They're in my little black notebook. You remember, the one I keep in my sock. The one you were looking for when you tore up my apartment. Oh, yeah. You thought I didn't know about that. Sherry called me in Winchendon — she told me someone had been in the apartment and searched it. I figured the only one with balls big enough to do it was you."

"You're wrong. It wasn't me."

"What does. . .it matter. . .now. You want the notebook? It's in my right sock. But be careful, Joe. You could hit a wire and blow us both to hell. Wouldn't that be a kick?"

"Not really."

I slow-walked across the room toward him.

"Careful, Joe," Muldoon warned me again. "Don't make a mistake."

"Fuck you."

I bent to one knee in front of him, took out my penlight and ran the beam over his feet and ankles. His legs were bound to the chair with wire just below the knees. Far as I could tell, there was no loose wire — nothing around the ankle that could trip an explosive. Whoever wired it knew what he was doing. Cut the wires, any wire, and bingo, everybody goes to the cleaners. Carefully, I raised the right pant leg of his blue jeans and checked the sock. A two-inch square notebook was wedged inside the arch. Gently, I inched my fingers into the sock and lifted it out.

I was still alive.

Strange, as I stepped back in the dark reading the names,

the beam of the penlight going over the pages, I found myself not really caring about anything at all. The names — some I recognized, some I didn't — they didn't seem to mean anything to me now. There was something more important to think about. Like getting the hell out of here. Wondering if I'd ever see the sun again. My children, Victoria.

I heard a moan. It was Tommy.

I went to one knee, reached out and shook him. "Tommy. It's me. Joe. You okay?"

Tommy looked up at me, rubbing his forhead with the tips of his fingers. "Where am I?" he said. "What the hell happened?"

"They shot us with drugs."

"Wonderful. Where's Muldoon?"

"He's here."

"Where?"

"Over . . . here," Muldoon said. "Welcome to hell."

Tommy looked around me. "Jesus Chist," he said. "What happened to him?"

I told him.

Tommy struggled to his feet. Wobbling, he made it to the cot and sat down. Rubbing his eyes, he said, "Feels like I've been on a four day drunk, for Chrissakes."

"Joe? Tommy?"

I looked at Muldoon. "What now?" I said.

Muldoon gazed at me, blinking in fear, his lips trembling. "Get away from me, Joe," he said.

"What?"

"I said get away. Get far away."

I saw in his eyes what he was about to do. "Hold it, Brendan!" I said. "Don't do it! Don't do it!"

"Too late, Joe." His eyes were wide now — maniacal. "It's the only way out." He began to struggle with the bindings, deliberately making his body move from side to side.

"Jesus Christ!" Tommy said. "Do something, Joe! He's going to blow us all to hell!"

"Brendan!" I shouted. "Cut the shit! There's got to be

another way. Don't do it!''

"No, Joe. There is no other way." Muldoon was crying, tears running down his face.

Tommy backed up. So did I.

Brendan's face turned bright red, his neck muscles bulged — so did his eyes, as the struggle with the bindings became violent and furious. Within seconds he had the chair rocking.

"The Muldoons!" he shouted. "The Muldoons! Ireland forever!"

The explosion was thunderous. The impact so sudden and massive, it spun me and Tommy around and tossed us against the wall like a couple of rag dolls. For an instant, I thought I had gone deaf. Wood, flesh, hair, and blood flew everywhere.

Prone on the floor, I looked up. Blue smoke. Everything eerily still and quiet. Slowly, I rose. It took me a few seconds to unscramble my brain cells and find Tommy. He was face down on the floor under the window, his head wrapped in his arms, some of Muldoon's inards mingled with shards of windowpane stuck to the back of his denim jacket. I thought I would vomit.

What was left of Brendan Muldoon, you couldn't scrape up and shove in an envelope.

"Tommy," I said.

His eyes crept above his arms, and looked around. "Are we dead?"

"No. You okay?"

"I'm breathing, ain't I?"

"Good. Get up."

A crack, outside the room, snaplike, echoing off.

I straightened, moved quickly to the door, and pressed my back against the wall. Tommy got to his feet. I motioned him to the other side of the door.

Whoever it was had stopped, obviously aware of the noise his weight had caused on the warped, cracked wood.

Silence.

Another crack. Closer now.

Again silence.

The door suddenly crashed open. I smashed it back, then threw my full weight against it, pinning the figure between the door and the frame. I pulled the door back and Tommy spun around and lashed his foot into the guy's midsection, folding him forward.

I reached down, grabbed some blond hair, and yanked the figure inside.

"Joe! Tommy!"

The voice came from the darkness somewhere outside the room.

We both froze.

"Joe! For Chrissakes! It's me! Jake! You've got Warren!"

I looked at Tommy, surprised.

Both of us looked down.

Warren was on his knees, his head down, his body limp, his hair still bunched in my fist. Gently, I raised his head.

Sonuvabitch.

Dazed, Warren looked up at me, his eyes glassy and huge. His lips moved but nothing came out. We'd knocked the wind out of him.

"Warren," I said. "Jesus Christ. Why didn't you say something, you stupid bastard?"

Warren's lips moved again. They said, fuck you, you sonuvabitch.

Jake stepped out of the shadows and showed himself, his shotgun lowered.

"Holy shit," he said, standing in the doorway, looking at Muldoon's parts. "What the hell happened?"

"Never mind that," I said. "Where are we?"

Jake didn't say anything right away, his eyes still surveying the carnage. "You're in East Boston," he said finally. "In an abandoned factory. Used to be the old W. T. Butz Tool Company. Remember?"

I did. Now it was part of the US Navy Annex located between the Chelsea River and McClellan Highway, a little way from Suffolk Downs Raceway.

"How'd you know where to find us?" Tommy said.

"We got a call," Jake went on. "The voice sounded funny — like some cartoon character."

I looked at Tommy. He seemed stunned by it all. So was I.

Warren finally caught his breath and stood up. "What the fuck?" he said. "You guys crazy? Couldn't you tell it was me for Chrissakes?"

"Sorry, Warren," Tommy said with a grin. "It was dark."

"Dark, my ass."

"You see anyone when you pulled up?" I said to Jake.

"Yeah," Jake said. "A red Firebird. Came through the gate doing a buck. We thought about chasing it, but finding you was more important."

My breathing stopped, a terrible realization becoming clear.

"Which way did it go?" I said.

"Back toward Boston."

I said to Tommy, "They're making a run for it. Let's go."

"Where?"

"The airport."

"How do you know that's where they're headed?"

"Trust me." Then I said to Jake. "Where's your car?"

"Downstairs."

I snatched the shotgun out of Jake's hand. "Give me the keys," I said.

He did.

We raced east along McClellan Highway toward Logan. I had the window down — the air smelled good, the rain sweeping in felt cool on my face. For a time I thought I'd never feel it again. As I jammed the accelerator to the floor, I promised myself never to bitch about the rain again.

Wheeling onto Airport Road, swerving to avoid a station wagon loaded with kids and luggage, I took a right at the lights and headed toward Butler Aviation.

Slowing for the lights near the Butler hanger, my heart-beat did triple-time.

There it was, the red Firebird parked inside the twelve-foot high chain link fence, behind a row of small planes. In it, three dark figures, waiting.

Skidding to a stop at the circle in front of Butler Aviation,

I jumped out and burst through the glass doors into the lobby, Tommy right behind me.

Running up to the glass door that led to the ramp outside, I pushed on the bar. It was locked. Moving to the counter, I said to the gray-haired guy, "I'm a Boston police detective. I need to get out onto the ramp. Unlock the door."

The man looked away nervously, his eyes showing panic.

I searched my jacket pockets for my wallet. Nothing. No badge. No ID.

Sonuvabitch.

"Look," I said to the guy, "I'm telling you. I need to get out onto the ramp. Unlock the fucking door before I bust the fucking thing in!"

Still the guy wouldn't look at us.

Tommy leaned over the counter. "Let me put it to you another way," he said to the guy. "We've had what you might call, a bad day. You know what I mean? Now be a good boy and unlock that fucking door before I break your ugly fat face."

Someone moved behind me. I turned.

Instinctively, I raised my shotgun and pointed the barrel at the man's midsection.

"Looking for this?" the man said, holding up a plastic bag that had my badge, my wallet, and my .9mm in it. "You dropped these last night."

I exchanged glances with Tommy. He wanted to blow the guy away. So did I.

"Who are you?" I said.

"I have an ID in my pocket," the man said.

"Reach for it slow," I said.

He did.

"Do me a favor," the man said. "Aim that shotgun someplace else. I'm a friend."

I jacked a round in the chamber. "Bullshit," I said. "Your hand comes out with anything but an ID, your're fucking history."

The guy's voice suddenly went funny. "If we wanted to

kill you, Joe, we would have done it long before now.''

I glanced at Tommy. "What do you know?" I said, surprised. "It's Cartoon Voice."

The man smiled and showed me his ID.

Whatever image I had of what a CIA agent was supposed to look like, this guy wasn't it. The ID said his name was Collins. William P. Collins.

He was maybe in his late thirties, early forties, tall and slightly overweight. He wore rimless glasses that continually slipped down his nose so that he had to keep pushing them back upwards again with a thick index finger. He did it so frequently, it seemed a nervous tic he couldn't do anything about. What hair he had left above a high forehead was curly and gray. The dark blue pin-striped suit he wore was expensively cut, the vest tailored to hide his swelling gut.

"What do you think of my Mickey Mouse impression?" the CIA agent said.

"Not much."

"Gee. I thought it was pretty good. It was a bit theatrical, I'll admit, but what the hell."

I shoved the end of the barrel deeper into his jelly gut. "Cut the bullshit," I said. "Where's the woman?"

Collins looked at me for a few seconds in silence, then he said, "It's over, Joe. Let it go. There's nothing you can do about it now."

"Bullshit there isn't." I moved toward the door, screamed at the guy behind the counter. "Unlock the fucking door before I blast the son-of-a-bitch in!"

The guy stayed where he was, motionless, afraid to move.

"Fuck it, Joe," Tommy said. "Blow the glass away!"

I took a step closer to the door and stopped.

Three stone-faced men appeared on the other side of the glass. Two of them opened their long raincoats and showed me automatic rifles. The third guy had on a tan waist-length jacket with sunglasses — the same bastard who stuck me with the needle.

We glared at each other. All I could hear were my two

brain cells, screaming at me. Back off! Back off!

I listened finally, lowered my shotgun, and stepped away from the door. I couldn't shut out the feeling of helplessness.

"Go home, Joe," the CIA man said. "Take your friend here with you. Her plane is due any minute. Operation Iron Hammer is terminated as soon as she goes wheels-up."

"It's not over, you sonuvabitch. She's a murderer. No way she gets on a plane and flies out of here."

Collins' smile faded. "You can't stop her. We won't let you."

"We'll see about that."

"You're a good man, Joe Knight," the CIA man said. "Frankly, you've made the game enjoyable."

"Game? You fucking asshole! You call killing people a fucking game?"

"That isn't what I meant. I was referring to your tenacity — your perserverance. The agency could always use more people like you. Someone with more balls than brains."

"Fuck you."

"I did my best to keep you alive, Joe. But you're a hard man to convince. I thought I knocked some sense into you that night at Muldoon's apartment."

"That was you?"

"It was nothing personal, of course."

My face was heating up again. "Whose idea was it to shoot fucking holes in my car at Franklin Park?" I said.

"Mine. She wanted you taken down. I convinced her it should be a warning."

"So Pasely did call you."

"Yes. He told me you were becoming a giant pain in the ass. I agreed. Pasely and I, we're good friends. We served in the army together at the State Department. He helped us with logistics."

I heard the high-pitched whine of jet engines, growing louder, drawing close.

I moved slowly up the floor-to-ceiling window and looked out, careful not to spook the goons with the rifles under their coats.

The jet came slowly down the ramp into view. A white DC-9 with no markings, just some numbers stenciled in blue on the tail. The rain was a heavy mist now. The tarmac glistened.

I turned around. "What I don't understand," I said to Collins, "is how you could stand by and let some bitch commit murder and get away with it. That night we showed and talked to Muldoon's girlfriend — the night she disappeared. You were there."

"My people were."

"The bitch was there."

"Yes, she was. Our responsibilities were to monitor her movements. Not to interfere."

"The bitch tortured and murdered an innocent woman for Chrissakes. Why? For what? Because she wouldn't tell where Muldoon was? Jesus Christ! This is still the United States. Not some jerkwater little country you people run over with your horseshit clandestine mentality. The bitch murdered people in my city. She killed people in New York. She's not going to get away with it. She can't get away with it."

"She already has."

"Bullshit."

"Don't do anything stupid, Joe. I've had a hard time keeping you alive. Don't spoil it now — alright. I'll admit she's a little crazy, but aren't we all sometimes. You're not exactly the sanest person I've met."

"I don't kill innocent people."

"She was only following orders — orders that came directly from Number Ten Downing Street. The arms and money pipeline from the United States to the IRA has to be severed. The Muldoons were a major part of that pipeline. They had to be found and taken down. MI5 requested our help, the CIA cooperated. Simple as that. The British are desperate. The recent bombings in London have got them panicked. They want it stopped."

I faced the window. Looking past the three goons, I saw

the jet swing around and jerk to a stop. A few seconds after the engines were cut back, the doorway opened. A crewman appeared and, holding onto a rope, lowered a set of stairs.

Tommy joined me at the window. "What do you think?" he whispered out of the side of his mouth, rubbing shoulders with me. "You take the three outside. I take care of fat-shit behind us. We rush the plane — take the bitch out before she knows what hit her."

I shook my head. "Not a good idea," I whispered back.

"I agree," the CIA man said, standing directly behind us now. "In a few minutes, she's on that plane and gone. End of story. We go home — you go home. If we're lucky, tomorrow we wake up again asshole deep in shit somewhere else. Nothing changes. Just the nameless faces. If what I know about you is true, Joe, you couldn't have it any other way."

The Firebird moved in slow from the right and stopped by the stairs. The car door opened and someone got out. A woman, tall and richly tanned, wearing a black raincoat, black gloves, and a black wide-brimmed hat that seemed to complement her long aburn hair.

I felt the weight of the shotgun still in my left hand, but there was not much comfort in knowing it was there. Watching her go up the steps, I felt helpless. Empty. Maybe for the first time in my life, totally inadequate.

Reaching the top step, she hesitated, as if sensing she was being watched. She turned slowly, and our eyes met.

Her large dark eyes were surprisingly soft, telling me something, telling me she had won. But there was pain — I saw that, too — a hurt so deep I felt I was an intruder watching some kind of private agony.

She was obviously intelligent. More than that; she was street-smart. She had to be. She had moved swiftly, decisively through her shadowed world. She was a killer, a paid assassin, and not of any world I was familiar with.

She continued to gaze at me, her expression warm and yet still distant, still observing. She nodded and smiled at me faintly.

My expression didn't change. Slowly I slid my right hand out of my pocket and, making my eyes as cold as they've ever been, I gave her the finger. It was all I could do.

I never did know her name.

24

Collins never knew her name either. Washington only told him she was a British agent assigned to MI5, to monitor her actions under the shroud of Operation Iron Hammer and clean up her mess — no questions asked.

Collins told me she was one of the best field agents the British had, a cold blooded assassin who spoke very little. The only conversation he could remember having with her was on the plane coming back from London the day the Albino was shot. She had talked at length how the Albino was a dangerous individual who needed to be taken care of before any move could be made against Brendan Muldoon. Just as the plane was about to land, the woman had simply stepped out of the restroom with the .25 caliber she had concealed between her legs and put two bullet holes in the back of the Albino's head.

Collins had also told me about New York. The woman had sensed Brendan Muldoon was there for reasons other than hiring a hit man. She had been positive Muldoon would eventually lead her to his brothers, which he did the night of August 7th, in downtown Manhattan.

One of the brothers — Collins wasn't sure which one — had just come in from Miami with twenty-five kilos of pure cocaine. Brendan Muldoon met him at an apartment downtown — the apartment occupied by a couple named Mitchell.

Shortly after Brendan Muldoon left the apartment with the cocaine, the British woman calmly went in and killed them all, butchering the couple, and shooting the two Muldoons. She had tried to cover it up, making it look like a crazed drug killing. She even paid someone to later identify a photo of Manfred Styles, accusing him of the murders.

Collins had told me about the cold look of satisfaction on the woman's face when she came out of the apartment covered in blood. All she had said was "Take me to a phone."

Collins had also talked about Morris. How he had fucked up by tailing me so close. Because I was once a close friend of Brendan Muldoon, it was possible I was involved. When it had been determined I was not, Collins told his superiors it would be in their best interest to bring me in on the operation. They had refused.

Before he left, Collins had offered his hand. I told him to stick it up his ass.

The first thing I did was call Victoria at her mother's and tell her I was alright, not to worry, that she could go home and I'd be home soon.

The second thing I did was tell the uniform who picked us up at Butler to drop me and Tommy off at Amrhein's for a double scotch over some ice. I hated the taste but I needed the alcohol bad. So did Tommy. What we didn't need was Jimmy the Nose.

"Hey, Joe. Tommy. Where yah been!"

"Around," I said. "Give me a Johnny Walker Black over ice."

"Scotch? You?"

"C'mon, Jimmy," Tommy said. "Can't you see the man's had a tough day. Cut the shit and make it a double."

He did.

"You guys look like hell," Jimmy the Nose said. "What happened to your clothes?"

I didn't answer. Neither did Tommy. We downed the scotch and held out our glasses for another.

"What do you think about the big news?" Jimmy the Nose said after filling our glasses.

"What news is that, Jimmy?" Tommy said.

"You're kidding me? Where the hell have you been?"

Tommy looked at Jimmy the Nose over the edge of his glass. "In the fucking Bahamas," he said.

Jimmy the Nose reached down under the bar, picked up a wrinkled copy of the *Globe,* and tossed it on the bar. "Take a look at this," he said. "You thought I was shitting you about the feds, didn't you?"

I spun the paper around.

The headlines read: POLICE PROBERS INDICT 7 — BOSTON DETECTIVES ALLEGEDLY TOOK BRIBES.

Somehow, I wasn't shocked. It didn't seem important to me now.

The story went on to say how the seven cops worked where temptation beckoned. District 4, now known as Area D — the South End where there was plenty of opportunity for off duty cops to shake down nightclubs and barrooms in the Fenway and Back Bay.

Of the seven cops photographed in various stages of shock as they entered federal court, the one I enjoyed looking at the most was the photo of Lieutenant Robert O'Keefe, chief of homicide, who surrendered at the Boston FBI office after being advised of the indictment and pleaded innocent before U.S. Magistrate William Joyce in U.S. District Court, then released on $100,000 unsecured bond for trial January 11th.

The article went on to say more indictments were expected.

I showed Tommy the paper, pointing to O'Keefe's photo.

He laughed hysterically, and ordered us another scotch.

It was midnight when I crawled into bed.

Victoria's head spun off her pillow. "Joseph," she said. "My God. Are you alright? Where have you been? I've been worried sick."

I kissed her.

"Whewww," she said, turning her head away from me. "You've been drinking. And your clothes smell."

Half in the bag, I flashed her one of my shit-eating grins. "You think I stink, you should see Tommy. We had to carry him in the house. At least I can still walk."

"Hurry up and take a shower," Victoria said.

I did.

In bed, I told Victoria the whole story. It didn't take long.

Maybe there wasn't that much to tell after all.

She gently rubbed my forehead with her fingertips. "My God, Joseph," she said. "It must have been frightening."

"Yeah. But I'm tough. Consider me on vacation."

"Oh?"

"What does that mean, oh?"

"Nothing. I just said, oh."

"The answer is, no. I'm not doing anything around the house. No painting. No hammering. No sawing. No yardwork. Nothing. All I'm going to do is lie on the couch and eat Cheez-Its."

"Did I say anything?"

"You don't have to. I know what you're thinking."

"Is that right?"

"Yeah. That's right."

She reached for me. Tired and drunk as I was, it didn't take long to stiffen.

"If you're such a mind reader, Mister Knight," she said, fondling me. "What am I thinking about now?"

Sonuvabitch. Am I easy.

The phone rang. I almost didn't answer it. It was interrupting something very important.

"Joe?"

"Yeah?"

"It's Sergeant Macky down at Area One. I know it's late, but I thought you'd like to know."

"Know what?"

"You know that transvestite, Ralph Monteria?"

"Who?"

"Ralphie, the fag you've been looking for. You know who I'm talking about — the one who was going around biting all those cocks off."

"Oh, yeah. What about him?"

"We found him."

"Wonderful. Tell him to take two aspirins and shove them up his ass."

"He can't."

"Why not?"

"He's dead."

I opened my eyes to the slit of cruel moonlight streaming in through the curtains. "What happened to him?" I said.

"Someone cut his prick off and stuffed it in his mouth," Sergeant Macky said. Then he let out a laugh. "Guess Ralphie finally bit off more than he could chew."

"I suppose. Goodnight, Macky."

"Just thought you'd like to know, Joe."

"Swell. Thanks for thinking of me."

"No problem. Have a nice night."

As I reached over to hang up the phone, Victoria slipped down beneath the covers.

No matter what, I never seem to lose the urge.

Three days later, I was reading the Sunday *Globe* over coffee in the kitchen when a brief headline on page two caught my eye. **TRUCK CARRYING DYNAMITE EXPLODES SOUTH OF LONDON.** The article, below an out-of-focus photograph of a firefighter silhouetted by flames, said the truck left the M4 Motorway ten miles south of London and ended up in a cow pasture shortly before midnight, killing the driver. The body had been burned beyond recognition, making identification impossible. A witness who observed the truck swerve across the road in front of her and leave the highway believed the truck had blown a tire but couldn't be sure.

Constable Oliver Greenleaf, the investigating officer at the scene, speculated the truck was possibly on its way to Northern Ireland, the explosives going to the IRA.

I lowered the paper and drank the last of my coffee.

I'd bet next week's paycheck it was Paddy Muldoon. And he wasn't headed to Northern Ireland.

The bitch had won again.